WHAT PEOPLE ARE SAYING ABOUT
STRAIGHT OUTTA EAST OAKLAND

Harry Williams is a new voice bringing immediacy and humanity to the experience of being black and poor in East Oakland yet fighting to **keep the dream alive**. *In defining so evocatively the struggles of a specific people, Harry Williams illuminates the struggle in each of us. He is an American Khaled Hosemi reporting with vivid prose, a keen eye, and a huge heart from the* **front lines of an American battle zone**.

SHARON S. L. LINNEA
Author of the best-selling thriller *Chasing Eden* and the Carter Woodson award-winning biography *Princess Kaiulani*

Shattering, riveting, explosive, captivating; Straight Outta East Oakland *is a roller-coaster ride. Reverend Harry Louis Williams II is a* **voice crying out in the wilderness of urban America**; *a prophet with a pen. The first time I met him he was seeking to assist a freshly released ex-felon in his quest to find a safe place to live. The people in the hood recognize and appreciate his ministry. I believe that in the future, he will be internationally recognized as an author. I live and minister in deep East Oakland, where it is* **not unusual to find a bullet-proof vest** *or a .44 automatic pistol on your front lawn in the morning. This book is real. I couldn't put it down.*

THE LATE REVEREND JOSSI OMEGA JONES
Alpha and Omega Foundation (East and West Oakland)

This is an extraordinary book that unravels the cruel and bitter realities that confront too many people of color in marginalized and impoverished communities across America. This book is powerful, **insightful, painful, and uplifting**. *The informed, authentic voice of the author is well schooled in all the disturbing dynamics that define urban street corners where terrorism and cruel indifference condemn, disrupt, and destroy the lives of thousands of American children of color and* their families. *We should all get to know the Firstborn Walker in Reverend Williams's powerful story because his tale teaches important lessons not easily understood in most writing on the urban condition. Equally important, after reading this incredible book, we should get to know the Firstborn Walkers in our communities, cities, and prisons and share with them the incredible vision and compassion revealed by Reverend Williams in this moving novel.*

BRYAN STEVENSON
Executive Director, Equal Justice Initiative
Professor of Law, New York University School of Law
(internationally acclaimed defender of death-row inmates)

[Reverend Harry] Williams, an ordained minister of the gospel, has crafted a book with vivid stories and milieu, representative of almost any ghetto but unmistakably characteristic of Oaktown. The Oakland-based author is a former rapper and an expert on hip hop culture. He takes the reader inside the minds of street hustlers and the world of drug dealing on the streets. These boys in the hood are caught up in a seemingly inescapable web of conceit and deceit. Straight Outta East Oakland is a gripping book that provides hope for one who will make the right choices in life.

RALPH GORDON
Columnist, *CityFlight* magazine

Harry Louis Williams, II is Donald Goines with answers.

DARREN GREGGS
C.E.O. Full Armor Records, Brooklyn, New York

Reverend Harry Louis Williams II is no joke. Like any man of integrity should, Reverend Williams tells the naked truth about the mean streets of East Oakland as well as the way it is on the streets of the central cities of urban America.

This book has appeal for many different kinds of readers. The young person of hip hop culture will find identity in this book. The young nerd living on an island of intellectual isolation will find a road map to use in **surviving the maze of violence and deception** *in a culture where everything is acceptable. Adults who need information in order to understand a world different from the one in which they grew up will find the book to be something they cannot be without. Church people will be led to reconstruct their thoughts about God, the church, and themselves. They will be* **forced to use a new approach** *in evangelism. Last but not least, this book, without the use of religious language, will change the lives of those who are into crime as well as the so-called good people who condemn crime but do nothing to make their communities better.*

We must thank God for using Reverend Harry Louis Williams II to teach us to **love the persons who are captives of underground culture** *while disapproving of lifestyles and values that destroy individuals and families. Reverend Williams understands all levels of life within our unholy cities, and he knows that only by addressing the roots of cultural dysfunctionalism will we bring health and harmony to our cities.*

DR. J. ALFRED SMITH SR.
Senior Pastor
Allen Temple Baptist Church, Oakland, California

Reverend Williams does not give us a novel full of church-based answers to the issues, challenges, and barriers of inner-city life, but he delivers (in a very powerful way, I might add) on taking us deep into hip hop, high-risk, urban culture. His story is real, provides characters of depth, and **doesn't hide the ugly side** *of under-resourced, under-loved communities. The rest is up to local urban churches around the country to wrestle with what to do about developing relevant ministry models in order to proclaim an ancient truth to urban youth and their families.* **May we read and be inspired to transform lives**.

EFREM SMITH
Author of *Raising Up Young Heroes* and *The Hip Hop Church*
(with Reverend Phil Jackson)
Senior Pastor of The Sanctuary Covenant Church, Minneapolis, MN

WHAT THE COMMUNITY
IS SAYING ABOUT THE AUTHOR

Early one morning in June of 2005, my twenty-two-year-old son took an AK-47 assault rifle and shot two men in West Oakland. One lived. One died. The courts **sentenced my son to life in prison** *without the possibility of parole. In the wake of this tragedy, I have dedicated my life to working with young men and the fathers of young men who are in danger of succumbing to the consequences of street life. Along my journey, I've had the pleasure to meet and talk with Reverend Harry Williams. He is a soldier in the* **struggle to bring peace to our streets**. *Give his message a chance. Remember, you always have a choice.*

MICHAEL GIVENS
Chairman/CEO
Fathers Saving Sons

Reverend Harry Williams (or Reverend Harry as he is affectionately known) has **a timely voice in this very critical hour**. *As my professor of Hip Hop Culture and Urban Sociology at the Allen Temple Leadership Institute, Reverend Williams guided me on a journey into the creativity, tragedy, and plight of our outer-city youth (a generation on the fringe and outer edge of our cities). Reverend Williams speaks the language of hip hop and knows how to* **reach the heart and soul of our young** *and disenfranchised. We are both members of the Allen Temple prison team. Behind the walls of the California state penitentiaries, Reverend Williams gives raw, real, and redeeming sermons to men who have been involved in* **raw, real, and gritty situations**. *Reverend Harry is a God-serving revolutionary with a very quiet, humble demeanor. He is a relevant mentor, preacher, and teacher. Preach on, Rev. Preach on! We will have our hip hop church.*

SHEILA WARREN

Straight Outta East Oakland *is a soon-to-be classic that talks about the lifestyles of* **individuals and families trapped on the dark side** *of a low-income, urban environment.*

Reverend Harry Williams has devoted his time, energy, and teaching skills to such communities. Not only does he reside in the community, he is an advocate for it. Additionally, he empowers these families and individuals through books, education, and other resources. Harry Williams not only talks about change, he is active in **bringing about change**. *He visits jails and prisons, ministering for change.*

I say all these things because I know Reverend Williams's work first hand.... Not only is he my brother in Christ, he's a close friend and was my professor in Bible college. It was there that he showed me how to move forward in making the **God-given dream and vision** *that I have for helping the post-incarcerated reenter and build positive relationships with their communities.*

ROMAL COOKS
J.E.T.T. For Life Ministries

I met Reverend Williams upon my release from the federal penitentiary in May of 2003. I needed to bring myself up from nothing. Unable to work in my trained field of expertise, and seeking a job in the construction industry, I decided to attend the Dr. J. Alfred Smith Sr. Training Academy at Allen Temple Baptist Church in East Oakland. There I met Reverend Harry Williams. He was a soft-spoken, kind, and **highly effective breath of fresh air**. *He was my case manager.*

When I met Reverend Williams I had low self-esteem and was depressed. Reverend Williams offered me help in the form of friendship. It was very important to him to know what, if any, problems I was having and what my obstacles were. If I missed a day of school, Reverend Williams would call to find out why. Eventually, I got a job in construction. Today, I am a successful business owner.

I have had **setbacks and triumphs** *since meeting Harry Williams. However, one thing has never changed. He is a true friend. I can talk to him if things are going well or not so well, and he will always give me* good advice. He has stuck with me through some of the hardest times of my life. He is a jewel in our community.

As a community leader, Reverend Harry Williams has dedicated his life to improving the quality of life for African-Americans and all the underprivileged in our community. He truly enjoys seeing others happy and is quite **aware of the obstacles we face** as a community. I feel blessed to be able to consider Harry Williams a true friend.

COSONDRA SATCHER

I met Reverend Williams about three years ago, while attending the Dr. J. Alfred Smith Sr. Training Academy in East Oakland. At first, I thought the Rev and the academy were all talk and no results for a poor sister trying to raise her children legally. I was wrong.

Reverend Williams made me feel like I am just as good as anyone else. There was **never a time that he was too busy to listen** *to my many problems. Sometimes there was no food in the refrigerator. On a few occasions I had no transportation to get my children to school. I know what it's like to have your PG&E turned off. These were just a few of the tricks that the devil sent to confuse someone who was seriously trying to change her life. Not only did Reverend Williams listen to my problems, he aided me in finding real solutions so that I could change the course of what was wrong.*

Reverend Williams (along with the Lord, of course) told Satan he couldn't have me. This is one man I love dearly, and you will also once you meet him. He is **one of the most humble people in the world**. *He never changes. I can truly say, you couldn't beat Reverend Williams with an egg beater. He's a very gifted man.*

SISTER TERRY LOVETT
East Oakland, CA

Over the past two years, I have had both the honor and the privilege of building with Reverend Harry Williams in San Francisco's Tenderloin community. We serve as community activists providing the elderly, chronically pained, mentally ill, drug addicted, homeless, and hungry with access to food, clothing, education, transportation, and employment, as well as mental, physical, and spiritual health care.

It is with God's life-giving breath that I express the utmost humility and gratitude for the love and friendship I've found in truth with a spirit and **soul that ever moves and inspires me towards higher heights,** *caring more than most think wise, risking more than most consider safe. He nourishes and strengthens my faith in the freedom of our birthright, reflecting and expressing the divine light shining in, between, and through us all. With him I stand tall, imagining more than most think possible, realizing more than most dream about the value of our lives, the necessity of family and of humanity, moving closer to one another, being honest with ourselves and each other about who we are as children of God, needing only to believe. And with this love, Harry Williams* **has my heart beating to new rhythms** *through his life's mission of community, our unity.*

LILLIAN M. BURNETT

Most of my life I have been lost to violence, drugs, homosexuality, incest, and penitentiaries. **I didn't think there was any hope for me** *to live a normal life until the day I met Rev. Harry Williams. In December 2003, he introduced me to Victory Outreach International in Oakland, California, and my life has never been the same. Rev. Harry Williams did not just introduce me to this ministry; he still follows up on me to see how I am doing, and he has inspiring words and a loving spirit every time I see him. Because of his dedication to souls, I am just* **one of many people he has touched and changed** *through the Lord Jesus Christ, who is instilled within him.*

Thank you, Reverend Harry Williams. May God always have a hand on you.

TAMMY CORTEZ
Victory Outreach International
Oakland, CA

I see Harry Williams II going far in life. The fire of God is in his eyes. He has a **compassion for the less fortunate who are being killed daily** *in the violent streets of East Oakland.* Straight Outta East Oakland *will be a best seller, reaching kids in East Oakland, because it's riveting, explosive, and just downright real.*

Harry Williams will become a well-known author who will touch the hearts and minds of the youth and maybe save a few by letting them know that **God loves them and there is hope and promise**. *I believe that he will tell them that they should not give up but press forward and achieve dreams and goals they might have never imagined possible.*

A word to the readers:

> *Quit the killing, 'cause there's another way to go.*
> *The pain is great, I know.*
> *I lost a daughter to the streets, don't you know.*
> *Just reach out, 'cause God cares.*
>
> *He's waiting with open arms.*
> **Just trust in him.**
> *Not with the metal of a gun cold and dark,*
> *But with the light of Jesus in your heart.*
>
> *There's people out here who care.*
> *Stop killing each other, brothers.*
> *Love one another.*

KAREN BALAWENDER
East Oakland

STRAIGHT OUTTA
EAST OAKLAND

IF YOU DON'T KNOW, YOU'D BETTER ASK SOMEBODY

a novel

HARRY LOUIS WILLIAMS II

SOUL SHAKER PUBLISHING
OAKLAND, CA
WWW.SOULSHAKERPUBLISHING.COM

Published by:
Soul Shaker Publishing
Oakland, California
www.soulshakerpublishing.com

© Copyright 2008, Harry Louis Williams II
All rights reserved

Printed in the United States of America
First Edition

ISBN: 978-0-9789133-0-4

Cover and interior design © TLC Graphics, *www.TLCGraphics.com*
Cover by Tamara Dever, interior by Erin Stark

DEDICATION

STRAIGHT OUTTA EAST OAKLAND IS HUMBLY DEDICATED TO MY number-one supporter and beloved second mother, Mrs. Irma McDaniel. (Ms. Irma is the mother of my late best friend Darryl "Mr. Heav" McDaniel.) From my teenage years until now, she has stood by my side through the valleys and the mountaintop experiences. I thank God often for her faithfulness, loyalty, love, and sacrifice. In the summer of 2002, when adversity struck, Ms. Irma split her last piece of bread with me. God only made a few Ms. Irmas. She has always been there for me. I've made few big decisions without her advice. She is the wisest person that I know. I often tell her that she reminds me of the character Oracle in the Matrix movie series. Until my last breath, I will be thankful that God placed her in my life.

This book is dedicated to Tamara Dever, Erin Stark, and Monica Thomas at TLC Graphics. They believed in my mission and blessed me with their creative gifts. They also brought in the mightiest pen in the west to serve as my editor. I am eternally grateful for the painstaking, meticulous work that Kathy Ide (www.KathyIde.com) performed on this book.

This book is also dedicated to Bishop Donald Hilliard Jr., presiding prelate of Cathedral Assemblies International, Perth Amboy, NJ. In the ensuing years since I first heard him preach, I have been blessed to hear sermons delivered by many a preacher. And yet I can still say with all honesty that in my opinion Bishop Donald Hilliard Jr. is the greatest preacher on the face of the earth. He is God's mouthpiece for the hip hop generation. Bishop Hilliard not only encouraged me to start college when I was in my thirties, he pressed me to get a master's degree. Bishop Hilliard believed in my future as a writer/preacher. I thank God for the day that I came under the influence of his ministry.

I dedicate this book to Reverend Dr. J. Alfred Smith Sr., senior pastor of the Allen Temple Baptist Church of East Oakland. Pastor Smith taught me that religion concerned with only the hereafter and not the "nasty now and now" is not faithful to the Word of God. Pastor Smith is the most intellectually astute minister it has ever been my great honor to meet. Although his opinion has been sought after by the most powerful people of our time, he still returns all of my phone calls. Pastor Smith has helped me in ways that could fill this book. He once looked at me and asked, "Don't I come through?" I could only answer, "Like a thoroughbred."

This book is dedicated to anyone struggling to leave street life behind, especially the incredible men and women I have had the great pleasure to journey with in deep East Oakland and the San Francisco Tenderloin. Peace to all of the incarcerated brothers and sisters I have been blessed to minister to in the prisons of California. Thank you for all your encouragement. God has a plan. Look up. I thank God for you.

Special thanks to Leticia at Image Graphics at Oakland, an incredible talent. Many thanks also to Brother Earl (the Ambassador) Nichols of Allen Temple Baptist Church who has graciously driven his limosine to the hood for years to pick me up for church. Special thanks to Deacon Hugh Blackmon, Deacon John Harrison, Deacon Douglas Cole and Deacon Glenn Phillips; all of Allen Temple Baptist Church,

East Oakland, CA. Thanks to Alan Korn, Esq. for generous legal counsel. Finally, thanks to my photographer, Karlya Benjamin (*www.karlya.com*). She is a person of excellence.

IN MEMORIAM

This book is humbly dedicated to the memory of Reverend Jossi Omega Jones of Alpha and Omega Foundation, one of the greatest inner-city social justice prophets of our time. She fed the hungry, housed the homeless, clothed the naked, healed the addicted, brokered peace between warring thugs, and fought the scourge of drugs in East Oakland. She was taken from us suddenly in the spring of 2007. I am thankful for her mentorship, invaluable counsel, and friendship. Pastor Jossi walked the killing fields not only preaching the gospel but living it. While she was with us, I had the opportunity to tell her that she was one of the greatest Christians I had ever met. Today, there is a hole in the universe above East Oakland where her great soul once dwelt.

MESSAGE FROM THE AUTHOR

"CLAP THAT NIGGA, BLOOD," A HOARSE VOICE HOLLERED OVER the screech of car tires. Gunpowder blasts echoed like high-power fireworks on the Fourth of July.

I rolled out of bed and onto the floor, resisting the potentially deadly urge to peek through the blinds. The shooters in front of my house meant business. They had come to separate the body from the head. Deafening bangs and booms told me they had heavy metal, probably .9 millimeters and .380s.

The shooters slowed down only to slap in fresh clips. Car windows shattered up and down the block. The automatic gunfire seemed endless. These cats were in no particular hurry. They had not come to squeeze off a few shots and then speed off into the night. This was war, and they were there to lay somebody down.

I don't care how hard you are, there's something about a drive-by that can almost make your heart stop. You can't see who is shooting or what they are shooting at. The smells of marijuana, hatred, and passion seep through the streets like poison in a gas chamber. You hear the death angel swooping down on your hood in a hunt for fresh blood. Life comes down to seconds because who knows whether one of those loud crackling noises outside is actually the grim reaper calling out for your life.

They weren't shooting at my house that night. But there is a proverb as old as gunpowder that says, "Bullets ain't got no name on them." In the heat of the battle, a live round came blasting through my living room wall. It knocked down a pastel portrait of a Latina Virgin Mary cradling a dove: the biblical symbol of both peace and the Holy Spirit.

I'm thankful it was just a wall and a portrait. That stray round could just as easily have busted through a neighbor's window to puncture some innocent grandmother's heart. It could have blown up a baby while she slept peacefully in her mother's arms.

Not long after that attack, the landlord climbed up on a ladder and patched up the hole in my living room wall. Upon close inspection, I realized that though the bullet had knocked the picture of the Virgin from the wall, it had not pierced it. Yes, there was an ugly, gaping hole where the bullet had ripped through the wall, but no bullet hole in the cardboard reproduction, not even a scratch. I took that as a sign. I believe God was telling me that the Holy Spirit was protecting me.

I also believe that God was telling me that the gospel was not meant to be locked up behind closed doors or shared only with people in sharp suits or floppy straw hats. If we do not bring the message of peace to people trapped in desperate situations where trouble brews, trouble will most certainly come to us. And so this book and its message are geared not only to East Oakland but to hoods all over the world.

Many fingers will touch this book. Fingertips that have squeezed triggers will flip these pages. I pray that you will allow your mind to open and that you will think about your life, your family, your decisions, and your destiny. I pray that you will understand that your life will impact more people than you can ever imagine. I pray that you will think about God and your relationship to Him.

You might be serving thirty to life in the pen or serving rocks on the corner, but I pray that you will come to realize that you possess in your hands the power to change the world. I don't care what happened before this moment. As long as you have breath flowing in and out of your lungs, you possess the God-given capacity to change. No matter what the judge pronounced, what the teacher prophesied, or what your mother predicted, you can change with God's help.

We all have to change. You see, the night those gunmen opened fire on my block, there was no reported citing of white-robed Ku Klux Klansmen in East Oakland. More than likely, the shooters looked liked me.

Brothers and sisters, self-hatred is eating us alive, and if we don't turn a corner we are headed for self-destruction. Yesterday it was Rwanda and Dafur. Today it's your hood. We are committing genocide and it's getting worse. If it doesn't stop, we will one day be no more than a footnote in a history book.

If God has blessed you to escape America's version of the Gaza Strip, look back; better yet, reach back. Remember, it's not "them"—it's "us." And none of us is innocent. We walk around with our iPods on full blast while children in the wealthiest society since the dawn of humanity suffer from cold, hunger, want, poverty, and hopelessness two miles away from our doorsteps. If God does not judge us, one day He will have to apologize to the rich man whom he condemned to everlasting hell fire because he let poor Lazarus starve at his feet while he feasted on leg of lamb.

The good thing is that it's not too late. We can turn this thing around. Like the late James Brown once sang, it's time to get involved. None of us are innocent, and in the war to knock down the walls of the ghetto, we can't afford conscientious objectors. Oakland, California has been rated the fourth most dangerous city in the entire nation. This is a time for heroes. Will you be counted among the faithful or the apathetic? Don't point fingers. Do something.

Be remembered for the lives you saved, not the hell you raised.

Peace.

CHAPTER
ONE

"THIS IS A FUNERAL, YOUNGSTA," I BARKED AT THE TALKATIVE young man in the pew behind me. "Show some respect."

"For who? The cat in the box?"

The kid had to have been around seventeen. A thick forest of dreadlocks concealed his glassy eyes from the world. He was so short that his black rubber soles dangled from the wooden church pew, barely touching the wine-colored carpet. The bottoms of his baggy black dress pants bunched up at the ankles. The tattoo under the short sleeve of his dress shirt was raw with red-and-green letters that bulged in cursive writing that said, *We still ain't listening!* He smelled like a marijuana bonfire.

I gave up on silencing the mocker and set my mind on taking in the preacher's eulogy. He was a good six foot two. A river of perspiration dripped from his bald forehead. He gripped the sides of the pine podium with thick brown fingers and shook. He scared me. I thought he was going to have a seizure. Intermittent bursts of shrieking and screaming from the audience members did not slow the preacher down. He just yelled louder.

"I'm talking to you young people sitting out there," he hollered at the sea of tear-streaked brown faces. "I want you to get a good look at this young man at my feet. He was blown off the face of the earth the day before he reached his twenty-eighth birthday."

The screaming and moaning simmered down to a trickle.

I used the balls of my fists to swab tears from my eyes. This gave me a better look at the mourners around me. Some of the young people wore black shirts with silk-screen images of Lonnie's face. The full-color photograph on the T-shirts had been snapped on a more festive occasion—maybe his mama's surprise birthday party or a New Year's Eve celebration. A smile seemed to swallow up the bottom portion of Lonnie's smooth bronze cheeks. His date of birth and date of death were printed in a short but final line beneath the picture.

Big iron overhead fans swirled the hot air around in invisible circles. The ceiling lights made me feel as though I were sitting on the sun. The preacher looked as if he had just emerged from a sauna. The black robe clung to his white shirt. His gold cross jumped off his big belly every time he lunged forward to make a point.

"The Bible says, 'Thou shalt not kill.' So when are we going to stop killing each other?" He lifted a sheet of paper off the podium. "I found these lyrics by a Bay Area hip hop artist on the Internet—boy calls himself Side Show Psycho. In this song, called 'The Paper Man,' he says, 'Get out my way when my AK spray, 'cause I be doin' niggas bad like the KKK. Don't need no burning cross or rope. I handle my biz with a clip and a scope.'"

The preacher slammed the page down on the pulpit. "Why, that's the epitome of black self-hatred. When are you young people going to wake up?"

The two young men on the other side of me were beginning to doze off. They'd likely been to a lot of these funerals. Like many teenagers, they put the preacher on mental mute the moment he said the words "you young people."

The older people were listening, though. People like Lonnie's mother, who rocked back and forth, a tear-stained black veil hiding her eyes. Maybe Lonnie's girl, Savonna, was listening. She held her bulging stomach, pregnant with my homeboy's baby.

"I'm going to tell you something else," the preacher hollered. "If you don't change your ways, another one of y'all is going to be up in a box taking this boy's place come this time next year."

Every eyelash in the room batted. Lonnie's mother had insisted on an open-casket funeral. So there he lay, with a volcano the size of a fifty-cent piece blown straight through the middle of his forehead. The guy who took care of the body was a mortician, not a magician. The ugly black hole could not be covered up. It stared back at us like an unblinking third eye.

I think Ms. Rendell was trying to either warn us or punish us. But she didn't understand that in East Oakland, nobody wakes up in the morning and walks outside planning to catch a bullet in the forehead; it just happens sometimes, especially if you're not living right. And Lonnie definitely hadn't been living right during the season of his untimely demise. I should know. I'm Firstborn Walker. I was his best friend.

Lonnie and I met ten years ago in a high school that was more gladiator camp than educational facility. They gave us ancient textbooks with purple and green Magic Marker swirls scrawled on the pages. The bathrooms were never stocked with toilet paper. The stairwells were littered with used condoms and empty rolling-paper packages. Substitute teachers who could barely read taught us English literature. And yet, against all odds, Lonnie and I scored well on our SATs.

Lonnie aspired to become a bank president or a stock broker. My goal in life was to become a great writer in the tradition of Richard Wright or James Baldwin. I read Camus, Kafka, and Proust the way other kids read Spiderman and X-Men comic books.

For years Lonnie and I dreamed of getting into Alston University in nearby Berkeley, California; neither us got accepted. The guidance counselor told us that a 4.0 at our inner-city high school didn't count like a 4.0 at, say, Pleasant Valley High School. We needed extra-curricular activities to prove our intellectual worthiness to the admissions counsel—things like participation in the chamber music ensemble or membership in the thespian society. Of course, our school offered none of these things. I can still remember the guidance counselor's explanation as he wound up our session: "It's nobody's fault. That's just the way it is."

Lonnie and I both enrolled in junior college. Along the way he got bored. And lost. Then one day he met a girl in the cafeteria: Savonna. They quickly went from cupcaking to sharing an apartment. He started cutting classes.

When she became pregnant with their first child, Lonnie had to drop out of school to work. Ironically, he landed a full-time job serving smoothies and lattes to the scrub-faced, sunburnt kids who matriculated at Alston University, the very school we had dreamed of attending.

My friend and I lost touch. Occasionally, we'd run into each other at parties or on the BART train to San Francisco. We'd laugh about the old times and play "Whatever happened to so-and-so?" When it was time to leave, we'd exchange numbers and say, "Man, I'm going to call you next week." And we meant to. But neither of us ever got around to it.

The day I received an acceptance letter from Alston, I leapt for joy. I wondered if my homeboy had received the same letter. The last time we spoke, he mentioned he'd moved in with Savonna. But he didn't have the address on hand. I had to visit his mama to find out where he lived.

When Ms. Rendell cracked the door, the metal chain gave a metallic pop. I stared at her through the six-inch opening across the chain. A great shock of white hair fell across her eyes. She had aged ten years since the previous Christmas. Anguish riddled itself deep in the lines of her forehead.

"Firstborn Walker, is that you?" she asked.

"I'm looking for Lonnie, Ms. Rendell. Do you know where he is?"

Ms. Rendell's lips pursed into a tight line. Her eyes dropped down.

"What's wrong?"

"Crack."

There are a few single-syllable words in the English language that represent enough catastrophic information to overload the Internet. Terms like *storm* and *flood*. And *crack*.

Lee Stringer described his first hit on the pipe in a book I read last year called *Grand Central Stories*. The initial euphoria of that virgin high made him feel transcendent and uniquely alive. Yet it wasn't long before rock cocaine left that writer groveling around in a dirt hole somewhere beneath the New York City subway system, emerging from the filthy, dark tunnels only to score more crack.

There was never a slave driver as ruthless as "Ole Massa Crack." Rock cocaine will chew you up and spit out your bones. It will drive you away from your kids and have you rummaging through a garbage can pinching cold peas from the remains of somebody's discarded TV dinner tray. Crack will leave you on your knees in some dark alley, tugging on a stranger's zipper for a single hit. A crackhead gets no respect from anybody. I've seen a lot of brothers who took one hit and never came back. Only a fool puts a glass pipe to his lips.

As smart as Lonnie was, I couldn't help but wonder how he ended up a smoker. If only he could see the bottomless pain in his mother's bloodshot pupils or see her bottom lip quiver as she spoke. "He can't come roun' here no more," she said. "I got weak 'bout a month ago and let him spend the night. He stole my weddin' band and the silverware my mama had given me as a wedding present. I don't know where he at, Firstborn, but when you see him, you tell him that his mother loves him but she can't help him if he doesn't change. You talk to him, Firstborn. Tell him to get help."

I couldn't think of anything to say, so I nodded twice and turned on my heel. I was now on a mission to locate my best friend.

It's never hard to find someone with a taste for crack. Sooner or later, they have to feed the eight-hundred-pound gorilla hanging on their back.

I went to all the places in the hood where gorillas feed and asked for Lonnie by name. Finally an ancient piper named Ernie pointed toward a bustling intersection of International Boulevard.

When I drew within arm's length of Lonnie, I could hardly believe what I saw. He was on his knees, his neck bent and his nose three inches from the sidewalk. He poked his forefinger against the filthy cement and then pressed it against his tongue. He moved like a lion through tall brush, hunting for something invisible to my eyes. He was hunting for a ghost rock—that lost pebble that he might have dropped by mistake.

Lonnie's hair was lumpy and matted and littered with bits of white cotton. A thick mustache drooped like a grapevine over his top lip. His red polyester pants had no belt. Every few seconds, he snaked a finger through a tattered belt loop and hoisted in an effort to stop the pants from sliding down his emaciated hips. Lonny wore a navy blue button-down shirt he must've received from a rescue mission giveaway box or found in an alley. The neck was four sizes too big and the sleeves swallowed up his bony hands.

Lonnie had always been clean shaven and meticulous in regard to his personal appearance. Seeing my homeboy in this condition nearly made me vomit.

He glanced up at me, startled. "Firstborn? Firstborn Walker?"

"What you looking for down there?" I asked.

"I think I dropped something," he mumbled, rising to his feet. A death rattle shook in his throat. I wondered where he'd been sleeping nights.

My facial expression must have betrayed my heart, because his gaze immediately slumped down to his bare toes.

"Where are your shoes?" I asked.

"Sold 'em."

"For what?"

"You been to see my mom?"

"Yeah."

"You know what, then."

He scratched the tip of his nose with a ragged, dirty fingernail. "So, how you been, my nigga?" He reached out his hand to shake mine. Dirt the color of indigo ink coursed in and out of the tiny grooves in his palm. His handshake was oily and limp. I fought the urge to wipe my palm against my pants leg.

"I got a letter from an alumni group on the Alston University campus called the Fraternal Order for the Upliftment of Humanity," I announced.

His nostrils flared. "Isn't that the radical right-wing Berkeley think tank that's always in the news for trying to torpedo affirmative-action programs?"

That wasn't the way I'd have put it, but I nodded.

"Why'd they write to you?"

"They've persuaded Alston University to admit me."

"After all these years?"

"They say that all of my credits from junior college will transfer. And on top of that, they're giving me a scholarship. In two years, I'll have a bachelor's degree. All I have to do is raise 20 percent of the first year's tuition and I'm home free. They say it's part of a research experiment."

Lonnie frowned. "Research experiment?"

"Yeah. If I can get that first 20 percent, they'll foot the rest of the bill from my junior and senior year…room, board, books, everything."

"What are they researching?"

"I don't know, and I don't care."

"Maybe the experiment is to measure what lengths the ghettoized, economically challenged brother from the slums will go through to get the words *Alston University* stamped on a diploma."

I shrugged. Lonnie was clearly unable to see this opportunity through my eyes. Grandma would have called the letter we were discussing "answered prayer." Maybe Lonnie was jealous. After all, he hadn't received a letter from the society. And if he had, he certainly wouldn't have been in any position to follow up on it now.

Lonnie reached down and picked up a flat cigarette from a crack in the sidewalk. "You got a match, homie?"

I shook my head.

"Firstborn, you go get that scholarship. Do whatever you gotta do to get up from around here, man, 'cause these streets ain't no joke."

The corner was deserted, yet Lonnie leaned forward to whisper in my ear. "I did something stupid yesterday, and somebody's going to kill me for it." Pools of tears welled up in his brown pupils. "I gotta go, homie."

He lumbered away, his shoulders slumped. I didn't follow him.

The next day he was dead.

Word on the streets said that Vegas, a stocky man with an ever-present grin, accidentally dropped a crack rock on the floor of a candy store. Lonnie picked up the package and hit the door like a bullet. The dealer didn't chase him. Two days later, Vegas caught Lonnie slipping out of a rock house on Avenue A, and he blasted him in the face with a snubnose .38. My homeboy lost his life for less than the price of a Lumberjack Special at Denny's.

Vegas committed premeditated first-degree murder in broad daylight, but the papers said, "There were no witnesses." No witnesses? That nigga *wanted* everybody to know who did it. He rocked Lonnie's world in front of an audience so the next basehead would think twice.

And so, on the night of the funeral, I sat there trembling as the preacher spoke. I could feel the devil blowing at the short hairs on the back of my neck. Lonnie's last words to me swirled around in my mind. *"Firstborn, you go get that scholarship. Do whatever you gotta do to get up from around here, man, 'cause these streets ain't no joke."*

Lonnie's mother let out a shriek as the pallbearers levitated her son's broken body through the back door of the funeral parlor.

My soul was crushed. I only had two friends in life, and now one of them was gone.

Outside, fine drops of summer mist bit my face like a legion of sand flies. Down the block, a pit bull chewed on an old soup bone. I crossed the street to avoid him. I was on my way to the bus stop. I had to see Maggy.

CHAPTER
TWO

STREET LIGHTS LIT UP THE HOOD LIKE CANDLES IN A DARK ROOM. A cool fog drifted in from San Francisco Bay. I waded through the darkness until I reached the crossroads of International Boulevard and Seventy-third Avenue. I waited at the corner for the bus that would take me to Maggy's hood. Monarch butterflies with butterscotch wings fluttered by in a cluster.

Down the block, on the other side of the great asphalt cross, hundreds of speeding cars burned rubber up International Boulevard, treating it as though it were the last lap of the Indy 500.

A lonely tear slipped out of the corner of my right eye. It soaked into my black lapel before I could wipe it away. I looked up at a passing cloud and whispered, "Good-bye, Lonnie."

I forced my mind to think about the woman I was trying to persuade to become my girl.

I'm not a chick magnet. I'm the type of guy who has to work hard to get a date. There's nothing about me that would make you look twice should you ever walk past me in

Southland Mall. I probably look like the guy who tore your ticket in half at the movie theatre last weekend. I'm not an ugly man, but I'm nobody you'd remember either.

Maggy has always had a thing for hood niggas, ridaz, dope dealers, hoo bangers, and thug lords with chrome-plated heaters up underneath their hoodies. She was attracted to shot callers who pulled bids in Pelican Bay and San Quentin. She loved the killer with a mouthful of gold teeth and pants that sagged almost down to his knees, the kind who couldn't form a sentence that didn't contain profanity. Maggy was attracted to the kind of man you might get shot for just standing next to. Her man might call her the B word as a term of affection.

I could never see myself being that type of man. Still, she answered my phone calls, and when the bitterness of loneliness struck she was someone to talk to about life's little things.

I stood at the bus stop, meditating on ways to win her over without changing. I couldn't come up with any.

A slim man with bony hands and a full head of pearl-white hair joined me, cursing the city of Oakland for having uprooted the yellow graffiti-stained bus-stop benches. I could smell the trail of liquor riding on the old man's breath. He weaved back and forth like a circus performer walking a tightrope in a tornado.

I knew his kind. He was one of those people who felt it was his divine calling to unravel all the mysteries of the universe for the next generation. That chilly April night I was his captive pupil. I wasn't going anywhere until the bus pulled up, so what was there to do but listen?

"Son, see that chicken joint 'cross the street? That's hallowed ground, blood cryin' out from beneath the stalks of grass. You heard 'bout the killing that went down there last week, didn't ya?"

All I could manage was a nonchalant shrug of the shoulders. Down here people get smoldered all the time. As sick as it sounds, another body dropping doesn't raise too many eyebrows. We've grown cold to it.

"Who got caught out there this time?" I asked.

"Two boys from Brookfield Village. Four young cats with bandanas wrapped around their faces jumped out of the back of a Dodge Ram truck. The dudes started hollerin' in Spanish and firin' at will. Blood and slugs was poppin' everywhere. When they got done with them d-boys, they blasted a sizzler in our direction. I guess so as to discourage witnesses."

It's not wise to admit to a stranger that you were an eyewitness to a felony, especially first-degree murder. But Johnny Walker Red had unhooked the old man's tongue.

A black-and-silver Raiders windbreaker brushed up against me as its owner walked past me. The hood, tied tightly at the chin, made his face nearly invisible. But two dark gray eyes flashed back in my direction. I made out the butt of a .32 revolver in the pocket beneath his right hand.

Man, where is that bus?

The newcomer was followed by a crew of young hardheads with shoulder-length dreadlocks and gold teeth. They spread out on the side of the fence that faced International Boulevard. Snippets of their conversation floated in my direction.

"So I tole da broad, 'Tell that fool your moms ain't home, and tell him he should come over.'"

"Me and my niggas was already on one, you know. We was back at the crib splittin' dem Swisher Sweets and sipping on Remy. So when I got the word that he took the bait, I told my dudes, 'Time to break a nigga's pockets.' And when that chump stepped in the doorway, we got it all, man." The dreads flashed their gold front teeth as they laughed.

Every few seconds one of the young cats glanced back at the old man and me, his hollow eyes scoping, searching, measuring. One kid flicked a razor blade out from beneath his tongue and through his barely parted lips. The moonlight struck it and danced along the stainless-steel edge. I shivered.

The old man, oblivious to the danger, chattered away. "They got this black-tar heroin now. They calls it Osama. Those two boys who got shot up 'cross the street used to sell it."

"How do you know they dealt Osama?"

He smiled, showing off a mouth full of pink gums. "These streets be talking, son."

The old man reached into his back pocket and extracted a half pint of Mad Dog 20/20. He unscrewed the cap, unleashing a strong, mint-flavored ammonia scent. He rested the neck of the bottle on his bottom lip and tilted. He finished his swallow with a smack, then rubbed the back of his hand over his mouth. He tilted the bottle toward me in a gesture of generosity. I laughed. I would sooner have drunk pee out of a toilet.

"Were you born here in Oakland?" I asked the guy.

"Naw. I come out here from Shreveport, Louisiana, back in '65. When I first got here, everybody who wanted a job could work. There were factories all over the place, scooping up any able-bodied man who wanted to do an honest day's labor. Shoot, you could work thirty years at the car plant, put your kids through college, and then retire. Now my son can't even buy a job. He thirty and he ain't worked in two years. What they doin' to us, young blood?"

"What do you mean?"

He snorted. "What we got down here in East Oakland is a breakdown of law and order. Too many young people, too few jobs. Rents goin' through the ceiling. And if you get down with that dope game, you better be clippin' good, 'cause it's life and death out here in the O. One of the young hardheads out here will buck you down and say, 'It was town business.'"

His eyes glazed over and a smile stole across his lips. His voice took on a singsong tone, as though he were chanting a toddler's song that didn't rhyme. "But that's not your fate, is it, son? 'Satan seeks to sift you like wheat. ... And when you have been converted, strengthen thy brothers.'" The old man reared back on his heels and cackled like a maniac.

"You're drunk."

"I may be drunk, but I'm right."

A bus finally dragged to a tired wheeze on the International Boulevard side of the asphalt intersection. The thugged-out dreads trickled in, two of them pausing to flash me gang signs and hard looks. My lungs expelled with relief. They have a saying down here where I live. "If you look like a come-up, you'll get come-up-on." Thankfully, it wasn't my night to get come up on.

A man and woman in identical ill-fitting gray janitorial uniforms joined us at the corner. Two minutes later, the bus I needed came to a screeching halt at our feet. I nodded to the elderly gentleman and allowed him to board first, out of respect. As I followed him down the aisle, I heard him singing, "Praise the Lord, I saw the light. I saw the light."

I found two empty seats in the rear of the bus. After plopping down in the seat next to the window, I draped my right leg over the adjoining seat, which faced the aisle. I leaned back, staring out into the night.

Far above East Oakland lay an expanse called the East Bay hills. This was the vault of heaven, where the streets had no names and twelve-bedroom Greco-Roman mansions, gleaming with opulence and wealth, taunted us from high above. Some of the palatial digs had telescopes positioned on their sun decks, allowing the well-heeled ample time to hightail it out of there should the poor people below ever start climbing the hills of the great divide armed with the decision to change the social arrangement.

The Bay Area is as far away from Los Angeles and Compton as Portsmouth, Virginia, is from New York City. Neighboring San Francisco is known as the City. Oakland is the Town. More than four hundred thousand people live in the Town, but you can't travel within its borders for a day without seeing at least one person you know.

The Town is known around the world for its swagger and style. E-40 says that hip hop artists borrow their lingo from the Bay. I believe it. The slang here changes almost weekly. In LA, gang affiliates refer to one another as either "Cuz" or "Blood." In the East Bay, both terms could be used interchangeably with "homie" or "potna." Here in Oakland, the terms rarely have any relation to gang colors. I could be talking to you and call you both of those names in the same sentence.

We also have our own unique hip hop sound. The Town is all about the hyphy movement. The frenzy of the music will make you "go dumb" or "get stupid." After a jam is over, we entertain ourselves at impromptu (and illegal) gatherings called sideshows, where people turn their cars in quick, tight circles and make their tires smoke.

If you read comic books, you know that superheroes live in mythical places like Metropolis or Gotham City. A couple of years ago, a comic-book superhero named Pariah was tossed out of heaven to make penance for his sins. Where did he land? You guessed it: the ghetto streets of Oakland, California.

I've spent most of my life in the flatlands. Down in our world, beauty parlors, dry cleaners, storefront churches, ninety-nine-cent stores, liquor holes, and Chinese restaurants sit sandwiched between plain white box-style apartment buildings stained with graffiti hieroglyphics.

Crack fiends with sunken eye sockets and emaciated bodies waltz by in soiled T-shirts and tattered Nikes. A steady stream of cars race down the boulevard, their stereos pumping East Bay hip hop royalty.

Magdalene didn't live far from where I had caught the bus. I could have walked, but living in the ghetto is all about calculating the risk factor. I would have saved the bus fare, but I might have run into an angry bunch of hardheads with empty stomachs and loaded pistols.

I walked up the steps to Maggy's building five minutes after disembarking from the bus. A brother in a Raiders jersey and shoulder-length dreads leaned against the lobby door, his girl collapsed in his arms. She giggled as he popped slanguage, which he'd probably picked up from listening to hip hop records. I squeezed past them and made my way up the stairs.

My heart thumped in my chest as I drew closer to Magdalene's apartment door. I wondered what she would be wearing. I wondered if she would kiss me.

I'd met Maggy back when I was slinging chicken and fries at a roach grease trap around the corner from her building. She used to come in and try to bum meals on credit. We started kicking it when business was slow. Eventually I started catching feelings for her. I used to dream of marriage to Magdalene, of enchanted evenings in Mamaris, Turkey, conversing over gray mullet and fried mussels at an outdoor café, of reading Rimbaud's *Departure* to her over almond tea and crumb cakes at Geladon's or the Flambergé in Paris.

Ah, yes. I had illustrious fantasies of the good life, but alas, no money.

Three weeks prior, my boss, Mr. Voneti, had called me into his office just before the end of my shift. He grabbed a letter-size manila envelope and slammed it into my open palm, never looking into my eyes. He said the layoff was temporary.

My work was good but business was slow. He promised he would have me back at the drive-through window within a couple of weeks, as soon as things picked up again. But the phone never rang. I know because I sat on my bed and watched it for hours, waiting for the slightest vibration. Nothing. Finally, the telephone company cut it off.

My living expenses forced me to pinch away at my tiny nest egg until the last straw was depleted. I was officially broke. All the money I'd saved was gone.

To whom could I turn? I was alone in the world. My mama had wrestled the death angel in the last throes of childbirth. I was named after the final word she uttered before she gave up the ghost: *firstborn*. So whenever I filled out a job application, I gave the world the only thing Mama had to leave me: my name. And the world threw it back in my face.

Mama was not the only one who left me with a legacy. Joshua Walker gave me my last name. Daddy took me to Granny Walker's house after Mom's funeral. The two-bedroom white house with the olive shutters in the Sobrante Park section of Oakland was the only real home I'd ever known.

My childhood memories are a suitcase filled with snapshots. I can still feel my granny's soft hands rubbing lotion on my arms. Her warm hugs smelled like Johnson's Baby Powder and lilacs on a warm spring day.

On hazy, humid afternoons, Granny took me to the Oakland Coliseum, where we would watch baseball and cheer for the A's. Granny was a die-hard A's fan, win or lose.

Daddy was tall, with strong hands and a dark-chocolate complexion. He and Granny argued a lot, mostly about money and what he was and wasn't contributing toward the household expenses. Daddy did most of his work for "the people" (pro bono). Granny wanted him to "grow up" and assume some responsibility now that he had a son.

Things got so hectic between the two of them that Daddy eventually packed up and left. He must not have gone far, because every other night around midnight he would sneak into the house and into my bedroom.

"How's Daddy's little man?" he always asked. I felt his palm cradle my head as my cheek came to rest on his black leather jacket.

I just shrugged. I knew what was coming next. Daddy would deliver the next installment in the Joshua Walker lecture series. He read passages from George Jackson, C. R. L. James, Che Guevara, Malcolm X, and others. When he was finished, he would lower me back down on the bed and say, "Good-bye, my little warrior."

I'd drift off to sleep again. When I awoke, Daddy was gone. But I always remembered the lessons.

I was about nine years old when the last visit came. Daddy crept in one night, the way he'd done a hundred times before. That night's reading was from Huey P. Newton's *To Die for the People*. The next morning, when I turned on the television searching for cartoons, Daddy's glowing face peered through the glass in the TV screen. His black marble eyes stared at me as if in a state of shock.

The news commentator said, "Joshua Walker, a Bay Area subversive, was shot to death early this morning while attempting to hold up a Safe Transport armored car."

I didn't hear Granny's footsteps behind me. Her high-pitched shrieking caused me to shove the heels of my hands against my ears.

When the funeral service ended, and the relatives had gone back to Louisiana, Arkansas, and Mississippi, Granny sat next to me on the thick plastic of the living room couch. "Firstborn," she said, "from now on, I'm going to be your mother and father."

And it was so…until a heart attack took her life from both of us. She was sixty-seven. I was seventeen. The bank foreclosed on her home.

After the place was sold, I lived in one rooming house after another, working at anything that paid minimum wage or above. I never seemed to fit in anywhere. I was a shooting star launched from a dying solar system. If it hadn't been for Lonnie and another close friend named Herbert Cook, whom we called "Drama," I'd have spent many a Thanksgiving meal beneath the golden arches.

My relatives down South might send a fruitcake around the holidays or a wristwatch on my birthday, but that was the measure of our relationship. After Granny's funeral we lost touch. Now all I had in the world were Drama and Magdalene.

I knocked at apartment 13 for a good four minutes before the door swung open.

Maggy's mom stood inches away from my face, flashing a radiant smile. Her white sweatshirt said in sky blue script, "Too Blessed to Be Stressed." Ms. Holmes was one of those religious people who always walked around with a glow on her face. Her brown eyes sparkled as though she had seen God Himself in the flesh. Her handshake was warm. Her smile made me smile.

I was twenty-eight years old, but Ms. Holmes started every conversation with "Hi, baby."

"Hello, Ms. Holmes," I answered. "May I please speak with Maggie?"

"Such a gentleman!" She winked. "Excuse the way the place looks. Maggy was supposed to clean up while I was at work, but the place looks just the way I left it this morning. She's a lazy thing, she is. Maybe you can do something with her."

"Mama, who's that at the door?" a familiar voice cried from the back of the apartment.

"Honey, it's Firstborn. Put something on and come out here and talk to him."

She winked at me again. Ms. Holmes was a genteel, Southern-born woman who wanted a man with a future for her daughter, one who would treat her with dignity and respect. I wanted nothing more than to be that person, but Maggy had a different ideal for a man.

I had no criminal record. I didn't have any dreadlocks. On the contrary, I kept my head shaved almost bald. I sported a neatly trimmed goatee. I was more likely to wear penny loafers and Docker pants than Timberland boots and baggy jeans. On the evenings that I came over to watch TV, I argued for the Discovery channel while Magdalene wanted to see the hip hop video countdown for the eighth time in a day.

Maggy's Tents of Kedar fragrance oil rushed up into my nostrils. My heart skipped two beats as she walked toward me. Magdalene's skin was dark and creamy. Her eyes were black ovals that exercised a magnetic pull. Dimples plunged into her cheeks when she smiled. Her extensions were tied up in a ponytail. Gold hoops swung from beneath her earlobes. Her figure was a perfect eight.

Magdalene politely opened the apartment door and walked out into the hallway. She popped purple bubble gum and stared at the ceiling while I tried to make conversation.

"How was your day, Maggy?"

"It was cool. Me and Monica went out to Bayfair Mall. I saw these bad new sneakers. Yo, I want dem joints bad! You hear me, Firstborn?"

Ms. Holmes walked out of the apartment and into the hallway. She brushed past her daughter, clutching a glass of lemonade. The ice cubes clicked against one another as she handed me the glass. "Here you are, son. I'm sorry we don't have anything to go with it. This child done ate up all the chocolate-chip cookies again."

"I did not," Magdalene whined.

"Well, it was either you or the Keebler elves. Ain't nobody else here but us and my older daughter, Monica, and she's allergic to chocolate."

Ms. Holmes's left eyebrow hoisted. "Firstborn, what you doin' out here in the hall? Don't you want to come inside?"

Magdalene's body tensed at the suggestion. Her squinting eyes telegraphed the message that I should decline any invitation to enter the apartment.

"No, thank you, Ms. Holmes. I'll be fine right here."

"Suit yourself." Ms. Holmes closed the apartment door behind her. I flopped against the hallway wall.

Maggy traced the inner circle of her left earring with her pinky finger. "You found a job yet?"

"Not yet, but I'm looking."

"You can't keep comin' around here with no paper, blood. I can't have no broke nigga sittin' up in my house, eatin' my mama's food and peepin' in her TV. Shoot, a sista want to go to the show, get her nails done. You feel me, dawg?"

"Is that all a man means to you?"

"Firstborn, my big sista Monica tell me, 'A brother who ain't got his paper right is a problem.' I can do bad all by myself. I'm nineteen, you know. So you kinda old for me anyway. 'Sides, I need a man to help me get out the house and see the world." Her gaze slipped from the top of my bald head to the tips of my freshly shined Payless penny loafers. "And I can see you ain't gonna help me do all that."

She reached for my lemonade glass. "I'm goin' inside to see the end of *Hell Up in Harlem* now."

"Wait, Maggy…"

She sucked her teeth. "What is it you want from me, Firstborn? We opposites, like sunshine and rain. I like rough-necks, bad boys. I got two pen pals in San Quentin right now, talking 'bout gettin' out soon, and they wanna come holla at a sister. And you always talking about wantin' to go to college, or always wantin' me to read some book." She wrinkled her nose. "You a nice guy, but I ain't feelin' you at all, homie."

I had graduated from junior college with a 4.0 grade-point average. My final papers were hoisted up to jealous students as examples of what an assignment should look like. I was the valedictorian of both my freshman and sophomore classes. My SAT scores were better than adequate. But none of that made a difference to Maggy.

Her voice switched to a sympathetic note. "I wish I did have some feelings for you. There's plenty of sisters out there who'd want a square like you. You know, the settlin'-down kind of sisters, like my mama." Her eyes widened. "Do you like older women, Firstborn?"

I couldn't believe the woman I loved was telling me I was better suited to date her mother.

Granny had led me to believe that if a man worked hard, he could reach the stars. My sights weren't high: I only wanted to escape the angst and poverty of the crumbling, blood-soaked streets of the American ghetto. I desired only the opportunity to prove myself. But soon the doors of Alston University would close to me forever. Where would I get the thousands of dollars needed to make up the difference between my scholarship and the full cost of a semester's tuition? Even though the scholarship was quite generous, I still needed 20 percent of the first year's tuition. To make matters worse, I was out of work and staring at the unsavory prospect of homelessness. To be frank, the future frightened me.

"You gonna get those tuition ends, Firstborn," Maggy whispered. "You been talkin' about going to Alston since I met you. You goin' to get in. It's just a matter of time. And then you gonna get yourself some square broad who'll be a bank manager or the secretary of state…somethin' corny like that."

"Magdalene, I'd sell my soul to the devil for such a chance. But I don't know where to sign up."

She shook her head. "Don't talk like that, blood." Maggy leaned her back against the wall and then patted at a spot next to her. I posted up next to her, staring straight ahead at the row of closed apartment doors. "Now, tell me about the funeral." Maggy said.

I didn't know why she thought that would make me feel better, but I obliged her. "It was awful. They shot Lonnie in the face but his mama still had an open-casket funeral."

"That's scandalous." Maggy wrapped her arms around me and pressed her soft, ebony cheek against mine. Her fingernails were stubby and plain, not radiant with intricate, swirling red, purple, blue, and white designs that young women often wore. I wished I could have offered her that luxury.

"Firstborn, what you gonna do if you ain't got a job?"

"I don't know. Guess I'll go see Drama tomorrow. Maybe he can think of something."

Her eyes squeezed shut for a second and then her lashes fluttered. "Drama's outta jail?"

"He's been out for two weeks. They couldn't make the charges stick. The guy decided not to testify."

"Blood, you know I don't like you hanging out with that fool. He ain't nothin' but trouble."

"Come on, Maggy," I argued. "So he chose one path and I chose another. We're still like family."

Magdalene frowned. "That's the kind of family that takes square niggas to the pen with dem."

"I'm broke, Maggy. I'm just going to go see if homie can help out."

She shook her head and sucked her teeth in annoyance as though she were explaining trigonometry to a third grader.

"Maggy," Ms. Holmes hollered out, "Clifford Smith is on the phone." Her voice quavered as though she were announcing news of a train wreck.

What would Maggy want with Clifford Smith? When we were in school, Clifford cut classes. He sold weed. And as far as I knew, he didn't graduate. The last time I saw him he was jacking people for their Hondas down in the Shady Eighties.

"Tell him I'll be right there," she hollered, all the while flashing a naughty smile at me.

"Why is Clifford Smith calling you?"

"Oh, Firstborn, don't be so uptight. Clifford and I are just friends. He said he was going to take me out to the mall and buy me this gorgeous outfit I'm just dying for."

"Magdalene, guys like Clifford don't spend money on a woman for nothing. He's going to want a return on his investment."

She put her hands on her hips and wrinkled her nose. "Why does everything have to be more than it is with you? Don't you think a man could be satisfied with the pleasure of my company?"

"Maybe in one of those Jackie Collins novels you're always reading, but not out here in the hood."

Maggie huffed. "You should stop comin' around here so much. People might think you're my dude or something. You know how fools like to run their mouths off." She turned her back on me and rushed inside.

The door slammed like a bass drum in a symphony orchestra. I stood in the hall, listening to its echo. Magdalene hadn't even said good night.

Maybe I shouldn't have made that crack about Clifford. Sometimes I didn't know when to stop. What I said was true, though. Guys like Clifford couldn't look past a woman's curves to explore her heart and mind. I wished I had the money to take Magdalene to the places she wanted to go and buy her the things she liked. I would be a much better man for her than Clifford Smith, but I was broke. So I zipped up my jacket and walked downstairs and outside, another lonely man drifting into the waiting arms of darkness.

On the way home I reflected on my friendship with Drama. Drama (or "D Montana," as the streets sometimes called him) was the type of thug who posted up in the middle of the street and grabbed his crotch at the sanitation truck crews because they left so much garbage on the streets of our hood. He had an unspeakable hatred for the police. People called him a crazy nigga, but never to his face. And when they said it behind closed doors, they were whispering.

I met Drama on the second day of first grade. (He cut school on the first day.) I used to prop up my mathematics book on the desk and hide behind the small print, terrified that the teacher might call my name. I was always shy. Drama was the opposite. He was always the center of attention. The pretty girls most of us dreamed of dating were always chasing him. His father was half Navajo, and Drama had inherited straight hair with just a hint of kinkiness. Sisters love a black man with what they call "good" hair, especially if it's long.

Drama was popular, a gifted athlete who always managed to find just the right comeback to make the whole class collapse in laughter. He was always sure of himself, confident. I was sitting next to him in fifth grade when our teacher, Mr. Gershwin, hung the name Drama on him.

Classroom comedy aside, Drama was a brilliant student. He used to help *me* with my homework. But all that changed when his daddy got shot to death for drug possession and resisting arrest. The police said they found two ten-dollar bags of heroin in his pockets one cool fall night when we were both thirteen. The funny thing was that Reverend Cook despised drugs and alcohol. He never touched them. He was also the gentlest man I had ever known. I had never once heard him even raise his voice.

Why would an unarmed, middle-aged pacifist decide to jump on two young, pistol-toting armed officers of the law? It didn't make sense. People said the cops beat Mr. Cook after mistaking him for a robbery suspect. How the dope wound up in his pockets has been a matter of speculation since his death.

Drama changed after his dad had what his mother termed "his accident." An explosive temper began to bubble in his guts. Once, during a high school lunch period, he pimp-slapped our friend Tiny because he passed gas without saying, "Excuse me." Mr. Bell, a six-foot-four-inch security guard with a jherri curl and iron biceps, heard the scream and saw blood dripping from Tiny's nose. The ex–college linebacker crossed the room in three steps and then swooped down to snatch Drama's wrist.

Drama reached for a carton of chocolate milk with his free hand and flung it at his captor. It was a direct hit. Instinctively, Mr. Bell dropped Drama's arm so he could wipe the chocolate rain from his eyes.

Drama leapt back and hollered, "Punk, don't put your hands on me! What you think this is?"

Eventually, Drama was wrestled to the ground. He was whisked away with his hand twisted upward in an arc behind his back. His eyes were screwed shut; his jaws clenched like a vise beneath the tight flesh of his fire-red face.

Drama cussed everybody from the principal to the janitor and then started in on their mothers. His fellow students went wild, hollering and chanting Drama's name like a war cry. That was the beginning of his legend.

Drama was expelled. When the school system found no further use for him, the streets claimed him.

Drama might take the point of your chin off with a left hook for no other reason than he was crazy like that, but if he called you friend, he was loyal to a fault. I saw that demonstrated on my fifteenth birthday. Grandma gave me the money to go down to Eastmont Mall to buy the new Jordans I'd been dreaming about since my fourteenth birthday. Drama and I bought the sneakers and then stopped off for a quick lunch. We were walking out of the fish-and-chips joint when Drama flicked his head up and back without blinking his eyes. Suddenly, I heard footsteps shuffling behind us. Without looking, I knew I had to either fight or run. Being that I was with Drama, the running option was out.

There were four of them, older cats. They acted as though they were just going to walk past us, but then they turned around and cut us off. I recognized the one who did the talking. I used to watch him shoot hoops in Mosswood Park for money. He was pretty good. They called him Endonesia.

"Where you niggas from?" he asked.

Drama spit out the name of our hood. He folded his arms over his chest and cocked his head to the side. "So, whassup?"

"We don't like niggas from there," Endonesia said, glancing around at his homies.

If I hadn't been with him, Drama might have utilized the element of surprise to put the smashdown on homeboy and then haul up out of there. Knowing him as I did, I believe he tried the nonviolent approach to keep me from being drawn into some street stuff. He sucked his teeth and started walking away. "Come on, Firstborn," he said.

"Firstborn?" Endonesia giggled. "What kinda name is that? Sounds like a girl's name, if ya acks me. Hey, where y'all going? Who told you you could leave? You young niggas can't turn your backs on me!"

In a flash they were on us. I tried to punch with one hand while protecting the shoebox with the other. Drama threw bolo punches and drilled his left jab into swollen eye sockets. "Come git it!" he hollered.

Eventually, a couple of guys five years older and a foot taller picked Drama up from behind and dumped him to the ground. Then they started stomping him. "Run, Firstborn, run!" his muffled voice called out from the bottom of the pack.

"Here," I shouted, tears streaming down my face. I threw down the plastic bag that contained the box of brand-new sneakers. "You got it. Now, leave us alone."

Endonesia scooped up the box off the floor and sneered. "Just my size." He walked away holding his swollen right eye with the palm of his hand. His boys stopped the melee and followed him out to the parking lot.

Drama's shirt was ripped. There were black footprints on his bare arms. His lip was busted and swollen. His mouth was bloody. There was an open gash over his left eyebrow that would leave a permanent scar. He tried to prop himself up, but he was still only semiconscious.

"Please, Firstborn, don't tell me you gave that fool your sneakers."

"They were gonna kill you."

"You mean I took that whuppin' for nothin'?"

I put my head down and mumbled, "Most people would have jetted. Why did you take that beating for me?"

Drama looked at me and rolled his eyes. "Are you kidding? My daddy used to say, 'All a poor man's got is his friends.'"

A security guard with an ample middle and tight shoes trotted toward us. "I saw what happened," he said, huffing for breath.

Drama glared at him. "Then why didn't you jump in it?"

The guard shrugged. "You want me to call the police?"

"If you wasn't man enough to get down for your mans, don't call nobody now!"

We went to the older cats in our hood and broke down what happened. They knew Endonesia, and by the code we lived by, they should have gone down to his block and taken turns breaking their feet off in the tender part of his posterior. But the answer we heard was "We got business with Endonesia and dem niggas."

Endonesia didn't have any love for the OGs from our hood, but drugs and money were being exchanged and business, as they say, is business. No one would help us. I never did get my sneakers back.

Drama made a deep antisocial transformation. He became worse than ever. He developed a new network of friends, dangerous cats who made their money the old-fashioned way: they stomped out fools and ripped off their pockets. Drama traded his perfect English for slang. He swapped the Boy Scout motto for the code of the block hog: "If it's got to be either me or you, best believe it's not going to be me."

CHAPTER
THREE

THE NEXT MORNING, A BLOOD-RED SUN PIERCED THROUGH MY dingy blinds like a razor. Out on the sidewalk, Blue Magic's old song "Sideshow" floated up from the stereo speakers in someone's low rider. When I stretched out my arms, I could almost touch each of the walls in my room at Ms. Chapman's boarding house. There wasn't much to the plasterboard cube, just an army mattress on a metal cot. Stacks of college textbooks filled the small space between the bed and the TV stand.

The clock said 8:00 a.m. I grabbed a blue tank top and some denim shorts and then slipped into my beach sandals. I grabbed the plastic grocery bag that contained my cologne, soap, and toothpaste. I slammed the bedroom door and rushed for the community shower down the hall. I needed to get there before Nelson the plumber did. Sometimes I didn't make it. On those mornings, Nelson often left me in the hall, dancing from one foot to the other while he colored his bald spot with cheap red hair dye and spent the next hour sitting on the bowl perusing *National Geographic*.

That morning, I got to the shower before Ms. Chapman, the landlady, came roaring through the halls, as she often did, howling and threatening, rubbing her thumb and middle finger together in the universal symbol for money. "Firstborn," she said, "you trifling, no-account deadbeat. You were a good payer for two years but now you ain't paid no rent in two weeks. You got three days to get my money or all your crap is going out on the street and I'm changing the locks." I had no reason to doubt her. I had seen her do this to others.

Leo, a chunky night-shift bread baker, came waddling down the hall as I left the bathroom, steam rushing out behind me like foam at the bottom of a waterfall.

"Hey, Leo, what's up with ya? They hirin' down at your place yet?"

His matching navy blue shirt and pants made him look like a blue hot-water bottle. He sucked his teeth in annoyance. "You ask me that every time I see you. And what do I always say?"

"Yeah, well, one day you're going to say yes."

I took the stairs two by two and snatched the front door open. I had to lower my eyes to shield them from the force of the sun. A strong Pacific breeze rolled across my bald scalp. Clouds hung like gray cotton balls suspended in midair.

A Mother's Finest moving van belched, filling my lungs with carbon monoxide. I covered my mouth and nose with both hands, but it was useless trying to keep the poison out.

The dull swirling of rotor blades caused me to look up. Ghetto birds circled overhead. The Oakland Police Department hunted evildoers down below with the aid of high-power binoculars.

I strolled past Greater Second Baptist Church, a sky blue storefront building squeezed between a liquor store and a funeral parlor. In the distance, the BART train hummed quietly on the elevated rails that carried commuters downtown and to San Francisco.

I tripped over broken sangria bottles, old phone cards, and cigarette butts. Someone had dumped green couch cushions with a pink floral print next to broken lamps and an old stereo right on the sidewalk. A few of the houses on my block had house numbers as long as your forearm nailed to their façades, just in case the police had to find them in a hurry.

Three bright-faced girls with braided hair skipped jump-rope as their worried mother stood in the doorway searching the block for stray bullets and potential kidnappers. An Oakland patrol car zoomed by as fast as a bolt of black lightning.

On the next block, a shrine comprised of helium balloons, empty Moët bottles, and blue votive candles surrounded a photograph of a young black man with his red, white, and gold San Francisco 49ers baseball cap twisted on backward. He flashed a gang sign as his boys stood back, arm folded over arm. The young brother was gone now to either heaven or hell. The image of his mortal self was nothing more than a memory left behind for the living.

I crossed the railroad tracks and made a right by a salvage yard. A pale gray pit bull with black stripes glanced up, homicide blazing in her eyes. The owner was known to mix hot sauce and gunpowder with the raw hamburger clumps in her feeding bowl. She flexed her gigantic shoulder muscles for me and growled like something otherworldly.

A brother with a fade-away haircut stood in front of a salmon-colored, three-story apartment building. His blue T-shirt exhibited a picture of Oakland's skyline. The words beneath the photo said, "Yay Area."

"What you want here, lame?" the guy in the T-shirt snapped.

"Norman, don't you remember me?"

He squinted harshly before his eyes burst wide with recognition. A smile puffed out his unshaven cheeks. "Firstborn, is that you? Give me some love, son!" He moved in to encircle me with both arms. He held me tightly for a moment and then released. It occurred to me that I hadn't seen my old high school buddy in about two years.

"Norm, where you been, dawg?"

"CDC, San Luis Obispo. Just got home yesterday."

"Welcome to the free world, my friend."

The brain-deadening roar of unmuffled motorcycle engines momentarily made conversation impossible. Beyond us two men in black leather suits, complete with chaps, popped wheelies on their chromed-out Harley Davidson choppers. They wore colors representing one of East Oakland's black motorcycle clubs. Norman and I stared at each other uncomfortably for a full minute before the din dissipated and allowed us to hear each other's voices again.

"Firstborn, you know where dey hirin'?"

"I'm out here lookin' myself. Man, if I catch on to something I'll get at you. Now, let me get up here and see what my man Drama's talkin' 'bout."

"Be careful out here, man. We done lost too many."

What a curious way to say good-bye.

Norman opened the iron entrance door for me. I felt him staring at my back as I trotted up the steps to the second-floor landing. I walked around the side of the building. The apartment doors faced the street.

As I searched for apartment 6, my mind's calendar flipped back five months to December 21. That was the last time I'd seen Drama. The Eight Ball Club was packed tight that night. The black walled box was equator hot. Humidity condensed on the ceiling and dripped down like a tropical drizzle. DJ Cake cut the hip hop funk on the one and two. Cats with dreads and blue hoodies went dumb with brown-skinned cuties in skin-tight dresses and gold hoop earrings.

The vast majority of the adults who live in any hood are law-abiding citizens whose only desire is to live in peace and be left in peace. If they are fortunate enough to own or rent a house, they keep their hedges trimmed and their lawns cut. They work every day, whether it's serving fast food or filing court documents. They go to the church, mosque, or temple. They love family cookouts and they participate in the block association. Most of their kids have never held a gun or sold a cocaine rock. But then there's that other small percentage. Welcome to that world.

Should the NAACP ever decide to create a chapter for thugs and ridaz, the Eight Ball Club would be a prime location for headquarters. Its was near Edes and Ninety-eighth in a warehouse behind a weed field. You wouldn't go in there unless you were trouble or looking for it.

Big Butch, an ex-Marine in a camouflage field jacket, patted you down before you walked through the door. R.G., the bartender, peered out at the strobe lights and dark corners through the blue lenses of his sunglasses while serving drinks in dirty glasses. The bass from the super-sized woofers hit your chest like a cannon ball.

Brothers and sisters from hoods all over the East were there that night: the Murder Dubbs, the Dirty 30s, the Shady Eighties, the Rolling 100s, High Street, 11-500, 65 Vill, 69 Vill, Funk Town, Jingle Town, and Stone City.

Drama's cousin, Sideshow Psycho, grabbed the mike and strolled back and forth with a pronounced gangsta limp. His gray-and-black Raiders cap hid his eyes. We called him Sideshow Psycho because whenever we closed the streets off to do our thing, he'd come racing through in his '79 Buick Electra, smoking up his tires and slamming into parked cars.

You never knew when he might come out of a donut and run you over.

People don't really appreciate some drunken fool bashing their car doors in. The only reason he was still walking around healthy was because of his bloodline. Sideshow Psycho was Drama's first cousin from New Orleans. He came out here after Katrina. I had to admit, homeboy could flow on that microphone after he had a couple of bottles of cold beer in him.

The one spotlight in the house flashed against his gold teeth as he jumped into his circa 1984 b-boy stance and started trash talking on the mike. "Is deep East O in this mutha? Then shout yo' mama's name. Lemme hear ya say, 'Ho!'"

Pandemonium broke out. Drama laughed and flipped him both middle fingers.

"Somebody say happy birthday, D Montana!"

"Happy birthday, D Montana!" the crowd hollered.

Drama and I sat with our elbows propped on the bar, ice-cold beer bottles in our hands. This was his night. His long, black hair twisted into a single braid that fell over his back like a horse's mane. A .9 millimeter pistol bulged in the waistband of his bulky black leather jacket. Cats from around the block came up one by one and hugged him, each greeting him with "Happy birthday." Fine-looking girls in miniskirts left scarlet lipstick prints on his cheeks.

A shapely eighteen-year-old with shoulder-length extensions and a two-piece camouflage outfit flanked Drama's left side. An olive green field commander's cap and mirrored sunglasses shielded her eyes. Renee curled her top lip in a snarl at any sister who approached Drama, but Drama had a hit-it-and-quit-it mentality. Renee was one of the many women he had run through.

Something in Renee spooked me. I couldn't put my finger on it, but I felt it deep down. She thought she was in love with Drama, but he believed that romance was for squares and marks. I wish I had a twenty for every time he told me, "Firstborn, a real playa don't fall in love."

Around midnight, two head busters from the block drifted in out of the darkness. Ray Ray was a dark tan brother with a bald head and scraggly goatee. His gut looked like he was hiding a bowling ball underneath his shirt. Every once in a while he would pat his paunch and say, "That's good living there, potna."

Ray Ray summoned Drama with a curve of the finger. Drama's body language told me he didn't want to hear from these guys. But he got up from his stool and went to the far end of the bar.

Drama kept me away from that part of his life. I was the aspiring novelist and he was the stick-up man. I knew how he made his money, but never knew enough about it to speak intelligently on it from a witness stand, which is how I wanted it. I nursed my beer and waited. Occasionally, I caught snippets of their conversation.

"Where da lick at?" That was the first thing out of Drama's mouth before a new hyphy joint drowned him out.

Drama's eyebrows rose and fell with reluctant interest. The thugs leaned forward as Drama drew an imaginary map in the palm of his hand with his index finger. The conversation ceased. Dollar and Ray Ray sauntered toward the door. Drama returned to my side. Before I could continue our earlier discussion, he said, "Look, man, I gotta go take care of some business. I'll be back in an hour. Wait for me."

Ray Ray waved at me, almost as an afterthought, before he followed Drama out the door. I waved back. Then he winked at a girl with green eyes who kept twisting her maroon bar stool in a semi-circle.

The next time I saw Ray Ray he was stretched out in a casket, wreaking of formaldehyde. Ambition killed him.

Drama's specialty was sticking up dope spots and gambling houses. He worked with a loose-knit team of lookouts, second-story men, and shooters. In the company of this riff-raff, he developed a trademark. He was always the first one through the door and the last to leave. If you did dirt with Drama, he was going to do his best to see that everybody on his team was safe.

On that fateful night, Ray Ray wanted to prove that he was as fearless as the legend himself. He insisted on going in the door first. As fate would have it, the mark was crouched in the dark, clutching a street sweeper in his sweaty hands. When Ray Ray touched the doorknob, the mark squeezed the trigger. The blast blew the door apart and sent fire-hot iron through Ray Ray's liver, heart, and intestines. Ray Ray didn't have time to holler, "Help me, Jesus!" before death shut his eyes.

In the confusion, the d-boy ran straight into Drama. He pulled his firearm back, ready to make it two for two. Drama seized the barrel and popped the mark with an overhand right. The victim bled from his mouth but held on to the street sweeper with both hands. The two of them fell to the dusty hallway floor, grunting and cussing in the semi-darkness, fighting for control of the weapon.

Who knows what the neighbors thought about what they heard. Not one of them opened a door. Someone, however, did call the police.

The mark pleaded self-defense for Ray Ray's murder, but pressed charges against Drama for terrorist threats and attempted murder. It didn't look good for D Montana.

Again fate intervened. One of our homeboys, Dwayne Richardson, aka "Street Life," was paroled from Pleasant Valley State Prison two weeks before Drama's trial was scheduled to begin. Life was a bad nigga, and few people wanted anything to do with him. His progress chart in elementary school had red letters scrawled out at the top of every page that read, "Emotionally disturbed."

When he was seventeen, Street Life broke into somebody's house along with two other brothers, G-Style and Hen. An inquisitive neighbor called the police, and Life and Hen got sent to the YA. Three brothers got arrested, two did time. It didn't take a brain surgeon to figure out who the snitch was. When Life got out he went looking for G-Style. Wisely, G-Style's family put him on the first thing smoking to Beaumont, Texas.

Life was furious at being outwitted. So one afternoon, he went down to the supermarket where G-Style's mom worked as a checker. He shot her while she was bagging groceries. He never went to jail for that, but everybody knew about it. Life wasn't exactly keeping it a secret.

Drama shot Life a kite from a holding cell in the Santa Rita jail. The situation was desperate. This wasn't Drama's first offense, and the best that "Jaws" (a high-priced Harvard-educated lawyer who specialized in mobsters) could negotiate for him was a plea bargain with a seven-year price tag tied to it. Drama needed help.

Why did Street Life get involved? Drama was a top feeder, an earner, a shot caller. Money had a way of dropping down in his shadow. Life wasn't so much helping out as he was putting in a job application.

Street Life went right to work. He combed the back-alley gin joints and trap houses for any word on where the plaintiff might have been holing up. He had to kick in a few doors, but he climbed through the right window one morning around three a.m. He had his witness.

It was a brief conversation but an effective one. A man like Life doesn't have to hold long conversations, especially after he's climbed through your bedroom window in the middle of the night, kicked your sleeping woman out of bed, and woken you up by pressing the cold, steel business end of a .9 millimeter pistol against your tonsils.

The witness walked into the courtroom the next day, trembling like a hypothermia victim. Life sat among a dozen spectators in the gallery, neatly turned out in a black pinstripe suit, his hair pressed and greased down into long, tight cornrows. He never said a word, never altered his facial expression. But the plaintiff took one furtive glance in Street Life's direction, gasped, and stiffened in his chair like rigor mortis was setting in. His lawyer whispered frantically in his ear but the star witness shook his head four times. He had just come down with a severe case of amnesia. Case dismissed. Drama was released.

I stood at the apartment door knocking, hoping Drama might have salted away a few dollars when he was rolling, at least enough to help a good friend in a pinch.

"Who is it?" a woman's voice inquired after my second knock.

"It's me. Firstborn."

Drama's sister squealed with delight when she saw me. She had café-au-lait flesh as flawless as sandalwood. She caressed my face with her long red fingernails and gave me a gentle peck on the cheek. Sandra was beginning to spread out around the waist and hips, but a blind man could tell you that the years had done her well.

"Mama, look who's here," Sandra screamed. She carried on like I had just returned from Iraq in one piece. She threw her arms around me a second time and rocked me back and forth. "My little brother, I'm so glad to see you! Come in. Drama's home."

A gigantic portrait of a white Jesus with moist blue eyes and flowing blond hair scrutinized the footsteps of anyone who walked into the living room. A golden plaque on the wall above the floor-model television set said, "Go ye into all the world and preach the gospel." Sandra led me to the kitchen, where roaches were running a marathon across the stovetop.

Ms. Velvet sat at the kitchen table in a blue house dress with a floral print. Oval-shaped sunglasses with steel frames and pitch-black lenses covered her eyes. Though she could no longer tell night from day, she still sat with her favorite Bible propped open in front of her. The Five Blind Boys from Alabama crooned "Amazing Grace" from a tiny transistor radio on the kitchen table. I leaned down to kiss the old woman's forehead. She touched my face, searching for recognition.

"Hello, Ms. Velvet," I whispered.

She smoothed the top of my head with her soft fingers and giggled. "Sandra, this boy's as bald headed as a cucumber. Boy, when'd you cut off all your hair? And why ain't you been to see me? Herbert don't have to be here for you to stop by."

"I'm sorry, Ms. Velvet. I've been trying to find a job."

"Found one?

"Not yet."

"You will. It's hard times, son. But be persistent. God will make a way for you."

I smiled and kissed her cheek. "I'm gonna go holler at Drama."

"Yeah, maybe you can talk some sense into that bad-behind boy of mine. He's not like you. You're a good boy. Herbert's got a bad bone in his body."

I patted her cotton-soft hand and started toward Drama's room. Sandra ran in front of me and pushed the door open. "Drama, guess who's here?" she hollered with glee. Sandra flipped on her heel and headed back to the kitchen.

Though it was morning on a sunny day, Drama's room was dim and humid and filled with posters. Pam Grier leered at me with a .45 Magnum in one hand, the other resting on her ample hips. A bald-headed Isaac Hayes stretched forth his bronze forearms, palms up like a man baring his soul. Gold chains swung down from Isaac's neck. Snoop Dogg held a bottle of St. Ide's malt liquor in his palm as though it contained sparkling water from the mystical Fountain of Youth.

Sideshow Psycho's vocals bounced out of two sets of twelve-inch woofers: "I put my nine in your mug. Then I watch you bug. I be that Bushrod thug. Ready to pop a slug."

"My nigga!" Drama hollered, flying over to meet me in the doorway.

His hair had grown in jail. It hung over his shoulders in pigtails. He was shirtless. The 510 tattoo across his chest was new, as were the block letters across his right forearm that read, "R.I.P. Ray Ray." "EAST OAKLAND" was scripted in a big semicircle that started between his shoulder blades and ended at the small of his back. Drama's blue jeans drooped down gangsta style, showing off his red-and-white-plaid Tommy Hilfiger boxers. A lightning-bolt scar cut through one of his eyebrows—a souvenir from that fateful afternoon in Eastmont Mall, thirteen years ago.

"Man, where you been?" he asked. "I been home two weeks and this is the first time I'm seeing you?"

Drama dropped his arms around me and pounded my back three times. He pushed me back and took a long look. I could see my reflection in his dark pupils. They danced with joy as he beheld me. He spoke so rapidly it seemed that everything he said was one sentence. "First, you lost weight. But you dress corny as ever. I went to that dump you lived in and the landlady cussed me out, said she wasn't leaving no messages 'cause you owed some paper."

Drama hollered out into the kitchen, "Hey, Sandra, Firstborn's hungry. Make 'im a plate of something."

"I'm making breakfast now," Sandra called from down the hall. "Our little brother knows he's welcome to eat with us."

"Can you stay, homie?" Drama asked. Without waiting for my response, he hollered back, "Sure, he can stay!"

Drama pulled me into the room and closed the door, then nodded to a shadowy figure in the corner. "Hey, First, look who's here." When he stepped aside, I nodded a greeting at trouble.

Street Life sprawled out on the velvet-cushioned chair, his head tilted back, a forty-ounce beer bottle clamped in his hand. He was about my height, five foot eight. His colossal afro was cut as round as a basketball. His eyes were narrow slits stuffed with darkness. Street Life's jailhouse muscles bulged in a T-shirt that said, "I ain't afraid a no Po-Po!"

A shirt announcing that one had no fear of the police could draw attention from the wrong people, I thought.

"What up wid it, folks?" I asked.

"From birth to the turf, reppin' that town all day, yada-mean?" Street life replied.

These were the brothers I grew up with. They weren't bad guys, but they lived by the rules of an alternate universe. Drama might have been a United States army general or a CEO at General Motors had he been born in Montclair or Piedmont. And if Street Life had been born in a more affluent neighborhood, he might have grown up to be the president of Enron.

Street Life lit fire to a stick of cherry incense and stuck the unlit end in a hole in Drama's bedroom wall. Drama unfolded a tiny plastic envelope with tiny green marijuana leafs printed on it. He took a copy of his work resume, ripped off a corner, and folded the bottom of the sheet. He poured the last of the purple weed into the crease. With expert dexterity, he twisted the weed into a cigarette. He put the joint into his mouth and rolled it around his lips, using saliva as an adhesive. He handed the finished product to me. "Spark it up, Firstborn."

I pulled the purple haze deep into my lungs. It tasted bittersweet, like ether. A cough started deep in my belly and shook my lungs. Street Life and Drama laughed. I forced down another hit and passed it to Street Life, who began a coughing fit of his own. Smoke enveloped him like a dragon spitting fire.

I leaned back in the darkness of Drama's room, my fingers burnt and my lungs on fire. The three of us were like orphans in a storm. I daydreamed of the numbing familiarity of high school, the purposefulness of the classroom, the strict order that the ringing bells represented, the love and nurture of teachers, the freedom of having no responsibility other than to oneself and one's peers. This new world I could not understand. We'd been out of high school for almost ten years, yet not one of us had ever been gainfully employed for more than eight months at a time.

Drama passed out tiny plastic cups. He poured a generous shot of Bacardi into the bottom of each one. "Ain't no soda in the house. Y'all gotta drink it straight."

Street Life frowned. "Your mama ain't got no Coke in the fridge, man?"

"Nigga, this ain't Burger King. You cain't have it yo' way all the time."

"Same old Drama, still wearing his behind up on his shoulders."

A white plastic fan swirled stale air around a room that couldn't have been much larger than Life's old prison cell. The morning sun blasted through the tightly drawn yellowed shades, casting a somber shadow over the three of us.

Ms. Velvet's gospel music wafted in from beneath the door. Drama cranked up the hip hop oldies station until Public Enemy's "Night of the Living Baseheads" drowned out "Amazing Grace."

"So, what's up, First?" Life asked. "I thought you'd be playing frat boy at some big college by now."

I yanked the wrinkled Alston University catalog out of my back pocket and flung it down at his brand-new Air Force Ones. "This is where I want to go," I said. "They've got the most highly respected Writings of the African Diaspora program in the country. Pervis Newhart just came over from Notre Dame to teach the Poetry of the Harlem Renaissance class. His book, *Sonnets of Freedom*, changed my life. It's my dream to take classes with him."

"So why don't you go for it, cuz?"

"I have a scholarship, but I still need a big piece of money to get in the door."

"How much we talkin' 'bout?" Drama asked.

"Major g's."

Drama's eyes blazed hot, like twin black suns. He picked up his curling bar and started busting out sets until sweat popped out on his forehead and biceps. "First, if I had my paper right, I'd pay for you to go to that school." He spit through clenched teeth. He stared over Life's shoulder as he flipped the college catalog. "You belong at Alston. You're as good as any of those white boys in there, probably smarter than most of them.

Look at that fool!" Drama nodded at the picture of waif-thin Louis Cronston, president of the lacrosse team.

Street Life cursed under his breath. Drama blanched red. We had learned to live with shattered dreams and speared expectations, but this one stirred rage in the belly. The governor had slashed millions from the higher educational system budget. Outreach programs and financial aid coffers that had once offered help to California's hoods and trailer parks had been raided. Affirmative-action programs that had once helped minorities escape the East Oaklands of California had been crushed. I was holding on to the last leaf of the last branch, and it had been greased to slip through my fingers.

"Was you at your boy's quiet hour last night?" Drama asked.

"Yeah, man, I was there."

"I heard it was open casket."

"True indeed."

"That's some foul madness, man. How you gonna have open casket when the nigga's face done been shot off?"

That was a good question, but my heart thumped with a more urgent matter. "Drama, do you have any money? I'm a little behind on my rent."

He shook his head. "Sorry, bro', the safe is empty. Jaws got it all. He don't open his mouth to stick a toothpick in it for less than two grand. They don't call him Jaws for nothin'."

"Then I may need to bunk up on your couch for a couple a weeks. The old lady's going to put me out any day now."

"You always got a place here, homie. We'll find somewhere to put you up long as we can. But we got our own problems. Came home two weeks ago and found an eviction notice taped to the door. Sandra said it's the third one."

Street Life rested his elbows in his lap. "I been out all week trying to put in applications and resumes."

"Any luck?"

"Not even a phone call." He folded his hands like he was praying. "Ain't nobody tryin' to hire a convicted felon with two strikes."

I felt Street Life's pain. Brothers released from the great iron house get put on the bus back to society with a prison record, no saleable job skills, no place to live, and two hundred dollars in gate money. For many of the dudes I came up with, a release date was nothing more than the revolving door of a vicious cycle. After the two hundred dollars was gone, they would go back out to the block to survive. They felt that crime was the only option society had left open to them. It wasn't long before they got arrested again. After a few months or years, the treadmill spun around again.

"I been home from Pelican Bay for three months, man," Street Life said. "I got kids I can't feed and my PO been breathin' down my back 'bout makin' restitution. They don't care how I get it. They just want they money. Man, I don't wanna do it, but I may have to take my game to the streets again."

I took a puff of the weed. He was trapped. We were all trapped. Personally, I was determined to escape the situation. "What are we going to do?"

Street Life and Drama exchanged glances. Life turned to me with a whimsical smile. "Look out the window, First."

I gathered myself to my feet, my head spinning in a cloud. I pulled at the bottom of the window but it was stuck. I could only budge it two inches, just enough to draw in a mouth full of exhaust fumes when the AC Transit bus lumbered past. Down below, a young brother with a Mohawk haircut and a T-shirt that stretched to his knees flashed me the peace sign. I nodded.

"What you see?"

Through the dirt-caked window, I looked out over deep East Oakland—concrete Hades. Lost, broken men sucked suds from broken beer bottles in paper bags. Middle-aged whores in platinum wigs and pancake makeup plied their trade in front of candy stores. Three liquor stores did business within the span of a single city block. "I don't see anything," I said over my shoulder.

"Look closer."

Young men with sagging pants and Nike sneakers flipped tiny packages of white powder into the sweaty hands of housewives, hustlers, bankers, and would-be ballers. Thousands of ones and tens changed hands. Dope, crack, weed, crystal meth, any poison your heart desired could be bargained for at this outdoor drug bazaar. I turned away from the depressing scene. "What am I looking for?"

Life sucked the joint, his cheeks ballooning as the smoke filled his lungs. He shook the ashes loose from the end. He took another hit, breathing in with a hiss, then he passed it to me. As the joint burned down to a roach, conversation grew virtually nonexistent.

Drama broke the silence. "Firstborn, do you think you could ever shoot a nigga in his face?"

My head felt like it could have floated off my shoulders. "Depends. I guess I could do it in self-defense. Why?"

"No reason."

Street Life traded glances with Drama again, then joined me at the window and gazed outside.

Street Life's fascination with the world of pimps, whores, and hustlers had earned him his nickname. Whenever someone got his throat cut, Life always had a theory about why it had happened.

That warm April afternoon, he studied the block from the window like a scientist peering at protozoa through the optical lens of a microscope.

On the corner, six black men smoked Pall Mall cigarettes and counted fistfuls of twenties and fifties. Two others argued over the lyrics of a popular hip hop song.

A small crowd crouched together like penitents at a Pentecostal prayer meeting, leaning over the bent backs of three gamblers as they cracked red cubes with white dots against the curb. "Shake the dice up, shake the nigga up," one of them hollered. A few teenage girls strutted by. The gambling group looked up and hollered X-rated comments at them. They passed by without replying.

I recognized these brothers. Our hood legends used to do business with those fools, but something went down grimy and there had been bloodshed on both sides. When the ATF broke down doors on some of our triple OGs, Endonesia and his crew stepped in like an occupying force. We didn't like it, but what could we do? They were strapped down like the National Guard. Even now, thirteen years later, Endonesia still walked around with black Jordans on his feet.

Endonesia came around the corner and circled the group like a big yellow rooster. His T-shirt hung over his belt line, and a white do rag covered his braided head. He was hollering something that I couldn't hear. My guess was that he was trying to motivate his greyhounds to get in the race. Those dudes seemed more interested in joking and playing at stacking chips. That's not to say that they weren't making money. But I saw it like this: if it was raining quarters from heaven one day, any fool with a Dixie cup could get ten dollars worth, but a hustler with some real game would fill up his swimming pool.

Uzi was looking to fill up the swimming pool. He did his business on the corner across the street from the crack slingers. Uzi was a five-foot-four Jamaican cat with a wispy mustache and glassy eyes. He wore a yellow T-shirt with the image of the late Tupac Shakur across the stomach. The words above the picture had been faded by too many washings, but they used to be the album name: "All Eyez on Me."

Uzi sold "zips": plastic bags each filled with an ounce of weed. If he got in a large shipment of product, he hired people to break it down into dime bags and loose joints and then sell it. Drama worked for Uzi from time to time. I never bothered. Selling weed didn't pay very well. It was bulky, and you had to sell a lot of it to make a profit. Selling it for someone else was pretty much a waste of time, especially if you smoked it like Drama did.

Uzi kept zips and half zips, filled with sticky green buds and stems, stored in a beat-up brown paper bag. The sack lay beneath a mailbox a few feet away from where he stood.

A car pulled up to the corner. Uzi held his thumb and forefinger to his lips and pulled them back and forth rapidly as though he were smoking a joint. The universal symbol for "I got it." The transaction took less than thirty seconds. Four more cars pulled over in about seven minutes.

I turned to Life. "The only one making any money out there is Uzi."

"You got it, First," Drama said, the joint glowing down to its final ember between his burnt fingertips. "That's why we're going to stick that nigga."

"What do you mean?"

"We gonna run up in his crib."

This is not good, I thought. Actions like this start the ring of violence that ends up in people getting killed. I wasn't raised to do burglaries. Plus, this seemed reckless, and I had always assumed Drama was a smart criminal, if there is such a thing.

"Suppose you can get his supply," I said. "What you gonna do with it?"

"Sell it." Street Life turned to Drama. "Where's your tools?"

Drama reached under his Mickey Mouse pillowcase and pulled out a carpenter's hammer with an iron block on the end. I was high, so my thoughts were muddled. But Drama's plan confused me further. Uzi was part of Endonesia's crew. These cats were hard hitters. They weren't going to stand still while Drama punked their homeboy.

I peered at Drama. "Do you know why they call him Uzi?" A mean laugh crept up from Drama's throat. "Yeah. 'Cause he's got a machine gun and he ain't afraid to use it."

Street Life glared at Drama, then turned to me. "Firstborn, that nigga is so soft he use Tampons." He said his words slowly, enunciating each syllable. "I can take care of that fool. My question is: Are you down?"

I couldn't breathe. Debt had wrapped its scaly fingers around my throat. In less than twenty-four hours, the landlady would go into my room, throw my belongings into garbage bags, and set them out on the curb like trash for neighbors to peruse. At that moment, I didn't have the luxury of choosing either right or wrong. My only choice was survival.

"Yeah, I'm down."

Those three words were going to haunt me for a long time.

AND THE DEVIL SAID,
"BOW DOWN, D MONTANA,
AND I WILL GIVE YOU
UNTOLD WEALTH."

CHAPTER
FOUR

THE NEXT DAY, TUESDAY, I SHOWED UP AT DRAMA'S PLACE around five p.m. He and Street Life leaned against the building's gate, passing a half-empty forty-ounce bottle of Old English 800 back and forth. Drama thrust the bottle toward me. I didn't care much for Old Gold, but I took a sip just to be social.

"Kill it," Drama demanded.

I hoisted the bottle up and sucked down the bitter brew until the bottle made a hollow *ping* noise. My brain felt weightless inside my skull. I tried to set the empty bottle down on the sidewalk but stumbled when I leaned over.

"You all right, man?" Street Life asked with a chuckle.

"I'm fine."

"Let's do the damn thing, then," Life said. "Drama, you set?"

Drama peeled back the lining of his Oakland Raiders jacket to reveal a baby sledge hammer. I couldn't see his eyes behind his pitch-black sunglasses. A headband with the silver Raiders emblem circled his forehead. His black jeans sagged halfway down his rear end, exposing blue-striped boxers and leaving excess fabric bunched up at his knees.

I yanked at one of Drama's plaits. "You and these pigtails, man. I swear…"

Neither of us had the money for cab fare. So we walked thirty blocks to our destination at Havenscourt and International Boulevard. As we neared the intersection, Drama nodded at a gray hovel where three young brothers sat on broken kitchen chairs on the porch, slapping down playing cards. Every few seconds they aimed casual side glances in our direction. They were wannabes, down with Endonesia's crew.

"I ain't really feelin' this, man," I whispered. "Too many witnesses."

Drama chuckled. "Stop trying to sound so hood. When I get stuck on a trigonometry problem, I'll call you. But when it come to the streets, I'm a straight-A student. Now, let's roll."

Drama gave a flip of his head and we followed him through an alley around the back of the house. A sea of weeds and knee-high grass pushed through patches of broken concrete that littered the backyard. The back door of the house was clasped together by an iron padlock.

"Lemme git that sledge, D."

Drama handed the sledge hammer to Street Life, who lifted it high above his head. His biceps rippled as the business end landed squarely on the lock. The hammer left a black mark but didn't seem to have any real effect.

"Life, you done gone soft on me while you was inside. Lemme get that, baby boy."

"Nigga, you must be mad," Street Life said, his manhood now in question.

The next whack sent broken metal flying. We were inside quicker than a match head could strike fire.

Uzi's woman, a petite twenty-year-old, stood in the middle of the living room, gripping part of a peeled tangerine in her left hand. Long dreadlocks fell down her back, wrapped in a green tie-dyed headpiece. Silver bracelets on each wrist collided with one another as she held up her hands and hollered, "Don't hurt me," in a horrified Caribbean accent.

"Do you know who I am?" Drama asked. He leaned forward, a smiling playing at the corner of his mouth.

Her lips trembled. "I've never seen you before."

Drama sauntered past her and made his way to a square wooden table in the middle of the living room. Life and I followed. Two of the chairs around the table had angel harps carved into the back rests and thick seat cushions reupholstered with daisy yellow fabric. The other two chairs had red plastic seats and iron legs.. A bowl of tangerines, oranges, and apples sat on the kitchen table.

Drama turned one of the chairs backward and sat facing the woman. "You're lying to me. You know who I am. It wasn't a month ago, I sat right at this table. You fixed curry goat with rice and peas for dinner for me and your man."

Her legs buckled slightly.

Drama raised his right eyebrow. "Remember me now?"

"What do you want, Mr. Drama?"

Drama clapped his hands and nodded. "You remember my name."

The woman's eyes narrowed and her backbone straightened. She pointed a long fingernail in Drama's direction. "I told my husband he was a fool to trust you. I said, 'That one has the eyes of a cobra and he'll harm even the ones who love him.' And I was right, wasn't I? You're here to bite the hand that fed you, aren't you?"

"So you know what I want?"

"It's not here. Uzi doesn't keep his business in the house with his children. If you were a real man, you wouldn't walk up to the house of a friend with two gangsters to face down an unarmed woman."

Drama gave Street Life a barely perceptible lowering of his chin. Life grabbed a handful of the woman's dreadlocks, then bounced her onto the bare wooden floor. A scream rattled the windows.

The woman shook herself and tried to rise, but Street Life kicked her back down. He plunged the instep of his sneaker into her windpipe. She grabbed his foot with both hands, but his iron calf muscles rose to the challenge.

Gurgling and grating sounds emanated from deep in her throat. Spittle formed at the corners of her mouth. Life continued to ground her windpipe with his foot. Tears streamed down the sides of her face as life ebbed away.

I felt like I was trapped in a movie screen during a horror flick. I was ten seconds away from being party to homicide and I didn't know what to do about it.

Drama reached into the bowl of fruit and grabbed the tangerine that sat on top of two cherry-red apples. He slowly and carefully peeled away the skin of the fruit and then slipped a slice into his mouth, never once taking his eyes off the woman, whose eyes stretched wide in torment. Fruit juice clung to his fingers. "You got a napkin around this joint?" he asked in disgust. "Damn it, where's a napkin when you need one?"

"Drama," I cried out, "he's going to kill her." I didn't sign up for a 187 charge.

"Then talk to her, man. Convince her to cooperate with us."

I scrambled over to the prone body and dropped to my knees so I could look her square in the eyes. Her knees pointed upward, her sandal soles planted flat on the floor as she struggled to dislodge the foot that interrupted her breathing.

"Please," I begged her, "tell them where it is. Give us what we want and we'll leave you alone." I was so terrified my heart felt like it wanted to dribble against the floor.

Her lips parted but no sound came out.

"Move your foot, you moron," I hollered up at Street Life, who looked ten feet tall from that view. "She's trying to tell us something."

Life answered my demand with a brutal stare, a silent warning that he'd be happy to let me change places with the victim. He lifted his sneaker from her neck and stepped back a few inches.

Uzi's woman sprang up like a jack-in-the-box. She rubbed her throat as she gulped for air.

"Well?" Drama said dispassionately, one leg crossed over the other.

"Fridge," she gasped. "In the freezer."

Drama jumped up from the chair. I followed him into the kitchen. He flung open the olive green door. Behind a half pint of Breyer's rocky-road ice cream and six all-beef hot dogs lay a dark brown plastic bag. The pungent weed told on itself even before we yanked it out of the freezer. There had to be a kilo inside that bag.

I followed Drama back into the living room, where the young woman stood. Her tiny frame trembled as she gulped for oxygen. Her fingertips raced up and down her neck. Street Life stood next to her, scowling, his arms folded.

"May we have the machine gun, please?" Drama asked like a third grader seeking a teacher's permission to use the bathroom.

"Big bedroom. Under the mattress."

Drama raced to the back of the house.

I stayed with Life this time. Uzi's girl stared at me as though I had just pinched the last spoonful of applesauce out of her baby's mouth. A glowing hatred pulsated from her eyes and radiated through her light brown pupils.

"Can I get you a glass of water, miss?" I asked.

As soon as the words came out of my mouth, I knew they sounded weird. Sort of like an executioner asking the inmate in the electric chair if he wanted his shirt collar loosened.

The woman wrinkled her nose at me in disgust.

Drama raced back into the living room, playing with the safety on the black machine gun. He threw the gun and four metal clips inside a white pillowcase and walked past the woman as if she didn't exist. Life and I headed for the back door.

As my companions left the house, I looked back. The woman fell to the floor and balled up in a fetal position, shivering and praying for God's mercy.

Shame covered me like a coat. What if someone had treated one of my loved ones the way we had treated her? "I'm sorry," I whispered. She looked away, denying me forgiveness. I followed my friends through the broken door.

We walked in silence until we reached the corner of East Sixty-ninth and International, where we passed the Martin Luther King Jr. Public Library.

"What was that all about, man?" I finally asked.

"What was what all about?" Drama asked.

"How about attempted murder, illegal detainment, assault during the commission of a felony?"

Street Life snarled. "Stop crying like a little girl. You wanted to be down with us—this is how we get down. You played your part well. Now just keep your mouth shut and your eyes peeled, and you'll be a'right."

"This is how you get down, beatin' up on women?"

"It's her own fault," Drama said. "If she'd told us what we wanted to know, we could've walked in and out like gentlemen.

It's only when she started talking back that Life had to break out his gorilla game."

"Das right," Life said.

We continued on a few more blocks, then stopped at a liquor store and bought two forty-ounce bottles of Old Gold. This time I was ready to do my share of the drinking. Drama split a Swisher Sweet in half with a silver door key. He emptied the pods of tobacco out on to the sidewalk next to a garbage can, then sprinkled the empty husk full of fat, seedless green buds.

We strolled on, drinking and puffing. But I couldn't get the picture of the woman with Life's foot against her windpipe out of my mind.

By the time we reached Drama's apartment, he was so high he could hardly fit the key in the door lock.

"Here, let me try," Street Life offered, but before he could grab the key, Sandra threw the door open. Drama walked past her without a hello. Life and I followed.

Ms. Velvet sat at the kitchen table, nodding to the beat of her spirituals. She turned up her nose and sniffed as we entered the room. "Boy, you stink of that marijuana."

"Aw, Mama, we ain't been smoking no marijuana."

Street Life burst out in a belly laugh.

Even though she was blind, Ms. Velvet looked in Life's direction like an exorcist staring at the devil. She turned to her son. "Herbert," she said quietly, "I had a dream about you last night. You was standing at the crossroads back home in the countryside in Louisiana. And Satan was trying to strike a bargain for your soul. He was shining like an angel, and he had pearly white teeth and pointy shoes. He grabbed you by the hand, Son, and took you up to the pinnacle of St. Mary's Cathedral in the French Quarter. And the devil said, 'Bow down, D Montana, and I will give you untold wealth.'"

Drama smirked. "Mama, you saying the devil called me D Montana? And what did I do then?"

"Son, you didn't just bow down, you lay prostrate at his feet. And when you looked up, you were back at the crossroads, and there was a sign pointing in one of the two directions."

Drama touched his chin, fighting to suppress his laughter. "And what did the sign say, Mama?"

"It said, 'Highway to hell.'"

"Zat right, Mama?"

"Yes, Son. That's what the Lord spoke to me in my dream."

Drama loved his mother but he didn't have enough respect for her, and that bothered me. She was a wise woman and it wouldn't have hurt to sit down and listen to some of what she had to say from time to time. He rarely did. Drama could take the most serious things as a joke.

"Well, I had a dream last night too," he said. "In my dream a cat with a green bandana on his head handed me a suitcase full of hundred-dollar bills and said, 'Do your thing, blood. Do your thing.'"

Ms. Velvet shook her head. "Boy, it sounds like we had the same dream."

Drama rolled his eyes and led us toward the bedroom.

"Herbert," his mother called down the hall, "you'd best take heed. God speaks to people in dreams."

"Yeah, Mama," Drama called back. "I believe that. In my dream, I was so rich I couldn't spend all the money."

He took us into his room and ordered, "Lock the door, Life."

Street Life stared at Drama as he did. "Is Herbert your real name?"

Drama smirked. "What you think, when I was born my mother named me Drama?"

He held the white pillowcase he'd taken from Uzi's house over his bed and turned it upside down, allowing its contents to pour out onto his Mickey Mouse pillow.

Life let out a low whistle. His eyes blinked rapidly. "Look a here!"

"Trick or treat," Drama said. He licked his lips like a child staring at a chocolate banana split.

There on top of Mickey Mouse's smiling face sat a brown plastic bag. I opened the top of the bag and ran my fingers through the buds and stems. It was at least a kilo of high-grade marijuana. It was accompanied by six clumps of bills, twenties on top, and a coal-black, ten-pound, Israeli-made Uzi submachine gun, small enough to fit into the palm of your hand.

"All the things an enterprising young businessman needs to start a franchise," Drama said in a voice that sounded like Robin Leach doing a real-estate infomercial. He took the money out of the bag and began to separate the bills into four piles, one for each of us.

"What's the fourth pile for?" I asked.

"We got a silent partner. How do you think I knew where Uzi's money was? Information is power, and somebody gave me some power."

"Who?"

"I promised I wouldn't tell."

I knew better than to press the issue. Trying to get a secret out of Drama was like trying to pry wisdom teeth from a pit bull's mouth.

"THE BIBLE SAYS SOMETHING LIKE,
'WHATEVER SEED A MAN SOWS
IS THE KIND OF FRUIT
HE'S GOING TO REAP.'"

CHAPTER
FIVE

BY THE TIME STREET LIFE AND I ARRIVED AT DRAMA'S HOUSE the next morning, Drama had about a pound of weed measured and packed into tiny plastic bags. We each filled our pockets with dime bags of sticky green and headed outside.

We stood in Uzi's old spot, hoping to collect his business trade. We got lucky. Everybody wanted to get high that sunny Saturday morning. A few of our friends stopped by, asking for a good deal. We let some of the dime bags go for six dollars. Why not? After all, they hadn't cost us anything. I sold nine dime sacks of weed in twenty minutes and asked Drama for more.

The clique across the street eyed us suspiciously, no doubt wondering what we were doing on Uzi's corner. But they were too busy serving knocks to get involved in whatever we were doing. Still, I felt a confrontation brewing. I studied their movements as closely as they seemed to be studying ours.

A thirty-five-year-old man called C-Storm owned this corner, though he never showed his face in the neighborhood.

He sat in his house in the suburbs of Antioch, playing John Madden Football with his kids. The drug runners took 90 percent of the risk and C-Storm took 90 percent of the profits. God help you if you shorted him. He was liable to forget that he was a member of the PTA in good standing.

Word on the street was that C-Storm was being extorted by a shot caller serving life behind bars who still had power on the streets. Still, the old guy had hitters on his payroll—state-certified killers who would bust your wig with just a phone call and the mention of your name in anger.

The game is no joke. I knew that walking in. One dissatisfied customer could end you. But it's your friends you have to keep an eye on. If you're set up, don't go after those haters down the block. Holla at your potnas. Talk to your woman.

By the time you have the life halfway figured out, some dope fiend walks up behind you and busts your skull wide open with a ball-peen hammer. Prison or death is the end of the game, and even the people who escape the inevitable don't walk away unmarked. The Buddhists call it karma. The Bible says something like, "Whatever seed a man sows is the kind of fruit he's going to reap." Everything you do comes back on you some way, probably when you least expect it. Balance is the law of the universe.

We weren't out on the corner for more than an hour before Uzi rushed up to us, breathing fire and talking crazy. He got so close I could smell onions on his breath.

He stabbed a finger in Drama's direction. "Drama," he sputtered, his words broken by rage, "you ain't nothin' but a scandalous, low-down snake. You break into my house in broad daylight and steal my heat and my weed and put your hands on my woman. And I treated you like my own brother. You put your feet under my supper table. You played catch with my children."

Drama dropped his jaw. He looked genuinely wounded by the accusation. "I never put my hands on your woman!"

"Show me another red nigga with pigtails and loc shades who calls himself D Montana. And now you've got the nerve to sell my weed on my corner. You got a death wish, man?"

Drama shrugged and giggled. Street Life plunged his forefingers into Uzi's chest and assumed a boxer's stance: his left foot forward, his knee bent, and his right foot back for balance. His fists balled on either side of his cheeks. His woolen beanie lay cocked over the side of his head, covering his right eye. Folds of flesh rested over his stormy black eyes.

"Nigga, don't put your hands on me," Uzi said, too blinded by visions of retribution to perceive the threat. "You don't know me."

Street Life laughed. He swung his shoulders from side to side.

"Hold it, man," Drama said to Uzi, half grinning. "If you got a beef, let's talk about it like brothers."

Drama said it so calmly that Uzi was caught off guard when Life flashed a precision-aimed upper cut into Uzi's jaw. His eyes rolled back in his head. He raised his open palms to ward off the punishment, but it was too late. Life smashed him in the nose with an overhand right. A river of blood slithered out of his nostrils.

Street Life ducked and came in on Uzi like a freight train. Uzi extended his arms as if he were trying to find a light switch in a pitch-black room. Life punched him in the head until blood and saliva poured out of his mouth.

"Bang dat nigga out, Life," Drama commanded. A Street Life left hook caused Uzi to do a back flip. He landed on the pavement with a thud.

Drama stepped back, unzipped his jacket, and flung it in my direction. I caught it and wrapped it over my arm. Life tossed me his jacket too. I held their garments as they circled their prey. My heart was doing the mambo. I was afraid Uzi was going to get beaten to death out in the mean streets. I felt sorry for him…but not sorry enough to interrupt the lump down he was getting.

The two of them took turns stomping Uzi's head and upper body. The fallen man lifted his knees and twisted his torso away from the rain of sneakers. Uzi covered his head with his elbows. He shuddered and moaned. A deep gash opened up under his right eye. Blood spurted from his ear.

"Stop! Stop!" Uzi cried out, holding the top of his head with both hands.

Street Life kicked the small of his back like a soccer forward aiming at a goal. I heard something crack. Uzi screamed.

"Firstborn, get the nigga's pockets!"

I stumbled toward Uzi, feeling as if I were sleepwalking. The concrete sidewalk felt hard and gritty beneath my knees. I squeezed my hands into his pants pockets. He groaned, struggling to turn away from my prying fingers. I found seventeen dollars in one pocket and fifty-three cents in the other.

Drama crouched down to stare into the puffy lumps that hid Uzi's eyes. The victim's breathing was labored. He needed a doctor.

"You got to know when it's time to quit, Uzi," Drama whispered like an old friend. "Go home now, nigga. You done here." He spoke as calmly as if he had been reading a story about crop failure in Eastern Europe. "This our corner now."

"But I got kids!" Uzi exclaimed.

Life smirked. "I got kids too—a gang of 'em. So just go on home now and clean yourself up. It's over."

Hardcore profanity showered us from across the street. From the corner of my eye, I saw Endonesia and his crew racing toward us like Olympic sprinters. Traffic came to a screeching halt. A black Subaru whirled around in the middle of the street and zoomed the wrong way down our one-way street.

"Drama!" Endonesia cried out from a few feet away. "What the hell are you and your savages doing, man?"

Drama gasped for breath. Uzi's dark red blood had begun to coagulate on his fists. "Nigga said I took something from him."

"Did you?"

"Yeah. I just didn't like him saying it."

Endonesia took a deep breath. "Nigga, you done gone crazy." He stuck his right hand inside his denim jacket and kept it there. I resisted the temptation to run. I knew what Endo's hand was resting on.

Uzi grabbed the door handle of a parked Pontiac Firebird and hoisted himself to his feet. Before he could stand upright, Life kicked him in the seat of his pants, sending him sprawling to the pavement once more. Uzi hit the deck face first. Two bloody teeth flew out onto the concrete.

Endo cursed us as if a hurricane were stuck in his throat. "You niggas is completely out of pocket," he hollered. The hand inside his jacket moved.

In an instant, I unzipped my jacket, reached in, and yanked out Uzi's machine gun. I handed it to Drama like a baton in a relay race. The *click-clack* of the clip insertion caught the whole clique off guard. Endonesia backed up, slowly raising his hands.

"You don't scare me," Drama growled. "This is *our* hood. Now, step off befo' I slip and chop sumpin' you might need."

Street Life and I peered over Drama's shoulders, unblinking. Endonesia's clique stood behind him, shoulders square. Joe Joe, Shazz, Ricky, and IZ were hollow husks with tattoos and battle scars on their faces and arms. They feared neither killing nor dying, for they were neither dead nor awake. They were all strapping and if they had started firing, Drama couldn't have got them all before they got us.

If I had known how to pray, I would have been doing it right then.

"Ya know what I think, D?" Endo asked.

"No, nigga, and I don't care. 'Cause I'm 'bout to leave your thoughts smoking on the sidewalk!"

Endo cussed under his breath. I thought he might still go for his gun. I was closest. I'd be shot first. The world's longest ninety seconds elapsed before Endo cocked his head toward the other side of the street. I glanced in the direction he indicated and saw half a dozen crack fiends, licking their lips, hungry for a blast.

Drama's eyes narrowed. I looked through them into the soul of somebody I really didn't know. Nothing about that menacing glare said that he would hesitate to shoot anybody who put a foot down in the wrong direction. This was his world. He knew his way around it. My best chance of surviving out on the block lay in listening to everything he told me to do.

Endo flashed a wicked smile. "There'll be another day, Drama. Come on, fellas. Let's go get his money." His clique followed him without a word.

Crack fiends began to walk away, taking their precious dollars with them. The crew was losing sales. But messing around with Uzi and his beef with us was more about machismo than money. Endonesia made a business decision. "Let's go get this cash," he snarled.

Uzi stood on the corner with his bottom jaw stretched out. "Y'all ain't gonna do nothin'?" he screamed, waving his hands frantically. "Endo, this nigga done pulled a gun on you in broad daylight. He broke in my house and put his feet on my woman. Y'all jus' gonna let him walk away?"

Obviously Uzi thought his boys should do something to protect his honor. But he was blind to the nature of twenty-first-century capitalism. Maybe he'd seen too many cowboy movies where the bad guys got locked up or hanged for violating the code of the Old West. But this was the New West and the crime game is different. It's all about the Ben Frankies, not the bull.

While Endo and his boys were playing games, potential sales were drifting away. So they turned their backs on us and went back to serving on their side of the street as though nothing had happened.

"Go on home, Uzi," Street Life suggested, "while you can still walk."

His head drooped down between his shoulder blades and he limped off.

As we strolled down the block, I handed Uzi's $17.54 to Drama.

"Keep it," he said with a grin. "That's just the beginning."

"YOU'RE A HUSTLER NOW,
ROLLING WITH THE BIG DAWGS.
I LIKE THE NEW FIRSTBORN."

CHAPTER
SIX

I SAT ON THE EDGE OF MY BED, LISTENING TO THE TRAMP OF BARE feet jogging up and down the hallway, my heart palpitating. Would the police come to my house? Would I be implicated for my role in Uzi's beating? I hadn't done anything wrong, just held my friends' jackets while they kicked and pummeled the living spit out of someone. Still, I felt guilty—like the prison guard charged with the duty of pulling down the electric chair's lever.

Why had they stomped Uzi? He liked Drama. And he was good for a loose joint when we didn't have any money. But now were selling his weed. We had stolen his corner...as if brothers can actually own the corners they stand on.

I paid my rent with my share of the profits from selling Uzi's green. Ms. Brown, the landlady, beamed when I pulled the bills out of my pocket and placed them in the palm of her cold, sweaty hand. She even called me Son. That was a first. I felt like death microwaved over.

A car horn tooted in front of the building. My window faced the aluminum siding of the building next to ours, blocking any view of the street. But I knew that horn. Maggy was here.

I bounded down the steps and out the door. She looked up at me through the driver's side window of her mama's mud-brown 1975 El Dorado with mismatched hubcaps. The door creaked when I pried it open.

"Hey, Maggy."

"Hey, Firstborn."

"Thanks for coming over." I opened the passenger-side door and scooted in.

She handed me a white paper bag with a plastic cup inside. It was hot to the touch. I peeled back the lid and inhaled the mocha flavor of hot cappuccino—my favorite.

"Thanks."

"No problem. What's the deal, blood? You sounded terrible over the phone."

"Would you just drive, please?"

"Where?"

"Anywhere."

Magdalene huffed as she grasped the steering wheel. The big brown whale swam down the middle of the asphalt, its brakes grinding and screeching at every stoplight.

Maggy clicked on the radio. Her mother's gospel music blasted in my eardrums. "Thank God I'm saved. Thank God I've learned to love everybody and treat my neighbor right. Thank God I'm saved."

I clicked the radio off. We both stared into the distance as dusk broke, leaving a hue of purple and black in the sky. Car lights flickered all around us.

Maggy took the freeway exit for downtown Oakland. We rode in stillness except for the sound of cars rushing past.

"Maggy, I did something bad today."

"What did you do?"

"I can't really talk about it."

"Then why'd you bring it up?"

I looked at my hands. They were trembling in my lap. "I needed money. That woman was going to put me out in the street."

Maggy's jaws tightened. "Drama got you caught up in some street mess, didn't he? You had to hang around that long-haired junkyard nigga. Y'all robbed somebody, I bet."

I rolled down the window, feeling nauseated. My brain filled with Uzi's screaming. I could still see his bloody teeth on the sidewalk.

The cappuccino burned my tongue and lips, but I gulped it anyway.

Magdalene gently squeezed my folded hands with her free hand. "I'm sure you did what you had to do."

She coasted the car down Broadway. Tourists in Bermuda shorts and Ray-Ban sunglasses strolled down the streets, arm in arm, staring at the stars. We parked two blocks away from Jack London Square and walked in silence. I felt the world spinning beneath my feet, tilting slightly on its axis.

Golden lights sparkled in the hills beyond San Francisco. The sun's last rays did their death dance on the waters of the bay. We took a bench at the water's edge and watched yachts with colorful names like *Majestic Queen* and *Lilo's Chariot* rock gently on the waves.

I grabbed Maggy's arm and placed it across my shoulders. "Magdalene, I want you to be my woman."

I knew I was presuming a lot. Magdalene liked nice things. She liked to go places. She liked men with buff muscles and tattoos who could spring for a dinner of barbecued ribs with a bottle of Dom Perignon.

Her eyes took on a vacant stare, as though she were looking right through me.

"What are you thinking about?" I asked.

"You're a hustler now, rolling with the big dawgs. I like the new Firstborn." She leaned over and kissed me. Twice.

CHAPTER
SEVEN

THE NEXT MORNING, I LANDED AT DRAMA'S CRIB AROUND NINE. I found him and Pimpin' EZ kicking back on the living room couch, smoking purple and watching hip hop videos. I plopped down in the empty space between them.

Pimpin' EZ was a vampire who walked the ghetto feeding on human dreams and sucking hope away like giblet gravy from a turkey leg. His eyes were two burnt-out olive pits, dark as the gates of hell. His slick perm lay on skinny shoulders. His fingernails were long, sharp, and shiny, like plastic daggers. Pimpin' EZ reminded me of a poem I'd once read about a man who was nothing more than a collection of shadows and lost days in the basement of time.

The first time I'd seen Pimpin' EZ, Drama and I were fifteen years old. Drama's dad had been dead for two years. It was Saturday morning and we were sitting on the living room couch, chewing soggy Cap'n Crunch cereal and watching college basketball. Suddenly there was a pounding at the door. Wood splintered. The iron hinges separated from the molding. Pimpin' EZ and his younger brother, Robert, darkened the entranceway.

Drama never took his eyes off the television set.

Ms. Velvet came bursting out of the bedroom, her hair in curlers. "Get out of here, you monsters!" she screamed.

The two intruders marched through the living room and back toward the bedroom that Sandra shared with Ms. Velvet. "Open this door, girl!" Pimpin' EZ demanded.

"No," came a tentative squeak from the other side of the closed door.

Pimpin' EZ raised the heel of his two-tone brown boot and plunged it through the door. Hinges and the bolt lock went flying. Robert followed his brother over the threshold.

I glanced at Drama, ready to spring into action. I expected to see horror, revulsion, or hatred etched on his face. I anticipated running into his bedroom and grabbing something from the arsenal of brass knuckles, razor blades, and billy clubs that he kept under his pillow. And I would have been down to back his play...if he would have made one. But he just sat there, transfixed. As though he were hypnotized by the Saturday morning cartoons. He never so much as blinked.

Sandra wailed as Pimpin' EZ dragged her out of the apartment by her long, jet black hair.

"Ho, you gonna get out on that corner and make me some money!" he hollered.

Ms. Velvet ran toward the fray, striking the air with her fists. Robert grabbed her chubby wrists and pushed her down in a kitchen chair. He held her there as his brother made his escape with Sandra.

When he heard the car door open, Robert released Ms. Velvet and ran down the stairs to the waiting vehicle. Ms. Velvet cried for Jesus. Drama never took his eyes off the television screen, not even during commercials.

Over the next several years, Pimpin' EZ's hairline receded like an ocean at low tide. His charm with the ladies followed the same route. Now he was a broke old hustler with a lot of exaggerated stories about the good old days. His bottom broad, Lydia, caught HIV a few years ago. In spite of her dangerous disease, he still sent her out to the block. There was money to be made from suburban husbands looking for a little innocent fun.

When Lydia's hair started falling out and her weight dropped off, Pimpin' EZ told her that her services were no longer needed. Rumor has it she moved into a welfare motel downtown, where she hustled tricks to buy black-market AZT.

Sandra told Pimpin' EZ that she loved him but was quitting the track. Pimpin' EZ moved into Ms. Velvet's apartment, where he shared a room with Sandra and treated her like a cash-strapped farmer treated the mule that refused to plow.

Ms. Velvet was a Christian if there ever was one, but she hated the ground on which Pimpin' EZ's shadow fell. He deflected her insults with laughter. The freeloader refused to go out and get what he called a "square" job.

Sandra eventually became a lot like the company she kept. She and Pimpin' EZ slept late and lived off Ms. Velvet's meager Social Security check. His "job" was thumbing through the *TV Guide*, and hers was mashing the buttons on the remote control.

Pimpin' EZ called Drama "brother-in-law." They watched football games together and got high together. But whenever EZ's name came up in conversation, I noticed something in his eyes that I could never entirely discern. Sometimes the glare was accompanied by a dark twist of the lips, but never any commentary.

The three of us could be enmeshed in a discussion about the upcoming heavyweight title fight when Drama would suddenly get a weird look on his face, then say something like, "You're lucky I need you, Pimpin' EZ."

EZ supplied Drama with "street knowledge." Pimpin' EZ claimed he knew the underworld the way a dentist knows teeth. I suspected that half of everything he said was a lie, but Drama seemed to get something out of it.

I still remember lesson number one: "A true hustler never gives anything away for free." Pimpin' EZ demanded dime bags of weed, forty ounces of malt liquor, and the occasional Big Mac in exchange for the information he supplied to his mentee.

Pimpin' EZ was a wanted man. I never knew who might be stalking him—police, some dead hooker's father, heavy hitters he'd crossed up or snitched on in the streets; it could have been anybody. I remember him pulling me aside one day and saying, "Firstborn, don't ever tell anybody that you seen me here or that you know where I am."

The morning after we did what we did to Uzi, I found Pimpin' EZ sitting on Drama's living room couch counting dollars on the scratched wooden coffee table. Looking at him licking his fingers and slapping down twenties, it wasn't hard to figure out who our fourth partner was.

Pimpin' EZ rarely had much to say to me, but he was in a fatherly mood that morning. A few sips of Old English 800 got his gums flapping.

"You can't show fear out there. Ya understand, Firstborn? I was watchin' this show on TV the other night, and they said a shark can smell a drop of blood in an Olympic-size swimming pool. These crackheads can smell intimidation the same way. Drama knows it. Street Life knows it. Now Uzi knows it. So do Endonesia and those other clowns on that corner. Y'all put a little fear in their hearts. You gave dem niggas something to think about."

"Niggas," "crackheads," and "sharks"—that was how Pimpin' EZ sized up the world, and everyone fit into one of those categories. In his mind, the whole planet was ghetto size.

"Remember lesson two and you'll last a while. Invisibility is the key to this game. The less people know about what you're doing, the longer you last on these streets. If you gonna be a criminal, don't throw it up in the police's face. Get a Volkswagen, not a Benz."

Drama smiled like the doting son. Was he that starved for a father figure? Something about that picture—Drama and the man who had turned out his sister, sitting there on the couch like old war buddies—twisted my brain around in my skull. I needed a drink.

I should have walked away from the game right then and there. But I didn't. Why? Money. That's why.

Fast money is addictive. I loved the feel of the bills, like velvet wrapped inside a red rubber band. They made me feel like a god to the poor who prayed to the heavens for something that came to me by just standing on a street corner. In America money is god. And everybody believes in that god—especially people who don't have access to it.

Two weeks after the Uzi incident, females who had never given me the time of day started staring at me like I had just won New Artist of the Year at the BET Awards. The hottest chicks in the hood would walk up to Sandra and whisper, "Who dat bald-headed nigga wit' your brother? He fine. Girl, slide him my number. I want to get at him after I get my hair done."

I had never, ever received that kind of attention from women before. I have to admit, I was feeling it.

Uzi made himself as scarce as the American bald eagle. But after two weeks, we had gone through his stash and needed to get more. Trouble was, we didn't know anybody who sold that kind of quality in bulk.

Drama reached out to some cats from South Berkeley who were known to handle the kind of weight we needed. Unfortunately, our block had experienced some major-league funk with their hood, and they were still leery about transacting business with us. But money talks.

We got a phone number for a brother named Tony who made his money on that turf. When we introduced ourselves, we got cold silence. But as soon as we started talking dollars, all beef was squashed. It was all love.

"You can't come here," he said. "Let's meet at the Berkeley Marina."

The marina was twenty miles away. We needed a car.

Ms. Velvet was hesitant to let Drama use the family hooptie. Not that she needed it. Being blind, she couldn't go anywhere unless Drama or Sandra drove. Her complaint was that every time Drama took the car anywhere it came back reeking of marijuana.

Drama concocted some story about wanting to leave a job resume in Martinez.

Ms. Velvet was so anxious to see Drama do something constructive with his life that she ignored the feelings of doubt she must have had and loaned him the car keys.

We took the freeway to Berkeley, then hit the dark strip that took us over marsh and swamp to the deserted outposts of the city. Gray raccoons as big as baby bears scampered through the thick growth of forest and sand.

We parked the car facing San Francisco. We sat in the darkness and stared at the lights surrounding the desolate concrete casket called Alcatraz. It lay like a lump of white coal in the middle of the icy blue waters of the Pacific.

Three minutes later Tony rode up on a ten-speed bicycle, his curly brown hair flying behind him like a tattered flag. I saw a large bulge beneath his black windbreaker.

Tony extracted a brown plastic bag half the size of a pillow from under his jacket. He flung it in into Drama's lap through the car window. Drama pulled a crumpled Gin and Juice tobacco leaf from his pocket. He opened the bag and took a generous pinch. He rolled it up, pulled out his gold lighter, and lit the tip of the blunt. Soon the sweet smell of sticky icky filled the car.

Drama took a hit, coughed, and handed it to me. I took a puff and nodded my approval.

Drama handed a pile of bills wrapped in a rubber band out the window. Tony did a quick count, then pedaled off into the fog.

"Man, this stuff smells like a pine tree," I said.

"This is gonna make us rich. It's gonna be like Christmas," Drama said with a glassy-eyed smile.

"Yeah," I said, "black Christmas."

We decided to call our joints Christmas trees. Weed heads from all over Oakland started coming to our corner to taste our stuff. We made so much money we were able to give some of our homies jobs.

People started calling our hood Black Christmas. The brothers started wearing red-and-gold Boston College baseball caps because of the initials. Some of the young cats branded themselves with Christmas tree tattoos. We were papered up and everybody wanted to get down with us.

We also drew attention from the other side of the street. The money we were making was still pennies compared to what they were pulling in. But Endo paced back and forth, watching and waiting. When he and Drama locked eyes, Drama laughed at him.

Drama was plotting something. He kept his mouth shut about it but his eyes told the story. I just hoped he knew that Endonesia was nobody to be played with.

CHAPTER
EIGHT

MR. CARTER WAS OUR JUNIOR HIGH SCHOOL JANITOR UNTIL THE principal started receiving complaints that he was gulping Jack Daniel's from his thermos every day. Mr. Carter had all the time in the world to drink now. He often came to our corner.

One morning, after sucking down an enormous slug of Pit Bull malt liquor, he gritted his teeth, held the can out at arm's length, and cursed it. After the next swig, light brown liquid floated on top his eye sockets. What used to be the whites of his eyes changed to a rose color.

"You want some of this, Firstborn?" he asked, extending the can toward me.

I sneered at him and twisted away. "It's nine o'clock in the morning, and that ain't orange juice you're drinking."

His eyes grew wide. He said my name softly, then his lips parted slightly in a silent prayer. He spilled a few drops of beer. That's when I knew something serious was about to go down.

I turned to face the street behind me. I saw a dark green unmarked police car with two young white men in the front.

The one who faced me wore a brown Marines-style buzz cut. He pointed a digital camera at me. Then the green cruiser sped down the block.

Mr. Carter shook his head slowly. "You done messed up now, boy. They got your face on file. They're already building a case on you."

"They'll never catch me," I boasted.

Mr. Carter laughed so hard he spilled another drop of beer. "Never catch you? Boy, what do you think they do for a living? They catch people doing what you're doing for a living. And while you're sleeping at night, they're figuring out ways to take you down. That's how they make their mortgage payments and send their children to college. Sooner or later they always succeed. In your line of work, there's only two ways out: prison or the pine box."

"I'm only flipping dime bags."

"Last time I checked that was still against the law." Mr. Carter sipped from his can. "Firstborn, you ain't gotta be that strong or even that smart to escape the streets. You just need three things: the vision to see yourself somewhere else, a plan, and the power to stand alone if need be. These Black Christmas niggas you hang with got no vision, they got no dreams, and they think they're tough. In reality, they so weak they can't make it without Drama to tell them when to pee and where to squat. They can't wipe themselves without having somebody else approve the kind of toilet paper they're allowed to use. These niggas crave validation. It's sickening. The Bible says, 'Where there is no vision the people perish.'"

I had to smile. My philosophizing friend was right. Street corners and prison cells are populated with brothers who chose against what was best for their families or themselves because of what another man might have thought of them. It seemed that if you wanted to motivate a brother to do something risky or stupid, something clearly against his best interest, the only thing that you had to do was question his manhood by saying something like, "Are you scared?"

Drama had used this tactic time and time again. It worked to perfection. And if that didn't work, he'd pull out the "but we're homies" card. Yes, Mr. Carter was as right as he was drunk.

"These young fools out here got street poison," Mr. Carter said. "They got no family structure. They got no vision. They got no skills other than slanging dope, and they seen so much blood they like to drown in it. They ain't never gonna escape. But you? You can still bust through the invisible walls of the ghetto. But ya gotta do it now, son, 'cause there's a little bit a Drama in you. That's why you're so tight. Every day you come out here, you become more like him. Soon there won't be no difference between you and him."

I shivered at his prediction. I liked to think of myself as a poor black man trying to get out so he could come back and maybe do some good. Drama didn't give a damn. I didn't want anybody to see me in that light.

"Mr. Carter," I said, "I can't get out without money."

"Pray. Maybe God will send you a miracle."

I'm not even sure I believed in God back then, at least not enough to commit my future to someone I could not see. "I don't want to bother God with my troubles," I told Mr. Carter. "I'm making my own miracle right here."

Sweat broke out on my palms. My throat constricted. I weighed the pros and cons of calling Drama and telling him about my impromptu photo op.

While I was making my decision, Maggy sashayed up, attired in tight black jeans and a backless blouse. Her dark-chocolate flesh radiated with the warmth of summer. Her hair was tied in a bun. She smelled like the San Francisco botanical gardens. She was the loveliest dime piece in the hood...and she knew it.

Drama didn't think Magdalene was right for me. "A woman don't respect a man who's too good to 'er," he'd repeat over and over again. "Take her money. Disappear for two or three days at a time and don't tell her where you're at. If she gets fresh about it, give her a little tap on the mouth. She'll run after you like you're the last man on earth. She'll be doing backflips in the bedroom. Trust me. That's how I be doin' these hos. And they *love* me."

I listened to Drama with half an ear. I wanted a woman like my grandmother: sweet and gentle, someone I could make a home with, perhaps grow old with. I would never hit a woman. And I loved Magdalene. I once wrote a poem for her. I wish I had saved it, but I still remember a couple of the lines. "I would give up my life for yours and be glad to die, but sad that I had just one life to give."

Magdalene touched her lips to mine. She pulled my head down until my face was buried in her neck. She laced her arms around my shoulders. The aroma of her Tents of Kedar body oil rushed through my nostrils. Her freshly manicured fingernails dug into my back.

"I want to acks you somethin', playa," she said so low her words ran together.

"Anything."

"Honey, can I get a zip?"

I pulled her arms from their lock. "Maggy, I'm out here trying to get the deposit on an apartment. And trying to get my tuition straight. You wanted your nails painted. You wanted new shoes. You wanted an outfit. You got 'em. Now you want to smoke up my profits too?"

She blinked those pretty brown eyes at me and I melted. "First, I be stressing. One zip ain't gonna hurt you. Please?"

I reached behind the mailbox and pulled up a wrinkled grocery bag. I put my hand in the bag and came out with a plastic baggie full of purple buds and stems.

Magdalene rolled a joint of Purple Haze. The brothers posted on the corner across the street eyed us coolly.

LG, a tall, thin cat I'd gone to high school with, sauntered up to me. "You got that Granddaddy Purple?" he asked.

"Sure, homie. How much you want?"

"I got seven; let me get a dime."

"A dime cost ten dollars. That's why they call it dime."

"But we go back, homie."

"I still can't take no shorts."

Drama walked up, wearing a black T-shirt with the black-and-white headshot of a young brother in a blue graduate's cap. The letters beneath the photo said, "R.I.P., Sandy." In small print it said, "The hood will miss you. Hold it down for us in heaven."

I was glad when Drama stepped on the block that morning. He knew how to operate on this planet. He sized LG up in a millisecond.

"What you want, LG?" Drama asked with a scowl.

"I want a dime but I only got seven dollars. Your man here is giving me a problem about it."

Drama snapped his fingers impatiently. LG dropped the seven singles into his palm. Drama fished around in his shirt pocket and then threw a dime bag on the ground. It looked light, as if he had already rolled something out of it. LG didn't notice. He scooped it up like it was God's phone number.

"Next time, come out here with ten dollars," Drama said to LG's back as he half jogged away without even a "thank you." LG raised his hand in acknowledgment and continued moving.

Maggy passed me the joint.

"Hey, girl," Drama said, "you takin' good care of my friend here?"

Magdalene scowled. She hated Drama. Thought he was too arrogant. She called him "ghetto" behind his back.

"Firstborn, this chick ain't really down for you. If niggas roll up and start blastin', you need a woman who ain't afraid to blast back. Ya feel me?"

Maggy pursed her lips together and then stared me down as if to say, "Firstborn, check this nigga. He's disrespecting me."

I rolled my eyes. "Drama, you're not looking for a wife; you want a codefendant."

Drama laughed. I giggled too. I couldn't help it. Magdalene froze me with a frown.

"Seriously, doe, we got some business to tend to," Drama said.

That was Maggy's cue to go home. She pecked me on the cheek and glided away, puffing on the spliff like a pacifier.

When she was beyond earshot, Drama clamped his hand down on my shoulder and whispered, "Look at all that money across the street, First."

Walking skeletons with uncombed heads shuffled past Endonesia, Rick, and IZ. An older guy, maybe thirty-five, lumbered up toward the crew, his head scrunched down into his frayed sports jacket collar. The brother was doing his best to appear inconspicuous, but he clearly did not belong here.

I guessed at his story. He probably held a position of some responsibility downtown, perhaps an office manager, computer programmer, maybe a third-grade teacher. He had begun fiddling around with crack cocaine on the weekends— nothing extravagant, just a few rocks to ease the tension. He fancied himself as something of a connoisseur. He laughed at the weak people who couldn't master the high. He had his under control. Then came the binge that ate up his entire paycheck. Next he was calling in sick and borrowing money from friends to finance his ever-swelling appetite.

IZ peeled himself away from the clique and tossed the guy a twenty-cent piece. He grabbed it and half jogged around the corner, tugging at the glass pipe in his pocket like it was the last bottle of water in the Mohave desert.

Bill, one of our clique from the old days, walked up to IZ, rubbing his palms together. I had heard rumors about Bill doing some strange things for drug money. But nothing a crackhead does for a hit would surprise me. Nothing.

Their next customer, a girl named NaNa, had flat-pockets disease. She rocked back and forth on her pink flip-flops, begging and pleading with Endonesia. He shook his head. NaNa had been fine back in high school. She had aqua green eyes and flesh the color of Arizona sand. NaNa had been captain of the cheerleading squad and she dated the quarterback. But she wasn't too wise about how she chose her friends. I'd seen her on the corner doing business with Endo's crew before. She was in deep.

NaNa bounced from one foot to another, shaking her hands and pleading for free drugs. Endonesia slapped her rump like she was an old, broken-down horse. He jerked his head toward his Escalade with a seductive smirk. Her begging stopped. She lowered her head in resignation; her eyes glazed over with submission.

IZ slipped a blue condom packet into Endonesia's hand. Soon the Isley Brothers' "Between the Sheets" was thundering from the Cadillac's stereo.

"Wow," I said. "I thought NaNa was married."

Drama shrugged. "Husband or no husband, she still gotta scratch that cocaine itch."

Ten minutes later, the back door of the Escalade popped open. Endonesia jumped out, tugging at his zipper, a wild grin stretched across his cheeks. IZ leapt in the open door. The truck rocked back and forth.

"What you think NaNa and IZ are doing in there, Drama?"

He chuckled. "Fool, you took sex education in health class. What you think?"

After IZ jumped out of the truck, Robert took his turn. I heard a high-pitched scream over the music that seeped out of the Escalade. Minutes later, Robert emerged, grinning. He sauntered up to his boys, who hugged him and shook his hand. They chattered like pals at an amusement park discussing the twists and turns of a thrilling roller-coaster ride.

NaNa opened the car door, tears spilling from her swollen eyes. The left strap of her pink sundress drooped down over her shoulder. She held her hand out in front of Endonesia like a beggar. He puckered as though he were about to spit in her open palm. Then he laughed. He hit her off with something. It might have been a twenty-dollar rock. She'd smoke that and be back in ten minutes.

We stood on our side of the street, staring at the crew for about an hour. I wondered how much money they were taking in.

Around ten thirty that morning, Street Life showed up. Drama's face flushed maroon. "Street Life, where you been? You can't lay up all day with those fat, broke-down rippers you love so much and then come out here like you're ready to handle business."

Life's uncombed hair was wooly as a big ball of black cotton candy. His sky-blue-and-orange Miami Heat jersey was so wrinkled I wondered if he had balled it up the night before to use as a pillow. He caught me staring at his outfit and burst out in a deep belly laugh.

"Chill, man. I'll treat for breakfast. How's that?"

It was fine with me. I had visions of grits slathered in butter, scrambled eggs with cheese, ham steak, homemade biscuits with jelly, and a liter of sweet tea. Street Life was thinking more in terms of the golden arches.

Micky D's was just a few blocks away. Still we decided to "borrow" Ms. Velvet's hooptie to make the trip. During the walk around the corner to the car, I noticed that Street Life never walked more than five steps without glancing back over each shoulder. He'd done so much dirt out in the streets he knew it was only a matter of time until it gained on him. I wondered if I could live like that.

When we walked into the McDonald's, I saw Mr. Carter sitting on a blue plastic bench, sipping on a small cup of coffee. He nodded in our direction. We nodded back and squatted down in the booth adjacent to the one he claimed. Street Life took our orders. Minutes later, he returned with two bags filled with everything on the menu except what we had asked for. I was too hungry to argue.

"I want to take that corner away from those fools across the street," Drama said.

"I'm down," Life blurted out, his mouth stuffed with freeze-dried eggs and microwaved sausage.

"What about you, First?"

I had reservations. "Endonesia and his crew aren't just going to *give* us that corner." My mind flashed back to the hostile stares that ran through me like razors the day we took that corner from Uzi. "Those busters will try to put some bullets in your head before it's all over."

Drama smirked. "That all that's troubling you?"

"No. There are a couple more things."

"Spit 'em out, then. Let's get it all on the table." He tilted his head.

"Po-Po drove by and took my picture this morning."

Drama's eyes narrowed. He extracted the cigarette from behind his ear, lit a match in the cup of his hands, and stared at me in silence. He cursed the police. "They tryin' to intimidate you, man. Thass all. Homie, the pigs got enough pictures a me to start a family album, and I'm still here."

Mr. Carter stared across the aisle at us. The blank look in his eyes told me he'd been listening to our conversation and had heard every word. "He's lying to you, son." Mr. Carter said. "The minute they snapped that picture, you got two steps closer to the chow line at Folsom Prison."

Drama glowered at Mr. Carter. "Quit ear hustling! Stay out of my business, old man. You just drink that watery coffee and keep your mouth shut." Drama turned back to me. He breathed in heavily, exasperated.

"Drama," I whispered, "crack ain't the same thing as weed. Slinging rock is like pouring rat poison in a baby bottle. It's the wrecking ball to the black community. We don't want to mess with the white plague, do we? It's genocide."

Street Life moaned. "Drama, I'm trying to feed my kids out here and this nigga here think he Chuck D or some damn body."

"Firstborn," Drama said, trying to draw me in with a voice of reason, "remember when we went to the Oakland Zoo back in eighth grade? There was these two skinny tigers walking around in a cage. Their legs looked like orange toothpicks with black stripes."

"Yeah, I remember." I laughed. How could I forget? The park ranger caught Drama sticking his hand through the bars while attempting to feed his strawberry ice cream bar to a spider monkey. He tossed the whole lot of us out of the park.

The teacher called Drama out of his name that day. I wonder if he ever figured out who slashed his tires.

Drama pointed at our competition across the street. "Imagine what would happen if you climbed on top of that cage and dropped a fat, juicy T-bone right between those two skinny tigers."

"They'd kill each other over that steak."

"Now, what would happen if one of the tigers was educated and he said, 'You know, brother Tiger, we've been maneuvered into this cage by the evil zookeeper and those people out there are standing around throwing popcorn at us. Instead of letting us walk around in the jungle, where we could get our own food, they put us in this unnatural environment and throw a steak down between us. What they really want is for me to kill you over that steak so they can have an excuse to come in and kill me and then take this cage back. So here's what we'll do. We'll let that steak sit there and rot. That'll teach them.' You know what would happen?"

"The spectators will get bored and leave the tigers alone?" I asked.

"No. One tiger will say, 'Brother, you right.' And as soon as the first tiger's back is turned, he'll kill him, eat the steak, and take his chances with the zookeeper."

I choked on the unmistakable moral of the parable. The tigers represented the uneducated, the poor, the broken of spirit, those tripped up by poverty and tossed headlong into a world maintained by rich absentee landlords and lazy politicians who came back occasionally to peer through the bars. The steak was the drug trade and the nickels and dimes it generated, tempting us to feed on our own brothers and sisters. The cage was the hood, which was being threatened by gentrification.

A splotch of ketchup dropped from Drama's burger and landed on his mustache. "It's ugly and it's bad, but when it's over, I'm gonna be the cat with the steak in his mouth. And

I'll take my chances with the zookeeper. Firstborn, give me three months and I'll help you make the bread you need to supplement your first year's tuition at Alston University. I promise. That 20 percent ain't nothin' to me, dawg. I'll help you get that and a little stake to get your life rolling."

Drama's eyes blazed with earnestness. He had counted the cost and now he was pointing out the path to the Promised Land. If I set foot on it, there would be no turning back.

I wavered but only for a moment. If I wanted out of East Oakland, I too would have to take my chances with the zookeeper. *Forgive me, Granny.* I said the magic words. "I'm down."

Street Life sat in a grease-induced trance, burping occasionally but paying no attention to the conversation. Out of nowhere he blurted, "You know, when I was locked up in Quentin, I saved Latin Caesar's life."

Drama smiled. "Seems to me I heard something about you and Latin Caesar. What happened?"

"I peeped some of his enemies 'bout to roll up on him in the yard and stick him. I gave him a heads-up on it."

"I heard different," Drama said.

"What did you hear?" Street Life cocked his eyebrow.

"I heard some heavy hitter, one of Latin Caesar's enemies, got some paperwork with Caesar's name on it. Somehow you heard about it and stuck the dude in the neck twice before he could handle his business. Niggas was furious. They say you jumped into something that didn't concern you. You didn't even know Latin Caesar and you almost started a war trying to save the dude's life. They say you crossed political lines and some triple OGs with stripes was looking to do unto you as you did to that torpedo—may he rest in peace." Drama looked down in mock remorse and made the sign of the cross.

"Yeah, it got messy all around. Our peoples was hot 'cause they wasn't feelin' it, but what those niggas didn't understand was that I was looking down the pipeline at my money thang. See, after I did what I did, Caesar was like, 'Yo, what's your name, champ?' When I told him, he said, 'I owe you one.' Those is the magic words, especially when somebody who moves coke by the key says 'em."

I'd never been arrested but I knew one thing from listening to brothers talk. Staying alive in prison is about who you associate with and who you don't. Street Life crossed political boundaries to do that favor for Latin Caesar, and it wasn't because his heart was so warm. He must have seen some great potential benefit in taking such a risk.

I had a newfound respect for him—the kind you might have for a pet snake that you just discovered had the potential to strike with a venom for which death is the only cure.

Street Life continued his story. "They didn't have no proof that I stuck anybody, but I still got drug off to the hole. Then they reclassified me and shipped me out to *Un*pleasant Valley. But it was worth it for the chance to get cut into Latin Cesar."

Up until that moment, I had imagined Latin Caesar as a legend, a folk anti-hero, an urban myth. I'd heard he and his brother Razor started GCD, which was a renegade set tied to a huge gang that had started in California but now existed in cells and sets all around the planet. GCD stood for Guns, Cash, and Dope. Cocaine kilos were GCD's product. Blood spilling was their trademark. They had the town on lock.

As Street Life searched his wallet for a tattered slip of notebook paper with Latin Caesar's number scratched on it, I remembered the story the old man had told me that night at the bus stop, the one about the heroin dealers who had been butchered in front of the chicken joint. I didn't feel the need to comment on it to the OG, but the killers he described wore GCD's colors.

Drama handed Street Life his cell phone. We listened to his end of the conversation.

"Whassup? Lemme holla at Caesar. This is Street Life. I met Caesar in Quentin. East Block."

There was a pause.

"Uh-huh. Uh-huh. What's the address?"

Street Life looked in my direction and started writing in midair with an invisible pencil. I took the hint and handed him a pen. He scrawled a street address on the outside of an empty burger bag.

"We'll be there in half an hour." Street Life clicked off the phone. "We in. He lookin' for us."

Drama jumped up, grabbed Street Life's head between his hands, and rubbed his knuckles on his forehead.

Life twisted away, grinning. "Nigga, you crazy."

"Street Life, can you drive?"

"Yeah."

"Do you have a driver's license?"

"What one thing got to do with the other?"

Drama tossed me the keys to Ms. Velvet's car. "You drive, First." He turned back to Life. "You got a gun?"

"Sure." He hoisted up his T-shirt to show off the butt of the shiny silver Desert Eagle stuck in his waistband. "You gonna acks me if I got a permit for this?"

Drama laughed at the brother with two strikes on his record.

Street Life's mood snapped in a millisecond. He turned his attention toward me, jabbing his forefinger into my chest. His eyes took on a stormy, distant glare. "Nigga, we been cool so far, but we only been playing Pee Wee League ball. Once you set foot in that car, you headed for the big leagues. You got judges handin' out centuries of incarceration down on

STRAIGHT OUTTA EAST OAKLAND 97

Clay Street to po' niggas with drug charges. If we get caught, you *will* be offered a deal. So, before you really get down, you gotta acks yo'self if you can handle yours without snitchin'. 'Cause if we get caught and you turn state's evidence on me or Drama, I will murk you. And if I can't get to you, I'll pay somebody ten cartons of cigarettes to X you out permanently. I put that on my kids, my mama, and everything I love. You feel me?"

My fingers trembled beneath the table. "I'm down. If anything goes wrong, I'll never bring up your name."

"You better not." Street Life rose from the table and smirked. "Nigga, you said you wanted to write some books. Well, in a little while you gonna have something to write about. Just don't put our names in it."

"Let's roll," Drama whispered.

We left Mr. Carter sipping lukewarm coffee and humming a Ray Charles song. We were on our way to kiss the kingpin's ring.

I stared at the oncoming traffic in silence, thinking, *It's about to get deep.*

FINALLY SATISFIED, HE GLANCED UP AT US AND SAID, "NOW, PREPARE TO SELL YOUR SOULS."

CHAPTER
NINE

LATIN CAESAR LIVED IN JINGLE TOWN, A SECTION OF THE CITY FAR removed from the desolation of deep East Oakland but joined by the International Boulevard pipeline.

Eleven miles from the block, salsa and hip hop collided. Two dozen workers stood in front of the Goodwill store, hoping for suburban patrons to drive up with promises of day labor. Taco trucks on each corner sold burritos and enchiladas to go.

Drama, Street Life, and I passed Victorian mansions with bright yellow-and-orange shutters and stores labeled "Carniceria" and "Bodega." Women with tiny children pushed handcarts, selling sweet corn and onion rings. "Border Brothers 94th" was spray painted in black on the front of a tacqueria. Someone had spray painted the bright red words "Rolling 60s Norte" on the side of a flower shop. Five-foot letters spelling "XIII SUR" were painted in blue on the side of a fast-food restaurant. Crossed-out letters and four-letter insults covered buildings and bus stops.

"Make this left, Firstborn," Street Life ordered.

The last house on the left was a Victorian mansion with Roman numerals spray painted on its face. Bullet holes checkered the steel doors. We'd come fifty blocks to fall through the trap door of destiny.

"Dis it," Life whispered. "Y'all ready?"

Dudes ranging in age from seventeen to thirty-two stood up from the porch steps as if they were preparing to salute the flag at a baseball game. Some wore sleeveless T-shirts revealing bulging biceps and green tattoo riddles painted across their torsos, necks, and heads. Three of the fellows wore wrap-around loc sunglasses. The set's color was represented in the bandanas that swung from their pockets, the laces in their sneakers, and the color of their T-shirts. Penitentiary stares stabbed us as soon as I pulled into the driveway.

The ghetto soldiers whispered and nodded, sizing us up from head to toe. One short, stocky fellow with a thick black mustache reached for a bulge under his shirt. The others blocked the stairs. Two monstrous pit bulls strained at iron-link leashes, their owners struggling to restrain them as they lunged at us with foam slipping down their jaws.

Street Life's right hand moved toward his Desert Eagle.

"Easy," Drama whispered.

A lanky shadow in a hoodie approached us. His pants and shoelaces were the same color as his hooded sweater. He was thick about the shoulders, twenty to twenty-five years old. A deep battle scar cut from his ear to the tip of his chin. Loc sunglasses hid his eyes. "What y'all want?"

"We here to see Latin Caesar," Street Life said politely.

The man with the scar snapped our pictures with his eyes. Then he swung the front door open and bid us enter. The other fellows from the porch followed us inside, where we were swallowed up in darkness.

"Put up your hands," our host demanded. "I want to search you." He snatched the Desert Eagle from Street Life's waistband. "You get this back when you leave. Caesar's in the back. Just keep going." He pointed the way with a nod of his head.

Wild flamenco guitars pulsated inside sixteen-inch stereo woofers. A Rent-a-Center TV with an extra-wide screen broadcast reruns of *My Three Sons*, but no one watched from the overstuffed couch. The house was a shell, a weigh station where human mules delivered their goods and coke, and money changed hands. This was the seat of Latin Caesar's power and we had come for the keys to the kingdom.

"He's in the kitchen," the guy in the hoodie mumbled.

A faint light flickered down the end of the corridor. I ventured a glance at Drama, who squinted in the darkness. Something didn't feel right. I never walked into a building unless I knew where the exits were. Drama had taught me that. But in this place, it appeared there was one way in and one way out.

We were holding thousands of dollars, every dime we could rake and scrape together, and everyone around us knew it. Drama never released the bag but he did have to let one of the soldiers peek inside. The kid smiled at the contents. I had stick-up visions. Still, we walked deeper into the darkness.

Finally, Life looked back at the man who had searched us. "Where is he, man?"

"He's in the kitchen," the fellow insisted.

We crossed over the threshold. A sea of fat red-and-purple votive candles adorned with the Virgin Mary's image lay spread out on a round, wooden table. The flames cast abstract shadows on a face that was covered by a Zapata mustache and black sunglasses. He sat back in a wooden kitchen chair and cocked his head slowly to one side. He wore a crisp white

T-shirt over his white undershirt and thick, iron muscles. I put him around thirty-seven or thirty-eight years old.

Seven of the soldiers from the porch squeezed into the tiny kitchen with us. I heard footsteps tramping back and forth in another room. There were other people in the house beyond our sight.

"Street Life!" Latin Caesar leapt up from the table and grabbed Life around his shoulders. He let go and pointed at Life's chest as if an S were sewn on it.

"Boys," Latin Caesar said to his followers, "while I was down, some fools tried to roll up on me. This vato stuck one of 'em in the neck with a shank. Then he looked at the others and said, 'Which one a y'all wanna back him up?'"

That story made Caesar's crew loosen their postures. Some of them even smiled. One by one, they shook Life's hand. "Good lookin', homes," the man with the scar said.

Latin Caesar dropped down in his chair once again. Four empty wooden chairs surrounded him. Still, he did not offer us a seat.

Latin Caesar's voice didn't rise above a whisper as he addressed his boys. "I told my man, Latin Caesar never forgets a favor. I told him, when he got out, to come see me. I owe him one. Now he comes to me."

Caesar's tone became more somber. "Now, what you want, homie?"

"Coke," Street life said.

"Razor, reach in the fridge. My friend here is thirsty."

The gangstas laughed.

"We want to buy some weight from you, Caesar," Drama said.

Latin Caesar's eyebrows bunched together. His jaw tightened. He stared at Drama as though he'd just bitten him on the hand. "Do I know you?"

Life coughed into his hand. "Uh…Caesar, this my home-boy, Drama."

Latin Caesar looked at me. I nearly melted beneath his hundred-degree gaze. "And who is this?" he quizzed.

"This is Firstborn. He our homie too."

Caesar studied me for a silent moment before he lashed out with the taste of poison on his whispering tongue. "I don't like his shirt. It's the wrong color. Get it out of my sight."

I swallowed. It hadn't occurred to me until that very moment that his enemies were identified by the color I was wearing. It was an honest but potentially deadly mistake.

Several voices cussed in unison. Drama shook his head in what could have passed for pity. He unzipped his jacket and flung it to me. I threw it on and zipped it up.

"What's this fool's name?" Latin Caesar asked.

"Firstborn," Street Life answered.

"Life, you come in here with one of your boys dressed like my enemies and the other one talkin' 'bout buyin' weight." Latin Caesar cocked an eyebrow. "You brought the FBI up in here or something?"

I froze. Then Caesar broke out laughing. "Had y'all going for a minute. FBI. Ha!" He eyed me coolly. "But don't you take that jacket off, fool."

The tension dissipated. Everyone in the room expelled a collective breath. I took it that Latin Caesar didn't make many jokes.

"How much weight we talkin' 'bout, big mouth?" Caesar asked, looking at Drama.

"A brick."

The guy with the scar giggled. "That ain't no weight."

A tattooed hand pressed a crumpled spiral notebook and a ballpoint pen down on the table in front of Latin Caesar. He scooped them up, paused for a few seconds, then wrote down a figure. He slid the pad toward us. The figure represented half the market price for what we were looking to buy. It was obvious that he was doing a favor for a friend. "Are we good?"

The three of us smiled at Caesar. "We're good," we said in unison.

"Where is it?" Drama asked.

"Give Razor the keys to your hooptie. When you leave, it'll be in the trunk."

I handed the car keys to the tall man with the Raiders jersey and the scar.

"Next time you come here, just leave the back door unlocked and we'll handle your order. While we're waiting I want to say something to college boy here." He looked in my direction.

"Why'd you call me college boy?"

"Because you don't talk like a thug and you don't look like one. Only a serious square would be dumb enough to walk up in my house with that color shirt on. You have been to college, haven't you?"

"Yes."

"Sociology major?"

"Philosophy."

"Ah." Latin Caesar sat back in the chair and spread his arms like an explorer announcing a great discovery. "I sit before Spinoza, Leibniz, Hegel...a rationalist. 'Always recognize that human individuals are ends and use them as means to your end.'" Latin Caesar smirked.

"Immanuel Kant said that," I blurted out in shock. "I see you've done some studying too."

Caesar continued. "When I was young, I wanted to be the Latino Martin Luther King. I wanted to organize voter registration drives, challenge the gringos' immigration policies, organize marches against factories that were paying our people slave wages. I wanted to run for political office. I wanted to make a difference for my people. I wanted to be a leader."

The starburst in Caesar's eyes faded as he took a personal journey into his soul. Somewhere along the way he seemed to get lost. I felt as though I had to say something to break the silence.

"It's not too late."

Latin Caesar came out of his trance and flipped mental channels again. "It's not too late for *you*, kid. You can still walk away. Do you know what you're getting into here? Fiends call rock cocaine the devil's candy. It turns out mamas and leaves them on the corner in mini-skirts flagging down tricks. It sends their kids to foster care. It sends daddies to prison and the homeless shelter. You gonna be sellin' to people who look like you. Could be your sister or your mother. Can you handle that? Could you stick a gun in a sucker's mouth and blow his brains out 'cause he shorted you ten dollars and you can't have fools in the street thinkin' you soft? What we doin' is genocide. You ever see that movie called *Pianist*?"

"No."

"A handful of Jewish traitors helped Nazi soldiers send their own people to concentration camps. We just like them."

I stood there with my mouth open. His words blasted through my skull like flaming arrows. My father had taught me that a race traitor was the worst thing one could ever become. I knew that selling drugs to black and brown people wasn't going to turn me into Frederick Douglass, but did he have to put it like that? *Traitor*. I choked on the word.

Latin Caesar chuckled. "Hand me my thirty pieces of silver!"

Life handed Latin Caesar a paper lunch bag stuffed with soft green paper portraits of Benjamin Franklin. Caesar thumbed through the stack twice. Finally satisfied, he glanced up at us and said, "Now, prepare to sell your souls."

CRACK HAD PICKED HER
BONES CLEAN. EACH YEAR ON
THAT PATH OF DARKNESS HAD
LOWERED HER HEAD ONE MORE INCH.

CHAPTER
TEN

DRAMA'S AUNT SONIA LIVED IN THE LOWER BOTTOMS PART OF Baby Baghdad. She was working as a law clerk in a downtown office when an old boyfriend gave her that first blast. Six months later, she was breaking into cars and houses and opening up her body cavities for ten-dollar rocks. Crack had picked her bones clean. Each year on that path of darkness lowered her head one more inch.

Sonia agreed to let us cook up our product in her kitchen. In return, we promised to hit her off with some rocks. She was waiting by the door for us to arrive like we were Ed McMahon there to bring her the million-dollar sweepstakes check.

Aunt Sonia had been meticulous about her dress when I was a kid. Now her clothes hung off of her like a burlap bag on a scarecrow.

Sonia's kids, ages six, seven, and twelve, sat in front of their one-eyed electronic babysitter. Sonia dropped a sugar-coated jelly donut down among them like a hockey puck. They threw knuckles and elbows in an effort to grab it.

Commercials about kitchen cleanser flashed unnoticed on the screen.

Drama and Life dumped the implements of our labor onto the kitchen table: latex gloves, a triple-beam scale, bent playing cards, Pyrex cooking utensils, baking soda, baby laxative, Manitol, and, of course, that kilo of raw.

I wasn't quite ready to go to work. I opened Sonia's refrigerator to see if there was anything for the kids to eat. A burnt-out light bulb stared back at me. There was nothing inside the box except two forty-ounce bottles of Old English 800, a box of baking soda, and a burnt spoon.

Drama sucked his teeth in exasperation. "Firstborn, get some gloves on. We gotta get busy, man."

"But those kids..."

Drama fished in his shirt pocket for a loose bill. He tossed a twenty down on the floor in front of the children. Sonia's older boy snatched it up and raced through the front door like a squirrel through a forest fire. The other children stood at attention, staring at the front door. Seven minutes later, the oldest boy was back with a Christmas-morning smile and big plastic bag of Chinese food. His siblings lunged at him, spilling a carton of fried rice on the linoleum. Not a drop was wasted.

Street Life stared at the fray in amazement. He whispered the Lord's name in vain and shook his head.

While we were placing our rocks in tiny cellophane squares, Sonia sat in a chair in front of us, her eyes skipping back and forth like a cat watching a Ping-Pong match. Her pupils took on an almost supernatural glow. She licked her lips over and over.

I make it a habit not to get into people's business. This time, however, I couldn't help it. "Sonia," I asked, "why don't you feed those kids?

"Shoot, they gets plenty to eat."

"It doesn't look like it."

Drama flashed me a look of exasperation. "What are you, Firstborn, working for CPS now?" He tossed four fat rocks down in front of Sonia. She scooped them up and then pulled a glass tube from her purse. She pinched one of the yellowish pebbles between her thumb and forefinger and slipped it into the stem. Next, Sonia took the lighter and tickled the black end of the pipe with the flame. She inhaled like a deep sea diver sucking on an oxygen tube, then flopped back on the couch. Her chapped lips parted slightly. She rubbed her nose with the flat of her hand. Her children hardly noticed.

As she sank into the couch, I noticed that her stomach was swollen. She was pregnant.

Life tucked the triple beam and the bulging plastic bag of devil's candy into a green duffel bag. Sonia's six-year-old daughter, Tracey, stared up at me as I reached for the door-knob. I sensed she wanted to say something to me, if only she knew how to talk.

THE SOUL-SEARING GRIT OF CRIMINAL LIFE SOAKED THROUGH THE PORES OF MY FLESH LIKE VINEGAR IN A SPONGE.

CHAPTER
ELEVEN

DRAMA TOLD ME TO DRIVE TO THE WILSHIRE MOTEL ON WEST MacArthur. It was a two-story fleabag dump, infested with meth and mice.

After a few words with the proprietor, Drama led Life and me to room 236, which boasted a magnificent view of the parking lot and the green communal dumpster. The room contained two single beds, a rusty sink with a dripping faucet, a faded portrait of George Washington, and a safe. The safe was the only amenity we had a use for.

Drama had paid the rent on these deluxe accommodations for six months in advance. In exchange for that generous consideration, the landlord agreed never to send the cleaning lady to that room. The place was crawling with dust mites and fat onyx water bugs that looked like baby dinosaurs. They crunched when stepped on.

Dark splotches made abstract designs on the camel-colored love seat. Were they blood or alcohol stains? I hesitated to sit down, fearing I might contract some incurable skin disease.

"Firstborn, why don't you click on the AC for a playa?" Street Life said.

I twisted the knob. The unit buzzed and knocked but no air came out. Drama laughed. Sweat ran from his brow. He handed me an ice-cold forty. "Crack this, man."

I poured a sip out on the carpet for "the brothers who ain't here," then took a long gulp. I passed the bottle to Life and clicked on the television. At least that worked. The reruns of *Good Times* sent canned laughter rolling through the room.

After the second blunt had been smoked, I lay back on the mattress, which curved into my spine like a sack of railroad spikes. I laced my fingers behind my head and stared at the ceiling. Drama and Street Life were almost invisible to me. The soul-searing grit of criminal life soaked through the pores of my flesh like vinegar in a sponge.

"You know," I said, still staring at the ceiling, "I think that with some direction, Latin Caesar could do some real good in this world."

Drama scoffed. "Firstborn, I can tell you look up to potna. But he ain't no Che Guevara or Emiliano Zapata. He ain't nothin' but a dope dealer, dawg…and a killer. He done killed enough of his own people to fill up a phone book."

"But he could be—"

Drama sucked his teeth. "Open your eyes, blood. You could put a pink dress and a bonnet on Street Life here, but that don't make him Mary Poppins. He's a straight husla from the Deep East, feel me? It's a thousand miles between could be and is. Latin Caesar ain't no revolutionary. He sell coke."

Drama snickered. "That fool reminds you of your daddy, don't he?"

Sometimes old friends don't even have to look into your eyes to know your thoughts.

I stared up at an army of ants marching across the ceiling. "No," I said. But I was lying. Latin Caesar had my father's charisma and leadership skills. He wore an Old World charm and wisdom like an invisible raincoat.

Street Life chuckled. "Can anything good come out of the hood?"

I deflected the question with a comment of my own. "Latin Caesar said we're selling death to our own people. What do you both think about that?"

Drama waved his hand to dismiss the thought. "You gotta get that Black Power crap out of your mind, man. When they put Malcolm X's picture on a hundred-dollar bill, that's when I'll pay that yip-yap any mind. Until then, I gotta do what I gotta do to bubble up."

Life curled his lips in disgust. "Forget that gang banger, man. You think he'd refuse to sell crack to somebody just because they could speak Spanish? Latin Caesar don't care what color a person's skin is as long as their money is green. He's just trying to play with your mind, homes. Forget that mutha. Black people ain't doin' nothin' for you. And ain't no such thing as good money and bad money. We get it how we get it."

Drama jumped off the bed and slipped on a latex glove, then shoved his hand between the two overstuffed mattresses. The butt of a .44 Magnum emerged in his fist.

"I got this from Reece over on Bancroft. Ain't no tellin' where it come from." He extended it toward me. "Take it. You need something to hold yourself down with. Just don't put no fingerprints on it. It may have some heads on it."

I grabbed a set of latex gloves from the duffel bag and slipped them on, then held out both hands. Drama placed the weapon in my palms as gingerly as a newborn baby. It felt warm and heavy to the touch. I bounced it in my palm. I had never held a gun before. I felt deadly, as powerful as Satan himself.

"Firstborn, the wild young niggas out there today was born in a room full of guns. They ain't afraid a dying. So don't be wavin' this li'l click-clack around trying to scare fools. But if a situation go down wrong, pull the heat and let it holler. Better to be judged by twelve than carried by six."

They were trying to bring home the truth that if something went wrong I would have to shoot somebody without hesitation or be shot. I usually thought exclusively about the money, not the cold, hard particulars. The fact was, I didn't know what would happen if I ever got in a situation where I would be called upon to blast a bullet into somebody's spleen. We'd just have to wait and see. You can best believe I didn't tell Drama and Street Life that I had any trepidation about killing, though.

"We gonna get you inside Alston University the hard way," Drama said. "You ready to get your grind on?"

"I just have one question."

Drama tugged his Boston College baseball cap down over his eyes in irritation. "What?"

"How are we going to get Endonesia's clique to share that corner with us?"

Street Life broke in with a laugh. "Who said anything about sharing?"

CHAPTER
TWELVE

I CELEBRATED THE ARRIVAL OF THE FIRST DAY OF THE WEEK BY twisting up a fat blunt. I poured all that I had left of a dime bag of purple into a zigzag and rolled it up the size of a fat man's thumb. I lit a match to the tip and hit it a few times before I walked out of my front door and into the heartless streets of the city of dope.

The air felt crisp and clean. There wasn't a cloud to be found anywhere in the sky. It was such a glorious day I decided to walk to Drama's house rather than hail a cab. The exercise couldn't hurt me. Besides, I had my blunt to keep me company.

I thought about Alston. Soon I would be packing my bags, shaking hands on the block, smiling as the old heads wished me a sweeter life in a better place. Berkeley was only twenty miles away from East Oakland but it felt like another planet.

A deep, hearty laugh sprang up from my belly. My spirit felt as though it could have sprouted wings.

I hadn't made it a full block before the roar of a car engine interrupted my meditations. I was as high as the space shuttle, but I had enough reflex response to whirl around in the direction of the speeding car. It was a black Crown Victoria, an unmarked police car.

The officer blurped me. I flicked the blunt down by the curb and kept walking. I did a quick personal inventory. I had rolled all my weed into that one blunt. I had no paraphernalia on my person, not even rolling papers. I didn't have a large, hard-to-explain money bulge in my pocket. Yet I could almost see my heart beating through my shirt.

Car tires whined and screeched behind me. A woman jumped out and hollered through my haze. "Get up against the car, fool! Spread 'em."

I gave an exaggerated yawn and placed my fingertips on the hood of the car. The officer kicked my ankles with her shiny black boots, forcing me to lean on the car for balance. I soothed my fear by talking to myself. *She's got nothing on you. She's just hunting young black men with bald heads and saggy pants. I just happened to fit the description. I'll play along and she'll let me go.*

"Mister, you smell like a Grateful Dead concert. Don't you know it's against the law to smoke marijuana? Hey, what's that by the curb?"

I gulped. "It ain't mine."

"I wonder if it's got your fingerprints on it."

I swallowed. Panic set in. "That ain't mine. I don't even smoke marijuana." My voice came out louder than I wanted it to.

"Yeah, right. And my name is Hillary Clinton."

I didn't know her real name. But I knew that people in the hood called her the Hawk. I'd heard that if she caught you doing wrong, it was nearly impossible to escape her. It was said that she could sprint like a deer and brawl like a dude. I also heard she knocked out a cat named Fred with a left hook just because he called her the B word.

The Hawk grabbed my right wrist and then my left. I was in steel bracelets before I could count to three. It was the first time I'd ever been in handcuffs. The metal edges sliced into the flesh of my wrists. My pants began to slip down but I couldn't pull them up with the bracelets on.

"They're too tight," I moaned.

"You'll get used to them. You'll be wearing them a lot in your line of work...*Firstborn.*"

How did she know my name?

She grinned at the shock that caused my lips to part slightly. "Get in the car, dope dealer."

"I ain't no—"

The Hawk placed her hand on top of my head and twisted it down like a corkscrew. Her long blue fingernails dug into my bare scalp like a crown of thorns. The squad car smelled like vomit, urine, and antiseptic.

Once I was in the backseat, she slammed the door and hopped in the front. She took Foothill Boulevard on two wheels. We raced down East Seventy-third doing eighty.

My seat was hard naugahyde. My wrists throbbed. I'd never been so scared. "Am I under arrest?"

"What do you think?"

"What am I being arrested for?"

"For mind waste."

"What?"

"A mind is a terrible thing to waste, and if I could arrest you for that, you'd be on your way to North County jail right now, Mr. Walker."

"If I'm not being charged, I want out of the car."

The Hawk swerved in the middle of the street. The speedometer dropped from eighty to zero in less than ten seconds. We came to a stop in the parking lot behind Eastmont Mall. The Hawk draped her arm over the back of her seat and stared at me through the black wire mesh. Her hair was teased and twisted. Long curly eyelashes shaded her gorgeous brown eyes. I couldn't help but think how fabulous she might have looked in an evening gown. However, there wasn't anything cute about her drab black uniform or the loaded .9 millimeter pistol holstered at her side.

"Firstborn, I knew your father. He was a righteous man. A warrior. A revolutionary. You know the corner where you and your crew deal poison to our beautiful black people? He used to stand on that corner and preach black nationalism and West African history to anybody who was smart enough to stop and listen. Your daddy was a brilliant man who loved his people. I've been watching you from a distance all your life, wondering if you would measure up to the man he was."

I didn't want to think about what she was saying. I had tried hard up until that point to keep from meditating on my actions. I remembered the look of anguish on Daddy's face when he recounted the day he saw his mentor, a once respected black leader, stick a needle full of heroin into his arm. It broke his heart. My father had called the dope game the "final solution; the annihilation of the black race." I couldn't do what I did every day and still think about Daddy and his teachings. But here was the Hawk force-feeding me my legacy. Her voice began to grate against my soul.

"The first time I saw you on the corner with those losers, I said to myself, 'That can't be Joshua Walker's boy!' But you look just like him. What are you doing out there, son?"

"I just like talking to my friends. I don't sell drugs."

STRAIGHT OUTTA EAST OAKLAND 119

The Hawk's teeth clamped together to make a grinding sound. Fury crackled in her voice like dry twigs in a forest fire. "Don't play me for a fool, chump. You've been consorting with the one they call Drama, aka D Montana, aka Dramacidal. He ain't headed nowhere but the pen or the funeral parlor, and he doesn't care who he takes with him."

I shrugged, studying the seagull formation high above us.

The Hawk's words slowed to a crawl. "Firstborn, do you know what prison is like? Do you ever talk to your fascinating friends about *that*?"

"I'm never going to prison."

She laughed so hard tears flooded her eyes. It took her a full minute to regain control of herself.

"I think the worst of it must be hearing those big iron doors shut after they walk you through the gates. You take that last big gulp of freedom. You know you're not going to be outside again for years, if ever. Guards with rifles and black sunglasses staring down at you from the towers. Razor wire circles. San Quentin's so crowded, you got ten men squeezed in a space meant for three. Sleeping on the concrete floor, on steel trays, packed liked sardines on bunk beds in the gym."

I tried to think about a movie I'd seen on television the night before about an astronaut stranded in space with a runway model. I counted my fingers over and over again. Anything to keep from listening to the Hawk's mouth run. The pinkie and index fingers on my left hand trembled slightly.

"The other inmates are brothers who have been sexually active since they were twelve, and now they're down till the casket drops and they'll never be able to touch another woman. The sex drive doesn't just dissolve because they can't have a woman. They start running through the younger men, ripping them off, trading them like old baseball cards, sharing them with friends."

Oh, God, make her shut up.

"You got hardened convicts who are pros at this game. They've been down for twenty years already. When you wake up one cold night with the point of a shiv stabbing your jugular vein and some crazy nigga named Bob, with bad breath and problem skin, telling you what he wants and how he likes it, what you gonna do? Who you gonna tell? You just better pray that Bob don't have full-blown AIDS. And he might, because it's hard to get condoms behind the walls. The governor expects his prisoners to be celibate."

I gritted my teeth and twisted in the seat like a corkscrew.

"So then you become Bob's punk, his slave…washing out his drawers, ironing his clothes, using Kool-Aid powder for eye shadow, following behind him with your fingers in the circles of his belt loops, submitting to risky, painful sex acts whenever he says, 'Spread 'em.' He'll force you to change your name from Firstborn to something catchy like Freda or Francine. And what a sight you'll be, flitting around in a nightgown. Dudes you grew up with acting like they never saw you before, and you in the lunchroom saying, "Bob, may I feed you the mashed potatoes now? Bob, may I sit now?"

"That'll never happen to me."

"It's happened to a lot of brothers harder than you'll ever be, running around saying, 'I'm a gangsta. I'm a thug.' You can't take no Tech 9 through a metal detector, playa!" She cackled like a wild woman.

I trembled. I wanted out of the car. I wanted to stop her words from seeping through my brain tissue.

"Son," she said, her voice gentler, "why don't you go to that college you want to go to? Alston, right? Then you could come back here and help people. You'd be a symbol of success to the youngsters."

How did she know about Alston?

"I can't afford the tuition."

"So you're out there on that corner trying to raise it?" She glanced at me through the iron mesh and broke into another hysterical laugh.

"Can I ask you a question?" I managed.

"Sure."

"How do you know so much about me?"

The Hawk's brows knit together. "Son, these streets talk. There ain't much that happens out here that I don't find out about sooner or later. I've got eyes and ears all around you."

She climbed out of her seat and opened my car door. My high was gone. The Hawk clasped the chain between my handcuffed wrists and gave a pull. I muffled a scream as I was jerked to my feet. She produced a key and unlocked the cuffs. I rubbed my wrists to get the circulation back.

She stood there, arms folded. "I'm going to let you go this time, son. But remember this: there's no code of the streets. There's no such thing as disrespecting the game. Crack killed all that. Now there's a new saying in these streets: *Why go to the pen when you can tell on a friend?* And friend, your name is already coming up in places you wouldn't want it to be mentioned."

My heart pounded as I considered this. I had no reason to doubt her. *Maybe you should get out of the game now, before it's too late*, a voice whispered inside my head.

She waved her index finger from left to right. "Out here, it's every man for himself. There are cold, nutty killers out here who would rat you out in a heartbeat if they thought I had a strong enough case to pull them down."

I shrugged, trying to appear unfazed. But I was pretty sure she was looking right through me, encouraged by the smell of my hot perspiration mingled with fear.

"I know your boys are always talkin' about death before dishonor. They call themselves men of honor. Firstborn, you're the walking encyclopedia. What does *honorable* mean?"

I bowed my head and stared down at my sneaker laces. I took a deep breath and the words spilled out. *"Honorable* means ethical, moral, or just."

"That's right," she said. "Honorable is the librarian providing a safe environment for little kids to study in after school. Honorable is what tutors and mentors are in the after-school program. Honorable is every father and mother who get up every morning to work an honest job so they can put food in their kids' mouths. Now, what does *dishonorable* mean?"

"Foul, shady, unprincipled, corrupt, without morals." I expelled the words in a whisper, as though a Mack truck were sitting on my chest. The entire Black Christmas crew paraded before the video screen in my mind, grinning.

"Your boys talk about death before dishonor but they are clearly dishonorable. They *brag* about being shady. They cheat people. They operate by con and deception. They survive by lying. They applaud when someone does dirt and doesn't get caught. They survive by being foul, unprincipled, corrupt, and without morals. According to the definition you just gave me, they are dishonorable. Are they really going to suddenly get honorable when I've got 'em in an interrogation room looking at ten to twenty years?"

I could hear myself breathe. I couldn't turn my mind away from the words. They made too much sense.

"Death before dishonor? What a load of crap! Criminals are the most selfish people on earth. Somebody who lies in bed till ten and then breaks into your house and steals your stuff while you're at work is lazy, selfish, and *dishonorable.* Somebody who steals your credit card numbers or rips off some elderly person's Social Security checks is *dishonorable.*

When I'm about to offer a criminal a deal, I say, 'Here's a chance to help yourself.' A true hustler will almost always help himself. If he doesn't tell on somebody, it's not because he's *honorable*. It's because he's afraid."

I didn't want to admit it, but everything she was saying had the ring of truth to it. I tried to act as though I wasn't listening, but that didn't shut her up.

"Nobody wants to go to jail. Believe me, you can't trust anybody on that block. You'd be surprised by who rings my phone. I'm a better friend to you right now than any of them will ever be."

"You gonna let me go, *friend*?"

Her head snapped back in surprise and dismay at my defiance. The Hawk's nose wrinkled and her lip curled.

"Firstborn, you better wake up. Go back home and think about your ways. I pray you'll decide to change immediately. I hope the next time I see you, you're on television giving your presidential acceptance speech before you take office. I hope that one day, you and I will look back on this little episode and have a chuckle."

Wow, the Hawk really believed that I had it in me to be the president of the United States? Those words caused my eyebrows to rise involuntarily. If only she had stopped there. But she didn't.

"If you choose to destroy our people by selling drugs, I will destroy you, a little piece at a time. And once I get you on paperwork, consider yourself officially screwed. 'Cause I'll slap you with a four-way search clause. Then anybody with a badge will be able to drag your pants down in the middle of the street and search your drawers just because they're in a bad mood or because they're bored and have nothing better to do. We'll be free to run up in your place and toss it upside down, rip open your mattress, and step all over your personal belongings whenever we get the notion, and we won't even need probable cause because you'll be on the lowest form of custody and your behind will belong to the state of California. That day is coming for you unless you change your ways."

I could get caught. That reality finally hit home.

"And one more thing. The next time I put you in the backseat of this car, you'd better have somebody else's name in your pocket or you're going to San Quentin to meet your roommate, Bob. Now, get out of my face, race traitor!"

The Hawk turned her back, leaped into the driver's seat, and sped off like Batman chasing a Gotham City hoodlum, leaving me in a cloud of dust stranded four miles from home. I hailed a cab and gave the driver Drama's address. From the backseat I pulled out my cell phone and dialed his number. When he picked up, I squeaked out, "We got trouble, cuz-o. Five-0 trouble." My voice was two octaves higher than normal.

"Don't talk on the phone. I'll see you when you get here."

Ten minutes later, I was standing at Drama's front door in a state of paralysis. He grabbed me by the arm and snatched me inside.

"Pimpin' EZ, come make Firstborn a drink," he hollered over his shoulder.

The star boarder sprang into the kitchen. The minute he heard the word *drink*, his tongue popped out of his mouth like Pavlov's dog. His bony ribs pressed against the cotton of his tank top. A plastic shower cap protected his perm from exposure to the heat. He got up on his tiptoes to search the top shelf of the kitchen cabinet where the alcohol was kept. Pimpin' EZ's sheer black socks almost reached to his knees. "The only thing you got up in here is some Beefeater gin."

"Well, crack it open, fool."

Pimpin' EZ poured one Styrofoam cup for himself and one for me. I gulped my liquor down like an asthmatic sucking on an inhaler.

"Give me another one," I demanded.

"Take it easy, playa. What happened?"

I told the story and finished it with "If she picks me up again, she'll want me to snitch on somebody."

Pimpin' EZ smirked. "Occupational hazard." Drama gave him a deep-set frown, but Pimpin' EZ continued to work his jaws like a parakeet on crystal meth. "They needed an inside man on that corner. So they went for the one cat with something to lose. Firstborn, you wanting to go to Alston and all—"

"Wait a minute," Drama howled. "How did the Hawk find out about Alston?"

Pimpin' EZ's eyes grew wide. He bounced his Styrofoam cup down on the kitchen table and backed up toward the front door like the soon-to-be victim in a horror movie.

"What, y'all think I'm a snitch? Is that what this is?"

Drama curled his bottom lip. His common-law brother-in-law stood condemned by the words that came out of his own mouth.

"You're lucky I need you, Pimpin' EZ," Drama spat out.

"I don't have to take this." Pimpin' EZ did his best imitation of the backward moonwalk.

After he slammed the door, Drama muttered, "I can't believe that mutha."

I looked out the window and saw Pimpin' EZ do a pimp strut out the front door of the building and straight into broad daylight. That was the first time I had seen him leave the apartment in two months. I wondered where he was headed.

"Drama," I said, "you have a snitch living in your house."

Drama peered into my worried eyes and shook his head. "I need that buster, First. Don't worry, though. You can control a rattlesnake if you got him trapped in an empty room with all the lights on. Ain't nothin' gonna happen. 'Sides, what does he know?"

"He knows your name and my name. That's enough to start a police investigation, isn't it?" I took another drink.

Drama rested his hand on my shoulder. "Cuz, I'll never let you get arrested or shot. You have my word on it. Now, get your mind right 'cause we got to tend to this business."

The doorbell rang twice. Drama froze for a moment before he twisted the knob open. "Is ya with me or not?"

"Till the wheels fall off," I answered.

Street Life met us at the door with a solemn glare in his eyes. I could see the butt of his pistol stuck in his belt band. It was going to be another long day.

CHAPTER
THIRTEEN

CROSSING THE EMOTIONAL DISTANCE BETWEEN OUR CORNER AND the other side of the street was a slow, cautious walk through an unfriendly world, somewhat akin to wandering barefoot from the equator to the North Pole. Piercing stares swept us in. The sun beat down like a bolo punch. Sweat tickled my brow.

Endonesia was sitting in the passenger seat of his black Cadillac Escalade. The door stood open. His right foot dangled outside the car door. A bright orange dew rag covered Endo's scalp. His cell phone was glued to his ear. Endonesia talked to his girl while absently sizing us up. He probably thought we were just trafficking loose joints and dime bags of weed. If so, he had miscalculated our ambition.

"What's up?" Endo asked without taking the phone away from his ear.

"We need to get at you for a second, man," Drama said.

"Go 'head." He continued to babble into the receiver. "So, girl, if I go through all that, what you gonna do for me?"

Drama closed the distance between himself and Endonesia, who was chuckling heartily. "Girl, you too much."

Drama snorted deeply and huffed. Phlegm and saliva sprayed out of his mouth and landed on one of Endonesia's black Jordans.

Endo's friends froze. His hand leapt for the glove compartment like a cobra striking at its prey.

"I wouldn't do that, man," Street Life said in a sing-song voice.

Suddenly he was met with three pieces of iron. His crew shuffled backward. I held the handle of my gun, struggling to keep it aimed straight and hoping I wouldn't have to shoot. Endonesia's mask of shock broke my concentration. His hard-guy, mean mug evaporated. I almost laughed.

"What y'all gonna do, stick a nigga up?" he asked with a measure of awe in his voice.

"We should," I cut in. "You stole my sneakers."

"Is that what you mad about?" Endonesia spat out. "Get a life."

Drama shook his head and waved me off. He had told me he wanted to do all the talking. "Lame, I came over here to talk to you like a gentleman, but you steady disrespectin' me. And when you disrespect me, you disrespectin' Black Christmas."

"Black what?"

"Black Christmas. Our crew."

"Drama, I know you probably brain damaged after that boot stomp we put on you back in the day. But to create all this tension over some bull—"

Drama gripped his pistol with both hands. "Shut your mouth. I'm the one with the gun. Now, as I was saying, this corner belongs to Black Christmas now, and tomorrow we gonna smoke anything standing here that ain't down with us. You feel me, dawg?"

"So, what you sayin', playa?" Endonesia asked.

"I'm saying, get down or lay down."

"I'm calling C-Storm!"

C-Storm was a heavy hitter. A phone call to him meant someone was soon to take a feet-first trip to the morgue. He rarely showed himself unless there was a serious problem out on the blocks, and even then he sent problem solvers to take care of it.

"Am I supposed to be scared?" Drama snarled, showing C-Storm no respect. "He a old man. Tell him I said he should retire."

As we walked away, Endo shouted, "You better watch yourself, Drama. You're playing with your life, dawg!"

Drama turned and stabbed his forefinger in Endo's direction. "No, you better watch yourself, Endonesia, 'cause tomorrow, I'll be playing with yours."

Drama spent the rest of the afternoon back at the crib, talking on the phone.

"Yeah, I know niggas like to yip yap at the lips. But if y'all get down with us, they finished. C-Storm's clique won't be able to pick up a wet food stamp on a rainy day in this hood. We gonna get this money and everything be lovely. Is you down, fam, or what?"

A cold summertime darkness fell over the California Bay Area the next night as we drifted through the courtyard and wandered down to the corner. Drama stopped in front of a red 1998 Chevrolet Camaro with a badly dented back fender. He nodded toward the vehicle and then cut his eyes in my direction. "Open it."

I tried the handle on the driver's side door. It wasn't locked. The door sprang open. "Whose car is this?"

"Don't ask so many questions, Firstborn. Just get in."

I got in and pulled up the latch on the passenger door. Street Life climbed in the backseat, leaving the front open for Drama.

It took a few seconds for my eyes to adjust to the darkness. What I saw hanging under the steering wheel told me that it was fruitless to ask for the keys. A multi-colored jumble of naked wires crisscrossed beneath the dashboard.

Street Life folded the hood of his sweater forward over his cornrows. He looked like a hip hop version of the grim reaper, complete with sunglasses and a toothpick swinging out of his mouth. He leaned over and tapped the tips of the wires together. I saw sparks. The engine roared to life. Life nodded at me. I pulled the Camaro away from the curb. I was too afraid to ask for directions. I just drove.

A .45 pistol with a pearl handle came out from the waist-level pouch of Street Life's hoodie. Life took a clip and plunged it into the butt of the pistol. "Hell, yeah!" he said to no one in particular. "It's on and cracking now."

We came around the corner like the plague of darkness ready to visit Egypt. Drama yanked his machine gun from its hiding place underneath the seat. "Time to show these niggas what's really up," he muttered.

"Do I need a gun, Drama?"

"You mean, you ain't got one?"

Street Life laughed like a maniac. "Man, just drive. We got dis." Drama looked at me and chuckled. "Firstborn, Firstborn, Firstborn," he said, shaking his head.

I was clearly in over my head. It was like I was standing at the mouth of a dark pit at midnight being pursued by wolves, with Drama at my side assuring me that I wouldn't hit bottom if I jumped. I didn't have much choice. I jumped. I took the car down Foothill Boulevard. We took a side street and ended up on Bancroft.

"Take a left on Eighty-second," Drama said.

"Where we headed?" I asked.

"It's judgment day for the suckers."

I knew what that meant. I turned toward Endonesia's corner.

A patrol car passed us, going in the opposite direction. The driver slowed down and stared into our car. My heart did a rapid tap dance inside my chest.

"Easy, Firstborn," Drama cautioned.

I was ready to peel out should he hit the wailer. He didn't. He took a right on Ninety-first and we took a left. I pressed my foot down on the gas pedal. There was no looking back now.

"Whatever happens, don't stop this car until I tell you to, you hear me?" Street Life said. I nodded.

Drama reached beneath the seat for a ski mask. He handed it to me. I pulled it down over my face while still driving. He and Street Life both wore identical masks. We looked like the triplets from hell.

It was hot beneath the black wool. I felt like another person, a lower self. I glanced at my reflection in the side mirror. I was a masked ghost, a stranger even to myself.

I could see shadows drifting back and forth on a street corner about a block away. I looked in the rear view. Drama put his finger to his lips. The front passenger window slowly slipped down. Street Life rolled his window down as well.

Endonesia was sitting on the curb, yapping away on his cell phone. IZ tossed two cubes of dice up and down in his palm. Eddie King slapped hands with a customer, slickly exchanging drugs and money.

Two young cats I didn't recognize stood watch. One of them stretched out a bony finger in my direction. They had made us, but it was too late.

Drama knelt on one knee, using the car seat for leverage. The nose of the Uzi rested on his window ledge, pointed toward the crack corner.

"Die, niggaz, die!" Drama hollered.

Thunder and hell spit from the business end of the machine gun. One of the lookouts reached for something in the bushes.

Street Life's trigger finger squeezed. "Uh-uh-uh," he muttered through gritted teeth. He missed.

Homeboy on the corner came up with a .22 and returned fire.

Drama climbed almost all the way out of the Camaro. He sat on the car's window ledge and fired at his prey with one hand. "Burn in hell!" he hollered.

The kid with the .22 fell as if he'd been knocked in the head with a sledge hammer.

Endonesia took off like an Olympic sprinter. His black do rag flew behind him like a cape.

"Turn around, Firstborn," Drama said.

"What?" I hollered. "Man, the police gonna be comin'!" I was ready to defy him and face the consequences later. I could smell death and prison in the air. I wasn't about to hang out and see how things played out.

Drama's door opened. He sprang out of the moving car. He slapped a fresh clip in the Uzi and took to the middle of the street in a dead run. All that weed smoking and good living had lowered Endonesia's stamina. Drama closed the distance between them in a matter of moments.

"Don't do it, Drama!" Endo pleaded. The ski mask hadn't fooled him.

"Get down or lay down, ain't that what I told you, trick? Now, get on your knees and pray!"

"Get away from him," a voice cried out from behind the blinds of a house we called the prison because of all the bars on its windows. Invisible witnesses all over the block were now staring at us from behind blinds and curtains and through dark windows.

"I'm a soldier," Endonesia declared, I guess to impress his phantom audience.

"You? A soldier? Well, here you go, Sarge, a souvenir from the enemy."

I heard the machine gun fire twice. Endonesia's scream came from deep in his bowels. He turned over in the street, rolling over to his left flank and then back to his right. Tears rolled down his smooth cheeks.

"You tore up my foot!" he screamed.

"Well, look at the bright side, Endo. Think how much money you'll save on sneakers now," Drama said, laughing like a madman. He jumped back in the Camaro and I stomped on the gas pedal.

"Slow down, Firstborn," Street Life warned.

My hands shook on the steering wheel. I'd never seen anyone shot up close. I had never been a part of anything like this. I felt like this would be on my soul for eternity.

"What should I do, now, Drama?" I asked.

"Just drive."

We took Ninety-eighth down to Avenue C. People stared at the car but not too hard. In the distance I heard the roar of traffic zooming up and down the International Boulevard thoroughfare. Car horns blared. Hip hop beats from passing cars blasted at volume 10.

Drama pulled a matchbook out of his pocket with a phone number on it. Street Life and I sat in silence while Drama pressed the speaker function on his cell phone.

"Hello, C-Storm? My name's Drama. We've never been formally introduced, but I suspect you've probably heard of me."

"How you get my number and what you doing calling me this late at night?" C-Storm asked.

"Oh, my. Did I wake you? Sorry about that, man. Look, I'll keep it short. Nigga, we took back our corner tonight, and if I so much as see somebody that *looks* like you in my hood, I'll blow your brains out."

"Yeah, a-right, just let me get at Endo and his goons," C-Storm huffed. "My niggas are out there in the East acting a beast. We'll see what they got to say 'bout all that."

"Oh, yeah, you can get at 'em if you want to, but I'll tell you now, you gonna have to call the Highland Hospital emergency room. Other than that, do yourself a favor: stay outta East Oakland. Consider yourself warned, hear?" Drama clicked off the phone and stuck it back in his pocket.

Street Life sat back and gave a deep belly laugh. Drama smiled like an actor who had just finished a role fit for an Academy Award. He shook his head. "These fools is too much!" He slapped my shoulder with his open palm. "My man, Firstborn. You a trooper, blood. We got much love for you."

"Hell, yeah," Street Life drawled out. "Much love." He nodded his grudging respect.

I smiled, the fear and anxiety dissipating.

"We gonna leave the car behind the chicken joint on International and East Sixty-sixth," Drama said. "We'll split up there and meet back at my crib tomorrow around noon. Cool?"

We nodded. And so ended the scariest night of my life up to that point.

C-Storm didn't just lie down. There was retaliation. K.R., a kid we'd grown up with, got his dome split by an AK-47 slug while he was coming out of the dry cleaners one afternoon. He wasn't even an affiliate. He lost his life because he played pool with us on the weekends. Anybody in our circle was a potential target. K.R. was a civilian causality who caught his because of evil associations.

In spite of all the gunplay and injuries, I didn't believe C-Storm and his team would ever get that corner back. There were too many of us. And Drama let everybody eat. We had heavy hitters holding us down; hungry niggas with Tech 9s and .380s were creeping everywhere.

For the next few days Po-Po came around the hood with pen and pad, asking questions. I guess they got tired of hearing, "I don't know nothin'." Soon they moved on to the next trouble spot and the hottest headline. We waited a couple more days for the attention to die down, then we set up shop.

Black Christmas had an opening-day sale: fat rocks for half price. We figured if it works for Macy's, why not us? By nightfall, patients were swarming over us like ants on a piece of sugar bread. Two days later, when the price went up, the knocks still came. And they brought friends.

A knock as tall as a tree, with square-frame sunglasses, sauntered up to our corner. A navy blue wool hat squeezed down over his ears. Specks of dried mucus covered his nose and mustache. Chocolate-chip cookie crumbs spilled down his beard. Tense black eyes beamed out from beneath a tight, solid black eyebrow. He rocked from side to side, flicking his soiled thumb over a thin wad of bills.

"What you got, man?" he asked.

"What you want?" I asked.

He squeezed off a wrinkled twenty-dollar bill, rolled it up small as a pebble, and tossed it up in the air. I grabbed it before it could hit the ground. I nodded twice toward Drama, who stood half a block away. That was the signal that said, "We're paid. Serve him."

"Thank you," I said as the addict shuffled in Drama's direction.

He froze immediately and whirled around. He glared at me as though I had just stabbed him between the shoulder blades. He twisted on his heel and inched back toward me until our noses almost touched. He was cussing under his putrid breath.

"*Thank you*?" he said, spraying droplets of lukewarm saliva in my face.

My home training dictated good manners. I'd said it from force of habit.

"You tryin' to clown me?" the knock asked. I knew I had crossed a line. You never insult the customers. There was so much to learn in the streets, and what you didn't know could get you killed.

The smoker cocked his head slightly to the side. His eyes narrowed into hate-filled slits.

"Look, man, just go down there, get your dub, and leave, all right?"

"Yeah, you got a lot to be thankful for, gettin' rich off a other folks' misery."

I heard a dull thud, like a basketball bounced on a nylon carpet. The crackhead screamed like a pregnant woman in labor. The customer dropped to his knees. Behind him I saw Street Life, with a death grip on a bicycle handle attached to the narrow end of a cut-off baseball bat. Street Life called his vicious invention the attitude-adjustment program.

A tear leaked from the corner of the crackhead's eye. He reminded me of a child who was about to receive the spanking of a lifetime. He huffed, his chest rising and falling as he knelt on the pavement.

Life pulled up his hoodie, allowing the knock a glimpse of the handle of the Desert Eagle stuck in his belt band.

"Gerry," Street Life said to the guy, "we came up together, and I got love for you and all that. But before I see you mess up my money out here, I'm gonna dump some bullets in your head. You know I ain't playing, right?"

The addict nodded, the wind depleted from his sails. He got his dub and left to smoke his brains out.

When smokers ran out of money, they tried to trade everything from postage stamps to oral sex for a hit. One of my best customers, a Silicon Valley engineer, moaned that he was scraping the bottom of his children's college fund to pay for his pleasures. Every two dubs that he purchased from us represented a college textbook. The way he was buying our drugs, he wouldn't even have the money to buy pencils so his kids could fill out the college applications come that next spring.

During the course of a single Friday afternoon, I made three sales to one of our home girls named Deena. The fourth time she walked up in my face that day she said, "Look, Firstborn, I ain't got no more money, but I want to get high. Let me get a couple of rocks on credit, baby. I'll hit you off tomorrow. You know I'm good for it. You know how I get down."

"I know how you *used* to get down before you started smoking," I said. We'd been friends since fourth grade. This was a cash-and-carry business. "Black Christmas don't take ATM cards and we don't do credit." I was sounding more like Drama every day. It kind of scared me. I tried not to think too much about it.

Deena flashed a tight frown. She muttered something under her breath as she walked away.

Half an hour later, she came back, this time lugging her five-year-old son, Chauncey, by the hand. He struggled to free himself from her iron grip. When strength could not pry him loose, Chauncey tried to scratch her arms with his long fingernails. He bit her wrist, but she yanked him into submission like a slave at the wrong end of an iron chain.

I remembered when Deena was a pretty girl with a walnut brown complexion and lips that glowed with gloss. She was never seen without her baby hair slicked down and greased forward. Two years ago, her closet was stuffed with high-fashion urban wear. She dressed her son in Phat Farm gear. Before the kid could even walk, she put Air Jordans on his size-one feet.

But home girl didn't walk into Eastmont Mall with a credit card. No, her renowned underworld skills made her the hip hop fashion-store nightmare. Deena could walk into a store wearing a T-shirt and a mini-skirt and leave with a whole rack of bomber jackets. After she had hit some fancy department store for a big score, she would sometimes unscrew the dressing room doorknobs and throw them in her shopping bag as souvenirs.

Then she started smoking rock cocaine. I'm amazed that people in the hood can watch a million smokers get strung out after even one hit and still believe that they are the exception, that they can handle it. Deena made that mistake. Now she was too strung to steal and too skinny to ho.

Back in the day, she could leave a crowd of men in a daze, hypnotized by the cloud of Passion perfume she left behind. But lately she smelled as funky as a grizzly bear with a pack of spoiled goat cheese tied around her neck. A black forest grew under her armpits and her hair spilled out all over her scalp, wild and uncombed.

The gorilla on her back also impaired her ability to care for little Chauncey. His face and elbows were ashy. He looked thinner than he should have for a boy his age. His purple shorts and soiled blue T-shirt made him look as though someone had dressed him in a dark room.

Deena's face wore a look of resignation. "Give me seven rocks and you can have him," she mumbled.

"Pardon me?" I rubbed my finger in my ear. I couldn't have heard her correctly.

"He's a good boy."

"What would I do with him?"

"Sell him."

"Girl, get away from here with that child!"

Deena shrugged and pulled the kid down the street by his tiny hand.

I trembled. *What am I doing? I don't belong here. This is hell.* If she would sell her child to me, who else might she sell or even rent him to?

I lost a few sleepless nights over that, but I didn't leave the block because the dollars kept stacking up.

We had no shortage of workers, what with cats coming home from the penitentiary every week with no jobs and no place to stay. Desperation put them on our doorstep, down for whatever. "Put me to work, Firstborn," I heard countless times. Or, "Firstborn, let me do some work. I need forty dollars to get a room tonight."

At first I would tell the brothers (and sometimes sisters), "Don't do this, man. You're on paperwork. You get popped with a couple of fat ones, you won't see your kids again till they're old enough to vote. Drama ain't paying no bail." Then I would stick some folding money in their hands. But the next day, they'd be back and I'd have to put them to work. When Street Life's younger brother, Billy, came home from Mule Creek, we gave him a job.

I met all kinds of people on that corner. There were even some kids from prosperous two-parent homes out there with us. They posed in front of the local liquor store with the rest of the hood because they needed to belong to something; they needed to be noticed. I never could understand why they wanted to be viewed as bad boys. Some of them even got branded with BCM tattoos.

Most of the people who worked for us had gotten themselves arrested somewhere in life and later found that it was difficult for someone with a ex-offender jacket to get a legitimate job in a tight economy. Some of the most intelligent people I've ever met—people who could have become nuclear physicists, Pulitzer Prize–winning journalists, or astronauts—stood around wasting their precious youth, slinging rocks on that corner and banging our clique.

Nineteen-year-old Petey had the brains of a molecular biologist. He was five foot six but he wore black jeans hemmed up for a seven-foot man. He glared at the world through silvery gray pupils. Petey was the oldest of five. When cancer claimed his mother's life, his grandmother stepped in to claim custody of Petey and his siblings. But money was tight and the refrigerator was always empty.

The family's rented two-story clapboard hut, with its peeling white paint and rusted gutters, raised eyebrows on a street full of meticulously cared-for homes. Without any warning the landlord upped the rent by three hundred dollars a month. The social worker threatened to split Petey's family up if they were evicted. It looked hopeless.

Petey was walking up and down East Eighty-eighth Avenue, collecting aluminum cans for recycling, when he nearly tripped over Drama. Drama noticed tears in his eyes. It's not often you see a young man crying in the streets of East Oakland.

His curiosity piqued, Drama asked, "What's up, cuz?"

"I need a job. They tryin' to split up my family."

"Do you know who I am?" Drama asked.

"Yeah."

"Do you know what I do?"

"Everybody know. It ain' no thang to me, mister. My family hungry. I'm ready to get down. I ain't afraid to do no dirty work, and I don't ask no questions. Just help me get this rent money. I'm tryin' to eat."

Drama stuck a crisp, new fifty in Petey's hand. "Go down to Safeway and buy your peoples some food. Then meet me on my corner. You know where it is?"

"Everybody know."

"I gotta test your loyalty," Drama said, "'cause I'll have to bring you close if you're gonna work for us."

"Bring it on."

Petey's entrance exam came that very day. Drama handed him a .007 knife and ordered him to gut a fifty-year-old smoker called Tubby like a blowfish. The luckless sucker owed us sixty-two bucks.

The brother tossed his lunch up the first time warm blood dripped off of his fingertips. But he couldn't quit. Drama kept groceries on his family's table.

Drama made Petey a button man, an enforcer. People took to calling Petey "Drama Jr."

If you don't pay your PG&E bill, they turn your lights off. If you didn't pay your cocaine debt to us, pretty much the same thing would happen. Petey took care of most of that. He recruited a group of goons and hard heads who would kick in doors and stomp people out with just a nod from Drama, Street Life, or—though I regret to admit it now—me.

We now had two corners cracking. If you drove in from out of town on your way to an A's game, you might have thought that all you were looking at was a swarm of aimless young black brothers milling around, talking trash. That was the intended illusion. In truth, we had it on and cracking.

Patients started lining up early every morning, seeking the Peruvian miracle cure.

Drama had enough street knowledge to help us survive longer than your average here-today-busted-tomorrow grinders. We invested a portion of the money into shady lawyers, sheisty bail bondsmen, and a crooked cop who fed us priceless inside information. By the time a task force hit the corner, the block was cleaner than the Vatican steps. I got tossed up against a police car more times than I can remember, but they never found anything.

Magdalene and I moved in together. We found a one-bedroom apartment in a three-story building not far from Grand Avenue. In the cool of the evening, we'd take a brisk three-mile walk around Lake Merritt. I never did business out of the crib. I avoided having affiliates come by my apartment. There was nothing flashy about me. I didn't want to draw attention to myself or my lifestyle.

With no visible means of income, I couldn't have rented the place in my own name. Magdalene's sister, Monica, leased it for us. The two of them crammed our tiny apartment with high-end furniture. They topped if off with a twenty-inch flat-screen plasma television and all the cable stations known to humankind, all of it on my dime.

"I don't know why you're collecting all this stuff," I told Magdalene. "When I go to Alston University in a few months, we'll have to live in a dorm. What will we do with all this furniture?"

She just giggled at me.

Still, I loved her. For her birthday, I bought her a twenty-four-carat diamond friendship ring with a gold band. Maggy never took it off. She even slept with it on.

I could afford little luxuries like that because Black Christmas was rolling. Street Life went clothes shopping almost every day. If it didn't say Prada or Moreschi on it, he wouldn't buy it. Life had the whole collection of Steeple Gate alligator shoes.

Drama bought his dream car: a 1978 Cadillac Deville with red candy paint, spinners, and a sound system that made windows rattle in China's Mai Ling province. The thing sat on brand-new twenty-inch chrome.

After my 1970 Pinto died of old age, I ran out to a used car lot on MacArthur and bought a two-tone blue 1988 Chevy Cavalier with a dent in the trunk. The first time I drove it down to the block, Street Life's jaw popped open. "Nigga, all the money you makin' and this is all the whip you could come back with?"

The truth was, I saved most of my money for Alston. I kept it in our Wilshire Motel safe, along with the unsold product and the mob's finances.

The scrilla was stacking but it wasn't all gravy. One afternoon Ms. Johnson glided toward my corner. I'd known her since I was seven years old. She'd been my second-grade teacher. In all of the time we'd been acquainted, I had never seen her leave the house with a shoe untied or a shirt button undone.

That hot summer afternoon there was clearly something wrong. Ms. Johnson's hair was disheveled beneath a green-and-yellow Oakland A's baseball cap. She wore a pair of beige poodle house slippers and squeezed a pink Kleenex in one hand. Her eyes were tear stained and bloodshot. She looked lost as she shuffled up to me.

"Firstborn," she whimpered, "have you seen my Johnny?"

I was anxious to get her away from the corner. I didn't want her to see what I was doing. At any moment, some smoker was liable to walk up to me and say something crazy like, "You got anything?" I didn't want the lady who had taught me phonics and mathematics to see that happen.

"No, Ms. Johnson. I ain't seen 'im."

"Don't you mean, 'No, Ms. Johnson, I *haven't* seen him'?"

"Yes, ma'am."

"You're an intelligent young man, Firstborn. I don't like to hear you talk like a hoodlum."

I glanced up and down the street, then stared at my watch. Ms. Johnson didn't budge.

"I must have fallen off to sleep watching my stories. When I awoke, the living room window was open and the TV was gone. Firstborn, are you sure you haven't seen my Johnny?"

"No, Ms. Johnson. I haven't."

The truth was, I had seen Johnny not ten minutes earlier. He was a notorious dope fiend who alternated between crack and heroin. Hepatitis C had turned the whites of his eyes pale yellow. His lips were eternally cracked and white. He lived off our drugs like a baby survives on breast milk.

Now, I hadn't seen Ms. Johnson's TV. Like I told all my knocks, "Black Christmas ain't runnin' no pawn shop." But I *had* seen the fifty dollars Johnny got after he'd sold his mama's TV set. In fact, it was in my pocket as she spoke to me.

"Well, if you do see him, send him home, all right, son?"

"All right, Ms. Johnson."

Why did she have to call me son? I hated what I was doing. And for the space of about sixty seconds, I hated myself.

How did someone as sweet as Ms. Johnson end up with a son like Johnny? He had stolen the china, the silverware, the groceries, even the car. And I'll bet that every time he got caught he promised, "I'll do better, Mom. I went to see about a program today." Yeah. Right.

There was a lot I hated about the game, and it wasn't just the fact that I had to take diaper money from mothers on

General Assistance and that lazy crackheads would some-times send their kids out to buy rocks from me. What bothered me most was the fear. Terror of the unknown became my constant chaperone. I rarely talked business over the phone. I never drove home the same way two days in a row. I made pick-ups in a bullet-proof vest. I sometimes worked the corner with the heat in my pocket and my finger on the trigger. I even made love to Maggy with one hand on the chrome-plated .44 under my pillow.

Anybody who tells you they're holding down a corner and they aren't scared is either dumb, crazy, or lying. Anybody could be in a car that pulls up to the curb: detectives, hungry young jackers looking for a come-up, or some crazy nigga from the other side looking for a big payback. I was scared every day.

I worked hard not to let my homeboys see the fear, but my heart jumped through my chest every time a strange car pulled up to the curb next to us. If I didn't feel good about somebody, I would whisper, "Undercover." That meant he or she didn't get served.

Magdalene took to this street life like a polar bear to snow. She loved running with the flashy pimps, hookers, and hus-tlers who populated our world, many of whom couldn't form a single sentence without profanity. She chugged down Remy Martin like it was water. Sometimes I had to say, "Wow, girl, why don't you take it easy on that thug juice?" She'd respond by crudely showing me her middle finger.

One day, over a slice of pepperoni pizza, she said the words I had waited my whole life to hear. "I love you, Firstborn." By that time, I had developed enough street sense to question everything that came out of her mouth, and therefore came to this conclusion: Magdalene loved hood life and the hustler

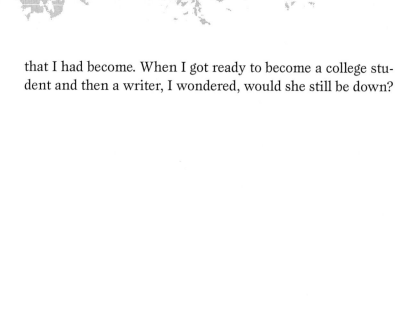

that I had become. When I got ready to become a college student and then a writer, I wondered, would she still be down?

CHAPTER
FOURTEEN

THE DAYS DRIPPED BY LIKE SPECKS OF SAND TO THE BOTTOM OF an hourglass. Broken elders with shattered lives sat on old milk crates, lying and testifying, drinking and winking at the young girls who walked past them into Butchie's Liquor Store. Billy, Frank, and Teddy were out there all day every day. We used to worship these guys when we were kids. Back then hustlers wore brand-new outfits to the corner. They'd occasionally tilt a wide brim at us, as if it took some great effort. They'd tip us five bucks to light their cigars.

When I was twelve years old, Frank once paid me twenty bucks to go get his newspaper, because he was talking to his whore and didn't want to get out of the car. Eventually, he got busted for pandering and made a long trip to the pen. I calculated once that if you took all the money Frank made out on the block and divided it by the number of years he spent in San Quentin, all his years of hustling earned him about fifty cents a day (not counting the pennies he earned wiping feces and urine out of prison toilets).

The game was moving too fast for the OGs by the time they left the little yard for the big yard. No matter. There was plenty of cheap wine to soothe their sorrows. By the time I made my way to the block, cats who had been rollin' in Benzes and Beamers were hitting us up for loose change and cigarette money. They spent their time reminiscing about the old days, when they were getting money and hating on the new school.

"I don't want no money if it ain't ho money," Dank D told me when I was ten. Dank wore suits that had been sewn on his back. He wouldn't leave the house without having his hair whipped and curled to perfection. The spokes of his Fleetwood wheels were so shiny they would blind you on a clear day. Now he was riding down the street on a rusted kiddie bicycle with a plastic saddle seat and red, white, and blue streamers coming out of the handles. I hadn't seen Dank D's afro combed in two weeks. He'd worn the same dingy tank top and cut-off blue jeans at least three days in a row. If I hadn't seen it with my own eyes, I wouldn't have believed it was the same man. It's funny how the world turns.

I kept a low profile on that corner. I was the quiet, bald-headed cat in the shadows with the red-and-gold baseball cap pulled down low and tight over his eyes. I nodded directions at my runners. I kept a mental tally of who had collected what. At set intervals, I led our workers into Butchie's, where I would relieve them of the profits.

Steady grinding sapped my strength. When my crew was grinding hard, I didn't even go home to change clothes. I took cat naps in the backseat of my car. I always had one eye peeled to catch every falling nickel. When I did go home, I didn't want to rise in the morning. I cursed the sun as it crept through my window before I headed down to the turf to face another day of tedium and terror.

After a few weeks, all I could think of was escaping to Alston. I promised myself that if I made it to August 31, I would never come back to the corner again.

The sun gleamed against the hood of a black Jaguar XKE as it slithered to the curb. I shook my head. I didn't want to speak to the driver, but how can you ignore old friends?

Darcy's lanky frame unfolded from the Corinthian leather seats. His blue boating sneakers were untied and folded over at the heel. He toted a camel-colored valise in his hand. He was tanned, as though he had just stepped off his yacht. A rubber band kept his dreadlocks from flopping all over his shoulders. There was a bounce in his step as he started in my direction.

"Hey, hey, man," I managed to say.

"Firstborn, what are you doing out here?"

"Just hanging."

Mr. Carter, the man who used to be the janitor at my junior high, stumbled up to me, belching. "Firstborn, let me get a pebble or something."

I flashed Mr. Carter the most hateful look I could muster. He didn't know my friend Darcy from Adam. For all he knew, Darcy could have been an undercover cop, and there he was, telling all my business.

Darcy's eyes popped out like golf balls with brown dots. "Firstborn, somebody told me you were selling dope down here. I didn't believe it. I had to come see for myself. What's out here for you, man?"

"Twenty percent of Alston's tuition for my junior year."

"Pardon?"

"The Fraternal Order for the Upliftment of Humanity offered me a scholarship. All of my JC credits are going to transfer. The only thing I have to do is get up 20 percent of my junior year's tuition. After that, it's a free ride. It seems somewhat generous, doesn't it?"

"Generous? Those neo-conservative kooks! Firstborn, those idiots are somewhere in a back room betting against you. They're using you to prove some kind of point about us. Negro, will you wake up? The devil doesn't give a free lunch buffet."

Darcy's eyes twinkled with amazement. Though he was a brilliant man, he couldn't make heads or tails of my new life. He had won second-place honors on the debating team in our senior year of high school. (I won first place.) He'd been the vice president of the chess team. (I was president.) I'd heard he had finished his undergraduate studies and was now preparing to start his third year of medical school. And I was running with block monsters and selling rock cocaine on the corner.

His lips curled in disgust, exposing the top row of his pearl-white teeth. His reaction caused me to look down.

"Look, man, I know your dream is to get into Alston, but this is no way to do it. Why don't you get in the car, Firstborn? I'll take you for a cup of java. We'll see if we can straighten this thing out."

"Why don't you just jump back into your daddy's Jag and get lost," I snapped, "before somebody thinks you're the police?"

Mr. Carter nudged me. "So, how 'bout that blast? Can I still get it?"

Drama's red Caddy eased up to the curb. He slammed the car door and stood just within earshot of our conversation. He flashed me a look that said, *Hey, man, it's not cool for your boy to be up in here. Let him go.*"

I nodded.

"Tell you what, Darcy. Let me get your card and I'll call you."

He eyed me suspiciously, as though he knew I wanted to get rid of him. Then he reached into his wallet and took out a business card. When I squeezed the card between my thumb and forefinger, he held on to his end of it.

"Firstborn, are you prepared to become the type of nigga you're going to have to be to survive out here any appreciable length of time?" He whispered so that only I could hear.

"I won't be out here long. And this experience won't change me, man."

Darcy let out a dry laugh. "If you ever come up short with these ruthless street niggas out here, they'll leave your dead carcass in an alley and then go out for jambalaya. Call me, Firstborn. Let me see if there's something I can do to help you."

Then, to my shock, Darcy hollered in Drama's direction. "Hey, man, I know who you are. You got Firstborn into this. I remember you from school, and you know what I think? I think you're the devil himself."

Drama smirked. "You got some money in your pockets?"

"No."

"Then I don't care what you think. Now, get outta here before I break my foot off in your—"

Darcy gunned his engine and raced down the street. I stood there, filled with both shame and thankfulness. That man and I had been colleagues in high school. We would sit around the library during study hall, peering into college catalogs and fantasizing about the marvels and wonders the future held for us. He was climbing toward the ceiling of possibility while I was selling my life in the bargain basement.

I was thankful that he cared enough to warn me. But I had to take this chance. I had no father with a government job to help me make my way. I had to make the best of what was available to me: a .44 and a friend named Drama.

Business started picking up that afternoon. Ms. Chelsea, a plump matriarch with gray braids, limped up to me on her steel walker. She slipped three twenties into my hand. I slipped her three fat rocks with the words "I wish I could say no."

She smiled. "Me too."

Just then I heard a scream. I shivered. The sky went inky black. Mr. Carter kicked his milk crate over and ducked behind a parked Toyota for cover. A pint of Seagram's gin shattered against the pavement. Street Life hollered, "Endonesia!"

An engine roared. Mothers snatched their children through front doors. Two thirteen-year-old girls, who had been jumping rope, dove for the concrete curb. I raced for the front door of Butchie's.

The clouds of perdition sank down on the ghetto as shrieks and screams rose from the block. Like the preacher man says, "Whatsoever a man sows, he also will reap." As I saw the big streak of speeding black steel whisk by, I knew that pay day had arrived.

A pistol swung out of a smoked-glass window. Smith and Wesson–brand lightning crackled through the sky. Dead shells fell like steel rain pellets.

Petey popped up from behind a silver Acura. I watched his trigger finger squeeze as he returned fire again and again. The invisibles in the black Cadillac Escalade never slowed down. In seconds they had hit the corner and turned left.

I heard screaming. A mother's screams. It was Deena. She shrieked, "My baby! My baby!"

I raced to the corner. There, stretched out on the sidewalk, was five-year-old Chauncey Hubbard, blood gurgling in his mouth as he kicked his feet in the air. The suffocating child scratched at his throat as though he were trying to extract the bullet from his windpipe. It was no use.

The fight left him and he lay still like a lost leaf in winter, his throat ripped open by talon bullets, the kind that enter the flesh and tear apart all organs in their path. Chauncey's blood ran bright red down the sidewalk and into the gutter.

Drama gazed at me. "Wow, what a way to go out."

Sirens screamed. We took off in a flash.

Back in Drama's room, Drama, Street Life, Petey, and I shuddered at the vision of the young child claimed by the cold, clammy hand of death. He had fallen just beyond my arm's reach.

"That nigga Endo," Street Life scowled. "We gotta dump some bullets in his head. And I think I saw Uzi in the driver's seat. We gotta lay dem niggas down, blood!"

Petey seconded the motion.

"What do you think, Firstborn?" Drama asked.

I stared through the window at a flock of oily black crows racing through the air for the shelter of a palm tree. I knew that if we didn't take Endonesia out, he would be back. But I wasn't a killer. Perhaps that's what Drama was counting on.

"Man," I said, "I think we should wait. Let them think we're too shook up to retaliate. Sooner or later they'll fall asleep, and you know what they say: Sleep is the cousin of death."

Drama shook his head. "Nah, niggas 'round here gonna be falling like raindrops. We gotta take it to these fools *tonight*."

"Well, I don't want to know about it," I said. "I'm not involved."

Street Life's left lip raised in a snarl. "You ain't gotta get down, but you *do* know about it and you *are* involved. So don't get so high and mighty on your niggas. This is how we get down, and you're down with us. When niggas start dying 'round here, people won't say, 'It was dem Black Christmas niggas, 'cept Firstborn. He could read real good.' They gonna know we wouldn't wet our enemies up unless you ordained it, even if you wasn't there. Real thugs never forget. And they never forgive. This is funk season, my nigga. In these streets funk lasts forever."

Who was I fooling? A month earlier, the police had popped a brother down the block for drinking beer out of an open container. The first words that leapt out of his mouth were "You gonna arrest me for something petty like drinking a beer in public when you got dem niggas down the block movin' keys in broad daylight?" Not long afterward, somebody in a black ski mask caught him slipping one night and cracked several vertebrae in his spine with a crowbar. I knew Petey did it, but I refused to talk about it, as if silence would wash the blood from my hands.

I was far from innocent. I was second in command. If something ever happened to Drama, I would be his choice to call shots for the Black Christmas Mob.

As my brothers walked away, I knew the coroner was going to get some business before sunrise. I might have been able to stop it. I didn't try.

The Friday after little Chauncey's murder, a local church led a cease-fire march through the hood. Two young African-American brothers in black suits stood on either side of a banner that said, "This is genocide." Other signs said, "Stop the Killing," "This Is Not Rwanda," "Turn to Christ, Not Crack," and, "Did Martin Luther King Jr. Die So We Could Kill Each Other?"

Women in black dresses and veils walked through the streets, tears streaming down their faces. Men in stark black suits came up to us on the corner and shook our hands. They said, "Put the guns down, fellas." They handed out gospel tracts, voter registration cards, and job bulletins.

I saw Dollar Dan, one of our runners, leaning against a wall with a homemade cigarette burning between his lips, listening to some folks from the church. Dollar Dan was a down-to-earth brother who took care of his business and never said too much. So I was surprised when he opened up to one of the missionary ladies.

"Ma'am, you don't know what it's like for the black man out here today," he said. "I got into it with my female one night, you know? It wasn't no physical contact, ya unnastan'. Next thing I know, she calling the bacon boys and I got a domestic violence jacket. The judge slapped me with a stay-away order and fifty-two weeks of domestic violence classes. I can't find no job. Can't see my kids. Police harassin' me. I got a prior now, and every job application says, 'Have you been arrested in the past seven years?' If I tell the truth, I'm screwed. If I lie and they find out, I'm screwed. Pardon my French."

I expected the lady to throw Bible verses at Dollar Dan. Instead she drew close to him and asked, "May I pray for you?" When he said, "Yeah," she bowed her head and started praying.

Dan looked as though he were about to break down in tears but he held himself in check. After the prayer was over, he embraced the woman.

Dollar Dan didn't come back out to the turf too often after that. I heard he joined the church. One of the members helped him find a job.

I appreciated what the church people were trying to do that night. But I was back on the turf the next day, doing my thing. I had tuition money to stack.

IF I MADE IT PAST THE RICH AND POWERFUL, I COULD EARN THE REST OF THAT 20 PERCENT FROM THE HUNGRY AND DANGEROUS.

CHAPTER
FIFTEEN

IN THE MIDST OF MY CLOUD OF MADNESS, I GOT A PHONE CALL from Alston University. A woman with a distinct Bostonian accent said, "The research team wants to conduct its initial interviews with you tomorrow, Mr. Walker. Can you be here at nine a.m.?"

I was up at dawn the next morning without the aid of an alarm clock. I lay back with my knuckles laced behind my head. A pile of goose-feather pillows swallowed me up as I stretched my legs out over the sheets. Maggy lay on her side, facing me with her closed eyes. Hot breath shot in and out of her nostrils.

My eyes closed again. Technicolor images shot by in milliseconds, like a montage from my subconscious. I shivered as Chauncey's tiny head bounced against the pavement like a ripe cantaloupe. NaNa ran past me with tears in her eyes, the sound of laughter echoing behind her. Uzi's woman stood in the middle of her kitchen in a red, black, and green head wrap. She stared through me as though I were made out of cellophane.

And there stood my daddy: tall, stately, almost regal in his black turtleneck sweater and black Ray-Ban sunglasses. Six inches of afro natural squeezed out from under his black beret. A lone teardrop raced down the split in the middle of his chin.

"I can't believe you, Son," he said. "I raised you to be a revolutionary, a warrior for our people. But you ain't nothin' but a low-life dope dealer...a race traitor. I have seen the enemy, and he looks like me with a bald head!"

I was trapped in a vicious nightmare. It felt like the real me was locked away in a basement. I struggled to climb up the dark, slick steps of my subconscious to the door that led to daylight.

Finally, I found the strength to crank my eyes open. I jumped up in bed like a rhino with a tranquilizer dart stuck in its side.

"Stop all that moving around, Firstborn," the sultry voice beside me commanded. "Go back to sleep, baby."

I trotted into the bathroom and cupped my hands under the flow of cold water. I wet my face with one handful after another. I struggled to catch my breath. My voice echoed in the small enclosure, soothing my nerves. "It was only a dream. It was only a dream." But was it?

I pulled a pair of black slacks and a white shirt out of the closet. I slipped my feet into a pair of black lace-up shoes. I splashed myself with cologne. I turned on Gil Scott-Heron's "Winter in America," then sat in an easy chair in my living room and waited for the sun to blaze.

Maggy got up shortly after seven. Soon after she stepped out of her shower, I heard the soft crack of eggs against the iron lip of a frying pan. The scent of freshly brewed coffee and the sounds of Gil Scott-Heron bubbling from the stereo served to soothe my jangled nerves. I heard the plate clang on the kitchen table and I didn't wait to hear, "Come and get it." I grabbed a fork and pulled up a chair. I got busy on the eggs and bacon.

As she crunched down on the last slice of toast, I said, "If you're going with me this morning, I want to be on the way by eight."

"I'm ready, baby."

And she was ready. Her hair was pressed and curled. She wore a tight, sky blue blouse and had touched her lips with just a dab of lip gloss. The air was sweetened by the smell of Tents of Kedar oil essence. I pulled her close to me. We shared a tender but passionate kiss.

"Leave the dishes." I grabbed a briefcase filled with papers and documents; it had been packed for weeks. I grabbed my car keys and slammed the apartment door behind us.

Talib Kweli's classic "Listen" pounded from the car speakers when I turned the key in the ignition. We didn't talk much until my car hit Fortieth and Telegraph.

"First, you don't ever tell me what's going on inside of that head of yours, but there's one thing I can't figure out."

"What's that?"

"Why don't you go to some other college? I know you got enough chips to get into any of them. What is it about *this* place? Shoot, when I was in high school, Mr. Hollenbeck, our political science teacher, took us to march at Alston. People were carryin' signs and chantin', 'Let us in.' They don't want niggas there, so why you wanna go?"

I could feel my guts tighten as I formulated my response. You sometimes wonder, if one right decision would have been made and followed through on, would it have changed the string of things that happened after the wrong thing was done? It hurt to think about these things. Still, I tried to explain it to my girlfriend.

"My daddy dropped out of Alston after his junior year. I need to finish what he started. I have to complete the circle for my family."

"And then will you be able to rest?"

"And then I can rest."

Alston was a city set on a hill. I parked the car on a steep incline and turned the wheels away from the curb. My heart raced as I opened the car door and considered possibilities once lost to me. I stretched out my arms as if to gather the whole scene within my embrace.

A bank of grayish blue fog drifted behind Alston's rolling hills and stone mansions. Ivy vines swarmed all over the buildings. The place breathed Old World earthiness. I stood for a minute and watched the students go by: young Chinese girls with shoulder-length hair and tight jeans, blond-haired preppies sporting the gold Alston emblem on their sweat-shirts and backpacks, professors with bow ties and cheap woolen suits, graying hippies who had lost their way home from the sixties. There was even the occasional black man, who held his ground like a commando and swung his books beneath his arm like a machine gun. This place was a planet unto itself.

The newspapers were right: there weren't many African-American or Latino folks here to walk through Alston's hallowed halls. You'd need a telescope to find someone of Native American origin.

Magdalene frowned. "Why you want to be here? It's clear you ain't wanted."

"Who cares what they want?" I pointed at a tall white guy sitting by the fountain in sagging blue jeans and a white T-shirt. He wore a blue doo rag over his straight blond hair, clearly in imitation of someone he'd seen in a hip hop video. I pointed him out to Maggie. "See that cat over there? One day he's going to put on a suit and control the world. Drama's holding a gun, but that kid's got a book. We'll see who's gone further five years from now."

We stopped in front of a six-story stone structure with a sign in front that said, "Founder's Hall." I took a deep breath. "Here we are, baby. Are you ready to face this with me?"

Maggy stared at me like I'd just spoken in Russian. She glanced at her watch. "It's ten to nine." She wrinkled her nose. "I can't roll with you. This ain't my world. You go inside and do your thing, baby. I'll wait for you out here."

"Might be a while."

She shrugged. "Maybe I'll do a little shopping down on Telegraph Avenue if you take too long. If I'm not here when you come back, page me." Maggy kissed me softly on the lips and sat on a granite bench outside Founder's Hall.

She blew me a kiss as I entered the lobby of the building. I pretended to grab it. A great shadow fell upon me as I entered the highest plateau of educational achievement in the western world—Alston University.

Papa Lou Alston's great marble bust stood on a petrified tree stump. His black eyes, handlebar mustache, and parted lips gave him a madman's leer. From what I had found out on the Internet, Lou Alston had been a degenerate gambler and moonshine runner who discovered gold while digging a hole for a whiskey still somewhere near Mariposa.

After luck found him, Papa Lou put away his wicked ways and became a philanthropist, donating millions to worthwhile causes. He left directions in his will for the construction of a great university that would offer education to the State of California's poor and working classes. Somewhere along the line something got crossed up. Today, the only poor on campus were ladling out ice cream in the cafeteria or cleaning up behind the president's French poodle.

I climbed the stairs and opened the door to Room 209. A magnificent oil portrait of Papa Alston stared down from the wall with lifelike exactness. He knelt on one knee, his head turned sideways to stare at the artist. He wore a brown duster and an open-collar white shirt. His crazed eyes were wider than in the other pictures I had seen. He held two cubes of dice in his open hand. His lips parted as if to say, "Get your hustle on, player."

A receptionist in a smart blue suit and pink blouse sat behind a desk behind the door in the waiting area. She smiled, her teeth as bright as an angel's robe. "May I help you?"

"I'm here about the research project."

"Oh, you must be Firstborn Walker. Have a seat."

I felt comforted by the fact that this stranger knew my name.

There was only one seat in the waiting area, a metal-frame folding chair that was bolted to the floor. A security camera in the ceiling pointed directly at the chair.

US World and News Today, Ebony, The Conservative Truth, and *The Source* sat neatly stacked on a small table. Flip Snow, the star of *Real Talk*, was on the cover of *Ebony*. I picked it up almost instinctively and then set it back down just as quickly. Something inside told me to make another choice. An unsmiling politician glared tight lipped from the cover of *The Conservative Truth*. The headline said, "Undocumented Immigrants? Stop Them at the Border. US Senator Fred Naworthy Speaks Out." I glanced up and caught the receptionist smiling at me.

A buzzer rang. The receptionist pushed a button on her phone and leaned forward to speak into a microphone by her computer terminal.

"Bring Mr. Walker in, Miss Lemons."

It was about time! I'd been sitting in that hard metal chair for nearly half an hour. My rear end felt like someone had kicked it. Still, I was so nervous I had to fight to keep my teeth from chattering. Miss Lemons walked in front of me like I was invisible. She pushed at a pair of heavy wooden doors.

"Am I to follow you, ma'am?"

She said nothing.

I followed a few feet behind her. She made a quick right through a glass door as if to throw me off. I trotted in her direction just in time to see her step inside an unmarked room.

The space was spartan; nothing more than a wooden table surrounded by three middle-aged men and a woman whose hair was pulled away from her face in a white bun. A closed-circuit television hung down from the ceiling. The screen was frozen on the image of the metal lobby chair I had just vacated.

"We've been watching you, Mr. Walker." The man who spoke was the only black at the table. His most exceptional features were the three lone strands of black hair that popped out of a cue-ball-bare forehead. He hid his ample middle beneath a sporty white golf shirt with a polar-bear emblem over the pocket.

"Must have been a slow morning," I said with a chuckle.

"You disappoint me, Mr. Walker. What part of this do you find entertaining?"

I had already stepped off on the wrong foot. I had made the comment as an ice breaker, taking a gamble that I could make them laugh. I lost the bet. Each of them furiously scribbled in an identical black composition notebook.

"Myra, take his temperature," the brother ordered.

The woman at the table produced a thermometer from her Gucci coach bag.

"What is this?" I protested. "The letter said I was to meet with the research team about my scholarship opportunity here. Now, I've brought my SAT scores, my report card, and an essay that was printed in our junior college newspaper—"

The brother put his hand up like a traffic cop at rush hour. "Myra, the thermometer reading, please."

Her eyes were chips of blue ice. Without a please or a thank you, she stuck the glass tube between my barely parted teeth and then studied her watch. Sixty seconds later, she yanked at the thermometer and held it up to the lights in the drop ceiling. The room was quiet as a tomb. She stared at the brother and nodded grimly. "Ninety-eight point six. He'll do."

"What was that all about?" I addressed my question to the brother.

"Research studies have shown that when a subject grows defensive or shows patterns of deliberate deception, the body temperature rises by two degrees. Of course, there are some people so acquainted with lying and cheating that they can actually control the temperature of their own physiology." The brother's bushy eyebrows rose slightly, as though he were wondering if I fit into that category.

"Let me introduce you to our team, Mr. Walker." He pointed at the woman with the blue eyes and the thermometer. "This is Betty Morgan, eminent social theorist. Next to her is Baron Michael Von Morris, behavioral scientist. To his right is Oscar Norton, anthropological studies. And last but not least, you have me, Mugo Smythe, building plant supervisor, Alston University class of 1975."

Building plant supervisor? This cat was in charge of making sure the floors got buffed and the manure got spread around the rose bushes. How did he land a chair on the research team?

Smythe snatched the essay out of my hand. "'My Struggle,' by Firstborn Walker." He read the title slowly, like a kindergartner trying to make sense of an advanced physics textbook. Smythe read silently but I could follow his progress through the story by watching the involuntary movement of his lips. A word or two seeped through out loud from time to time.

When he reached the last page, his head shook violently, as though his pinky had just been slammed in a door. "Liberal, whiny, tripe, faddle," he blurted out. "This will never do." He dropped the essay as though it were tainted with toxic waste. "Tell me, Mr. Walker, do you see yourself as a victim?"

I couldn't have heard him correctly. My heart fell like a stone toward the bottom of a wishing well. My hesitation merely exacerbated his smoldering rage.

He repeated the question. "Are you a victim, Mr. Walker?"

I had thought I was being invited to the welcome table, but the looks on their faces made me feel like I was the guest of honor at a crucifixion.

Oscar Norton thumbed through the essay. Norton had been introduced to me as an anthropologist, and perhaps that was his major back when he attended Alston. Everybody who could read *Esquire* knew that Norton's real "job" was being the heir to the Norton fortune. His life's "work" was bench pressing martinis at stuffy, upper-crust cocktail parties and entertaining bored housewives. What right did he have to question anything in my essay?

Norton's eyes grew cold. He wheezed like a man trying to draw a breath in an airtight room. "Mr. Walker, you write here that your high school principal had the library chained and padlocked due to budgetary restraints the week before exam time during your senior year. You write that your high school teachers were often unaccredited and ill prepared to train you for the rigors of academic life in an institution of higher learning. You write that your high school had but one guidance counselor per thousand students. You say the bathrooms were filthy, and you say, 'I was in fear of my life because violent human predators would sometimes sneak into the school and skulk boldly through the halls, searching for a dry place to hang out.'"

"That's true. But I'm not—"

Betty Morgan cut me off. "It sounds like you're looking for an excuse, boy. You want a free pass through life because you've faced some hard times. But haven't we all? I grew up in Walnut Creek, and my father was an industrialist, but that doesn't mean I didn't have any setbacks. My life may be one of greater privilege than yours, but I've had to climb obstacles to reach my plateaus. Wouldn't you agree that everyone's obstacles are tantamount to the same thing?"

I looked into her eyes. "Did you ever see your best friend after somebody blew a hole through his forehead?"

Her face blanched. "No."

"Then I would not agree. But I didn't come here seeking to blame anybody. That isn't what this is about."

"Don't you see, Mr. Walker?" Ms. Morgan continued. "That's exactly what the Fraternal Order for the Upliftment of Humanity is about. We've all lifted ourselves up by our own bootstraps, and we don't see why you can't do the same thing…like Smythe here. Smythe is the new voice of black America. He is the new Martin Luther King. He will lead your people from the slums of victimhood to the mountaintops of the Promised Land."

Smythe sat back in his chair with his eyes closed, soaking in the moment like a prophet recently anointed to lead his people out of the desert. If someone would have risen from the table to stroke his bald head for luck, the picture would have been complete. I wouldn't want to set foot in any

Promised Land that Smythe could lead me to, but I wasn't about to argue.

"I don't need a handout," I said. "I just need a hand. You helped me get admitted into Alston. If you'll just help me with that scholarship, I can do the rest."

Norton squinted at me and leaned over the table. He rubbed his hands together, revealing the results of a high-priced manicure. "Son, we have fifteen thousand students here at Alston. Four hundred of those fifteen thousand students are African American. Now, of those four hundred blacks, one hundred are here on athletic scholarship. Tell me, why should you be one of the fortunate four hundred?"

I stared at the well-fed faces around the table. The members of the research team tried to appear disinterested, but I could sense great anticipation for my answer. They all leaned in like a den of hungry lions trying not to notice a fried chicken leg thrown down in the midst of them. I licked my lips and responded with the only thing that I could think of: the truth.

I said, "In post-industrial America, an education is everything. You can't compete in today's job market without a college degree. A high school teacher once told me that a degree can be the difference between living in the hood or living in the hills. It's the key to economic stability and social mobility in our society. A degree from this particular institution of higher learning would turn me into someone who could do more than earn a living. As a graduate, I would be in a place to make a wonderful contribution to society. If you gave me this chance you would never be sorry."

Oscar Norton glanced into the stone faces of his teammates. "Well said."

Smythe didn't look satisfied. "What about the twenty percent of the tuition?"

"I'll get it," I assured him.

No one shook my hand at the interview's conclusion. I think they had expected me to tiptoe in there and plead, to make excuses, to beg for a break on the 20 percent, perhaps throw in a little hand wringing and tap dancing for good measure. No, not Joshua Walker's son. I would never take that route.

Smythe dismissed me by saying, "Miss Lemons, you may lead the candidate away."

I left the interview scratching my head. I had thought the research team would embrace me with open arms. They clearly hadn't done so. I felt as pressured at that meeting as I had on a hot day on the block with five-0 out in full force. I left reasoning that if I made it past the rich and powerful, I could earn the rest of that 20 percent from the hungry and the dangerous. And I was almost there.

CHAPTER
SIXTEEN

TWO WEEKS AFTER THE ALSTON INTERVIEW—FRIDAY NIGHT, JULY 1—the block was buzzing. Shots ringing out. Niggas scheming on girls. Hood fellas getting their shine on. Brothers speaking on what party or club they were going to slide up into that night. Talking about who was about to get shot and who'd shot whom. Laughter. Trash talking. A full moon. Cars streaming by like ripples on a lake.

First of the month, smokers showed up with ready cash. Food stamps were accepted. Money flowed.

Two young boys walked by. One opened a bottle of water and poured out a sip for the brothers who weren't here. He couldn't have been more than twelve.

Ghetto CNN had it that Shorty from Brookfield caught strike number three for boosting a pack of Kools from the Rite-Aid. He was looking at thirty with an L. "Wow," Petey remarked. "When that nigga comes home, we'll be wearing spacesuits."

Two white boys from Montclair—wannabe niggas with practiced Southern accents and Oakland A's hats—drove up to the block in a beautiful black Mustang 4.0. The kid on the passenger side sported an expensive-looking black leather jacket. He stuck his head out of the window and said, "Hey, bro, y'all got that Black Christmas blow?"

War Thug, a youngsta with a thick mane of dreadlocks, happened to be hanging with us that night. He got the name War Thug because he kept a Ruger on tuck at all times and was quick with it. Half of the houses on the block had bullet scars due to his overactive trigger finger. He was a loose Black Christmas affiliate known for his gun game. He would rob you as soon as ask you for the time of day. Unfortunately for the wannabees in the Mustang, his girlfriend's rent was due and War Thug was broke.

"Whatcha'll want?" he said, leaning into the car.

"I wanna spend a hunnerd," the driver said in a fake Louisiana drawl.

War Thug looked up the street and then back again. He beamed at me with his trademark golden-mouth smirk. He knew full well that I couldn't abide the strong-arm game he tried to run on our customers. He also knew I wasn't going to allow those two to get served. That made them fair game.

"Let me get in," he whispered to the young fellows in the shiny black car. "I'll take you around the corner. They don't sell Black Christmas here. You don't want these niggas' stuff. It's whack. It's bootsie."

The young man on the passenger side sat up and let War Thug climb into the backseat—Ruger .9 millimeter and all. He winked playfully at me through the back window just before the 4.0 rolled off.

War Thug was back an hour later, wearing the driver's black leather jacket and flipping through a stack of bills like an accountant. He had a brand-new pair of sneakers on his feet. Their previous owner had left his suburban digs that morning, never dreaming that those sneakers would end up on someone else's feet before midnight.

I sucked my teeth in disgust. "War Thug, I'm just going to tell you this one more time. I don't want you running up on marks down on this block. We don't want the police comin' down here to see what we're doing."

War Thug looked up from counting his money with a naughty smile. "I feel you, boss. Ain't goin' happen again. But you gotta admit, it was too easy."

I waved a finger in his face. "I'm telling you, fam. That's the last time."

I was done talking. You never knew who might walk up while you were posted up on the corner.

That night, Phil came whistling by. He had just landed in Oakland courtesy of Greyhound and the State of California penal system. That was the first time I'd seen him in five years.

Phil was never without a twisted smile. He was the kind of guy who was always cracking jokes on people. He'd been a halfway decent point guard back in high school, but he gave up his chance at a college scholarship to make fast money on the block. Well, at least he could claim he was successful at something. Phil invested in sneakers. I never saw him wear the same pair twice.

When Phil was rolling, diamond-studded rings sparkled on his fingers. Now his bare knuckles were ashy and crying out for a manicure. He was so thin, he looked like he'd just stepped out of a "Save the Children" commercial. The brother had traded in his shiny black gators for clunky brown brogans. He was outfitted in loose-fitting tan khakis when I saw him that night. Phil's eyes used to twinkle with laughter; now they were two swollen holes of despair that sank down in their sockets, rotating only on occasion.

"Fellas!" he hollered. We took turns embracing him. I could feel the structure of his rib cage when I wrapped him in a bear hug.

"I got a stay-away order. I can't even be seen between East Seventy-third and East Hundred and Sixth. If they catch me down here, I'm soaked. But I had to come see my dudes. Drama and Firstborn, your names are ringing back on the yard."

I knew he was lying. We weren't making the kind of money that would have dudes in prison discussing our business. And cuz-o wasn't risking his freedom for the privilege of shaking our hands. The second a cop with a good memory for faces rolled by, Phil would have been washed all over again. No, he had to have been taking this risk for a high-priced reason. Maybe he wanted a ghetto pass so he could slang rocks on his old turf. Perhaps Phil wanted to borrow some muscle and bullets to reap a little payback for the terrible thing that happened before he went away.

"What happened to my nigga TC?" he asked.

"TC's dead," Drama said with a tinge of sadness in his voice. "Dude was the big winner in a cee-lo game on Auseon. Somebody peeped how much paper he was checkin', went in the bathroom, and made a phone call. TC walked out the front door half drunk at four in the morning. Young head busters caught him slippin'. They didn't even give homes a chance to act wrong. Just started bustin' on a nigga."

Phil's neck dropped like there was a noose around it. "What about my old road dawg Albert? He never wrote or came to visit while I was in the pen."

"Twenty to life—been gone 'bout three years."

Why was Phil back? I waited for that information to come out in conversation. When it didn't, I spit out the question. "Didn't your mama get kidnapped once?"

That may have seemed harsh but I was thinking about my personal safety. Phil could have been sent out there to trap us. I didn't trust anybody. The cops might have dealt Phil out early so he could get inside Black Christmas and set us up for grand jury indictments. The thought of it made me anxious. I needed to see inside that ex-con's skull.

Phil's lips pursed tight. His eyelids fluttered. If he'd had a gun in the pants pocket of those beat-up khakis, he might have shot me.

"Yeah," Drama asked, taking the heat off of me. "What happened that time when those niggas snatched up your mama, dude?"

Phil cocked his head to the side, but his eyes remained stationary, as though glued into position. The street-light glow revealed three green teardrops tattooed beneath one of his eyes. He folded his arms and let his soul loose with a sigh. "I was standing right where you standing right now when I got the call. Nigga said, 'Phil, shut up and listen. We got your mama.' Thass all he said. Then he put the phone to Mama's mouth and let her scream."

"Then what happened?" I asked.

"Dude say, 'You look like a hundred-g nigga. Bring it to the phone booth at Bancroft and Seventy-eighth, and it better not be a dime short.'"

"What'd you say?" I asked.

Phil waved his hands and bounced on the balls of his feet as though the incident was happening all over again. "'Look, man, I ain't got no hundred g's. I might got seven, eight g's da most.'"

Drama's jaw dropped. "Nigga, you was livin' large and talkin' larger. You mean all that gold you was flashin' and you ain't had but eight g's?"

"Das all. That money was going out as fast as it was coming in."

"Well, I'll be."

"The voice didn't say nothin' for 'bout a minute. Then the voice say, 'Well, dis yo' lucky night. We got a sale on mamas tonight.' I told 'im, 'You better not hurt my mama!' The cat on the other end sounded cold as Tahoe snow in my ear. He say, 'And what you gonna do if I blow Mama here away, Phil?' I could hear Mama trying to scream in the background. But they had stuffed a dirty old black sock in her mouth so she couldn't get the words out. It was still in her mouth when they found her."

"What'd you do, Phil?"

"I played my hand. See, after a while I recognized the dude's voice. It was this li'l young nigga named ChaCha who used to be one of my runners. I said, 'ChaCha, I know this is you. Boy, you shoulda never touched my mama. You's a dead man. I know where you live.'"

"What did ChaCha do?"

"He hung up the phone."

"Then what happened?"

"That was the last time I ever heard Mama's voice. ChaCha shot her in the head and dumped her body out in a field by Oakland Airport like she was an old dog. The police found her three days later."

"What did you do about it?"

"Would it make any difference what I did? Could it stop Mama from being dead? What y'all got to remember is, if you in this game, your mama, your woman, even your kids is in it, whether they wanna be or not. Last time I heard my mama's voice, she was screaming 'cause of the choices I made. You tend not to forget thangs like that. Her screamin' wakes me up in the middle of the night near every night. Mama was a casualty of the game."

He stared into Drama's eyes. "You betta think 'bout what you doin', D Montana. Nigga, that could just as easily be yo' mama."

Drama swallowed. His eyelids fell like guillotine blades dropping down on chopping blocks. That didn't stop Phil from talking.

He said, "If fools decide to spray up your crib in the middle of the night, you think they gonna holla, 'We 'bout to light up your crib, so send out the babies first'? Hell, no. And the beef don't stop if your mama or the kids is wit' you."

Phil was keeping it real. He was saying things we all knew to be true but never discussed out loud.

"Y'all better listen to the former prince of the game now," he continued. "If some fool catches you slipping at a red light, and if he hates you enough, or he thinks he's gotta get you before you get him, or if there's enough money in it, he'll blow up a whole zip code to get to you. And he won't care who dies as long you don't walk away."

"Niggas around here know betta, Phil," Drama responded. "They'll never hurt my family. I got too much gangsta in my blood."

"That's what I thought, too, D. And you know the type a nigga I was out here. But truth is, anybody can get got...just let the right dudes get hungry enough or scared enough or desperate enough. It's scandalous, but you know it's real."

The corner grew as quiet as an underwater cave. People began to reflect, visualizing Phil's terrible misfortune, wondering about his feelings of guilt. Guys who had loving parents or infant children put themselves in his shoes and shifted from one foot to the other.

Drama's voice trembled slightly. "Phil, that ain't never gonna happen to me, and don't say that again. You tryin' to throw some bad luck in the game. You hatin' or something?"

Phil smirked. "I'm done with it, OG. I've learned my lesson...a little late but I got an A plus. Drama, with all the dirt you doin' out here, the whole world's got a green light out on you and these renegade niggas around you. You 'bout to get twisted up and you'll end up doing the high end of fifty years or dead."

"Shoot, I don't give a damn. I'll go out in a blaze."

"And if they cuff you before you get that chance, you'll end up an old man wheezing and coughing in the prison infirmary, handcuffed to the gurney. And everybody you knew out here will have forgot you ever existed."

"Phil, why you come back, man?" I asked.

"You gonna laugh at this, but I got saved in chapel one Sunday morning last year. And I promised God that if he let me make parole, I would make one trip back to my old corner to warn my dudes not to wind up like me. I'm just keeping my promise to the Man Upstairs."

"Well, Phil," Drama said, "you kept your promise to God. So now let's change the subject. I'm a little hungry. You hungry?"

"Yeah, I could eat something," he said.

"Anything else you wanna ask me before we go?" Drama cocked his left eyebrow.

Phil looked up at the stars for a minute and then said in a singing voice, "Well, if you got a few dollars you could loan me..."

Drama laughed. "Don't say 'loan,' Phil. Say, 'Drama, do you have a few dollars you could *give* me?' I don't want to have to kill nobody about my money."

They both laughed as Drama rifled through a stack of dollars and handed Phil a generous sum.

Drama slapped a hand over his bony shoulders and said, "Firstborn, my man here ain't had a plate of barbecue in a while. I'm gonna take him to Larry's Pit on San Pablo and get him hooked up."

I told Drama to bring back a plate for me. "And don't forget the cole slaw," I said. "You always forget the cole slaw." I told him I could hold down the block until he came back. I stuck a fifty in Phil's hand and wished him well.

After they left, I heard Marvin Gaye's classic "Inner City Blues" droning from someone's window. It was the first of the month, Mother's Day in the hood. Every crack fiend in town came out to spend part or all of his check with us. We counted money and marinated in the madness.

A lookout on the next block sent a signal by calling us on his burner. In thirty seconds, the rocks were gone. Seconds after I passed some product off to a ten-year-old kid on a bike, he cleared out of there like a cyclone was chasing him.

The Hawk swooped down. She crept slowly down the street, her car tires gripping the black asphalt. Her long manicured nails rested on top of her steering wheel.

What was she doing, trying to catch a brother wrong? I was too fast. Too slick. Our game was too tight. I cut her the razor-blade stare. She flashed it back with a curl of her glossy crimson lip. Petey showed her the crease in his middle finger. The Hawk tossed her head back and grinned.

When the unmarked Crown Victoria burned rubber, I took a deep breath. Somebody sparked up a joint. Sixty seconds later, we were back in business.

"What was that all about?" Petey asked.

"The Hawk be trippin', man!"

A high-pitched male shriek echoed in the distance. I waited for the signal. There was none. Then it hit me. It was a setup.

"Rollers!" Petey hollered on the run.

Task-force cops dressed in black helmets, ski masks, full body armor, and jack boots climbed down a fire escape above us. Two unmarked cars raced up our one-way street from the wrong direction. A black-and-white van with the words "Oakland Police Department" flew toward us, its engine humming. Mayhem and confusion had us running into one another.

A stiff, militaristic voice yelled, "Freeze!" They might as well have dropped a checkered flag and hollered, "Run for your life!" I was out of there like an Olympic sprint champion. Sirens whined. Red lights flashed in tight circles.

A uniformed cop with wrap-around sunglasses pinned Petey up against Butchie's front door. OPD poured down on the block like black rain. Three jogged up the steps that led to Ms. Velvet's place; one of them was toting a battering ram. I headed for MacArthur Boulevard.

"There's one of them!" a black ninja hollered through his mask.

I was moving like a human missile but not making much progress. Cops had the hood covered like a black blanket. Ghetto birds circled the skies above me. Spotlights from the clouds lit up our hood. Sirens nearly made me deaf.

A young white cop, who looked as though he had just fallen out of the academy yesterday, took up the chase. He was half a block away and gaining on me. We took it to the middle of the street. My pockets were chock full of the stuff that felonies are made of: ten crack rocks and close to three thousand dollars wrapped tight in a fat red rubber band. I wanted to throw my package away, but I knew that if the rookie behind me picked it up, I was through.

The gates of San Quentin opened before my mind like the turnstile to the bottomless pit. I saw myself with an ill-fitting blue shirt on my back, mean mugging on the chow line. My lungs burned. My legs turned to rubber. Yet I couldn't slow down. All that weed smoking had shortened my breath. I wanted to quit, but the Hawk's story about Bob kept my legs pumping on automatic pilot.

I heard a voice whisper, "Over here, brother."

I twisted between a gold Toyota Celica and a red Chevy Malibu that were parked at a red light. The interior light shone from the open door of a royal blue Blazer 4x4.

"Get in," a gruff voice demanded.

I slipped inside and ducked down, quickly closing the door behind me. My heartbeat sounded like a basketball dribbled by a Harlem Globetrotter. I was afraid my loud gasps for air would give me away. I heard the sound of scampering feet outside the vehicle. Other cops had joined the hunt.

"Can I look inside your car?" someone asked the driver next to us.

The light must have changed. My savior mashed his foot down on the gas pedal. I peeked at the driver. He was forty to forty-five, with salt-and-pepper shoulder-length dreadlocks. A neatly cut goatee encircled his chin and upper lip. "Deep East Oakland" was tattooed on his thick, muscular neck in green cursive letters. There was a stylish blue-and-white pinstripe on his back. A black leather book lay on the seat between us. The name in gold leaf at the bottom of the Bible said, "Oliver Jones."

"Stay down," he whispered.

Within seconds we had entered the flow of traffic that poured onto the freeway. A few minutes later, my accomplice said, "Rise up, young blood."

I picked myself up from the floor, half expecting to see a detective's badge flash in my face, but all I saw were his lips splitting into a broad smile.

"Man, you saved my life. Who are you?"

"My name is Oliver. Who are you?"

"Firstborn Walker."

"Firstborn—is that a street name?"

"No, it's on my birth certificate. So, Oliver, what's this going to cost me?"

I tugged on the thick wad of bills encircled by a red rubber band. I could hardly get it out of my pocket.

"Put your bank roll away, man. I want you to make a little run with me tonight."

"Run? Where?"

"I was on my way to church when God dropped you into my life. I'd still like to get there if that's all right with you. We're just in time for praise and worship. You cool with that?"

"Church?"

I was so glad to be rescued I'd have tap danced through hell in a gasoline raincoat if he'd asked me to. But church? Oliver sure didn't look like the holy-roller type. The word *redemption* was tattooed on his right hand above his knuckles in fat green letters. The edges were not properly outlined; it was a jailhouse tattoo. I wouldn't have taken him for a church man, but I certainly wasn't one. I hadn't been inside a church in years, except for funerals.

"Look at me, man," I balked. "I ain't got no church clothes on."

"God doesn't care about the clothes on your back. He's looking at your heart and your life. And I certainly don't care."

That ended that argument.

We pulled into a crowded parking lot on East Twenty-first Street. A heavyset, auburn-colored woman in a two-piece lavender pantsuit jogged up to Oliver and tossed her arms around his thick neck. She planted a big red kiss on his cheek.

"Oliver, when are you going to stop visiting and join us? You're here more than I am."

Oliver laughed. "It's not that simple, Belle. Greater Grace is my family's church."

Belle shook her head. "But is it God's church?"

Oliver coughed nervously into his hand. "Belle, this here is Firstborn. It's his first time here."

"Welcome, Firstborn. I pray the Lord meets you here."

She started toward me. I stuck out my hand, hoping she would get the hint, but soon I too was buried in her thick, cotton-soft arms. She gave me a red print identical to Oliver's. I could smell her perfume on my clothes even after she'd pulled away.

I received a lot of hugs that night. People treated me as though I had wandered into a family reunion. I had to admit, it was kind of cool. Ninety percent of the people who walked up to us were African American but there were a few Latinos, Asians, and even some whites in the bunch. The people looked so happy. Religion seemed more like a night out at a ball game than a solemn obligation.

Oliver was the only person in the building wearing a suit. Most of the crowd was in street gear: Nikes, white tees, and jeans. I didn't feel a bit out of place.

The music wasn't at all what I remembered from my days in Sunday school. I unconsciously nodded as three teenage girls sang, accompanied by keyboards, bass, guitar, and drums. A young cat in a Raiders jersey and blue jeans started rhyming on the break.

Let me tell how I used to get down.
I used to go to work with an automatic four pound.
The block got hot when I was raising hell.
Never backed down; I liked my beef cooked well.

Suckers caught on late, but soon they learnt
When my Glock got hot, noodles got burnt.
Go back to my hood, and do your research.
I was thug; I would never, ever lie in church.

I was a slave to sin; I wore an evil grin.
A one-way ticket to hell I was gonna win.
But then my cousin got shot while he was working for me,
And my eyes peeped open so that I could see.

At the funeral where my cousin lay stone dead,
I listened to the preacher, and this is what he said.

Teenage girls behind him sang the chorus:

Change, change, change,
You gotta change.
The streets will take you under,
But God has got a plan. You gotta change.

The kid started rhyming again.

You gonna look cute in your brand-new suit,
From your button-down collar to your eel-skin boot.
You painted the streets red, put the suckas to bed,
When they tread on the block where you made your bread.

Now it's your turn to be dead as Fred,
With a headache from lead bullets in your head.
You better clear your ears, while you can hear,
Run while you can walk, drive while you can steer,
'Cause I've been around, and here's what I found:
Any coward with a gun can lay a thoroughbred down.

And you ain't got a clue to what they can do to you.
But you ain't bulletproof, and neither is your boo.

Change, change, change,
You gotta change.
The streets will take you under,
But God has got a plan. You gotta change.

I looked at Oliver and asked, "What kind of church is this, man?"

He smiled.

The walls were barren and pale; no portraits of Jesus Christ, no candles. The pastor was a fortyish brother who wore a red, white, and blue Philadelphia 76ers throwback jersey that fit snugly over his round middle. He drew a black leather book from his side in the same fashion that Pharaoh Taharkah might have drawn his sword. He dropped the book down on top of a Plexiglas stand, licked his fingers, and turned the pages.

"Open up to Matthew 25," he commanded. Pages rustled like scattered leaves in late fall. "Let us stand for the reading of God's Word."

Oliver pinched his suit jacket shut and stood. He pressed his own Bible toward me so I could follow along.

The man on the podium read some verses from the Bible, then said, "Let us pray." He closed his eyes. "Father, bring your Word alive for us tonight. Strengthen us to know and do your will. Rain, Holy Spirit. Rain on all who hear. In Jesus' name, amen."

The preacher motioned for the crowd to sit down. After we did, he started preaching.

"Today, I want to talk about the end of the world. One day the clouds will part, the skies will split, and eternity will touch time. One day the end of this present world will be announced by the blast of an angel's trumpet. Oh, it'll start off like any other day. On that morning, you'll turn on *The Today Show* and pour yourself a hot cup of decaf coffee. But I'm telling you, at some point on that day, all the clocks will stop ticking. Jesus Christ will return to the earth, accompanied by a squad of angels. This Scripture tells us what will happen that day."

The preacher had my attention. My grandmother hadn't been a particularly religious person, but every time the weather took an unexpected turn, she started talking about how the Bible was being fulfilled. The preacher had caught my interest.

"On that great day, the righteous and the evil will be separated; one headed for paradise, the other to the bitter smoke and unquenchable flames of hell. And this passage of Scripture tells us there will be some surprises on that great and terrible day of judgment."

In his songs Tupac used to ask if there was a heaven for thug niggas. Drama and I talked about it once. He said, "Hell, no," and laughed.

As the preacher talked about judgment day, I shivered slightly, surprising myself. It wasn't cold in the auditorium.

The reverend said, "The Bible says that Jesus will call forth one group of people—the folks who made a practice of visiting the incarcerated, clothing the naked and the homeless, putting out a plate for the hungry—and the Lord will welcome them into paradise.

"And there will be another group present that day. On the earth they dressed nice, they drove well, they had fat 401Ks, and they smelled like exotic fragrances. They held down the Grand Puba positions at the lodge and the most prestigious chairs at the church, but they turned a blind eye to the poor fifteen-year-old hookers they passed on their way to worship God. They did little to bridge the gap between themselves and those who lived under the freeway underpass or in that tent city on the outskirts of town. They had nothing for the brothers on the corner but contempt and criticism."

If that preacher was right, three fourths of everybody riding past me on the way to church on Sunday morning was headed straight to hell, along with us.

"Before I came to know the Lord," he continued, "I chased after fast women. I cheated at cards. I broke chumps with loaded dice and I smoked weed like a Tasmanian devil. I served Satan from dawn to midnight, and sometimes I got up in the middle of the night to put in overtime. I was a faithful employee of the prince of darkness; ask anybody who knew me back in the day. Or just check the police blotter."

My mouth fell open slightly. Rev was keeping it real up there. I felt something warm inside my heart. I checked Oliver. He just sat there, nodding. What kind of church was this?

The preacher wiped the sweat off his brow with a white handkerchief. "But one day I met somebody who was like Jesus to me. This person came out to the turf where I was slinging dope. My crew was funkin' with these OGs just home from the pen talking 'bout we was on their corner. Just that morning this heavy hitter had walked up on me sayin', 'Fool, you don't know who you messin' with. You could get murdered out here!' They were saying they would heat us up if they came back and saw us on that corner again.

"I thank God for Brother Henry, who left the safety of the church pew and came out to the block where I was living low to tell me, 'Son, there is a better way. Have you met Jesus? Have you repented of your sins? Have you made him the shot caller of your life?'"

I couldn't believe this. I hadn't given a lot of thought to God, but maybe Oliver was right. He had said that his life had intersected with mine when it did because of divine intervention. Maybe there was something to it. Considering the message the man of God was spitting, I couldn't brush away the whole thing as coincidence.

The preacher half sang and half preached as he continued. "I was tired of the life I'd been living. I was putting my family in danger. I hated always having to watch my back. I knew the only future in the dope game was prison or death. So about two weeks later, I came down here to this church and found Brother Henry. I said, 'Brother Henry, I'm ready.' Today, I'm the pastor and he's the head of the deacon board. Stand up, Brother Henry."

An old man in the front row stood, his back slightly bent from the weight of at least eighty years. He wore his regal gray hair trimmed close to his scalp. He was dressed in a two-piece gray suit with a white shirt and black tie. Tears mixed with pride and joy came streaming from his eyes. He waved and sat down.

"I'd heard the salvation story a million times," the pastor continued, "but the day Brother Henry shared it with me, it all seemed to make sense. The devil could give me a lot of things, but he couldn't give me peace in my soul. Now I have tasted and seen that the Lord is good. I've got joy deep down in my heart. Christ died on the cross and rose again. He defeated death so that by trusting in him I could have eternal life. He has forgiven me of all the mess I did in the past. I can sleep at night now, without the faces of dead people waking me up screaming."

I had to tell myself to breathe. All of this was so real and so heavy. I could see freedom in the preacher's eyes; I could hear it in his voice. In that moment I wanted nothing more than to be free. I leaned forward to hear the rest of the sermon.

"I've found my purpose for living, and I'm on my way to heaven. I'm going to serve the Lord at least as hard as I served the devil. That just makes sense, doesn't it? And if Jesus loved the poor, the busted, and the disgusted, you can bet your last piece of chewing gum that I will love them and serve them, and so will any church I call myself the pastor of.

"Saints, there is something wrong when we say we are followers of Jesus but we're afraid to get out in those streets and tell the sinners that God has a plan for their lives."

So, Christianity isn't just about the afterlife, huh?

People around us were clapping and nodding. A voice from the back of the room hollered, "Tell it, preacher!"

"Some of us wear little bracelets that say, 'What would Jesus do?' Yes, what *would* he do if he were living in Oakland today, where young brothers are out on the corners shooting dice and shooting at each other, burning up with self-hate? What would he do if he came to a world where sisters, the precious fruit of our African tree, were selling their sacred bodies across the street from the church? What would he do if he landed in a world where hope, educational opportunities and employment had evaporated and young men aspired to be pimps rather than poets or political figures? Yes, what would Jesus do?"

I answered that question in my heart. In the twenty-first century, Jesus wouldn't be walking around in a robe and sandals. He would be straight out of the hood. He'd be rocking a black hoodie and some Tims. Jesus would be a serious revolutionary. There would be no one out there like him. The hood would hear him.

"I tell you, this will not be the kind of church where ministers sit up on the rostrum, legs crossed, nodding and hollering on cue but too holy to minister to the brothers in front of the liquor store. If you say you're called, I ask you, 'Called to do what?' We got too many preachers who are called to strut and preen around like royalty on coronation day but feel they are too good to touch the very people Jesus spent his life trying to save.

"Jesus didn't live in the hills. He lived in the hood. He lived in the Lower Bottoms of Nazareth. He lived in Dog Town, Jingle Town, the Murder Dubbs, Ghost Town, the Iron Triangle of his day. And today, he would have lost sleep praying for a way to reach these young people lost in the killing fields. If you agree, we ought to be about our Father's business, you feel me?"

Wild applause, whistling, and stomping feet made up the response.

The muscles in the preacher's neck bulged. He twisted as though the words had gotten stuck at the base of his tongue.

"We got to find a way to reach 'em. I'll tell you, I'd rather the prostitute knew my name than the president, the dope dealer than the diamond merchant, the pimp than the Pope. I'd rather my name rang out in the crack den than the country club, the projects than the palace, the penitentiary than the penthouse. I'd rather my name be written in the Book of Life than the social register. Because on that great day of judgment, when Jesus comes back, he won't ask, 'So, what make of automobile were you driving?' No, he'll ask, 'What did you do for my brothers languishing in prison, guilty of nothing more than being poor and dark, and rotting away because they couldn't afford a decent lawyer? What did you do about those little 11 and 12 year girls forced into prostitution by heartless pimps right there a stones throw from your church building? What did you do about the hungry children in the projects? Did you ever write that letter to your local congressperson, telling him how you felt about the issue of slavery in the Sudan? What did you do about the HIV/AIDS crisis in the black community? What did you do about those little ones who had no parent to carry them to your church's

Sunday school?' Some of us will look back at Jesus with a blank expression and say, 'You mean, those hoodlums? Lord, what did you expect me to do?'"

The room got so quiet I could hear the breath slipping in and out of the preacher's pulsating nostrils.

I wondered where he was going with all this.

The reverend's voice slipped several octaves, from bombast to whisper. "There is one here tonight who has never accepted Jesus Christ into his life. You've never asked him to be the boss of your life. You've never confessed your sins and asked him to forgive you. You've never accepted the gift of new life and soul salvation. If that's you, raise your hand."

I had never made such a decision, but I was afraid to raise my hand. Even though I had never been much for religion, I knew it came at the price of a powerful commitment, and I wasn't ready to make it. A few other people raised their hands, though.

"There is someone else who is here who has said the sinner's prayer but your life hasn't changed. You're still caught up in the same mess. You have no compassion for the poor. Your only use for religion is the promise of personal prosperity. But tonight, you're ready to surrender all to Jesus. If that means going into the projects to bring the Word to his little ones, so be it. If it means building houses for Habitat for Humanity, so be it. If it means mentoring a child without a father, so be it. You're ready to surrender all to Christ. If that's you, raise your hand."

The preacher called all the people who had raised their hands to the front, where he prayed with them. After he sent them back to their seats, the choir fired up a final song and we got the go-ahead to walk out.

The human beehive swarmed between the rows of chairs and formed a bottleneck in the main aisle. Some people waved at Oliver. Some smiled at me. A hand clamped down hard on my shoulder. I twirled around, half expecting to see a patrolman with handcuffs in his free hand. Somehow, I wasn't any less disturbed when I found out that the grip on my shoulder belonged to the preacher.

"Hello, sir," I said. "I really enjoyed the sermon."

Sweat dripped from his bald forehead as if he had just finished playing a full-court game in the summer basketball league. He wiped a white hand towel all over his face and head. Then he leaned over to whisper in my ear. I barely caught every other word, but what I heard caused me to tremble. It sounded like he said, "Son, I don't know you...never laid eyes on you before tonight. But I hear the Lord tellin' me that Satan wants to put you face down in the gutter with a bullet in the back of your head. But God has his hand on your life. Now, I can tell you're in the streets, but you ain't built for the streets. You gonna mess around and get your wig tore up. Get out of that life while you still got a life. God's got a great plan for you, but you have to choose. He never pushes himself on anybody. Get out now, before you give Satan something you can't get back."

The pastor peered deep into my eyes, as if to see if the message had penetrated my skull. Something he saw satisfied him. He nodded and then pressed his way back toward the stage. My legs turned to jelly. I forced them to walk toward the front door but my eyes followed the man of God as he glided through a door at the side of the platform and vanished.

In a minute, I was riding in the shotgun seat of Oliver's 4x4. It was a silent journey. That preacher had me scared to death. I wondered what I could give to Satan and never get back.

Twenty minutes later, we were wheeling through the streets of my hood. Oliver glanced at me and said, "Well, it was nice meeting you, Freeborn."

"That's *Firstborn*. And you aren't getting rid of me that easily. Didn't you say that God dropped me in your path?"

"Yes."

"Man, I want to come out to church with you on Sunday, and I want to bring my homeboy."

Oliver stuttered. His smile evaporated.

I raised an eyebrow at his hesitation. "Something wrong?"

"No. It's just that I go to another church on Sunday. It's my home church, and it's a lot different than this one."

"No problem; we'll come to that. One church is probably as good as the other. Where is it?"

He gave me the address.

"Cool, that's right in the hood. We'll be there."

"Where do you want to get put out?" Oliver asked.

"Take me back to my block," I said. I wanted to check on the family business.

I turned my jacket inside out and slipped down an alley between two apartment buildings. I found War Thug standing at the mouth of the alley, facing the street and smoking a fry daddy, a joint laced with crack. He peered out at me through his purple stunna shades.

"It was a sweep, man. They hit niggas all over the Town tonight. They ain't get nuthin' over here, though. Petey be out by morning. Most they could hit him with was loitering. Willie the only one caught a possession charge. They found three dubs within two feet of the nigga and he on parole. We ain't gonna see Willie for a couple years but he'll be a'right."

"What about Drama?"

"Drama was still on his way to Larry's Barbecue in West Oakland when they hit. Even if he wasn't, you know they ain't goin' get yo nigga. Drama can smell cops like old people say they can smell rain comin'. I seen 'em run up in his crib, though. Somebody told me Ms. Velvet had a heart attack and they had to take her out in an ambulance."

My heart skipped a beat at that news. I loved Ms. Velvet. I could hardly bear the thought that she was that ill. I left War Thug smoking his drugs and took off for Drama's apartment building.

I raced through the courtyard. The front door of the building swung open. I raced through it and up the steps. What I saw forced me to slow down. Drama's front door had been caved in by a battering ram. Sandra swung the broken door back and pulled me inside. Her hair looked wild like she'd stuck her finger in a light socket. She threw her arms around me.

"Don't worry, Mama be all right. They just took her to Highland for observation."

"What happened?"

Sandra bid me to enter the apartment. A table lamp lay sideways on the floor with a hole in the shade the size of a jack boot. The stuffing was out of the big living room couch, piled where it had been slashed open. The rest of the place looked like the aftermath of a hurricane.

"Sit down, Firstborn," Sandra said. She handed me a cold soda. "They tried to cross us up but my Drama got the call about thirty seconds before task force hit. He paged that lookout kid on the corner to try to warn you all, but they snatched the kid up before he could give the signal."

"What happened to…?" I couldn't even finish the question.

Sandra smiled. "All the stuff Drama had in his room? That what you wanna ask?"

I nodded.

"He had a .9 millimeter pistol, two clips, body armor, an ounce of bud, and two eight balls. I wrapped it all up in a sheet and chucked it out the back door. My girl Alisi lives next door. She took it and hid it. They didn't have a warrant for next door."

I got a picture in my mind of what must have happened to poor Ms. Velvet. She was listening to the Christian radio station when suddenly, out of nowhere, the front door exploded into splinters and policemen with riot gear and black helmets rushed in with their German shepherds howling and tugging at their leashes, and a masked man with gloves and goggles waved a warrant in the air.

Sandra filled me in on the rest. "When they hit the door, Mama went crazy. She start praying, hollering, 'Herbert, Firstborn—Jesus, where is my boys?' She started crying and then she clutched her chest. I said, 'I got to get my mama to a hospital,' but they call me out my name and told me I wasn't going nowhere. If something happens to Mama, we got a case, First."

A case wasn't going to bring Ms. Velvet back if she died from a heart attack. So many people who had nothing to do with the game were suffering for what we were doing. Ms. Velvet was the kindest person I had ever met, and now she was maybe on her deathbed, at least in part because of our buck-wild lifestyle.

I got up from my seat and kissed Sandra's cheek. The night sky was on fire. Storm clouds swirled around like cyclones in the distance.

Five-O had come close. Too close.

YOU HAD A WAY TO MAKE A DIFFERENCE FOR PEOPLE IN THE HOOD, BUT YOU DIDN'T GIVE ENOUGH OF A DAMN TO WALK OUT OF THIS FUNERAL PARLOR AND DO IT.

CHAPTER
SEVENTEEN

I woke up Sunday morning to Maggy's whining and the sharp sting of her fingernails slapping me against the back of my neck. "Firstborn, get up. You're supposed to be going to church with that long-haired street nigga a yours."

I fought to bring myself back to consciousness. "What time is it?" My tongue felt like a damp flannel blanket, and I could barely open my eyes.

"Ten thirty."

I threw the sheets away from my body and jogged toward the shower. Maggy turned over in bed, facing the window.

"Do you want to go this morning?" I asked before shutting the bathroom door.

"Are you mad? The way I'm livin', the church roof'd prob'ly fall in. Why you goin', crack man?"

"God didn't let Ms. Velvet have a heart attack. The doctor said she was all right and sent her home. Me and Drama made a pact that if God made her all right we'd go to church. I always keep my end of a bargain."

I made my way to the shower. I didn't have time to iron anything, so I grabbed the first things I could slip into.

As I returned to the bedroom, Maggy giggled. "That's what you wearing to church?"

"Sure, why not? You should've seen what people were wearing the other night. Oliver says God looks at the heart, not the clothes."

Maggy chuckled softly and turned her back to me, her figure-eight frame sinking into the mattress. I flicked off the light and let her go back to sleep as I tied up my sneakers.

When I got to Drama's crib, he snatched the brand-new door open before I could knock. A cloud of Eternity cologne flooded the hallway. Drama's black Bertolini suit fit him like a glove. The hallway lights sparkled against his black alligator shoes. A diamond stickpin speared his flame-red tie to his eggshell-white shirt.

"The billion-dollar baller looks the part," I said in admiration.

He grinned. "I see you didn't go to too much trouble."

I told him what Oliver had told me about God's view on church clothes.

As we walked the streets I wondered what would happen if Drama decided to get saved like Oliver. Well, first Black Christmas Mob would be over. Second, people who had never darkened the inside of a church would be walking into places like this on Sunday morning. The whole hood would be looking to God. As I listened to Drama talk on the way to church, I wondered if this might be a day people would be talking about twenty years from now.

"Firstborn," he said, "this ain't no kinda life. When I found out the SWAT had done stomped through my mama's house, leaving footprints on the pillow cases and throwin' fried chicken out the fridge, I start thinking, man, I can't keep puttin' Mama through this. Hear what I'm saying, fam? It's a good thing Sandra was slick enough to get the product and the gun next door before they busted down the door, or that could be my mama sitting up in Santa Rita 'cause of how I'm living. I can take a bust, but what if they had shackled up Mama and thrown her in a cell? Mama's sick. That might have killed her."

There were two things Drama never talked about: the possibility of being arrested and changing his ways. This was going to be interesting, I thought as we walked through the courtyard gates.

The block was dead. Crackheads were probably all off stealing something so they could buy that next hit. There was fresh blood on the sidewalk. The sound of organ music wafted from down the block. The sun blasted through palm branches that spread out like lizard claws over the mean streets of East Oakland. A sultry breeze lifted old cigarette butts and condom wrappers off the broken sidewalks and dropped them back down again.

The corner was still that morning. Dust and flies circled the turf where we made our living. It was as though the underworld had respectfully sounded retreat so the church people could have their two or three hours to pray and then leave.

Mr. Carter stood flat footed in front of the liquor store, scrutinizing every step the delivery man took, from his disembarking from the truck to his journey into Butchie's Liquor Store. He had been decked out in the same khaki shorts and Marine World T-shirt that we had seen him wearing for the past week. Mr. Carter had also neglected the shaving ritual that morning. He rubbed his hands together and stomped his feet and licked his lips in anticipation. His gaze was fixed on the truck's insignia. It said, "Pit Bull Spit Malt Liquor."

"Good morning, Mr. Carter," I said.

He nodded.

I squinted to adjust my eyes to the darkness that enveloped me as I stepped inside Butchie's Liquor Store. Steel racks and refrigerated glass cases were lodged in every nook and cranny of the store. A television set high above the store alerted customers to the day's winning lottery numbers. Superball, Pick-a-Winner, and a half dozen other shiny, multicolor cards told the desperate and the adventurous that they were just pennies away from a fortune.

A chunky woman with light blue curlers in her hair made her choice from the grandest selection of cheap liquor in the free world. "Gimme two packs of Kools, some pork rinds, and a bottle of Remy," she demanded.

About ten years ago, the owner, a Middle Eastern man, had bought the place from Butchie, who took the proceeds and moved his family back to Louisiana. The new proprietor was a human enigma, a deeply religious man who would never indulge in anything this woman was purchasing from him. He even had a sign above the hard liquor cabinet behind the counter that said, "Alcohol is slavery." In his home country, the government officials would have cut off his hands for selling liquor and pork rinds. Yet he thought nothing of selling it to poor black and Latino people.

Who was I to talk, though, considering how I was living?

Drama purchased a pack of breath mints and we walked two blocks to the Greater Grace Memorial Church.

Drama's back stiffened as we drew within a block of the church building. "Blood, I ain't been inside a church on a Sunday since my daddy was living. I wonder what's gonna happen."

"The roof is gonna cave in. That's why Maggy isn't here."

"Stop playing, man. I'm serious."

Eric B. and Rakim's masterpiece "Paid in Full" bounced in my memory banks. Rakim Allah might have been talking about hip hop money in that song, but one look around this parking lot told me who was getting the real money. African-American professionals from the neighboring suburbs slipped out of Benzes and BMWs. "That's the new Bentley," Drama cried. "I gotta get me one of them."

When we hit the front door, a silver-haired woman in a white nurse's uniform handed us pieces of folded paper with pictures of orchids on the covers. The music grew louder as we cracked open the sanctuary doors.

"You sure this ain't a funeral?" Drama asked. "I heard that music before."

"It ain't no funeral," I said. "That's God's music. That's what it sounds like in heaven."

"Negro, are you crazy?" Drama whispered. "They got hip hop in heaven."

"Why would you think that?"

"'Cause Mama's always quoting this Bible verse that says, 'Make a joyful noise.' What's more joyful than hip hop music?"

"May I lead you to your seat?" the usher asked with a wave of his white glove.

"Thank you, sir," Drama responded.

"My name is Amos Kipfield. Let me welcome you both to the Greater Grace Memorial Church." He turned around and stuck out his hand. Drama shook first, then I did. I liked the old man's smile. He really seemed happy that we had walked through the doors of his church. So far so good.

He pointed at two vacant spaces in a bench near the middle of the church. We took our seats and waved at him as he made his way back to the entrance. I couldn't remember when I'd been treated with such dignity.

Drama and I sat silently, drinking in the view around us. There were maybe sixty folks spread out all over the sanctuary that could have easily seated three hundred. Except for a handful of elementary-school kids, the congregants were almost all over fifty. Stained-glass windows with portraits of northern European people in red-and-purple robes blocked out the view of East Oakland.

The organist played three chords over and over. I was in the early stages of hypnosis when a loud thump startled me. An elderly woman in a pink straw safari helmet had just slammed the back of my wooden bench. I nearly jumped out of my seat. She must have put her lipstick on in the dark that morning. Her pearl bracelet shook when she pointed her finger at me.

"Whass up?" I asked.

"This seat belongs to me and my family. Y'all are sitting in it."

Butterflies floated around in my stomach. I certainly didn't want to cause a scene. I knew Drama would walk out at the slightest provocation. He was already nervous about this.

"Lady, this seat doesn't belong to you. It doesn't have your name on it."

She frowned and then slapped the back of the pew with the flat of her hand. I looked at the spot where the fingers had landed, and sure enough, there was a brass plate with black writing that said, "This pew was purchased by the Hanratty Family in 1966."

"Well, can't you sit somewhere else just this Sunday, Ms. Hanratty?"

The woman trotted away, muttering something under her breath.

"Did you hear what that lady said when she was walking away?" Drama asked.

"I think she was praying to the Virgin Mary. I heard her say mother-something-or-other."

"Mary must be black."

"Why you say that?"

"'Cause I heard her say, "You black mother—" Drama covered his mouth as if to stuff the laughter back inside.

A queasy feeling settled in the pit of my stomach. Ladies with blue hair and diamond necklaces whispered into waiting ears. A woman with swirling black hair and butterfly spectacles pointed out my shirt to her seven-year-old girl and scowled. She read the writing out loud: "Penitentiary Chances." The corners of her mouth creased in a frown.

The choir, draped in yellow robes with emerald trim, sang a hymn. Oliver stood in the front row, right in the center. He sang along with the rest of the choir, but he didn't appear to be having a very good time. At one point, he caught sight of us, broke protocol, and waved. The man next to him gave him an elbow nudge to the ribs.

During the second number, a woman with a blonde wig stepped up to the microphone and sang the lead in a song that sounded like it came from a French opera. When she hit the high notes at the end, Drama frowned. "Man, are you sure this is what heaven is going to sound like?"

A rail-thin fellow with glowing eyes and a silver handlebar mustache rushed to the microphone. "We want to thank the Lawd for the gift of Sister Sylvia Watts's voice. What a soul-stirring rendition of 'Feast on a Distant Mountain.' Did not our hearts warm within us? Now, would all of our visitors stand?"

I joined Drama in his sudden admiration of the purple carpet. I felt like a prison escapee when the bright spotlight from the guard tower hit its mark.

The deacon cleared his throat as he looked down at us. He was waiting for the only two visitors in the house to jump to their feet. When it became clear that we were intent on maintaining our anonymity, he said, "Well, saints, greet the person next to you with a hug or a handshake."

The organ sounded again. All around us, men in black suits and women in ball gowns skirted over to their friends.

"Good to see you, Arthur. How did those preferred stocks I suggested work out for you?"

"Why, Lilly, that's a lovely dress. Did you buy it at Nordstrom's?"

I scoped the audience in search of anyone who looked like they had come in from the hood. I found only one familiar face: a quiet girl with long braids. I'd gone to high school with her. She sat in the pew, staring at her shoes. Sunglasses covered her eyes. She kept dabbing under the black lenses with her forefinger. I think she was crying. Perhaps the preacher would offer her some hope.

A thick-built woman in her late sixties twirled around in the pew in front of us. She read my shirt as though it were written in Braille and she were blind. "'Pen-i-ten-tia-ry Chances.' Good day, Mr. Chances. I'm Helen Crane. Welcome to our church." Her left nostril trembled as she stretched out her hand for the obligatory handshake. She closed her eyes and bit her lip when she shook, as if it pained her to touch me. She acted like she was trying to pull her lost house key out of a pile of dog excrement. When she reached for Drama's hand he shook his head and kept his hands at his side.

"Who she mean, muggin' up in here?" he whispered in my ear as Ms. Crane turned to sit back down. "Satan will get an engraved invitation to heaven before they let her in."

"She sure is a big girl," I said. "That dress looks like somebody sewed pockets on a tent!"

"If she did make it to heaven, the construction crew would have to tear up part of the pearly gates to let her in." Drama's comment made us giggle like second graders.

Finally, the organ grinding ended. The grinning and back-slapping was over until next week. Everyone returned to his or her seat so the service could resume.

Up in the pulpit, six middle-aged men in blue suits sat on wooden thrones like the gods of Olympus staring down at the minions below. They offered an occasional nod, scoping out familiar faces in the audience. The men looked as if they were plotting a holdup, but I guessed they were praying. At uneven intervals, one would catch sight of us, lean over to the next man, and whisper in his ear.

"What you think they're talking about?" I asked Drama.

"They're reading your shirt."

When the offering was announced, I expected a snide comment from Drama about the church and money, but he didn't give it. Instead he reached inside his pocket and pulled out a thick wad of bills. He shielded it with the palm of his hand before I could get a good look.

The basket looked like a wooden hat turned upside down. It was almost brimming over with ones. Drama slapped the bankroll down on the top and passed the hat to me. My eyes bulged when I glimpsed the wad that Drama had placed in the basket. There was a hundred-dollar bill on top of it. He must have dropped three thousand dollars in that basket.

Drama used to make fun of his mother for sending her Social Security money to any radio evangelist who had a good rap and could pronounce the name of Jesus correctly. I never thought I'd see the day when he would put that kind of money in a church collection plate.

After the offering had been lifted, a balding man with a thick paunch beneath his shirt rose up from among the group of wise men and came to the pulpit. His voice betrayed a Louisiana upbringing, yet he adopted Alfred Hitchcock's classic South London accent when it came time to do the Lord's business.

"Shall we pray?"

The organ played the same three notes in soft, hypnotic repetition as the preacher prayed. "Eternal Gawd. The one who separated the sun from the shadows. The one who created Bach and Mozart and Shubert. The maker of the Imperial Gardens of Babylon and the Riviera of France. He who observes the splendor and goodness of humankind and blesses us daily with words of thank-you and amen…"

I fell asleep somewhere around that part.

Drama woke me up with a nudge. "What's he doing?"

"He's leading us in a prayer to God."

"Oh."

"And Lawd, you have brought us here together, the saint and the sinner, the righteous and the infidel, the children of Gawd and the criminogenic sons of mammon. But on that last day, oh blessed Father, you will separate the sheep from the goats. Let these words serve as our prayer. In Jesus' name. Amen."

The entire congregation said, "Amen."

When we opened our eyes, the preacher's gaze fixed on me like an arrow headed toward a bull's-eye.

Drama leaned over to whisper in my ear. "What's a criminogenic son of mammon?"

I shrugged, though I knew perfectly well what the preacher was saying and who he was saying it about.

"Before I begin my sermon, I want to introduce a few special guests. Bill Thisby, stand up." A smattering of applause rang out. "Bill here has just been elected fire marshal over in Lakeview."

A tall, gray-headed man with beady eyes stood and waved like Prince Charles facing the English hordes.

"And I see Lois London, hiding there in the last row. Lois was in the newspapers last week for the work she's doing to promote lower prime lending rates down at the bank. Let us thank God for Sister London." More applause.

A few more people were celebrated, some for their sorority affiliations, others for their contributions to the arts and sciences—none for anything connected to the Christian faith.

Drama turned to me and whispered, "What the hell does all this have to do with religion? I mean, who really gives a damn?"

"Shhh. And stop cussing in church." But I knew he was right. We were hustlers. In our world, if we celebrated people, it was because they'd gone on a mission for us or moved a lot of product. If the church's mission was to help people be more like Jesus, it would seem as though the church should celebrate people who were on a mission for Jesus.

This church was nothing like the place I had visited with Oliver. I should have risen up at that moment and invited Drama to leave with me, but I felt compelled to wait around for the train wreck.

The preacher read something from the Bible and then faced the audience. "Today I want to talk about the subject of free will. Even an idiot knows that Martin Luther's great revelation threatened to meld the empire into one great episcopos. Say amen, church."

"Amen!"

"And now, here we are, children of the basiliea, the priesthood of all believers. But should it be so? Now, I'm not angling for some type of theocracy. Not unless I'm going to be named the Potentate Exemplar."

The room erupted in laughter, as though everyone in the church was in on a private joke except us. Drama's face turned red. I stared at the floor, hoping the service would end soon.

"And even an idiot knows Pope Leo's famous quote..."

Drama's eyes grew heavy.

"Pope Leo, that beneficent leader of the Catholic church, said..."

Drama eyes shut tight.

I nudged him. "Are you listening?"

"I'm trying, but I don't know what he's talkin' 'bout."

"Back in Arkansas in 1945, when I was just a young pup..."

Drama closed his eyes again and was soon snoring softly.

"I was watching the news yesterday when that rascal Sideshow Psycho was being interviewed."

Drama's eyes popped open.

"I hate that back-alley doggerel they call hip hop music. What a pathetic charade at poetic expression. But that Sideshow Psycho exemplifies the worst in our people."

Drama looked as though the preacher had slit his throat while he'd been dozing. "Firstborn, what is that fat, liver-lipped fool talkin' 'bout? He don't know Sideshow Psycho. That's my blood cousin!"

"Just chill, man. It's almost over."

The preacher launched into a tirade against the evils of hip hop, young people today, and the falling interest rates of blue-chip stock. I didn't notice him quoting anything from the Scriptures unless the phrase "God will bless those who invest" is somewhere in the Bible.

He asked every head to bow and every eye to close. "Are you without a church home? It is no accident that you wound up in our loving grasp this morning. You need a place where you can worship God, serve him in the beauty of holiness alongside people who will love you and take you into their hearts. Someone here is lost."

I ventured a glimpse to my left. Drama had bowed his head, but he had not closed his eyes. Sweat beads popped out on his forehead. He shuddered violently. He bit one of his white knuckles. He rocked back and forth, moaning, "Jesus help me. I don't know what to do. Help me, God."

Drama squeezed the bridge of his nose between thumb and forefinger. Then he rose to his feet. Before he could make his way to the aisle, the preacher said, "That concludes our services for today. Join us next Sunday, when our sermon title will be 'Heaven: Who's Going to Be There?'"

Drama slumped back like a balloon that had landed on a pin cushion. The light of hope vanished from his eyes as quickly as it had appeared.

People stepped over both of us, racing for the exits as if the building were on fire. I glanced at the lone sister from the hood. She still had not looked up.

"Firstborn, I'm gonna straighten that fat little preacher out for talkin' all that yang 'bout Sideshow Psycho."

"No, you're not." I squeezed his bicep like a drowning victim holding on to a lifeguard.

"No? Watch me." He wrenched his arm free.

"Excuse me. Pardon me," Drama said as he elbowed his way through the startled crowd like a boxer making his way toward the ring.

The preacher stood in the narthex of the church with a smile spread across his chubby cheeks. He bent down to peck someone's grandmother on the cheek when Drama's angry voice echoed with danger.

"Preacher, I wanna acks you somethin'!"

The pastor bristled. He straightened up, ready to square off. "How can I help you, young man?"

"Why was you talkin' all that yang about Sideshow Psycho?"

"By 'yang,' I imagine that you mean viewpoint or opinion."

"I mean that ole bull—"

"Drama!" I hollered.

The preacher waved me off like a mosquito at a barbecue. "Sideshow Psycho promotes violence and antisocial behavior through his lyrics. He disrespects women, he glorifies gang culture, and he is the standard bearer for the thug-life culture. He is destroying black people."

"He just makin' records. Nobody ever got shot with no CD!"

"You're wrong, son. Words are more powerful than bullets. The words he sings and the images he interjects into young minds shape thoughts. And thoughts shape actions."

"Why you so down on us, Preacher?"

The man's shoulders slumped in his black robe. His voice took on a softer, more grandfatherly tone. "Because I don't understand your generation. I was born into abject poverty. My daddy and momma were Mississippi sharecroppers. They couldn't read or write. I didn't have my first pair of shoes until I was seven years old. But I always knew there was better. They couldn't give me the finest things in life, but they gave me hope."

If he had been almost anybody else, by this time the preacher would have been stretched out on the red carpet staring up at the ceiling lights with Drama kicking at his ribs. But for some reason, Drama stood there and heard the preacher out. Then he said some things that I thought might make the preacher think after he'd walked away. But the pastor didn't seem to think that Drama could teach him much of anything, his being from the ghetto and all.

"Son, you are nihilistic," the pastor charged. "You live without hope. You sell drugs on the corner to your own kind. You and your people disrespect women. You make babies that you can't take care of. The only accomplishment your generation has contributed to our race is a new spelling of the word *nigger*."

Worshippers skipped the niceties of the parting handshake to rush for the safety of their automobiles. A couple of beefy deacons took up posts next to the pastor. But they didn't intimidate Drama.

"Rev, niggas ain't comin' down to this museum you got set up down here. You da preacha. You da man a God. Instead a hatin' on us, why don't you come down to the corner where niggas really *need* God and give 'em some hope? The hardest cats on the block gonna be your audience."

"They'll never listen," the pastor said, folding his arms across his chest like Pharaoh facing down Moses.

"Rev, if Jesus Christ was here in the flesh, he wouldn't be hidin' out in here. And if he *were* to walk up in this mausoleum, you wouldn't even recognize him. Jesus hung out with the thugs and the ridaz. Shoot, Matthew was a tax collector, and he turned around and became Jesus' homeboy. Back then, being a tax collector was the same thing as being a d-boy or a pimp today. I know—my daddy was a preacher."

I encouraged Drama with phrases like "Tell it" and "That's right" and even an "amen" or two. But he didn't need my help. He could aim his arrows where they couldn't possibly miss their target.

"The pimps and hookers of Jesus' time knew his name, and he wasn't too high and mighty to kick it. If he was living in East Oakland today, Jesus might be a little like Tupac. He wouldn't be preaching outta no dictionary. Real live brothers would be able to feel him, ya dig it?"

The preacher smirked.

"My daddy used to always tell the story of the Good Samaritan. He said this cat was walking through the hood when he got jacked by ridaz. They shook his pockets and left him butt naked with a hole in his head. Well, this preacher walked up to the brother who was laid out on the ave barefoot 'cause they'd even took his Jordans. The preacher glanced around to make sure nobody was peeping him.

"Then a deacon came through. He saw the dude laid out and caught the other side of the street. But then one cat, sort of a thuggish fellow, who wasn't particularly religious and didn't speak the white man's English, came gangsta limpin' down the block, rapping the words to an old NWA joint, bottle o' Thunderbird in his hand. He looked down and saw bro and had mercy. He put bandages on the mark, put him inside the shotgun seat of his bucket, and took off for the private hospital."

Drama didn't talk about the Bible too much. I was surprised that he knew this story so well. I understood his message much better than the pastor's, even though Drama had never been inside a seminary.

"Rev, the Good Samaritan didn't preach no sermons. He helped his brother man when the brother man couldn't help himself. And not with no words, but with food and bandages. You should do the same thing. We done heard enough sermons. The hood needs food and bandages. Why don't you help brothers coming out of the pen to get a GED and a job? Do something for all these li'l youngstas in the hood with nowhere to go and nothing to do but get into trouble. And some of the single moms 'round here'd be glad for some help too. You show some mercy and you won't have to worry about them hearin' what you got to say about Jesus. They'll see him."

The preacher smirked. "And I'm supposed to trust you to know what the neighborhood needs?"

"Who better than me?"

A tall, beefy deacon with a gray jherri curl snapped, "Mind your tongue, boy. Don't you know this pastor is the premier black leader in this community?"

"Maybe back when people was walking around in bell bottoms and your haircut was in style. He ain't no black leader now until he can get brothers like me and my man here on line."

The pastor's nostrils trembled. He licked his lips. "Son, I wouldn't know what to say to those young men on the corner. This is God's house. If you and your friends want to meet him, come down here and find him." He glared at me. "Preferably without a dress-long T-shirt that says something about the penitentiary and without their drawers showing. Have enough class to put on a good suit when you come to God's house!"

"Do you really think God cares about what clothes folks wear to his house as long as they get there?"

"Maybe not, but I do. And I'll tell you something else. I know who you are. I've seen your friend here on the corner mingling among the thieves, whores, and the enemies of all that is good. Now, depart from me, ye that worketh iniquity. But before you go, hold out your hand."

Drama complied.

The preacher reached inside his robe. He pulled something out of his pants pocket and slammed it into Drama's open palm. Benjamin Franklin's portrait sat on top of a fat stack of green paper wrapped up in a red rubber band. "Thanks, but no thanks," the preacher hissed. "God can't use dope money."

Drama flinched and then took a step backward as though he had just been shot in the chest with an AR-15. A tear formed in the corner of his right eye. He turned around so that those behind him couldn't see.

Drama wasn't invincible. He'd been stabbed and shot at more times that I'm sure even he could have remembered. And yet, none of those things had ever brought a tear to his eye. The preacher hurt him that day in ways that no thug in the street would ever be able to do. Drama and I had been friends since kindergarten, and that was only the second time I'd seen tears fall from his eyes. The first time was at his father's funeral. It unnerved me. It was like watching Superman weep.

Drama reached under his black suit jacket and clicked the safety off his .9 millimeter handgun. "You think you better than me because you ain't got no tattoos and you got a college degree? Preacher, God is going to judge you before me, because you was the last hope. You had a way to make a difference for people in the hood but you didn't give enough of a damn to walk out of this funeral parlor and do it. You too busy thinkin' about your reputation than keepin' it real."

"I have a feeling you're not going to live too long, son."

"Well, I've got the same feeling about you, Rev."

The preacher cocked an eyebrow. The beefy deacons moved in closer for protection.

"How many people under thirty you got in that church?"

The pastor remained silent.

"How about under twenty?"

Still the preacher did not respond.

"How many teenagers you got in your church, Rev?"

The pastor stared ahead blankly.

"You ain't got no young people in your church, and you don't want poor people from this hood in here. Sooner or later, peoples is gonna get tired of driving thirty and forty miles to get here for church, and this church is gonna be dead. One fine Sunday morning the only one here will be the janitor hired to take the padlock off the door of this ghetto social club."

The preacher stood as still as a statue, with a bewildered look on his face.

"You see, Rev, we both made our choices and we goin' down together." Drama turned to me. "C'mon, Firstborn, let's go." He pressed the handle on the white wooden door and flung it open. Sunlight plunged inside and flooded the lobby.

The church members jumped back as we walked past them to the parking lot. They eyed us as though we were the devil and his accomplice crawled out of hell to wreak havoc on their country club. The stares and frowns merely served to underscore the preacher's words.

From the corner of my eye I saw Oliver, without his choir robe, stomping a quick pace in our direction. He looked at Drama's face and stuttered, "What did the reverend say to you in there?"

Drama quick-stepped past me in a half jog, obviously ashamed of his tears.

"Go back and ask the preacher," I said. I never stopped walking.

Oliver's feet stopped as if they'd been stuck in quick-drying cement. "Firstborn, I'm sorry," he called after me. "I should have told you not to come here, but in my wildest nightmares I didn't see this coming."

My brain was swimming inside my skull. I remembered Oliver's hesitation when I mentioned visiting his church. But I had always had the vision of church as a place where everyone was welcome no matter what you dressed like or who you might be. I thought of the sermon I sat through on the night my path crossed with Oliver. If that preacher was right, a whole lot of people at Great Grace Memorial Church were on their way to Brimstone City.

I could still hear Oliver behind me, crying out my name. I glanced back and saw horror etched across his face. This guy really wanted me to make it. He was deeply concerned that I would walk away from God's outstretched hand. I could see it in his eyes.

"Brother man, hit me later on my cell," Oliver hollered.

I was up the block and almost out of earshot.

Life brings us to moments that clarify the reason we have been placed on God's earth. I'll go to my grave believing that preacher's destiny was to meet Drama and show him another path. He missed it. And because of his blindness, many people would indirectly lose their lives. God had placed him there to be the light. Instead he caused an eclipse for one D Montana.

Drama was never the same after that day. That preacher had stolen hope away from him.

CHAPTER
EIGHTEEN

ONE DAY MELTED INTO ANOTHER, WITH NO MORE TALK OF church, the preacher, fear, love, or God. A glass divider had fallen between Drama and me. I sensed tension, coolness, uneasiness. Oh, we shared meals together. We smoked weed together. And we spent countless hours on the corner chasing down the almighty dollar. But the sweetness of our friendship had disintegrated. That Sunday morning, I had seen through Drama's cloak of invulnerability. I had witnessed his thirst for faith. I had seen him cry. He felt ashamed. And that made him feel weak.

I was counting crack money in the back of Butchie's one morning when an idea hit me for how to repair the breach. I would invite Drama and Street Life over to my crib for dinner. I extended the invitation to Ms. Velvet and Sandra as well.

On the big night, I simmered steaks in the frying pan, smothered in fried red onions. Magdalene poured Chablis. When the doorbell rang, I snatched it open, eager for the night of reconciliation to begin. But what I saw turned my smile into a scowl.

An uninvited guest stood next to Drama. Pimpin' EZ spread his arms wide. "Looka here," he said, rubbing his hands together rapidly and sniffing the air. "Steak, my favorite!"

Sandra wrapped her arms around me and pecked my cheek. She was welcome in my house anytime. But I had no idea what she saw in that slime ball.

I cut Drama the meanest stare I could manage.

He shrugged. "He was in the car, man," he whispered. "I couldn't get rid of him."

I went back into the kitchen to help Maggy serve the food. We set the table with brussels sprouts, baked potatoes, and filet mignon. Everybody chowed down.

Halfway through the meal, Drama looked up from his plate and said, "Firstborn, I'm 'bout ready to change my mind about this girl a yours. She sho' can burn in the kitchen!"

Everyone else concurred. Nobody talked about much of anything besides the delicious food.

We had peach cobbler and strawberry ice cream for dessert. After the last spoonful had been devoured, we gathered in the living room. I was thumbing through my bootleg DVD collection when I heard a rustling noise behind me.

Pimpin' EZ yanked a small plastic baggie out of his vest pocket. Tiny pebbles sat in the bottom of it, glistening like chips of yellow snow. He picked up my Smokey Robinson and the Miracles "Greatest Hits" CD and poured out the entire contents of the baggie on top of the word *Miracles*. He pulled a glass stem and a Bic lighter from his vest pocket. He picked up a rock and pinched it into the end of the stem. Then he licked his thin pink lips and glanced around the room. "Who wanna hit it?"

Sandra shot him a pleading look. "Let me get a hit, baby," she whimpered.

"Sandra," Drama snarled, "if you touch that pipe, I'll slap the taste out of your mouth." He turned on Pimpin' EZ. "You better not be giving that poison to my sister!"

Pimpin' EZ was ruining what should have been a wonderful evening.

Crack rocks sizzled as he teased the blackened end of the glass stem with the lighter and inhaled greedily. "You Black Christmas niggas got some good stuff."

"Look, man," I said, "why don't you go in the bathroom with that?"

He looked at everyone but me. "Who else wanna taste this?"

I recoiled in disgust. Drama remained expressionless, but I knew the veneer of calm on his face was just a veil for the rage that brewed behind his eyes. It was too bad Pimpin' EZ couldn't see that.

"Here, Life," he said, "take a hit."

Street Life waved his hand and laughed. "Naw, playa, you know I don't mess around."

Pimpin' EZ's visage grew dark. "I don't understand you Black Christmas niggas. This is y'all's money maker. This is what put those Versace suits on your backs, bought you those Cadillacs. This is the foundation of the empire. But y'all won't even try it. A wine connoisseur samples the sangria before he serves it to the public. A chef'll cut off a little piece of prime rib before he sells it a customer. But y'all got half a East Oakland strung out on this stuff and you won't even taste it!"

Street Life stared at Pimpin' EZ with his lip curled in disgust. No amount of teasing could have shamed us into smoking crack. I worked with it every day. I knew what it did to people. I wouldn't have inhaled it at gunpoint.

"I'll give it a try," Magdalene said.

I was so overwhelmed by disbelief I couldn't speak.

"Atta girl!" Pimpin' EZ's eyes lit up. For the first time, I noticed he had dimples when he smiled. "Well, come on over here and get it."

Magdalene rose from her chair and made her way toward the pipe.

I jumped to my feet. "Maggy, are you crazy?"

Pimpin' EZ grinned. "C'mon, Firstborn, let the girl have a little fun. One hit won't hurt her. I grew up on it like corn flakes and milk. It turned me into a man."

I was half a minute from kicking Pimpin' EZ's rump. "Nigga, I want you out of my house!"

He reared back as if to challenge me. "You puttin' me out?"

"Yeah. Now."

He crossed his legs and chuckled.

I took a step toward him. Street Life rose from his chair at the same time.

"Come on, Sandra," Pimpin' EZ growled. "I know when I'm not wanted." He started toward the door.

"Pimpin' EZ, you ain't got to go nowhere," Maggy said.

I couldn't believe my ears.

"This place is just as much mine as his. My sister's name is on the lease." Maggy stood there with a pout on her face, one arm folded over the other.

"But yo' sister ain't paying the rent," I said. "I am. And as far as I'm concerned, you and Pimpin' EZ can both get out." The minute the words flew out of my mouth I regretted them.

Magdalene strutted into the bedroom in a huff. She emerged seconds later in a leather jacket I'd bought her the week before. She had her purse in hand. She followed Sandra and Pimpin' EZ through the door.

I wanted to yell out, "I'm sorry, Maggy. Don't go!" But I couldn't. What would the fellas have thought?

The door slammed. The shuffle of feet pounded on the steps. The front door of the building shut, this time more softly. I heard their voices trickle off into silence. Pimpin' EZ needed a new muffler. His mustard brown Ford Mustang roared down the street louder than judgment day.

Loneliness chewed away at my soul like a school of piranhas mugging a guppy. So far I'd been incredibly lucky to have avoided being imprisoned or shot. But I could see the minute hand on the clock ticking. I was walking through triple-stage darkness and I could not find the way out.

GOD LOVES YOU. HE'S REACHING OUT HIS HANDS TO YOU. THE ONLY THING YOU HAVE TO DO IS REACH BACK TO HIM.

CHAPTER
NINETEEN

As THE SUN CREPT THROUGH THE WINDOWS, I REACHED FOR THE touch of Magdalene's warm, supple flesh beneath my fingers. My hand landed on cold linen. Maggy hadn't come home last night.

I tried to reach her on the cell. No answer. I called her friends. No one had seen her. Finally, I made the phone call I dreaded most. To Maggy's sister.

"Monica?"

"What you want, nigga?"

"Is Magdalene there?"

"Why would she be here? She's living in sin with you, remember? I don't know what she sees in you. But I do know how you make your money."

"Monica, when I was starving, you used to laugh at me. You told Magdalene she didn't want a man who couldn't get a new pair of Jordans. You told me to get money. I did."

"I didn't say *get* money. I told you to earn it."

"I looked for a job. Couldn't find one. But I'll bet you like that new living room set I bought you."

Monica sighed. "I like it just fine."

"Will you call me if you see Magdalene? There's a hundred-dollar bill in it for you."

"Yes, Firstborn, I'll let you know."

After I hung up, I lay back in bed with my hands behind my head. Outside, Oakland was slowly rising. The milkman was delivering eggs, cheese, and butter to the corner store. I heard his laughter as he greeted Mr. Song, the store owner. Kids were clamoring and cussing as they headed toward the bus stop. But I was still. I hated stillness. In moments of tranquility my conscience exploded behind my eyeballs.

In the darkness, I visualized Magdalene in a room somewhere with a glass pipe to her lips. I'd never given her crack. But I had let her walk out with a back-alley cutthroat named Pimpin' EZ.

When my conscience started whipping me, I thought about God. And then I thought about Oliver. I phoned his number.

"Good to hear from you, Firstborn. How you doin'?"

"I got some big problems, man. My girl walked out. I'm feeling a little lost this morning."

"Well, understand this: God loves you. He's reaching out his hands to you. The only thing you have to do is reach back to him."

"To tell the truth, I'm not sure how I feel about God. And I'm not really feelin' that church thing. I've felt more love on the block than I did from those church people."

"I know what you mean. Reverend Avery had no right to say what he did. Drama was absolutely correct. In fact, I believe God was speaking to the pastor through him. We should be takin' our message to the block. But he thinks that if we occasionally do some nice things for the poor, God is pleased. He obviously ain't read his Bible lately."

I wondered why the people in that congregation went to church. Was it just to show off the high-fashion clothes that nobody in our hood could afford? Was it to trade stock-market tips? Was it to network their businesses? What did it mean to them to be Christian? I had been to two radically different churches that preached basically the same message but practiced two different lifestyles. The paradox made me scratch my head.

"Brother, not every church is like Greater Grace," Oliver continued. "If you go to a restaurant and they burn your fried chicken, you don't swear off chicken. You go to another restaurant. Right? If you get hurt at a church, you don't swear off the church. You keep searching for one that's for real."

Oliver and I spoke for another twenty minutes. Mostly he spoke about what God could do in my life. He said Jesus had died and rose again so I could have a new life. He said God wanted to forgive me but first I had to repent.

I almost did it right there and then, but I caught myself. What would the fellas think if I walked out to the corner and said, "I can't do what we've been doin' no more, because I just made Jesus Christ the shot caller of my life"?

"Not today, Oliver. Would you just pray for me?"

"Lord," Oliver said, "my new little potna, Firstborn, is a good man but he's twisted up in the game. It's hard for a brother who wants to hold up his head like a man in front of his family and his community. Lord, Firstborn is out on the corner sellin' poison, living fast, and looking to die young or do some hard time. God, you know all about him. But you love him. Lord, get this young brother's attention. I believe he could do something special to help our people. And Father, please send his girl back home. Thank you for listening. In Jesus' name, amen."

When the phone line went silent, I felt at peace deep down inside. I couldn't explain it, but at that moment, somehow I knew Maggy would be back.

Not a half hour after I hung up, I heard a key twisting in the front door lock. High-heeled footsteps lumbered heavily toward the bedroom. Maggy opened the door softly. She looked as though she'd been wrestling in her clothes. Her hair was tousled all over her head. Her eyes were fire-engine red.

I flipped over in bed and flicked on the light. "Where you been?" I asked in a harsh tone.

"Out with my friends," she said with annoyance in her voice.

"I called all your friends. None of them have seen you."

"I'm talking about Sandra and P.E." She said it in the way a weary parent might when trying to explain to a child why two plus two would always equal four.

"Pimpin' EZ is your friend?"

"Nigga, you don't even know what's happening."

I didn't know what was happening? I couldn't believe she'd let that come out of her mouth. I could feel my pulse rate quickening and sweat pouring through my scalp. I propped myself up one elbow and shook my head. Maggy was getting disrespectful and I didn't like it. If I'd been like most of the guys in our hood, I would have jumped up out of that bed and slapped the spit out of her.

"Magdalene, you never went outside your block before you moved in with me. So let me lace your boots here for a second. Pimpin' EZ doesn't have any friends. He uses people. That's what hustlers do. A true hustler never gives away anything for free."

"Yeah, whatever." She flipped her head to the side and chomped down hard on her chewing gum. She peeled off one sandal and then the other. Her bangles clanged when she dropped them on the dresser. She was barely paying attention to me.

"Girl, next time you walk out of here like a crazy woman, don't forget to take all your stuff with you. If you don't, it'll be waiting for you at the curb when you come back."

Magdalene dropped her clothes in a pile on the floor and slipped between the sheets. She rubbed my neck with the back of her hand and cooed, "Aw, honey…"

I leapt out of bed as if the sheets were on fire. "Magdalene, I ain't going there with you right now. For all I know, you've been laying up with that shade-tree pimp, and that nasty fool probably has diseases that medical science doesn't even have a name for yet."

She sighed and rolled over. She was snoring in less than a minute.

I put on a clean pair of jeans and a blue button-down shirt. I glanced at Magdalene on the way out. The diamond friendship ring I'd given her was not on her finger.

My life was beginning to unravel. I was losing Magdalene. The thought of Pimpin' EZ using her for his own carnal lusts disgusted me. Why him? Anybody but him. As I walked down the steps of the building, my stomach churned. I almost threw up. The game was tearing me apart.

YOU KNOW WHEN WE GET THIS DEEP INTO THE GAME EVERYTHING IS ABOUT MONEY.

CHAPTER
TWENTY

I GOT LOST TWICE LOOKING FOR DOVE'S SOUL FOOD RESTAURANT on San Pablo. It was on the other side of town, and I wasn't used to West Oakland. Drama wanted to talk business, but he didn't like doing it in our neighborhood. Whenever we had a sit-down, it was always somewhere outside the hood in a spot where what we said wouldn't hold much interest to people.

Dove's fried and sautéed soul food was legendary. The proprietor was an ex-pimp who had invested his savings into the same black community where the women he had exploited earned it. Dove's was a place where everybody minded his own business. It was just the spot to satisfy two appetites at the same time: greed and hunger.

Drama's red Cadillac sedan was already parked outside, right behind Life's pimped-out royal blue Olds '98.

A bell rang when I opened the door.

Manu Dibango's old-school classic "Soul Makossa" thumped against the walls. Bus drivers leaned forward on the round red stools, staring at their laminated menus. Housewives and a few lost tourists sat around square wooden tables in the front of the restaurant. The hustlers sat in the back.

Drama beamed at me when he spotted me. He flashed a smile, revealing gold fronts covering his teeth.

"Cuz-o, look at you!" I said, laughing as I approached the table.

"I been to the dentist," Drama said. "No cavities."

"Well, I guess I know where your money is going."

"Aw, sit down, nigga. You sound like Mama."

I sat next to Street Life and we all stared at the menu for a while, trying to decide what to order.

At that moment it occurred to me how far we'd come since that day back in Drama's room where the idea of the Black Christmas Mob had been born. My partners were dripping with money. Drama sported a gold Christmas-tree medallion suspended by an eighteen-carat Cuban link chain. His nails had been freshly manicured. He had tattoos I'd never seen on him before. "510" was tattooed on his trigger hand. "BCM" for "Black Christmas Mob" was burned in black impact letters on the back of his neck at the point where his braids separated. A fat diamond earring sparkled in his left ear.

Life sported a black hand-stitched silk shirt and Italian-cut pants. His shirt sleeves were rolled up. The names of his children had been tattooed on his right forearm. They spread from the heel of his palm to his elbow. A gold wristwatch dangled from his left wrist. We had definitely come up.

An olive-complexioned waitress in a tight black dress tugged an order pad from the pouch of her frilly pink apron. She asked for our orders.

Street Life went first. He ordered salmon croquettes, grits, and scrambled eggs with a side of sweetened iced tea. "Make that two," Drama said. That sounded good to me. I put up three fingers. The waitress nodded and walked away. No one said another word until she was out of earshot.

"Homies," Drama said, "a couple days ago I woke up with a strange feeling. You know this thing we're doing can't go on forever. I think it's time to think about steppin' out of the life for a while."

Street Life stared at Drama like he was watching the Hindenburg burst into flames. "Step out from this good money? How the brothers gonna eat?"

"I've always told our dudes to save their chips. All this could end at any time, and you can't collect unemployment for breaking down O's. That's why they call it hustling."

Street Life rested his elbow on the table and leaned his frowning face into his hand.

"Life, Pimpin' EZ say—"

Street Life shot up as if he'd sat on a porcupine. "EZ?" Saliva streamed through his lips. "That broke-down, triflin', wannabe pimp? If some sorry snake ever had the audacity to even *think* about turnin' my sister out, I'd chop the nigga's head off and throw it in San Francisco Bay. That's real talk, playa. I put that on everything I love, feel me?"

This was the first time we'd ever had any real beef within the ranks. Street Life was going straight for the jugular. Right or wrong, he was saying things that he had no business commenting on. I knew this was not going to end well. I shifted uncomfortably in my seat.

Street Life's laugh turned into a snarl. "Are you tellin' me that Pimpin' EZ is tellin' you how to run the Black Christmas business?"

Drama slipped his hand from the top of the table. It fell beneath the white linen tablecloth.

I heard a click under the table. The type of click that has a way of stopping conversation.

"Put your hands on top of the table, Street Life," Drama said.

"Drama, I—"

Drama sucked his gold teeth. Hate flashed in his eyes. "Shut up. Beggin' don't look good on you…'specially after all the blood you done spilled."

I glanced around the room, anxious to see if anyone else had observed what was happening at our table. I crossed my fingers and wished for the waitress to come back to freshen our water glasses. I wished that Dove would come over to shake our hands and welcome us to his place. If I wasn't in the middle of plotting criminal activity, I might have tried to pray that Drama would put the gun down.

Drama's eyes glazed over. His top lip trembled. "Street Life, do you know what happened to the last person who talked crazy to me like you just did?"

I remembered. Drama had beaten a dude named Benji in a game of 8-ball. Benji owed Drama $63.00. He looked up from the pool table with a sheepish grin and said, "Drama, I ain't giving you squat."

Drama got this look on his face, like a shadow inside of a storm cloud. He didn't even look at Benji. He looked at me and said, "Firstborn, you've known me since first grade. Have you ever seen me promise to get at a dude about my money and not do it?"

"Never."

"So if a fool owes me money and he don't want to give it to me, what should he do?"

"Make a will."

Street Life's lips trembled slightly. Now, that amazed me. As many lives lives as he had destroyed, as many people as he had waylaid and blasted, as many funerals as he had caused, he was afraid to die.

"Aw, D, I ain't mean nuthin' by it. You know how I get. Put that heat away."

"Don't move, fool," Drama barked. "Now, I'm going to tell you one more time to stop beggin', 'cause that don't move me at all. You know when we get this deep into the game, everything is about money."

I was a slow learner when it came to the streets, but there was nothing wrong with my hearing. Drama talked a lot about the importance of trust and loyalty. And now he was singing a new song. It made me think of the Wu Tang Clan hit, "C.R.E.A.M. (Cash Rules Everything Around Me)." I had trusted Drama with my life because of our lifelong friendship. He used to say, "All a poor man's got is his friends." Now he was saying that there was one thing that he placed above friendship and loyalty. That was cash. I filed that one away in the back of my mind.

"Now," Drama said, "I got a decision to make. But first I wanna tell you a story."

I was glad he had a story to tell. That meant Street Life had at least a few more minutes on this earth. Drama wasn't going to shoot anybody until he'd made his point.

"Once there was three broke brothers who were looking for a come-up. One of these young brothers had an OG who knew the streets like Michael Jordan knew a basketball court."

"I wouldn't go that far." I wouldn't have put Pimpin' EZ's name in the same sentence with Michael Jordan, even as a metaphor.

"This older gentleman—for lack of a better name, we'll call him Pimpin' EZ—gave this young playa knowledge on how to get riches. Being the type a nigga that he was, this young baller brought his friends on the road to the riches. But this young playa—whom we'll call Drama—came up with a plan to stack a bank load full of paper. He realized that haters were lurking and plotting against him every day. Po-Po was snappin' pictures of him and his partners, getting their supreme hustle on. But before the trap gets sprung, this young playa hatches a plan to get a monster-size package fronted to him from his new friend, who we'll call Latin Caesar. With that kind of money, Firstborn could get through graduate school. I could open a rim shop or start this record label me and Sideshow Psycho been playing 'round with. And Street Life, you could get a whole year of services from those broke-down strippers with stretch marks you always be runnin' around with."

Drama raked his right hand across the top his head. I noticed a few strands of gray. I also sensed a touch of fatigue in his voice.

"My niggas," he said in a barely audible tone, "we gotta cool out on the cocaine business. I got a phone call a couple of days ago. The feds is got our pictures up on the blackboard down at headquarters. I'm thinking exit strategy. We need to get a big package of yay fronted to us. We break it down, move it, and then close down the shop. We had a good run. I ain't greedy. I promised Firstborn I would never let him get busted or shot, and that's a promise I plan on keeping."

Drama squeezed his eyes until they were almost closed. He said the next sentence so softly I could barely hear him, even though I was only inches away. "Street Life, is you in or are you dead?"

"Uh…I, uh…I'm in, Dramacidal," Street Life stuttered. He leaned forward, his eyes begging Drama not to blast him. "I'm in."

I heard the gun click again. Drama had put the safety back on. Street Life was going to be sucking in God's fresh air for at least another twenty-four hours. I breathed a sigh of relief.

Drama's lips flipped up into a smile but his eyes smoldered with hate. He glanced around the room to see if anyone had been observing us. Satisfied that no one was staring in our direction, he flashed his infrared stare in Street Life's direction. Uncomfortable with thirty seconds of silence, Street Life said, "I'm sorry about that crack about Pimpin' EZ, Drama. That was way out of line."

"Don't worry about it, man. We all say things we don't mean once and a while." Drama let out a smirk and stuck a toothpick between his barely parted lips.

I knew Drama would never forget how Street Life had disrespected him over lunch. One day he would make Street Life pay, with interest.

We finished our food in silence. Life tried to make some small talk about a new trade acquisition the Golden State Warriors had made. Drama iced him with a frigid stare.

Street Life looked at his cold salmon croquettes and eggs.

Drama sucked down the last of a gravy biscuit and then looked at me. "Ya done with that?"

I hadn't touched the last salmon croquette on my plate but I had planned to work on it.

"I'm ready to go," he said. "Life, you sit there and eat your food." Drama stood. "I need to get at potna here about a thing or two."

Street Life eyed Drama like an Old West gunfighter at high noon. "What's so important you can't talk to him right here?"

"It don't concern you."

I was up and out of my seat before Drama's lips could move. I tapped Street Life's arm. "What do you say we hit a sports bar tomorrow night and see the fight?"

"Sure, playa," he said without taking his eyes off Drama. "Let's do that."

Drama fished in his shirt pocket and retrieved a fifty-dollar bill. He dropped it in the middle of the table. The bottom of the bill was damp with blood.

Drama caught me staring and shrugged. "Hard money."

I walked out past the hoods, hustlers, bus drivers, and housewives who made up the local color at Dove's. Drama followed me out into the sunlight.

"You wanna talk about what just happened in there?" I asked as we walked up the block.

"Forget Street Life. I needed him to help me cut into Latin Caesar. Now I'm ready to give him his pink slip. But later for that. What I want to talk to you about is your girl."

"My girl?"

"Sandra came home last night beefin' 'bout how Pimpin' EZ dropped her off around midnight and then went somewhere alone with Magdalene. The nigga came in this morning about seven, singing 'Didn't I Blow Your Mind This Time?'"

I blinked. My mind was tangled in a knot of disbelief, doubt, and dismay. Drama was wrong; he had to be. "Magdalene told me that Sandra was with them the whole night."

Drama stared at me like a doctor diagnosing a stubborn disease. He whipped out his cell phone and punched a button. Sandra's voice hollered from the receiver.

"Sandra, this is D. I got my man here. Tell him how it went down." Drama thrust the phone in my direction.

"Hello, First," Sandra said with distress in her voice "That tramp of yours kept my man out all night. She ain't nothin' but a two-dollar hooker."

I mumbled something to Drama and handed the phone back to him.

He hung up. "Man, you got to cut her loose. We can't have no distractions. Don't let nothin' get in the way of our business. Do what you have to do."

I walked back to my car and climbed behind the wheel, tears streaming down my cheeks. My head slumped down. My chin fell against my chest.

Drama's car pulled up alongside my Chevrolet. "No distractions!" I heard him yell as he drove by.

I knew he was right. Distractions in this game could be fatal.

THE MONSTER I HAD SOLD TO STRANGERS WAS NOW IN MY CRIB MAKING A HOUSE CALL THROUGH MY GIRLFRIEND'S BLOODSTREAM.

CHAPTER
TWENTY-ONE

BACK AT MY APARTMENT, I COULD STILL HEAR DRAMA'S WORDS echoing in my ears. "*No distractions.*"

My footsteps were so heavy climbing the steps, I felt like I was scaling Mount Everest. I was drenched with sweat by the time I reached the second-floor landing. I turned the key and opened the door.

Maggie sat in the easy chair in her silk housecoat and pink pajamas, watching *Another World*. She barely looked up to acknowledge my presence.

I shut the door. "Maggy," I said as calmly as I could, "what's happening between you and that nigga Pimpin' EZ?"

Maggy grabbed the clicker and turned up the sound.

I stepped in front of the television and blocked the screen. She climbed up on the arm of the chair, craning her neck in an attempt to see around me. "Move!" she commanded. "I'm trying to see my stories."

"You want stories? I can give you some stories." I placed the heel of my shoe against the television screen and thrust.

Glass shattered all over the carpet. Sparks flittered in the smoke.

"What you doin'? That TV set cost money."

"*My* money. Now, I'm going to ask you one more time. Were you with Pimpin' EZ last night, ripper?"

"Don't trip," Maggy said while walking to the refrigerator. We just rode around all night." She rolled her eyes. She reached inside the fridge and grabbed a cold beer.

I felt like slapping her, but my grandmother's words flashed through my mind: "A real man doesn't beat up on women." Besides, I had plenty of furniture if I needed to break something.

I sat on the edge of the couch and stared at her. Her eyes were glassy. She sniffled once or twice. "You're high right now, aren't you? What'd P.E. do, give you a souvenir to take home with you?"

"No, First. I don't be smoking no rocks!"

I knew she was lying. The monster I had sold to strangers was now in my crib, making a house call through my girlfriend's bloodstream. Drama was right. I couldn't tolerate anybody as close to my business as Maggy smoking drugs. Soon money would end up missing. If she ever got stopped for speeding, she'd give the cops enough information on me to write my biography. If she ever got bad enough, she might even try to have me set up. But how do you ask someone you've made love to a hundred times to get out of your house?

"I think you'd better go back to Ms. Holmes. This relationship isn't working out. Besides, I'll be going off to college soon. Maybe you should be thinking about the same thing."

Maggy fell down at my feet and grabbed my ankles, whimpering and moaning. "You said you was gonna take me with you!"

"I never said any such thing. Now, get up off your knees, girl." I tried to pull free but she tightened her grip on my calves. "I want you to pack your stuff and go."

I felt so disgusted with myself I couldn't breathe. It had been a matter of months since I'd decided to get involved in the streets to earn that tuition money. Now I was living off of crack addicts and my girlfriend had taken the first step toward hell.

The phone rang. I wrenched free from Maggy and ran to it. I was out of breath when I answered the phone.

"We got a meeting with the king of the jungle in an hour," Drama said. "Can you be here in twenty minutes?"

Magdalene lay on the floor, bawling like an infant. "I don't want to go home!" she wailed.

"Man, what is that?" Drama asked.

"Nothing."

"Twenty minutes?"

"I'm there."

As I hung up the phone Magdalene leapt to her feet and started toward me. She threw her arms around me and slowly unbuttoned the first two buttons on my shirt. She squeezed my body close to hers.

Once, this might have made me late for my meeting with Drama. But now? I kept visualizing Pimpin' EZ with his arms around Maggy, slobbering over those luscious red lips.

I pushed myself away and started for the door.

"I know you got to handle yo' business. But don't believe everything Drama be saying. That long-haired nigga be lyin', First."

I cursed Maggy. I called her the B word, something I had never done before.

THEY'RE ONLY YOUR HOMEBOYS AS LONG AS Y'ALL ARE STACKING THAT PAPER. IF TOMORROW FINDS THEM STARING AT TWENTY-TO-LIFE, AIN'T NO TELLING WHAT THEY MIGHT SAY.

CHAPTER
TWENTY-TWO

I STARED OUT OF THE TINTED GLASS IN DRAMA'S CADILLAC AS HE drove Street Life and me to Latin Caesar's house. Caesar's words circled around in my skull like painted wooden horses on a carousel.

"Judas!"

"Thirty pieces of silver."

"Can you sell it to your own people?"

I tried to put my mind on other things. I counted telephone poles. I started a conversation about the Oakland Raiders, but it died quickly.

I figured Drama was as nervous about the next step as I was. All the money I'd earned in the streets sat in a briefcase beneath my feet. Drama and Street Life had put in equal shares. I suspected that Drama still had a small stake somewhere that he wasn't talking about, but everything I had was on the line. Even so, we would still need Latin Caesar to extend us a line of credit for the kilos we needed. It was dangerous asking for credit from killers, but it had to be done. I needed to get out of this world as quickly as possible, and I trusted Drama's instincts.

My stomach tied into knots as Drama turned onto Latin Caesar's block. I slapped a clip into the brand-new Glock .19 holstered on my belt. Drama told me to carry the briefcase with the money in it.

Three gangstas with bandanas tied around their heads stood on the front porch, leaning over the railing, spying out the passing cars. They barely flinched when we pulled into the driveway.

One kid, barely sixteen, ran into the house to alert Latin Caesar that company had come to call. As I watched his back, I recalled the first time Drama and I had come here to do business. The house was swarming with hard, seasoned gangstas, guys with tattoo sleeves and teardrops on their faces. They'd been replaced by young wannabe thugs, kids who were trying to catch some of Caesar's light. There was no warm blood on their sneakers yet. Latin Caesar had let his guard down. Business was good and he had come to trust us.

I liked Latin Caesar but I didn't relish these visits. I was anxious to get this over with so I could go on to college and then begin my illustrious career as an author.

Razor, Caesar's twenty-nine-year-old brother, leered at me as I approached the front door. "What up, college boy?"

Drama and I raised both arms. We'd gone through this routine so many times we didn't even wait to be asked. They searched Drama first, then Street Life. I was searched last.

Razor grabbed my Glock. "You get this back on the way out," he said, then pointed us toward the kitchen. We knew the drill. He followed behind Drama, Street Life, and me.

Zapp's old school jam "More Bounce to the Ounce" ricocheted off the walls at the highest volume on the stereo. The sweet scent of barbecue meat wafted from the backyard.

The beige carpet was worn and tattered. Black boot prints led the way to the kitchen like landmarks on a map. The light in the room streamed in from the windows. A half-eaten burrito wrapped in aluminum foil sat on a paper plate next to a half-chewed green pepper on the table in front of Latin Caesar. His face was pressed into the Metro section of the *San Francisco Press.* He glanced up when we came in. "Eastside O is in the house," he hollered with a tinge of sarcasm.

"What up, Caesar?" Life asked the shadowy figure in the dimly lit room.

"The price of rent in the ghetto, thass whass up." He turned the newspaper in my direction. The headline read, "Gentrification and Redlining Threaten Community."

"College boy," he asked, "you know what gentrification is?"

"Yeah. That's when your favorite burrito spot gets converted into a Starbucks and the catfish restaurant is turned into a tanning salon. The neighborhood gets stripped and poor people get shipped out to the Central Valley to make way for the yuppies. It's a phenomenon that's happening all over the country, especially the Bay Area. This is the most expensive real estate in the country. First they raised the prices so none of us can afford to buy houses here. Next we won't even be able to afford rent. Then it's over. At least the schools will be better and the sanitation will improve. But we won't be here to see it."

Caesar sneered. "How can you know what the word *gentrification* means but you're out there selling dope with these fools?"

Drama's face wrinkled. "Listen, mutha—"

"I'm out here trying to finance my education," I cut in. "Besides, these are my homeboys."

"I feel you on that first part. I was in college until I got caught up. I was an education major." Caesar pursed his lips and rolled his hazel eyes. "I was just hustlin' up a little spending cash on the side until I messed up a cat's money, and I had to get deep in the game to work it off.

"Caesar Chavez said, 'The end of all education should surely be service to others. We cannot seek achievement for ourselves and forget about the progress and prosperity of our community.' That was my theme, man. I also wanted to be a high school teacher back in the day." Latin Caesar balled up his right fist and rubbed it slowly with his left hand.

It wasn't hard for me to picture the leader of GCD in front of a blackboard with an open history book in his hand. Caesar was much more than the clothes and the tattoos. His voice sounded like it belonged to a hundred-and-fifty-year-old man. There was a certain sad wisdom in it.

Latin Caesar caught himself and snapped back. "But these guys..." He nodded at Drama and Street Life. "They're only your homeboys as long as y'all are stacking that paper. If tomorrow finds them staring at twenty-to-life, ain't no tellin' what they might say."

My mind went back to what Drama had told Street Life in the restaurant about the crack game being about money and not friendship.

Caesar sighed. "Firstborn, you betta wake up and get out a this game while you still ain't got no state number. 'Cause once they got you on paperwork, it's hard to get out of the system. The police will be at your house hassling you every time somebody spits on the sidewalk."

Latin Caesar snatched the black leather briefcase from my grasp. He tossed it on the kitchen table and flipped the metal tabs, opening the lid. He licked his thumb and picked up a stack of bills, counting every one. It took him all of four minutes to flip through the stacks of thousands. When he was finished, he glared up at the three of us.

"Life," he scowled, "you told me over the phone that you wanted the monster bundle. But I ain't countin' no monster-bundle money in this bag. We ain't *givin'* away coke up here, you know. What's up?"

Life ambled over to the czar of GCD and placed a heavy hand on Caesar's shoulder. "That's all the money we could scrape together. There's enough in that briefcase to get us half of what we need. We gotta get the rest on credit. Can you front it to us?"

Latin Caesar glared at Life and then at Drama and then at me. The room seemed to grow smaller and darker. A deep belly laugh erupted from Latin Caesar's gut and roared through his mouth. His red nostrils trembled like fish fins.

"We're good for it, Caesar," Drama said. "You'll get your money back with interest."

Latin Caesar clapped his hands twice. "Rudolfo! Get in here."

The floor shook. From the back room came a short, squat, 250-pound thirty-something Latino. He toted three plastic bags, each with brown tape strips around it. That was more coke than I had ever seen at one time.

A luminescent graphic design of a goat's head graced Rudolfo's shirt. Its eyes were dull and burned out. Horns swirled through the top of the skull. Flames erupted at the base of the neck. The whole thing was surrounded by a five-pointed star. The pentagram was a symbol of the devil.

Rudolfo slammed the three packages of cocaine into my open palms. "It's a sixty-forty split in our favor."

"And I want my money back in ten days," Latin Caesar added. "You got it?"

"We got it," Life said.

"Good. And Street Life, I hope you know what you're doing. You're a good man. But if you mess this up, I can't be responsible for what happens."

Drama stepped in front of Street Life. "He knows what he's doin'. We cool."

Latin Caesar's smile evaporated. "What are you, his puppet master? I asked *Life* a question. You got to talk for him?"

Drama's head twisted to the side. He flashed a hate stare at Latin Caesar. But he kept his mouth shut. That made me happy, because if he had openly disrespected Caesar, I was sure there would be more than one corpse laid out in that kitchen.

Street Life diagnosed the situation and pressed for calm. His lips pursed with anger when he looked at Drama. Life had cultivated this delicate partnership and Drama was acting as though he had no appreciation for how fragile our situation was.

Street Life spread out his hands. "This nigga is crazy, Caesar. We got no problem with you. You been cool with us. We cool with you."

"You better be careful this fool don't get you killed, Life," Latin Caesar said, pointing at Drama.

"Easy, Caesar," Drama said. "You gettin' disrespectful here."

Caesar frowned. His lips pressed tight but he didn't say anything else.

When we hit the front door, Street Life slapped Drama on the shoulder. I gasped. Drama hated to be touched. Even when Sandra grabbed him, he cursed her and pulled away like her fingertips were on fire.

I grabbed Drama's arm and pulled him toward the car. "Let's be out, D. Come on, let's go home, man."

He ignored me. He walked double speed toward the car, but before he could open the door, Street Life went off on him.

"Nigga, is you crazy?" Life hollered. "That dude can say whatever he wants in his house. Those vatos could have chopped us up with machetes and no one would ever know what happened to us."

"That gang banger don't scare me. You getting soft or something?"

Life took a couple of steps toward Drama. He was close enough to grab him should Drama have reached for his chrome-plated equalizer.

Drama flashed a hateful smile at him, the sunlight causing his gold teeth to twinkle. "C'mon, let's rock up this work. We got money to make."

Black Christmas was crumbling. Four or five months ago, we were homies; smoking weed, chasing females, and making money. We had hung together and protected one another. Now we were at each other's throats. Tension was rising like smoke levitating through the lips of a volcano. I should have walked away right then and there, but I didn't. I reasoned, in a few weeks, this thing would come to its conclusion and I'd walk away with my tuition money and a nice little nest egg with which to start my new life.

Or so I hoped.

SHE WAS THE ONLY
WOMAN I HAD EVER LOVED.
A TEAR SLIPPED DOWN FROM
BETWEEN MY FINGERS.

CHAPTER
TWENTY-THREE

Just after midnight I sat in the shotgun seat of Drama's Cadillac, bone weary from the business of cutting and bagging crack cocaine. My face felt numb from breathing in the cocaine powder and occasionally getting coke flakes in my mouth (an occupational hazard). As Drama's car pulled up in front of my house, I hesitated to open the door.

Earth, Wind & Fire's "Devotion" thundered from an open window on the second floor. Was someone having a party up there? I craved sleep. My fingers ached from rolling rocks inside little cellophane squares. The music grew louder as I climbed the steps.

When I reached my door on the third floor, I heard ice cubes tinkling in glasses, men talking trash, and women giggling. My heart skipped a beat. That bass-popping thunder was coming from inside my apartment.

I reached for my key, but there was no need. The door stood propped open by a woman's high-heeled shoe. I glanced around my living room in amazement. I didn't recognize a soul. My house was filled with straight hood rats, sipping my beer, smoking my weed, even chomping on my TV dinners. A woman with wide hips and an LA Lakers hat danced alone in the center of the room. A tall, reddish-complexioned man with dreadlocks flicked Marlboro Light ashes on my freshly cleaned carpet.

"Oh, no, you didn't!" I hollered. But I couldn't even hear myself over the music.

Where was Magdalene? I pushed past couples who were twisted up like pretzels, slow dragging to the music. I saw her in the kitchen sandwiched between the refrigerator and the bread counter. A thirtyish woman with a short yellow afro and a silver thumb ring had her arm wrapped around Magdalene's shoulders. Part of her tongue came through the wide gap between her teeth when she smiled. Magdalene held a glass pipe in one hand and a cigarette lighter in the other.

"Maggy?"

Shock caused her jaw to drop. "Oh sh- –" Maggy whispered.

The woman beside her sneered. "Who's that, your old man?"

I crossed the room, ripped the pipe from Maggy's hand, and threw it on the linoleum floor. The pipe shattered. I ground the bits of glass into the linoleum with my sneaker heel.

The older woman's nostrils wrinkled. "Nigga, is you out your mind? That was Black Christmas in that pipe. That rock cost money. I should break you off right—"

I pimp slapped her. She reared back, raising her fists in a boxing pose.

"Listen, Butch," I said, my voice sounding shockingly like Drama's, "you wanna step to me like a man, you gonna get knocked out like one. Now get the hell out of my house before somebody has to call an ambulance to come carry you out."

The back of my hand had left a red print on her cheek. She touched it gingerly.

I raced back to the living room and yanked the stereo's electrical cord from the wall socket. The music went dead. A soft female voice whispered, "Ooh, das her nigga!"

I raised my hands in the air like Moses before the Red Sea. "Party's over. Get out of my house."

Magdalene leaned against the kitchen sink, staring at the bits of glass that sparkled on the linoleum.

"You, too, Maggy. I can't have no crackhead in my house. I want you out of here tonight."

She jogged out of the room with tears streaming down her face. Her head hung down as she shuffled down the hall.

The crowd made quick steps toward the front door. As I watched them leave, I heard luggage being tossed about in the bedroom. Bags were zipped and unzipped. I heard the clang of clothes hangers unhooking from the closet. Then I heard Magdalene calling for a taxicab. "I want to go to Bancroft near Ninetieth Avenue."

That was where Pimpin' EZ lived.

It took Magdalene two trips to get all of her clothes down to the curb. After the second trip, she walked past me like a complete stranger. The door slammed behind her.

With the apartment now empty, I sat on the living room couch with my head in my hands. I wished I'd left Maggy at her mother's house instead of moving her in with me. Now she was on her way to destruction.

I've screwed up bad, I thought.

I couldn't look up for a long while. She was the only woman I had ever loved. A tear slipped down from between my fingers.

IF THERE WAS A GOD, I KNEW THAT ONE DAY WE WOULD HAVE TO ANSWER TO HIM FOR OUR PURPOSEFUL SPOILAGE OF HUMAN POTENTIAL AND OUR VANDALISM OF HIS DREAMS.

CHAPTER
TWENTY-FOUR

THE BLACK CHRISTMAS MOB DIVERSIFIED. THERE WAS PLENTY of demand for rock and flake cocaine, so we sold it retail. Before we put our cocaine on the street, the normal Black Christmas Mob ritual was to stomp on it four or five times. We cut it with B-12 vitamin, Manitol, baking soda, pseudo-caine, baby laxative…whatever we could find. We were extreme capitalists.

Six percent of what our customers sniffed was grown in Bolivia; the other 94 percent could be purchased over the counter from any head shop in San Francisco for pennies on the pound.

This was to be the last batch of drugs that our team would ever put out in the streets. We only tapped the merchandise twice and priced it to move. It didn't take long for word to get out that Black Christmas down in Deep East Oakland had quality merchandise at bargain-basement prices.

Phone calls started coming in from as far away as South City. Petey had a cousin who came over from Modesto to cop two ounces of flake and fat lumps. The cat wasn't home for ten minutes before we were getting calls from his homies.

I had to spend more time on the corner, which I hated. But the workers always seemed to grind a little harder with a pair of eyes locked on their backs. We had to hire more neighborhood kids to act as lookouts.

I had a tinge of guilt about it at first. Our capitalistic enterprise was wicked and depraved, and if there was a God, I knew that one day we would have to answer to him for our purposeful spoilage of human potential and our vandalism of his dreams. But I pushed all that out of my mind. Besides, where else could we sons of the American ghetto stack hella paper like that?

The older people in the neighborhood, the ones who had owned their houses since post–Civil War reconstruction, considered us the enemy. One afternoon I plopped down on Ms. Fredericks's brick stoop and rolled up a fat spliff. I needed something to calm me down. Life out here on the block was no joke. I had to look both ways at all times because I never knew when task force was going to fall on us. They would swoop down from nowhere and then toss us up against the wall and search us and then our vehicles.

When this happened, I could count on the fact that Ms. Fredericks would be watching through her window, nodding with smug satisfaction.

I couldn't blame her. Our trade drew desperate crack fiends and ecstasy-pill-swallowing thugs to her block. It must have been unsettling to look out the window at nine in the morning and see some cat with a glass pipe in his mouth defecating in your vegetable garden or some strung-out crackitute turning a trick on your back porch.

Ms. Fredericks yanked back her gold curtain. She frowned at me as I took a deep pull on the grapes. I really wasn't tripping. I was just a few weeks away from reaching my goal. I had done what no other man or woman before me had been able to do: I had solved the riddle of the streets. For a minute, I felt like I was Neil Armstrong walking on the moon.

The girls were out thick on the stroll down the street. Truck drivers slowed down to holler out their wish lists. I couldn't see the attraction. Most of these chicks looked wrinkled, sick, and old in their low-cut blouses and miniskirts.

I noticed a new girl on the track. She was young and fresh. She walked with an exaggerated swagger designed to accentuate her curvaceous hips.

Something about the girl in the spiked heels and cheap purple lipstick looked familiar. Suddenly a feeling harsher than death overtook me. "Petey, hold things down for a minute. I'm gonna go check something out."

I bolted down the block and across the street for a better look. It couldn't be her.

But when I looked into her face, my brain convinced me to trust my eyes. When I spoke, my voice quivered. "Maggy?"

"What?"

"Girl, what are you doing out here?"

"Gettin' money, same as you."

"Magdalene, selling rock ain't the same as selling tail."

"We all do what we got to do," she said matter-of-factly.

"You ain't got to be out here like this," I exclaimed with outstretched arms and open palms.

"I wouldn't be if you'd hit me off with a couple of rocks."

I thought my knees were going to give way. I held on to a light pole in case I should fall.

An old maroon Ford van with a blue handicapped-parking sticker in the window puttered to the corner. The unshaven man in the driver's seat could have been a stunt double for Tutankhamen's mummy. Magdalene trotted over to the driver's window. She leaned in and whispered something. They negotiated for about thirty seconds and then she opened the passenger door. The old geezer licked his chops and clucked his tongue against the roof of his mouth. He was actually drooling. Pink woolen blankets pinned over the back windows of his vehicle discouraged prying eyes.

"Magdalene," I cried.

She stared out the van's front window as if in a state of hypnosis. The old man's blinker signaled a right turn, then he disappeared with the woman I had once desired to bear my children.

I stood there, lost, motionless, and mute, afraid that if I took a deep breath my atoms and molecules would scatter to the four winds. It took several minutes to collect myself enough to walk back to the corner without breaking into tears.

Cats were staring at me. Some of the guys snickered behind their hands.

What had Pimpin' EZ done to Magdalene? I was ready to give the fool a long-overdue straightening out.

Half an hour later, Drama appeared. His long hair hung down in a single ponytail, a new style for him. He wore a black two-piece denim hook-up with brand-new red-and-white Adidas. "My nigga, Firstborn! Show me some California love, son." He folded me into a bear hug.

I stared back at him blankly. "Man, Pimpin' EZ got Maggy out on the track. Can you believe that? I been waitin' for you to get here so we can get at that nigga. You strappin'?"

Drama sighed. "I told you 'bout that girl, man. How you know she don't just want to get out there and make him some money?"

I was incensed by his insinuation. He was talking about my woman. I started toward my car, cussing under my breath. I picked the Glock .19 off the back tire of my car, where I had hidden it. I tossed it in my jacket pocket and leapt behind the steering wheel. "You comin' with me or not?"

Drama shook his head and frowned. He clearly didn't want to get into this, but he followed me to my car just the same. I jammed the key into the ignition and revved the engine. Drama sucked his teeth. "Aw, man. All right, let's go."

We rode in silence. I drove straight for the pink house in the middle of the block where the pimp god lived with his mother.

The front yard looked like Yosemite National Forest. You could have lost a baby elephant in those weeds. The sorry chump could have at least cut his mama's lawn. I felt sure he was living there rent free.

Pimpin' EZ's dented, mud-colored bucket was parked out front. "I hope that nigga be home," I muttered.

Drama led the way to the door and knocked twice. Pimpin' EZ opened up without looking through the peephole or asking who was there. That was dumb.

I aimed the business end of my Glock between his eyes. It took all the self-control I could muster to keep from squeezing the trigger and just accepting my murder case.

"Wha- –?" I detected a slight smile twitching at the corners of his lips.

"You gonna put my woman out on the street? How can you disrespect me like that?"

Pimpin' EZ put his hands up in mock terror. "Ooh! The gangsta has come to get me!" He laughed. "Lame, get out my face. Don't you know betta than to pull a gun on a thorough-bred nigga like me 'less you intend to use it?"

What did it take to get through to this fool?

"I don't know what you mad at. That freak chose me."

The gun felt heavy in my right hand. I let it drop to my side. "Magdalene's barely outta high school. She ain't no hooker."

"She ain't? What was she doing when you saw her, studying for her SATs?"

I grabbed the muzzle of the gun and pistol-slapped him across the crown of his head. The harder I gun-butted Pimpin' EZ, the better I felt. I'd have to break his skull to feel any real sense of relief. No problem, I had a little time on my hands.

Blood gushed from a cut above his left eye. I slammed him just under the ear. He went down.

"Drama," he screamed, "get your boy!"

My friend tried to reason with me, but the demon of killing had jumped on my back. Blood beat in my ears like conga drums.

P.E. fell to the carpet and curled up in a fetal ball, his hands covering his head. I smashed his fingers with the gun butt as if I were killing roaches. "That was my woman, you low-life son of a—" I took aim.

Drama wrapped his arms around me. "Remember Alston, man. He ain't worth it. You gonna get out the East. Soon you can forget about Magdalene, forget about him, forget about all this. Don't throw it away on account a Pimpin' EZ. 'Sides, she's strung now. Murking him won't change that."

As Drama pulled me toward the door, Pimpin' EZ screamed, "That's right, nigga. She's strung out on crack. Black Christmas crack!" He gave a weird laugh.

I broke away from Drama and busted him one in the mouth. My knuckles throbbed. His front two teeth had made indents in my flesh.

Drama locked his arm in mine and dragged me toward the door. It was no easy task.

Pimpin' EZ hollered at me all the way to the door. "I'm gonna teach you a lesson 'bout these streets, playa. I'm gonna make you sorry for puttin' yo' hands on me."

He cursed me from behind the closed door.

I didn't trust myself to drive. Drama took the wheel and turned my car back toward ho track. Magdalene stood out on the block, swinging her pocketbook by its chain. Her wig was crooked. Her lipstick was smeared. I couldn't get over how quickly she had aged in such a brief span of time.

The track stole light from the eyes of many a young girl. Sadistic tricks and greedy killer pimps worked some of the young women until their good looks were erased and all the youth was squeezed out of them. The pimps threw them away when they couldn't earn anymore. Maggy's future was now written in stone. And I'd have to take some of the blame for that.

Maggy quick stepped away when she saw us drive up. I should have hopped out of the car and thrown my arms around her, but I was too proud.

"Magdalene, get in the car," I said with a flick of my head. "I'm taking you home."

Her head dropped. She dabbed at a tear in her right eye. But she didn't stop walking.

Drama zoomed away from the curb. "Forget her, man. She's lost inside that pipe now."

He's right, I thought. Still, all the feelings I had for her swelled inside my chest. I wanted to burst out crying, but I dared not.

Within two weeks, Magdalene became the star of whore stroll. Every hour or so, Pimpin' EZ's moldy Mustang would pull up to the curb. She'd empty her purse into his smooth, manicured hands and then watch as he drove off. Sometimes he sat at the end of the block with the engine off, reading the newspaper with one eye and watching Magdalene work with the other. Some days, he taped black garbage bags across the side windows of his car and let her take her tricks in the backseat.

Everybody knew that Maggy had been my girl. It was embarrassing. Cats looked at me and cupped their hands over their mouths to whisper about the talk of the hood. I had to get Magdalene off that corner. Kidnapping crossed my mind. For two grand, I could have hired a couple of heavyweights I knew from Hayward to roll up, toss her in the back of a stolen car, and zoom off. We'd meet at an agreed-upon location and then I'd zip my homegirl over to a rehab. But no, she'd escape back to the stroll the first chance she got.

I thought about dropping a dime to the police. I knew that wouldn't do any good. Cops drove by whore stroll day and night, rarely stopping. And why should they? In a city where black men shot one another like rabbits during hunting season, who's going to look twice at a bunch of hookers?

Three weeks went by since we'd exchanged our last words. I watched Maggy one morning as she sashayed beneath the palm branches in white hip boots and a tight black miniskirt. Not much was moving on our end of the block. We might have sold four rocks in the span of an hour. Around eleven, Petey said, "Firstborn, I'm running up to Butchie's to get us some sodas. You want a sandwich or something?"

"Naw. Thanks, though."

A black Lincoln Town Car with tinted windows slid up beside Magdalene. She leaned into the driver's side window. I cursed under my breath.

A dark shadow fell over me and tapped me on the shoulder. A grisly voice growled, "Nigga, break yo'self."

I was being robbed.

"Keep your eyes front. Don't look at me."

I didn't recognize the voice. The stick-up man poked my ribs with the iron barrel of a gun. I weighed my options in a nanosecond. If I gave this guy trouble, he might blast me. If I gave him the money, every thug this side of the San Francisco

Bay Bridge would feel compelled to try me. I'd be labeled a mark. I cursed myself for being so careless.

I slowly reached into the left pocket of my hoodie and pulled out a wad of bills. Cold fingertips with long, scratchy fingernails scraped my hand as the gunman snatched the bank roll.

"The other pocket too."

I complied. He snatched a larger clump of bills that were folded over and held together with a rubber band. He got close to three thousand dollars.

The jacker cackled like a mother hen. "I been watching you, Firstborn."

The guy knew my name. I ventured a glance over my shoulder, hoping to see something that might help me identify him. His nose had been broken, probably more than once. He wore a thick goatee. There was a gold wedding band on his left hand.

"Nigga, I told you not to look at me! I should blow your brains out."

Out of the corner of my eye, I saw Petey emerge from Butchie's. A pretty young Tongan girl from up the block was gabbing in his ear. She wrote her phone number in the palm of his hand.

Petey cracked a smile. Then his gray eyes glanced in my direction. He studied the situation like a gypsy reading tarot cards. The smile evaporated.

"Nigga, you soft," the gunman sneered. "This is easy money. What you got in your socks, fool?" He hadn't brushed his teeth that morning. His breath smelled like spoiled buttermilk.

Petey jogged toward us. When he made it to the corner, his hands reached into his windbreaker pockets.

One of my boys hollered, "It's a stick-up!"

I felt the pressure of the gun against my ribs cease. The stick-up man pushed me to the side and took off down the street like a track star.

Twin .38 caliber pistols sprung from Petey's left and right pockets, barking fire. Petey was shooting with both barrels. A rush of gun smoke filled the air. I ducked for cover. The windshield of a new canary yellow Corvette exploded. The car alarm shrieked. Empty bullet casings clicked on the sidewalk. The jacker flew down the street with bullets whizzing over his head. He turned the corner and disappeared.

The fellas surrounded me and checked for bullet holes.

Petey turned me around in a circle, inspecting my torso. "You all right, First?"

"What are you, a doctor?"

His jaw dropped.

"You're supposed to wait until I'm out of the way before you start shooting," I hollered. Petey could have killed me.

Drama pressed his way through the small crowd. "What happened?"

"A cat robbed me, that's all."

"That's all? Firstborn, you can't be slippin' out here. Don't you know the first rule of the street is that sleep is the cousin of death? You gotta keep your mind on your business. Sometimes I don't understand you, man. I swear..."

He looked down the block at Pimpin' EZ, who was lounging next to his car with the *Wall Street Journal* stock report open in his hands. "Now I see what's on your mind." Drama shook his head and bit his bottom lip until the blood ran. "Pimpin EZ," he said so softly I could barely hear him, "you done finally torn your behind."

I was a nervous wreck. I had lost my woman to the streets. I'd been robbed and nearly killed. Drama was losing faith in my ability to hold down my end. What else could go wrong? Unfortunately, I was about to find out.

CHAPTER
TWENTY-FIVE

DRAMA AND I MAINTAINED A ROOM AT THE WILSHIRE MOTEL under my name. I was the only member of our team who was supposed to visit room 236, where we kept the company finances and stash. I always went alone. That was the way Drama wanted it. Too much traffic would bring suspicion.

My responsibility was to get the drugs to the cut house and then out to the streets. After a package was through, we split a percent of the profits. The majority of our money was invested back into the business and ended up at the motel. Most of the money we'd earned so far was tied up in this last major deal with Latin Caesar, so the iron box was bulging with paper. I also kept most of my personal savings in that safe. I couldn't very well take it the bank.

I realized I was taking foolish chances. I knew all too well what Po-Po would do if they ever found me in that motel room with all that yayo and cash. I kept my fingers crossed every time I turned the key to the room.

One afternoon, when it was time to re-up, I climbed the steps of the Wilshire. I walked into our room and slid the closet door open. I twisted the heavy black dial on the safe, left, right, left. I reached inside and yanked out half a brick of raw. I threw the cocaine in my backpack, left the room, and closed the room door behind me. I glanced both ways before trotting back down the steps and making my way to the car.

When I got back to the corner, Drama was holding a conversation with two of our runners. He never stopped talking but I noticed that he was watching my approach from the corner of his eye. I flipped the duffel bag off my shoulder and handed it to Street Life. Life threw it into the back of his car. He was going to take it Sonia's place, where it would be rocked up.

My job done, I headed back toward the car. I needed to go to the library. The Fraternal Order for the Upliftment of Humanity had written to me, requesting an essay on why inner-city students should be admitted to the institution. I had several ideas whirling around in my mind.

Seconds after I hopped back into the driver's seat, Life pounded on the hood of my car. He peeped at me through his yellow shades. "Hey, man, come out here and spark this joint with me."

I really didn't want to. I couldn't spare the time. Besides, I needed my full creative mind to write the essay. But I dared not deny him. Life wouldn't have understood. He lived to drop fifty-dollar tips on his barber and lay up with any female foolish enough to say yes.

Life and I never hung out. We rarely even spoke to each other except about things relating to business. I shrugged and got out of the car.

"Man, I gotta say, you've surprised me," Street Life said. "I didn't think you'd last out here. In the beginning I wondered why Drama even put you down with us. But you've held up your end and you kept us off the radar screen. You took care of business."

While I listened to Street Life babbling, I saw Pimpin' EZ drive up to whore stroll. He got out of his car sporting a two-piece Brooks Brothers suit, a pair of Stacey Adams lace-ups, and a Stetson hat that only half covered a bandage on his head the size of small child's bedsheet. He looked down the block in our direction and raised both of his middle fingers.

Street Life glanced at Pimpin' EZ and then back at me. He busted out laughing. I assumed that he'd heard what had gone down in P.E.'s living room.

Pimpin' EZ loped his arm across Magdalene's shoulders. I shuddered. She looked like she'd aged ten years.

Maggy shrugged at his touch. They exchanged angry words. I heard snippets of profanity coming from both of their mouths.

Pimpin' EZ grabbed Magdalene by the shoulder and flung her around. Then he slapped her.

One of the boys on my corner hollered, "Firstborn, you better go see 'bout your woman!"

I took half a step toward the corner. Drama clamped his hand down on my shoulder. "Cuz, you already tried to help her. She didn't want your help. She done chose, so let her handle her business. Don't let yourself get distracted."

Magdalene connected with a slap of her own.

"Handle that nigga, Magdalene!" Life's brother Billy hollered.

I gasped in horror. I remembered Pimpin' EZ's rule: "Never let a nigga put his hands on you in the street and walk away." I wondered if that applied to women.

In a dazzling streak of silver light, the sun struck the tip of a .007 survival knife. A blood-curdling scream turned into a moan, then a shudder. It sounded like Magdalene called my name, but I couldn't be sure. Her frame dropped to the pavement.

I broke free from Drama's grasp and raced down the street. I pulled back one spectator after another until I finally reached Magdalene. She lay in a puddle of blood, deep gashes on her neck and chest.

Sirens sang in the distance. The eyewitnesses split like roaches when the lights come on. Drama grabbed my shoulders and yanked me away from Magdalene's lifeless form. He uttered four words that I knew would echo in my sleep for the rest of my life: "The streets got her."

Drama whirled his finger twice in the air. Our runners read the signal. In thirty seconds the corner was deserted.

CHAPTER
TWENTY-SIX

Drama shoved me into the passenger seat of his car. We could not maintain vigil over Magdalene's body. The police would be there any minute. So we did what we had to do. We left her bleeding corpse on the sidewalk and drove off.

The image of Magdalene's broken body tortured my mind. But I fought to conceal my weakness in front of Drama. I didn't want to let him see me weep.

I cursed under my breath. *Why did I put my hands on Pimpin' EZ? He told me he'd make me pay.*

"Where do you want to go?" Drama stared pensively at the concrete-and-asphalt corridors of his ragged kingdom, his left hand on the steering wheel.

"Anywhere. Just get me away from here." I buried my face in my hands. "Magdalene is dead, man. She's dead!"

"I'm sorry, man."

"That's all you can say? 'I'm sorry'?"

"What do you want me to say?"

"Nothin'."

"Tell me what you want me to say and I'll say it."

My brain was splitting in two. I felt like a passenger on a jet plane that was falling out of the sky over the ocean. My woman was dead and I had as much to do with her killing as Pimpin' EZ had.

Drama's expression never changed. It was just another day on the dope track for him. I wanted him to say that everything would be all right, but Drama wasn't God. He couldn't resurrect Maggy.

"Was this really worth it?" I heard myself ask.

He sighed. "We did what we had to do. Magdalene made her own decisions. She was a big girl. And Pimpin' EZ...he's low."

We crossed the San Francisco Bay Bridge and zipped past the upscale boutiques of the center city and across Market Street. Twenty minutes later, we stopped in front of a posh little spaghetti nook on Columbus Street in North Beach.

"I'm hungry," Drama said. "Let's get some spaghetti and sausage."

I didn't need food. All I wanted was a drink. I wanted to get blind drunk.

When we walked into the restaurant, a waiter in a shiny black suit and spiked haircut flashed a "Leave me a big tip" smile. We were the only blacks in the place.

Drama asked for two bourbons and then told the waiter to come back for our food orders.

The waiter was back with two shot glasses filled to the brim. When I reached for mine, my hand shook. Drama started to say something comforting but his cell phone rang. It was a crooked cop feeding Drama information.

"Get down to the Wilshire right now."

All of our business money, our drugs, our entire future was in room 236 at the Wilshire, and this crooked cop was telling us to get down there. He hung up before Drama could ask for details.

I threw two twenties on the plastic red-and-white-checkered tablecloth. Two white-haired tourists in baby blue Bermuda shorts and knee socks gaped at us as though we had rap sheets stenciled on our shirts.

Drama dashed through the doors and out to the Caddy, with me on his heels. He twisted the key in the ignition and hollered, "Hold on."

We took the hills of San Francisco like a roller-coaster. The front bumper banged on the asphalt, momentarily lifting us off our seats. The tires squealed as they peeled around tight corners. Drama mashed down the accelerator.

We took the Bay Bridge and then flew down 580 to the all-too-familiar whine of sirens and the flash of red lights.

When we arrived at the Wilshire parking lot, I saw black-and-white police cars parked at weird angles. We came to a stop about half a block away from the action.

The door to motel room 236 stood open. Two beefy white cops wrestled a heavily muscled black man down the stairs. He twisted and resisted like a runaway slave, but he could not escape. They had cuffed his hands behind his back. His ankles were shackled.

In unison Drama and I identified the captive. "Street Life."

A pretty young girl in a black miniskirt followed him with her head bowed. A policewoman walked behind her. The girl's hands were cuffed behind her back. Tears of sorrow and remorse dripped down her face. *That's somebody's daughter.* I thought of all the young men who would give anything to date a beautiful young woman like this—guys on their way to college with good careers ahead of them. What did she want with a thug like Street Life? She was going to follow him to the penitentiary pining about how much she loved him. I'd seen it time and time again. Still, I could never understand it. I chalked it up as one of life's mysteries.

It took two cops to carry the safe down the steps. I cussed out loud. Drama slapped his face hard with the palms of his hands.

I was counting lost money in my mind. All of my risk taking and long hours of street struggle were now sitting in the back of a police van. My tuition money was gone. Where would we get the cash to pay Latin Caesar back?

Drama looked at me grimly. "We dead now, homie."

I knew he was right.

CHAPTER
TWENTY-SEVEN

DRAMA'S TIRES SMOKED AS WE PEELED AWAY FROM THE CURB. Not a word was spoken as the red Caddy sped back toward my apartment building. There was nothing to be said.

Latin Caesar's drugs were gone. So was his money. And we had less than twenty-four hours to produce the fortune we owed him.

Ten minutes later, we were sitting in front of my building. I was too drained to open the car door. I just sat there and watched the ice cream man serving cones to little kids still innocent to the ways of the world.

"Do you think Life will snitch us out?" I asked.

"Why would he?"

"The brother's looking at a third strike—possible life in prison. Plus you and he have some major-league funk between you."

Of course, he knew all that.

"How much money you got saved?" I asked him.

"Why?"

"We got to get up some bail money for Life. Maybe you should call your lawyer," I said.

"Wake up, Firstborn! Life is washed, man. He had a good thing going. The only thing he had to remember was to take his broke-down hos to some motel other than the Wilshire. But the fool had to bring her there. That chick looked no more than fifteen years old." Drama played with one of his braids. "You can't even *give* some niggas money."

"We have to get out of town for a while."

"Where?"

"I have family in Mills Creek."

"Louisiana?"

I nodded.

"What'll we do for money?"

"I don't know. But at least we'll be alive."

Drama took off his burgundy-and-gold baseball cap and blew at a speck of lint. "I'm alive here, Firstborn. The town is my home, and I ain't runnin' nowhere."

I stared up at the car roof, too emotionally wrecked to utter a single syllable. How could I explain my financial shortfall to the research team at Alston? What would I say? *"The tuition money was confiscated in a police raid"*?

Drama looked at me and smiled. "It ain't too late, ya know."

"What you talkin' about?"

He cocked his right eyebrow and folded his fingertips into a triangle. "What if I said I had a way to get the money we lost and more? And what if I told you I could get it in two days?"

"Without bloodshed?"

Drama tilted his head to the side. "Firstborn, do you remember when I asked if you could shoot a nigga in the face if it came down to it?"

"Yeah."

Drama grinned like a grandfather giving a child the answer to a riddle. "It's come down to it."

He started the car and we drove back to my neighborhood in thick silence. When we arrived at my front door, I opened the car without a word passing between us.

Drama sped off without so much as looking at me.

I knew how Drama got down. If you pressed his back against the wall, you had to expect him to come out blasting. That's what he knew. So far, I had journeyed through this great ordeal without having to squeeze my gat at anyone's dome. According to Drama, that was going to have to change.

My girl was dead. My money was gone. And Drama was talking about going toe to toe with a homicidal maniac to whom we owed a fortune. There was nowhere to run.

I glanced up at my apartment windows. I almost expected to see Maggy staring out, waiting for me to come home. The windows were dark. I walked up the stairs and then twisted the key in my apartment door, holding my breath in the silent hall.

When I opened the door, Magdalene's perfume swelled in my nostrils. In my mind's eye, I saw her punctured corpse, flung cold and lifeless to the curb like a broken rag doll, old bubble gum stuck in her hair.

I reclined in my brown leather easy chair and stared into the empty cavity in my television set. Broken glass glittered in the beige carpet.

A bizarre thought came to my mind. I attempted to squash it out like an old cigarette but it kept coming back. I fished in my wallet for Oliver's wrinkled card. I called his number before I could change my mind.

"Firstborn, my main man. Praise the Lord. How are you?"

"Not good. Magdalene got stabbed to death today. And some head busters from Jingle Town might kill me tomorrow."

Oliver gasped. "Let me come get you. Where do you live?"

"I wish it was that easy. But Drama—"

"Son, you better start taking care of yourself. I grew up in the East. I know something about the Dramas of this world. He only cares about himself. You need to think about you. I know the streets. You're not safe where you are. You can't be afraid of what the homies might say if you get outta Dodge."

The thought had entered my mind.

"Boy, if you don't wake up soon, your tombstone is gonna read 'Here lies Firstborn Walker. He worried about what niggas thought.'"

I almost laughed.

"I've told my wife about you. We can put you up until you decide what you want to do. Let me come and—"

I clicked the phone off. I came close to giving Oliver my address and packing a bag. But Drama was like my brother. I couldn't leave him. Latin Caesar had an army and an arsenal at his fingertips. And we owed him a big chunk of money. It wouldn't be long before he sent a reconnaissance team across East Seventy-third, strapped down with AK-47s and AR-15s, hunting for two out-of-luck crack slangers named Drama and Firstborn.

I reached under the couch cushion and snatched up my .44 and a box of bullets. My fingers trembled as I filled the Magnum with shells. I shivered in the dark, the loaded elephant stopper in my lap. I sat motionless for a half hour or so before walking to the bedroom like a zombie. I flopped onto the bed, the pistol cradled in my arms like a teddy bear.

Before I closed my eyes, I wondered what I would have to do to get the money Drama had dangled in front of me like a carrot before a greedy rabbit. For a moment I wished I'd never heard of Alston University.

CHAPTER
TWENTY-EIGHT

BLACK CHRISTMAS OPENED FOR BUSINESS WITH JUST ENOUGH coke to last until the close of business that day. About eleven, an unmarked black car hovered around our corner. The Hawk descended from it and waved in our direction. She held up a burgundy-and-gold Boston College baseball cap. Street Life's cap.

The Hawk pulled a disposable lighter from her pocket, flicked the flame on, and set the cap ablaze. She dropped the burning cloth in the street and stomped out the fire with her shiny black boots. Who could have mistaken the message? Street Life was sitting in the Santa Rita jail, staring at thirty to life.

Two little girls with pigtails and missing front teeth raced up to the Hawk's car like it was Santa's sleigh. She bent down and embraced them, pecking each one on the cheek. They grinned bashfully.

I had no love for the Hawk. She was slowing our flow. When the police showed up, our trade disintegrated. And with everything that was going on, we sure couldn't afford to have our money supply interrupted.

A ten-year-old boy paraded down the steps of his apartment building with an NFL football tucked under his arm. The Hawk clapped and held out her hands. The kid heaved the ball in her direction. It bounced ten feet away. The Hawk ran to the football and scooped it up. "Go out for a pass!"

The kid took off like he was Jerry Rice in his prime. The Hawk lobbed a nice spiral right into his arms.

I felt conflicted. In a perfect world, that kid should have been able to come out on his block day or night to play. However, this world was far from perfect.

Mr. Hall, the local mailman, marched out of his front door and down the street with a glass of lemonade in his hand. He handed it to the Hawk.

Needless to say, we weren't making any money.

Drama sat on the stoop of an abandoned building, his lips forming a tight line of anger. About noon, Renee plopped down on the steps between me and a silent but red-with-rage Drama. She had purple-and-white strands mixed into her long weave. She chomped down hard on two clumps of well-chewed grape bubble gum.

"What it do, baby?" she asked my business partner.

Drama grunted.

The Hawk clapped as the kid snagged his seventh catch in a row.

"Having a hard day?" Renee asked.

He twisted his head in her direction, curling his top lip. "What you think?"

The Hawk caught another pass. Drama cursed her under his breath.

"I'd do anything for you, Drama, you know that. It's almost like you my man."

Drama wagged his forefinger back and forth. "Don't even go there, Renee. I ain't *almost* anything. Just 'cause I rocked your world four or five times, that don't mean I'm your man."

Her eyes flickered with pain.

Drama stared back at the corner. "My woman would have to be down for whatever. I'd have to be able to trust her with my life."

"You can trust me, Drama. That's on the real."

"How real?"

"Like I said, I'd do anything for you."

Drama glanced up at me and Petey. "Boys, you heard her."

Drama was never one to talk just to feel his lips moving. Everything he said emerged from deep contemplation and planning. Everything meant something—one could only wonder what.

About one in the afternoon, the Hawk jumped in her car and sped off. We all breathed a collective sigh of relief. She wasn't gone for five minutes before the patients started lining up. Whores rushed down side streets and popped out of alleys. The ten-year-old wide receiver ran back upstairs. Football practice was over.

Pimpin' EZ climbed out of whatever hole he'd been hiding in. He posted up in front of his Mustang with one ankle folded over the other.

"Come on," Drama said. "Let's go upstairs to the crib."

Sweaty palms poked out at us, all squeezing folded bills. Eyes stared at us, hungry and impatient. Petey gawked at Drama and then back at me. I knew how he felt. If you could have looked into my eyes at that moment, you would have seen twin images of Benjamin Franklin staring back at you. I was going to need money to either make a fast getaway from Oaktown or to bribe Latin Caesar into allowing us to stay alive for another twenty-four hours.

"We should get this money before the Hawk comes back," Petey said.

"We got business to tend to," Drama responded.

What business could there be to attend to upstairs?

Drama turned his back on the line of patients. Petey and I followed. After a few steps, he made an about-face and turned to Renee, who had remained on the steps. "You comin', girl?"

A broad grin broke out on her face. She jumped up and trotted behind us.

Ms. Velvet's head popped up as we burst through her front door. She turned up the radio volume a few notches. Taut lines stretched across her forehead. "What good is it for a man to gain the whole world, yet forfeit his soul?" she hollered behind us. "Or what can a man give in exchange for his soul?"

"Yeah, Mama, whatever," Drama said.

We followed him into the bedroom, which doubled as our business office. I picked up a wrinkled T-shirt from off a chair and sat down. The air was so thick with tension that I struggled to breathe.

Drama pried a plastic bag from his pocket. He took a big pinch of purple from the bag and dropped it in a tobacco leaf. After the blunt had been rolled, he handed it to me. I lit it and took a big pull. The first couple of hits were all tobacco leaf, but on the third try I could taste the herb. I passed it to Renee, who sat on the bed next to Drama.

She took a big hit, held it in her lungs, and expelled. She did this three times and then passed it to Drama. After he had smoked some, he passed the weed to Petey.

Drama folded his hands over his stomach and stared into Renee's bloodshot eyes. She ran her fingers through his long hair.

"So," he said so softly I could barely hear him, "you want to be my woman, do you?"

"Sho' you right, Drama."

"And you'd do anything for me?"

"Anything."

Drama leaned forward and whispered something in her ear. The blood rushed from her face. Her left eye twitched. She shook her head twice.

"If you wanna be my woman, you gonna have to put in work."

Renee's eyes wandered around the room as if she were searching her heart for the courage to do whatever evil Drama had tempted her to perform. I knew what she was wondering. Did she love Drama enough to walk past the point of no return for him? She'd have to answer that question quickly. Drama was not a patient man.

"I can't do it!" A tone of desperation vibrated in her voice.

Drama bolted up from the bed and turned his back to her, his arms folded over his chest. "Get out of my face. I don't even want to look at you. You ain't worthy of me, Renee."

She tugged at his bare arm. It remained tight and unyielding.

"Petey, get her outta here. I can't have nobody 'round me who won't sacrifice."

Petey lumbered toward her as if invisible chains were wrapped around his ankles. Before his shadow fell on her, she threw up her hands in resignation. "Okay, Drama, I'll do it. I'll do it."

Drama bolted across the room to his closet, which was brimming with expensive, high-fashion hip hop wear. Stuffed in the rear, behind a row of six hoodies, was a bulletproof vest. Drama yanked it out and tossed it to Petey. "Strap her up, dawg."

Petey hesitated. "You sure you're up to this, Renee?"

She bit her lip and then snapped, "Put it on me, fool!"

Petey shrugged. Renee stuck out her arms, allowing the black Kevlar body armor to be slipped over her head. Petey pulled down the two side straps. The vest fit like a tailor-made body bag.

"Now, that's my girl." Drama slapped on a latex glove and slipped his hand under his pillow. The gloved hand came out with a jet black Glock .19. Its serial numbers had been shaved off. We had kept that gun for a desperate day—the day we needed to do somebody with a piece that couldn't be traced back to us. Judging by the way things were shaping up, this was that day.

Drama's hand dove between the mattresses; this time he came up with two clips. He loaded a clip in the chamber, handed the pistol to Renee, and slipped the second cartridge into the jacket's side pocket. Renee's body trembled.

"All right, girl," Drama said. "It's time to go handle your bidness."

Petey stepped up to Drama. "Don't do this, man. That girl ain't like us. She ain't never gonna come back from this, blood. You got some business you need handled, let me handle it. I ain't afraid a no dirty work. Why you wanna do this to her?"

Drama's face flushed. He cussed so loud that Ms. Velvet yelled, "Boy, what's going on in there?"

Drama ignored his mother's question and glared at Petey. "I ain't paying you to ask questions."

Since Petey wasn't getting anywhere, I decided to speak up. "What are you doing, Drama?"

"Will you niggas *please* stay out of my personal business? This is between me and my woman." Drama cupped his hand over Renee's ear and whispered, his right eye cocked in our direction. He looked like a quarterback in a huddle, calling a play.

Renee started crying again.

"You love me, right?" Drama asked.

She nodded three times.

"You gonna do it?"

She nodded again, tears running from her eyes.

Renee took a deep breath as if she thought it was her last. She snatched a blue windbreaker from Drama's grasp and put it on over the vest. She stuck the pistol in the jacket pocket. She grabbed Drama's arm and leaned forward, begging for the kiss that would strengthen her, fortify her will, steel her nerves.

Drama twisted away. "Handle yo' business first."

Drama slapped his burgundy-and-gold Boston College baseball cap down on her head. That and the oversized jacket made her look like a child playing dress-up in Daddy's clothes. Petey rolled up the sleeves so she could use her hands.

She opened the bedroom door, head bowed, shoulders slumped. A parting wheeze escaped from her cherry red lips.

The past few months had been filled with puzzles and mysteries, but the game had now gotten deeper. I felt like I was on the greased sliding board to hell and traveling too fast to jump off.

I heard the clump of Renee's clogs as she jogged down the stairs.

Drama raced to the window. Petey and I peered over his shoulders. Renee strolled halfway through the courtyard, then stared up at the window. Norman, my homeboy from back in the day, sat in a broken wicker chair, his feet resting on a discarded baby stroller. He tilted his cigarette to the side of his mouth and hollered at Renee, "What up, beezy?"

Ignoring him, she marched toward her mission.

She reached the corner, where crack fiends wandered like the damned in Dante's *Inferno*. Mr. Carter sat on a milk crate, a can of malt liquor tilted up to his lips. Two teenage girls with teased hair popped bubble gum and threw gang signs at a passing bus. Renee scampered past them all unnoticed.

Pimpin' EZ wore his two-piece, cream-colored suit with the Stetson's straw brim tilted sideways. He peered at the newspaper, with one eye on his whores. He hardly looked up at the strange-looking teenage girl in the sky blue windbreaker who quick-stepped toward him.

Renee drew within arm's length of Pimpin' EZ before he flinched. She leaned over and said something I couldn't hear from the safety of Drama's window. The newspaper dropped to the asphalt. Pimpin' EZ screamed like a wild boar wounded by a tranquilizer dart.

Renee stretched out her arm. A pistol muzzle emerged from the oversized sleeves of the windbreaker. Her skinny finger squeezed the trigger. Sparks flew. Gunfire clapped. Pimpin' EZ covered his face, perhaps praying that the last dignity of an open-casket funeral not be taken from him. Renee drilled a slug through his navel.

He slumped to the pavement, writhing in agony. A round through his forehead closed the show.

The corner went silent. Everyone vanished. Renee stuck the Glock into her pocket and walked back toward us.

"She did it." Petey's head dropped down and his chin touched his chest. He swished his head back and forth. "She did it," he whispered.

"Sho did!" Drama grinned. "That freak do love me, man."

I stared at Drama like he was a science project gone wild in the lab.

He cocked an eyebrow at me. "Nigga, what is your problem?"

"I hated Pimpin' EZ, too, but that doesn't mean I wanted to see him face down on the sidewalk with his brains blown out."

Drama walked back to the window and shook his head. He hollered down at the corpse, "Pimpin' *ain't* easy, and you should never have put your hands on my family, fool!"

Renee burst through the bedroom door and raced into Drama's arms. Her chest heaved in and out. Her whole body vibrated like a live wire. Drama squeezed her waist and stroked her extensions.

"Do you love me now?" she asked, her voice trembling.

"Always and forever, baby."

Drama looked over her shoulder at us, rolling his eyes and smiling, all the while patting Renee's back.

At that moment I recalled the time months ago when I told Drama that I was down. I really had no idea what that meant. No wonder he and Street Life had smiled at each other when I said those words. The desire to be down took me places that I never thought I would go.

I had just seen a young girl kill a man in cold blood just because Drama had asked her to do it. My partner and I had sipped beer out of the same forty-ounce bottle with Pimpin' EZ, and now he was laid out on the sidewalk, separated from his soul.

"Renee," I asked, "what made Pimpin' EZ scream like that? I mean, you hadn't even pulled out the heat yet."

"I just told him what Drama told me to say."

"Which was?"

"I said, 'Drama say he don't need you no more.'"

Petey removed the jacket and vest like an army medic tending to war wounds. He peeled the BC cap from her head. He grabbed the pistol she had used to commit first-degree murder and stuck it in his own pants pocket.

"Get rid of that properly," Drama ordered Petey. Without another word, Petey spun on his heels and left to obey Drama's command.

"Now, Firstborn, you go on home and leave me to my business." He kissed Renee's cheeks and massaged her hands.

I was only too glad to leave. But before I hit the door, Drama shouted, "Be back here tonight around ten. We got to go to Jingle Town and take care of that little business."

Drama was still keeping me in the dark. I could have asked what he had planned for Jingle Town but I was afraid. I knew it wasn't going to be pleasant.

By the time I walked down the steps, a circus-like crowd had gathered on the corner, watching the coroner placing Pimpin' EZ in a blue rubber bag. His left hand flopped out, its middle finger extended toward me. Magdalene's diamond friendship ring sparkled on his pinkie finger.

Even dead, Pimpin' EZ had to have the last word.

CHAPTER
TWENTY-NINE

SEA FOAM WASHED UP ON THE HUGE BOULDERS THAT NESTLED the shoreline. A mauve, crimson, and gold sunset married the creamy blue in the soft twilight sky. Kayaks and motorboats bobbed on the whitecaps.

A man and woman with silver hair strolled down the railed walkway that led out into the San Francisco Bay. They were the picture of love, the postcard of understanding. They spoke softly, intimately, telegraphing paragraphs with winks and half phrases, the shorthand of a lifelong journey. Fishermen smiled at the pair as they threw their lines in the water.

Cool air flushed through my lungs. I closed my eyes and let the breezes wash over me. This was the closest thing I had felt to peace in months. I sat on a bench and stared out at the sea. I'd come to the Berkeley Marina many times over the years to think and plan. As I thought about my impending meeting with Latin Caesar, I comforted myself with warm memories of my father.

I thought of Daddy making funny faces over the breakfast table. Of riding on his shoulders as we wove through the dense crowd at the Oakland Zoo. In my mind's eye, I saw Daddy sitting in the overstuffed recliner in Grandma's living room, reading. Daddy was forever studying.

If my dad had lived, how would my life be different?

"Joshua Walker was a brilliant man," Granny said over and over after he was gone. "If only he'd gone to college. If only he'd taken that incredible opportunity that was offered him by the faculty of Alston University."

But Daddy turned down his full-ride basketball scholarship. Nine years later, he was shot to death trying to appropriate reparations from a bank in the name of the people.

When Drama told me he had a way to get me the tuition money I needed to escape the streets of East Oakland, I knew it would be something over the line, but whatever it was, I had to go for it. I didn't want to end up like Daddy, face down in a pool of warm blood and dead dreams.

"Young blood!"

The voice from behind startled me. I spilled soda all over my shirt.

Oliver laughed. "Sorry, man. Didn't mean to scare you."

"Thanks for coming, man." I stood and gave him a hug. A few drops of soda clung to his dusty denim jacket.

He looked different from the two other times I'd seen him. His camel-colored construction boots were worn and scuffed. A yellow plastic hard hat covered his dreadlocks. This was the first time I'd seen him in his work clothes.

Oliver pointed at an empty bench that faced the San Francisco Bay and skyline. I plopped down next to him. "How you feelin'?" he asked.

"I'm sinking, man. Little Chauncey is dead. Maggy is dead. Pimpin' EZ is dead. Street Life got busted in a room full of coke and money. And tonight—"

"Let me guess. Your homeboy Drama has a plan to get crazy money and deal with these killers at the same time."

"How'd you know?"

"What does the tat on my neck say?"

I didn't have to look. I knew it read Deep East Oakland.

"Homie, it's time for you to get ghost."

"That's what I told Drama, but he doesn't want to leave."

"Then let him stay."

"I can't do that."

"Why not?"

"I need the money. 'Sides, me and Drama came up together. I can't leave him hanging."

Oliver stared at the rise and fall of the ocean. "Young blood," he said, not taking his eyes off the waves, "did you know they trade privatized prison stock on Wall Street?"

I shrugged. He was touching on things I knew but didn't like to focus on. I sensed that he was going to tell me to take responsibility for what I was doing to black people. That was something I didn't want to think about.

Oliver looked at my glazed expression. "A prison guard makes twice the salary of a public school teacher. In the past twenty years, California has built one college but twenty-one prisons. Add to that the overtime that parole officers and police rake in every year, and the beast is getting fat on the flesh of our brothers and sisters. And what are you doing? Boy, you're helping the machine destroy us!"

I bit my nails, hoping Oliver would make his point and move on to another subject.

"I was like you once. Greedy. Thought only of myself. Never looked into the bloodshot eyes of the people I was destroying. I was so blind."

Oliver let out a short laugh. "One day that will be your blood on the gears of the machine. It'll be your life rotting away behind iron doors. You're on your way to becoming a twenty-first-century slave."

I rolled my eyes at him. "It'll never be me."

"Maybe God has raised you up to fight for us. Maybe you're the one who's supposed to go downtown and tell the mayor we want the same garbage pick-up service in East Oakland that they have on Lakeshore Drive or Piedmont Avenue. Firstborn, maybe you're the one who's supposed to raise Cain about the schools. Maybe you're the one who can help us get some jobs and some after-school programs for the kids. Why, I'll bet you could even *be* the mayor one day."

I clucked my tongue against the roof of my mouth. "Man, are you one of those bleeding hearts who feel they have to help the whole world?"

"Not the whole world, just you," Oliver said, his eyes narrowing. "If I reach you, you can do the rest. God gave you all the tools. If I could just help you see...make you care..."

"My father cared. Know where that got him?"

"Who was your father?"

"Joshua Walker."

Oliver shook his head slowly. "Yeah, young blood, I knew your father. And you're right: he did care."

"You knew my dad?"

"I knew him when I was out in the streets. He used to stand on the corner, preaching about black nationalism and black unity. I used to laugh at him. For me, if it didn't make dollars, it didn't make sense. But when I was in the joint, I did something he once told me to do."

"What's that?"

"I started memorizing quotes from famous black people. I still remember a lot of them. Marian Wright Edelman, a great advocate for children, said, 'Never work for power or money. They won't save your soul or help you sleep at night.'"

I couldn't speak to the soul-saving part of that, but I reasoned that if I had Donald Trump's money I would sleep just fine at night. Still, I listened as Oliver kept the quotations coming.

"Martin Luther King said, 'A man who will not die for something is not fit to live.'"

I had a lot of respect for King. But Drama's words drowned him out in my mind. "Don't get sentimental. It's all about the money. Everything else is pure nonsense." I folded my arms over my chest. Oliver wasn't living in the real world. Yet out of respect I listened as he continued to spit knowledge.

"'I have no mercy or compassion in me for a society that will crush people and then penalize them for not being able to stand up under the weight.' That was Malcolm X. My favorite quote is from boxer Joe Louis: 'I made the most of my ability and did my best with my title.'"

I cut Oliver off. "I come to you for advice and you're quoting from the encyclopedia?"

"Brother man, will you open your eyes and peep some *real* game for a second? I'm talking about you, son! God has blessed you with the ability to help our people. You can't throw that away chasing a dollar. What if Moses had said, 'Forget those Hebrews. If I play my cards right, I'll be the next Pharaoh'? What if Frederick Douglass had said, 'Forget those Negroes in bondage. I've got my freedom.' Why, we might be back in Mississippi today, picking this season's cotton crop."

Oliver's voice was beginning to rise. He had probably rehearsed this speech all day at work, thinking he was going to get me to repent and turn over a new leaf. Well, it wasn't that simple. I had seen too much to just turn around. Still, he had my interest.

"What if Mahatma Ghandi had said, 'Forget this struggle. I can stack my chips if I go into private law practice. Think of the mansion I could have!' History would have been changed. Son, you're trying to gain the whole world, but you're going to lose your soul in the process. Wake up, young blood. Wake up!"

I whistled softly.

"You can't hear me because you're a nigga."

I bolted up from the bench, my muscles tightened. "A nigga?"

"Isn't that what you and your boys call each other? The word stems from the Latin root *Niger*, which means 'dead one.' Every time you look at a black man and call him nigga, you're calling him 'dead one,' and you're right. You're all mentally dead, spiritually dead, intellectually dead. You're in spiritual darkness, yet you shun the light. You are mentally dead, yet you revel in your death and curse the resurrection."

I never met a hustler who didn't think about death. And though most people in the streets aren't churchgoers, almost all of them believe in God. When you look at a friend with his head blown off because he walked through a door one step before you did, you tend to believe that Somebody you can't see has spared your life. When a judge sends you home when you should be doing life, you know that Someone has just given you another chance to get it right. People in the game wear crosses not only as jewelry but because they believe. They might not have repented, but they do believe.

Belief came hard for me. I wasn't ready to let go of my freedom. However, my hold was slipping. Two months ago, I would have greeted everything Oliver was saying with a cynical grin.

But folks say that the great Somebody has a time for things to happen. Perhaps this was that time. I sat forward to hear Oliver speak.

"Firstborn, if you choose the light, you could save a lot of brothers. They would listen to you. But first you gotta assassinate that house slave who's livin' inside you, the one who's got you sellin' poison to your own people."

I couldn't breathe. I was fuming with wrath and indignation. I wanted to curse Oliver, but I couldn't. Because he was right.

I folded my arms over my chest. "Man, you carry a Bible and go to church, but I can still see the streets all over you. You talk about Jesus, but you can't hide where you come from. You're just like me and you've probably done worse."

He sighed heavily. "I'm not proud of my past. I don't like to talk about it, but I guess I have to now." He looked at his boots. "Fifteen years ago, I was rolling down Hegenberger with two of my hood niggas. Po-Po pulled us over. They found two eight balls in the car. None of it was mine, but I wasn't no snitch. I caught five to ten."

It didn't surprise me that Oliver had done prison time. A huge percentage of brothers in the hood have been inside at one time or another. But Oliver didn't talk about it like it was a badge of honor.

He said, "I hated everything about the penitentiary. Most of all the fact that there weren't no females in there, and I thought of myself as somewhat of a ladies' man." He shook his head. "I became the evilest gang-banging nigga in the institution. I had fools writin' home to dey mamas, 'Put some money on my books or this cat gonna shank me up in here.'"

Oliver's visage darkened. For a moment, he looked like he had walked back into hell to resurrect a portion of his rotting past.

"So what happened, man? How did you get out of the game?"

"It was Christmas. I had done four years. I don't care how hard a man is, something happens in your soul around Christmas. The rest of the year, I walked the yard plotting and politicking, but on Christmas Eve I started thinkin' about Mama and the look on her face when the judge pronounced that number and slammed the hammer down. I started thinkin' 'bout my kids and how I couldn't protect them from the wolves outside when I was behind bars. I couldn't put no groceries on the table. And at night, when nobody could see, I started cryin' into my pillow."

I felt a bit embarrassed when he started talking about crying. I associated crying with softness, with weakness. Oliver looked hard. I couldn't picture him with tears in his eyes.

"The next day, these church people from Oakland came out and sang Christmas carols for the inmates. The preacher was this older cat from Oakland. He told us he'd done a little time himself. He told us that Jesus had lived in the hood and that he chopped it up with thugs and thugettes on the block. He talked about how Jesus was executed as an enemy of the state but how even the grave couldn't stop him from coming back because he loved us so much."

My heart started pounding, though I tried to stay calm and collected.

"He told us that Jesus rose from the dead. And that if I repented of my sins and gave my life to him, I could have a new life—eternal life. I needed a new life because I had worn out the old one. He told me that God loved me in spite of all the dirt I'd done and how badly I'd hurt my family and my other victims. He said God wanted to give me a new start."

"And you changed, just like that?"

"No, not just like that. In fact, I'm still changing. A little bit every day. But I knew at that moment my life was different."

I had heard about Jesus. Ms. Velvet talked about him all the time. My father wasn't a Christian but he read the Bible. He used to quote Jesus the same way he quoted Che Guevara. Daddy also used to read to me from the book of Amos in the Bible. I made a mental note to get a copy of the Bible and read it. I needed to find out more about Jesus.

"The hardest part was tellin' my homies I had accepted Christ," Oliver said. "I don't know what it is about folks like us, but no matter how sleazy or low-life our friends are, we want their approval. But those guys weren't really my friends, because they started saying, 'You can't quit us. You the man. We need you to help fight this war. 'Sides, you too strong for that religion stuff.'"

"What did you tell them?"

"I told them they could kiss my—" Oliver cut himself off with a big belly laugh. "Like I said, I'm changing a little bit every day, all praises to God."

"A lot of brothers get saved in the pen, but they go back to the hood when they come home. Why are you different?"

"For me, it wasn't about religion. It was about a relationship with God. I was tired, young blood. I'd tried everything else. So I said, 'Why not give God a chance?' It was the best decision I ever made."

Oliver's face had a glow. He seemed so peaceful. I could see that his decision for God had really worked out well for him.

"First thing I did when I got out of the pen was join a church. Then I went to this free training program for construction. That's where I learned carpentry. The trade unions don't really look at your record as long as you can do the work. I signed up with the local, and I started working steady and making good money. I stepped up and got married to the mother of my children. We were able to buy us a house last year. It needs some work but it's our house."

Oliver pulled the collar of his denim jacket up to meet his chin. The wind was picking up. The sky was almost dark.

"So, what you wanna do, homie? I got a place to take you if you want to walk away from all this, start a new life. And if you're smart, you'll take it. 'Cause I gotta tell you, the stench of death is all around you."

I shivered. I had to change the subject away from death. "If there really is a God, where has he been? Why'd I have to go to a school where the principal padlocked the library because of funding cuts while somebody born in the suburbs ten miles away had their dreams handed to them? If there really is a God, why did the city close down all the health clinics in the ghettos? And why does God let factories and trucks in West Oakland pollute the air with poisonous carcinogens so young kids suffocate with asthma? If there really is a God, why is there such a thing as gentrification?"

Oliver sighed. "Man, God doesn't have a magic wand that he waves over evil to make it go away. He uses people to do his will. When he heard his children crying in Egypt, he didn't send down a laser beam from heaven to blow up Pharaoh's palace. No, he sent Moses. You think the school system is cheating our kids out of a good education? Well, God has given you the strength, knowledge, and wisdom to go down to the next board-of-education meeting to confront whoever's running the school system. God will give you the power to deal with every evil you just mentioned."

Oliver made me think of a quote that my father used to say all the time: "Dare to struggle, dare to win."

"If Alston University is unfairly blocking black kids from enrolling, maybe God is raising you up as a prophet to speak truth to power. If the city doesn't want to improve sanitation pick-up in the East, it's up to you to go to city hall and get on the speaker's list at the public forum. God has put you in a free society where you can hold elected officials accountable. You're asking, 'Where is God?' Well, God is asking, 'Where are you?'"

Oliver rose from the bench. "I've got to get home to my wife and kids, but I'm gonna leave you with an African proverb your father taught me. 'Every morning in the Tanzanian jungle, a gazelle wakes up. It knows it must run faster than the fastest lion or it will be killed. Every morning the lion wakes up. It knows it must outrun the slowest gazelle or it will starve to death. Whether you are a lion or a gazelle, when the sun comes up, you'd better be running.'"

"What does that mean?"

"It means make your decision, young blood. The sun is about to come up on you."

Oliver reached in his pants pocket and pulled out a red felt-tip marker. "Hold out your hand."

"No way." I instinctively recoiled.

"Firstborn, I gambled with five years of my life to save your up-to-this-point trifling life. If it wasn't for me, you'd be in Santa Rita right now, facing possession and trafficking charges. The least you could do is hold out your hand."

He gripped my wrist with one hand and scribbled in my open palm with the other hand.

"Man, what are you doing?" I snatched my hand back, anxious to see what he had written. "Luke 4:18–19" lay emblazoned in dark red ink.

"What does that say?"

"Go get a Bible and look it up."

Without another word, he turned and walked away.

I WAS A MILLION MILES
FROM HOME, SURROUNDED
BY A SEA OF KILLERS TO WHOM
I OWED AN OCEAN FULL OF DEBT.

CHAPTER
THIRTY

I ZIPPED HOME TO CHANGE CLOTHES. I FOUND AN ALSTON University sweatshirt hanging in the closet, and I slipped it on for luck, hoping I'd live through the night. I drove to Drama's place, wondering what the night would hold. How would we escape Latin Caesar's wrath?

As I got close, I saw Petey's shiny, black '74 Ford LTD parked in front of Drama's building. My eyebrow twitched. Petey never went to the pick-up spot with us. Latin Caesar didn't take kindly to uninvited guests. In the dope game, any stranger is a potential witness.

I flew up to Drama's apartment, still wondering what I would have to do to get this tuition money. By this time, most of what Oliver had said had gone in one ear and out the other. I was back in the real world.

When I knocked, Sandra pried the door open. She hugged me and kissed my cheek. Her eyes were red from crying. I could smell Captain Morgan's rum on her breath. She had probably been drinking to dull the pain of a lost love.

She waved me inside. "You going to Magdalene's funeral?"

"I don't think I should. Her family probably ain't feelin' too good about me right now. I don't think I could look her mom in the face." I couldn't tell this to Sandra, but the truth was, I wasn't even sure I'd live long enough to attend that funeral.

She twisted a damp handkerchief around in her hands. Her lower lip quivered. "My baby's gonna be cremated. We're having a private ceremony next Wednesday, just for the family. You're welcome to come out. You know P.E. thought of you like a son." She dissolved into weeping. "Firstborn, who would want to kill my baby?"

I could have named about a dozen people, present company included. It was a good thing Sandra didn't keep two ears in the streets. If she knew who killed her "baby," the household would have been grieving over its second homicide in a day. Renee would have no longer been with us.

I coughed. "I'll try to make it. Right now, I got some business with Drama."

I dashed into the kitchen and saw Ms. Velvet sitting at the table, her Braille Bible propped open in front of her. As I gave her a kiss on the cheek, I looked down and saw what Oliver had written on my hand. "Ms. Velvet, what does Luke 4:18–19 say?"

She didn't even hesitate. She knew the verses by heart. "'The Spirit of the Lord is on me because he has anointed me to preach good news to the poor. He has sent me to proclaim freedom for the prisoners and recovery of sight for the blind, to release the oppressed, to proclaim the year of the Lord's favor.'"

I chuckled. I was a hustler, not a prophet. How could God's Spirit be on me to say anything to anybody? How could God send me to preach freedom to the prisoners when I was throwing rocks at the jailhouse?

"What are you laughing at, boy?"

"Nothing, Ms. Velvet. Somebody told me to look up that Scripture in the Bible. It's some sort of message."

"Ain't nothin' funny 'bout it. Whoever gave you that Scripture is tryin' to tell you that God done set you apart to do his work. You supposed to join hands with the poor and help lift 'em up like Jesus did. Are you ready to do that, son?"

"Not yet, Ms. Velvet. Maybe when I get old."

"'Behold!'" Her voice rang out like thunder as it ricocheted off the dingy clapboard walls. "'Now is the day of salvation. In the day that you hear His voice, harden not your heart.'"

Feeling uncomfortable, I inched my way toward Drama's door.

Ms. Velvet must have heard my sneakers sliding away. "Son, don't go through that door tonight."

I froze. Why did she say that? Had she overheard one of our conversations? Had Sandra whispered something in her ear? Or did God...no, it couldn't be.

"Why not?"

"'Cause I know what you boys have been doing, and I got a feeling about tonight. Son, you can save yourself and many others. My boy Herbert, he done made his deal with the devil. He won't hear me. But you.... Firstborn, turn around and go home before it's too late."

I almost obeyed her.

"'There is a way that seems right to a man but at the end of it are the ways of destruction.'"

"What does that mean?"

"It means, son, that if you lie down next to Satan, sooner or later you're going to have to fornicate with him."

My hand trembled as it twisted the bedroom doorknob. The scent of pinewood incense permeated the air. The Intruders' old-school hit "It's a Thin Line between Love and Hate" jumped out at me from Drama's high-tech stereo speakers.

I walked into Drama's room to face the unexpected.

Petey sat in the folding chair, puffing on light green, high as the Goodyear blimp. Renee sat on the bed next to Drama. Her face glowed. She and Drama shared a blunt. His right arm encircled her shoulders. He held her right hand with his left.

Black gangster shades covered Drama's bloodshot eyes. He squinted at the letters on my Alton University sweatshirt. He smirked. "God bless a man with a dream."

I didn't care for his sardonic tone, so I spoke to Renee. "How you feeling, girl?" I had never killed anybody. I wondered what it felt like afterward.

"Don't call her Renee no more, man."

"What should I call her?"

"From now on, we callin' her Mamacide."

Renee giggled.

"So," Drama said, "you ready?"

"I'm ready. But where *they* going?" I nodded at Petey and Renee.

"They coming with us. Come on, y'all."

Renee squeezed the neck of the blue windbreaker around her neck. I could see the bulge of Drama's bulletproof vest beneath it. Drama's Uzi machine gun sat in her lap. Her burgundy lip gloss glowed in the semi-darkness.

"You ready to use that, *Mamacide*?" I asked.

"Sho' you right."

My legs grew weak. I dumped myself into a folding chair a few feet away from Drama. "What's the plan?"

"It's going down like this. We rollin' up in the spot like always. Just me and you. Of course, they'll search us. Three minutes after we get in, Mamacide and Petey come in blastin'."

"You want to rob Latin Caesar?"

"I wanna murk that sideways-talkin', disrespectful gang banger."

I looked at him like he had just stepped out of a Martian spaceship. "Blood, they got soldiers hanging out in front of that house. We've never seen the complete inside of the house. He might have bodyguards in the bedrooms. We'll never get out of there alive."

"Well, what's *your* plan?" Drama asked.

"My plan is that we tell Latin Caesar what happened and ask him to front us two more kilos. Then we go back on the block and get his money back. When it's done, we walk."

Drama took a deep hit on the blunt. "I like my plan better." He exhaled. Then he turned to the others. "What y'all think?"

Petey shrugged. The weed had almost closed his eyes. "Whatever, man. I'm ready."

"What you think, Mamacide?"

"Let's blast them fools!"

"It's settled. Let's go, y'all."

I stood still as a rock. "Drama, is you crazy? If GCD don't kill us when we walk through the door, they'll hunt us down till they find us."

"We ain't leavin' no witnesses, so who's gonna know? We do our thing, then we take whatever's in the house."

Panic seized me. This was suicide. "I ain't going."

"Yeah, you going. You know too much about my business to walk away now."

Petey stared at me as though he'd never seen me before. Renee's eyes squeezed into a menacing glare.

I glanced back at Drama. "So it's like that now?"

"Yeah, it's like that. We ain't got much time. So let's go."

I felt like a captured enemy preparing to face the firing squad. I cursed myself for ever having involved myself in

Drama's business. I knew there was no way this could come out well. I was going to die for nothing.

The four of us marched down the apartment complex stairs and through the courtyard. I took the shotgun seat in the Cadillac. Renee and Petey followed in his LTD.

Drama was silent for the span of four blocks before he decided to empty his mind. "Firstborn, you sounded like a little girl back there. When I first told you we was goin' out to the block to get this money, you tole me you was down for whatever. You tole me you could shoot somebody in the face if it came down to it. When I tole you I could get you that tuition money, you was down. Now when I need you, you draggin' your feet."

"I'm here, aren't I?" I muttered.

He popped Sideshow Psycho's new album, *The Purple Pill Formula*, into the CD player. The first cut was called "Glock .19." The beginning of the next song raised my eyebrows and then lowered my bottom lip. Sideshow Psycho was spitting rhymes about the Black Christmas Mob.

When we pulled up to the light, Drama stretched out his arms and waved his hands up and down to the rhythm of the music. He sang out every word.

I grabbed the CD cover and scrolled down the song titles. The song we were listening to was titled "Funky Black Christmas: We Got that Snow." The beginning of the first verse said:

The cash hauler
The shot caller
The block hog
The billion-dollar baller

Drama is the don of the BC clique.
Empty out yo' pockets or get blasted quick.

Firstborn is the capo, the number-two nigga,
The one who can order ya done with the trigger.

"Drama, that fool is testifying about our business in his music! What you trying to do, catch some federal time? 'Cause they'll enter this madness as exhibit A at the trial."

Drama wrinkled his nose and curled his top lip. His voice rose above the music. "Man, will you stop crying like a sissy? This is my cousin flowin' on that mike. I pay for dat studio time. The nigga is showing us some love. He tellin' fools out there what time it is. And that slap beat is sick, ain't it?" He gave an exaggerated nod.

I gave up trying to argue. Drama wasn't hearing me. He had become an ardent believer in his own myth.

The next cut was called "Witness Stand." The lyrics said:

Helen's main hustle was prostitution.
Now she's the star witness for the prosecution.
They found a half a gram of blow in her place.
But they will erase her case
'Cause they want Scarface.

So they shift the blame
'Cause in the high-stakes game,
They want the nigga rollin' high with the hip hop fame.
So Helen's on the stand giving up transcript.
Tell the bail man, "Sorry but I had to skip."

Had Drama lost his natural mind? I wondered how many of those CDs were in circulation. Didn't he know that cops listened to hip hop? He had let his cousin put our thing out on front street.

Song number three was called "Nigga Killer."

I ain't trying to hear no conscious rap
But you 'bout to hear my .9 milla clap.

'Cause I'm riding through your hood with my goon battalion.
We'll put a slug straight through your Africa medallion.

I knew I wasn't exactly leading my people to the Promised Land, but Sideshow Psycho was making songs that the Ku Klux Klan could play at their cross-burning rallies.

Drama loves this stuff, I thought. What did that say about how he felt about himself? What did it say about how he felt about other blacks? My stomach felt queasy.

When we reached Latin Caesar's driveway, Drama cut the headlights and clicked the music off. I fought not to look in the rearview mirror.

Drama read my thoughts. "They stopped about a block behind us."

Latin Caesar's soldiers posted up on the porch steps, nodded their heads to the fat beats of Muerte Clique, a Spanish-speaking gangsta rap group. I didn't understand the words, but when one of the MCs hollered, "Buck! Buck! Buck!" I knew what he was saying. Gunshots speak a universal language.

The tatted-up hell raisers who used to evil eye us from the driveway to the front door were a thing of the past. Also gone were the pit bulls. Three youngsters hardly out of their teens sipped out of the same forty-ounce. They barely stirred when we got out of the car.

Razor cut his eyes in our direction. He said something in Spanish and all the fellows on the porch giggled. The front door opened and he bid us enter with a sweep of his hand.

Rudolfo emerged from the darkness, motioning for us to raise our hands. We submitted to the pat-down. Satisfied that we were unarmed, he grunted and pointed Drama and me toward the kitchen.

Drama glanced back at me and smiled with an arch of his eyebrow. He gave three deliberate nods, one for each minute that lay between then and the second that Renee and Petey were scheduled to come blasting through the door. My heart was beating so fast my chest hurt.

Latin Caesar slouched down in one of the brown wooden stools, one leg folded over the other. He was reading the newspaper. A young woman with golden skin stood behind him with a pair of barber clippers. Her shiny black hair cascaded down her back and landed at the beltline of her blue jeans. She looked like a Mayan princess.

Caesar's bark took my mind off of her stunning beauty. "Y'all got my scrill?"

Drama looked at the linoleum, playing his part to the hilt. "You see, it's like this. Street Life—"

Caesar raised his hand, showing us his palm. "If I wanted *Entertainment Tonight*, I'd watch TV. Now, where's my money?"

"The truth is, we need a few more days."

Latin Caesar sprang up from his chair. He was in surprisingly good shape for a man in his late thirties. His biceps were tight from jailhouse push-ups.

I glanced at my watch. Three minutes had passed. Something must have gone wrong. Drama's eyes stretched in panic.

"You fools are out of tomorrows," Latin Caesar barked. "I want my money tonight!" He slammed his hand down on the open newspaper that lay on the tabletop. The headline read, "East Oakland Drug Kingpin Arrested: Guns, Coke, Cash Confiscated."

Street Life's face stared at the camera. His lips were swollen. His left eye was black and blue.

"Firstborn," Latin Caesar said, "I want to talk to you about something. It's about my little sis here. I thought I could ask for your help. You being a college boy and all." The angry glow seemed to dissipate from his eyes. "You said you used to be a philosophy major, but what did you want to be when you graduated?

"A writer," I spat out of my cotton-dry mouth.

He looked at his sister and winked. "I knew it. I got James Baldwin sitting up here in the crib!" Latin Caesar strolled over to the cabinet and reached for something on the second shelf. I saw his fingers reach for something between the paprika and the olive oil.

Drama leaped up and grabbed Caesar's waist before he could put his hand on it. Caesar struggled to free himself, but Drama held on for dear life. His pigtails bounced up and down as he wrestled with the drug lord.

"What are you doing, man?" Latin Caesar asked.

"Help me, Firstborn!" Drama hollered.

The princess let out an ear-splitting scream. "Razor! Rudolfo! Help! They've got Caesar!" She picked up a steak knife from the drainage board and aimed it at Drama's back like a dagger. I caught her wrist.

The clump of heavy footsteps shook the floor. I heard cussing in Spanish. Then I heard somebody rack up a .12 gauge shotgun.

A woman shrieked. The sound of automatic gunfire lit up the night like the Vietnam Tet Offensive. Glass shattered. The front door flew off its hinges.

Renee burst into the kitchen. She slapped a fresh clip in the Uzi and sprayed the ceiling.

I choked on the bitter taste of gun smoke. Plaster dust particles rained down from the ceiling. Renee's screeching forced me to cover my ears. Petey's .12 gauge blasted a flaming black hole through the refrigerator door.

Razor and Rudolfo ran into the kitchen toting a .32 and a Mac-11.

"Drop that heat, fools," Petey hollered as he stomped into the room, the front door swinging behind him. He was leveling the sawed-off shotgun at Latin Caesar's nose. Dark blue sunglasses blotted out Petey's eyes, but the murderous tone in his voice said it all.

A Mac-11 and a .32 hit the floor. Drama swept them away with his foot. "Now, lie down!"

Latin Caesar wore an expression of pure shock. "What is this? You killed my boys outside?"

"Didn't have to," Drama said. "They ran."

Latin Caesar's sister stood statue still, as though she were in suspended animation. Then she startled all of us with a blood-curdling scream.

"You better shut that up," Drama said through gritted teeth.

She cupped her mouth with her hand.

"All right," Drama said. "Where the drugs?"

Latin Caesar stuttered, "Everything is taped underneath the table. Take it. Just let my family go."

Drama ran his hands under the kitchen table. He smiled. I watched him tug at something beneath the table. I heard the sound of gauze tape ripping. Three kilos of uncut raw dropped into Drama's hands. The packages were imprinted with the GCD logo.

Drama grinned at me. "Nigga, didn't I tell you? You can *buy* Alston University now if you want it."

"Okay, you got it," Latin Caesar grumbled. "Now, get out of here!"

"Shut up," Drama barked. "I'll leave when I'm good and ready."

"Drama," Petey squeaked, "tell me what you want me to do. But whatever it is, we gotta do it now. You know those fools outside went for help."

"You right." Drama took a step backward. "Mamacide, chop 'em up." He said it as casually as if he were asking for mustard on his hot dog.

Renee took aim at the four prone bodies. She squeezed one eye shut and gripped the trigger.

I don't know what made me do it, but I dove in front of the muzzle. I waved my arms like Shaquille O'Neal guarding the basket. I was the only thing standing between Caesar's family and the coroner's slab.

Renee gasped. "Firstborn, is you stupid? Nigga, what is you doin'?"

"No more blood, Renee. No more killin'. Drama, you got what you wanted. Now, get out of here."

Drama's jaw dropped. "Well, I'll be damned. You pick this particular moment to stand up and grow a pair? Firstborn, you know they got an army, and I'm not talking about those young wannabees on the porch trying to get some of Caesar's light. I'm talkin' 'bout hardcore, thugged-out killas. Nigga, if we let him live, they'll come after us. They will hunt us down and shoot us."

"Don't call me nigga!" My knees were shaking but my voice was steady.

"And when did you stop being a nigga?"

"Just now."

"Firstborn," Drama said, "I don't want to have to shoot you, man, but I will."

"Yeah," I smirked. "All a poor man's got is his friends. Remember that?"

Drama dropped his head and sucked his teeth. His shoulders slumped slightly.

Renee stared at Drama for direction. Petey aimed his .12 gauge at my chest.

"Petey, don't do it," I pleaded.

He turned to Drama.

"First, I can't believe you goin' out like a sucker, man!"

"I can't stand by and let you kill these people in cold blood."

Drama placed his arm across Renee's outstretched wrists. The Uzi lowered to her side. Petey picked up the artillery that lay on the floor.

Drama sighed. "All right, let's go."

I took a deep breath and stuck my hands in my pockets. "No."

Shock forced Renee to swallow her bubble gum. "Firstborn, you been reading too many books. You done lost you mind. You want us to leave you here?"

Drama backed up toward the door. "Please, man, come on. They gonna kill you as soon as we hit the door."

"I'm tired, Drama. I'm finished with this."

"What'll I tell Mama?"

"Tell her I love her and that I believe. She'll understand."

With one last stare of confusion, they left. My heart sank as I listened to the sound of his car drive away. I was a million miles from home, surrounded by a sea of killers to whom I owed an ocean full of debt. And they were plenty mad.

"Help me up, Firstborn," Latin Caesar said. I reached my outstretched hand in his direction. He grabbed it and I pulled his weight upward.

Razor and Rudolfo climbed to their feet.

The goddess's eyes broadened with fear. Her body shook. Tears dripped down her light auburn cheeks.

Latin Caesar draped his arms around her and patted the back of her neck. "Shhh. They gone now, li'l sister. It's all over."

Latin Caesar released the girl and turned to me. His eyes burned smoky black with rage.

I felt certain I was breathing my last.

"You are a brave man," Latin Caesar said. "You saved all our lives, and for that we will spare yours and erase your debt."

I let out a sigh. I felt the strength leave my body.

"But Drama…that's another story. What was that fool's problem?"

"You started reaching for a gun, and he—"

"A gun?"

Latin Caesar flung the cabinet all the way open. The second shelf contained two blue spiral notebooks and a box of ballpoint pens. He picked up one of the pens. "Does this look like a heater?"

"We thought you were going to kill us because we messed up the money."

"This is business. If I take y'all out, I never see that money again. Y'all are good earners. Things happen. I would have given you a chance to get my money back. But I never got a chance to discuss that with you."

"I told Drama that."

"Firstborn," he said, pulling the girl close to his side, "this is my sister, Marisonia. I brought her here to meet you. I want her to go to college, but we were having problems with the essay part of the application. Punctuation is a mutha! I wanted you to look at what she wrote here on the essay section."

A footstep on the porch made me jump. The front door crashed open. Cries of outrage echoed in the living room. At least a dozen pair of sneakers pounded the floor. I was sure these cats had stomped in strapped with enough hardware to win back the Alamo.

A barrel-chested man with a beard and tattoos on his face ran into the room with the business end of an AK-47 pointed at the bridge of my nose. The others pointed Lugers and semi-automatic rifles at my head.

A stocky cat with a shaved skull and machine-gun biceps stuck the end of his .357 Magnum against my temple. Something about the way he squeezed his cold brown eyes at me told me he'd been down this road before and he was ready to take it again, no questions asked. He glanced at me for an instant before his gazed shifted to Latin Caesar. "What's up, *carnale*?"

I could hear myself breathing. For the first time since I'd started slinging rocks, I realized that I didn't want to die.

"Put it down, *bro*," Caesar said. "You're scarin' my man here to death."

The gangsta didn't crack a smile. "GCD fo' life, homes," he said in a deadly whisper as though for some reason he didn't want me to hear. "Caesar, it's time to bring the pimp hand down hard on these fools. Let's start with this one."

Latin Caesar's brow wrinkled. He pointed at four of the young men who surrounded us in a semi-circle and then barked commands. "Three of them," he hissed. "Drama and two others. They're in that Cadillac, the one with red candy paint, sitting on dubs. They're headed for the deep east. They got three keys. Bring their heads back in a Hefty bag and get my coke. Andale!"

The soldiers ran for the door. I heard car tires peel away from the curb and engines zoom. The cat with the .357 hadn't flinched a centimeter. Meanwhile, Latin Caesar paced the floor. His face betrayed no emotion. Eventually he smiled and beckoned toward the love seat. "Sit down, Firstborn."

I obeyed but I didn't blink. My heart pounded like a kick drum.

Latin Caesar bent forward to look me squarely in the eyes. He folded his arms over his chest. "Your boys and that crazy broad got as much future in these streets as Elvis," he said without raising his voice. "But you...you saved my life, and for that you will live…unless, of course, you choose to walk in the shadows of the dead."

Well, that wouldn't be difficult. My friendship with Drama ended the moment he left me to die here in the killer's den. I planned with everything in me to follow his order. I was going to take this chance to live. That great "Somebody" was blessing me with a second chance and I was going to run with it.

"Listen closely to what I'm about to say to you." Latin Caesar dropped his hand down on my shoulder. "I was in college when I started grinding. It was the worst mistake I ever made. I'm in too deep now to look back. I got too much dirt on my soul. But you got another chance. God done smiled on you, homie. Before too long, that fool Drama is gonna be laid out in a body bag, staring up at his own eyelids. But God gave you a second chance, my friend. Use it."

"I'll think about what you're saying."

Latin Caesar gripped my hand, rubbing my knuckles against one another. His gaze stung me like a scorpion. "There's nothing to think about. Just do it."

I nodded.

"You wanna call somebody to come get you?"

"Yes. But let's have a look at that essay first."

Latin Caesar sat back in a wooden rocking chair with his fingers laced behind his head.

Marisonia handed me the application and three typed pages. The essay was actually quite good. I made a few spelling corrections. That was all it really needed. I'll never forget the essay's last words: "I was born in the ghetto, but the ghetto was not born in me."

I felt that great Somebody's voice speaking to me through that last sentence.

"That's tight," I told Marisonia. "I really like it. You're going to be somebody in this world. On your journey, people are going to try to tell you otherwise, but never lose sight of what you wrote here." She smiled and blushed as she reached out for the essay pages.

The gang banger with the tattoos on his face smirked. He looked at my forehead as if there were a shooting-range target painted on it. I shivered at the ghastly sound of his grinding teeth. I knew that if Latin Caesar so much as walked out of the room to use the bathroom, he would shoot me with that AK and have as much remorse about it as a lion might have for swatting a fly with his tail. But Latin Caesar never moved from his seat. Thank God.

It was time to think about making my exit. I contemplated walking out of the front door and heading for the Fruitvale BART station. I chose against that. It would be too easy to get cut off by ridaz looking for payback. Staying alive in the streets had taught me nothing if not how to be resourceful. I plucked the wrinkled business card out of my wallet and dialed Oliver's number. The conversation was short. His end of it was "Just give me an address."

Latin Caesar pointed at a seat across from his rocking chair. "Sit down, Firstborn. Let's talk."

I sat in the seat as he commanded. He talked. I listened.

"Did you ever learn about Pancho Villa in school?

I shook my head.

"Why doesn't that surprise me?" Latin Caesar said with a grimace. "Pancho Villa worked on a farm. One day a man put hands on Pancho Villa's sister. Villa killed the man. He was only seventeen. He became a wanted fugitive. Pancho Villa got with a gang and became a rider. Pancho Villa went from being a hardcore vato to one of the leading figures in the Mexican revolution."

We hadn't learned too much Latino history in school, which was really a shame. This story piqued my interest. "What happened to Pancho Villa?"

"The outcasts and the hoodlums, the despised, the cats from the hood, fought for Pancho Villa. It started as a clique and it turned into an army. On March 9, 1916, Pancho Villa invaded Columbus, Texas. The president of the United States had to send almost twenty thousand troops and the United States Air Force to push Pancho Villa back across the Mexican border. Years later, he was caught up in an ambush. He went out blasting.

"The point is, Pancho Villa went from being a stick-up man to being a general. And he took cats from the hood and turned them into revolutionaries. The last words he said before he died were "Don't let it end like this. Tell them I said something."

I smiled at Latin Caesar. "So Pancho Villa's life didn't really end when he caught that slug. Latin Caesar, you are Pancho Villa."

The gangsta with the tattooed face drawled, "Hell, yeah." He said it like he had just come up with the answer to an algebra problem after a night of study. His grip on the barrel of that AK-47 tightened.

A car horn blared outside. I knew it was Oliver.

I walked over to Latin Caesar and shook his hand. "It looks like we've both got some choices to make."

He nodded. I twisted the doorknob and never looked back.

When I opened Oliver's car door, I didn't even say hello. I just said, "I'm choosing life. The nigga is dead."

EPILOGUE

DRAMA WAS RIGHT. THE MAJORITY OF THE MONEY I HAD SAVED for college was lost in the big raid. I never did get into Alston. However, I was able to continue my college studies at a California state university. I would tell you which one, but C-Storm has a contract out on my life. People rarely forget, especially when the conflict involves money. In the streets they say, "Funk is forever." Although it's doubtful that anyone would come way out here looking for me, you never can tell.

I carry a solid 3.8 grade point average. When I first got here, I zipped through algebra, chemistry, English, and the language courses. Ironically, it was the creative writing course that tripped me up.

The English professor was a stocky white fellow with a Sherlock Holmes hat and corrective shoes. I was doing well enough in my other classes, but this guy was giving me Cs and Ds for idiotic assignments like "Write a paper on what it would feel like to be one of George Washington's soldiers."

George Washington was a slave holder. How could I weigh in on that assignment?

The next week, my homework was to do a thirty-page autobiographical sketch. I wrestled with brief shards of memory: my grandmother sitting down to the dinner table with me...my first day of school. But it was flat, meaningless.

Then inspiration struck. I started writing and I couldn't stop. Thoughts swirled around in my skull, then jammed down through the ink in the point of my pen and raced out onto the pages.

After the essay was finished, I handed it to my roommate, Salaam, who read aloud, "Why dey shoot dat nigga in his face, cuz? Dat's what I wanna know."

In my mind's eye, I visualized the kid who had said that. He had to have been around seventeen at the time. A thick forest of dreadlocks concealed his glassy eyes from the world. He was so short that his black rubber soles dangled from the wooden church pew barely touching the wine-colored carpet. The bottoms of his baggy black dress pants bunched up at the ankles. The tattoo under the short sleeve of his dress shirt was raw with red-and-green letters that bulged in cursive. They said, "We still ain't listening!" He smelled like a marijuana bonfire...

NEXT BY HARRY LOUIS WILLIAMS II:

Straight Outta East Oakland
Part 2: Track Star

CONTACT US

Join the Soul Shaker Publishing family.
Stay up on the newest releases and write to your
favorite Soul Shaker authors. You can find us at
www.soulshakerpublishing.com or write to us at:

SOUL SHAKER PUBLISHING
4096 Piedmont Avenue #558
Oakland, CA 94611

Reverend Harry Louis Williams II
is available for speaking engagements.

Harry Williams would love to hear from you.
You can e-mail him at *innercityhealing@yahoo.com*
or write to him c/o Soul Shaker Publishing.

Out of the spiritual legacy of the black religious experience, the Reverend Harry Williams has had the audacity to write as if the Christian faith has efficacy for the 21st century and the third millennium. The journey of Firstborn Walker is **riveting and reminiscent** of the struggle of the apostle Paul. In that struggle, Paul seeks to rediscover the spiritual power of God in a new and altered social reality. In spite of his dogmatic presuppositions, false class consciousness and religious bigotry, Paul discovers God anew.

The scene in chapter five where Firstborn's two companions give a "beat down" to a drug dealer, vividly portrays the real tragedy of contemporary drug culture and the nihilism that both drives it and produces it. It is also an **indictment of the racial-capitalism** and social oppression that continues to plague black America and similar communities of color and marginalization.

Likewise, Reverend Williams effectively demonstrates the manner in which a young black man in East Oakland negotiates the terms of existence in the violent nihilism of post-civil rights ghetto life. Williams demonstrates that the **battle for the souls of young black men** and women, trapped in the grip of a street culture defined by Guns, Cash, and Dope is a microcosm of the way in which these same values are undermining the dream of America on a much larger scale. Both in and beyond the urban ghettos of Oakland, Baltimore, Chicago, Cleveland, Detroit, Los Angeles, New York, Philadelphia and Washington, D.C., the Gospel of Jesus Christ is the power of God for our salvation as families, communities, and as a nation struggling to **reclaim its soul**.

This book is a must read for those who seek to discover the demands that God is placing on the religious community to find new forms of communication and style for outreach and witness. It is also a clear challenge to the young people of urban and suburban America to reconsider the power of God that can be found through an intense relationship with Jesus Christ. This relationship yet offers **true freedom**, power, and love. It is an offer that we can ill afford to refuse.

In his writing, Reverend Williams beckons us to consider that the God who sustained our grandparents and great grandparents must become our God as well.

DR. DONALD FRANCIS GUEST, PASTOR
Glide Foundation/Glide Memorial Methodist Church,
San Francisco, CA